AMERICA'S FOOL

AMERICA'S
FOOL

LAS VEGAS & THE END OF THE WORLD

A NOVEL BY
JAY AMBERG

Third Edition, Revised 2020   ISBN 13: 978-0-9708416-7-4
AMIKA PRESS   466 Central Ave #23 Northfield IL 60093   847 920 8084
info@amikapress.com   Available for purchase on amikapress.com
Edited by John Manos.
Cover photography by Tony Savino, Shutterstock, and Sebastien Leboef. Designed and typeset by Sarah Koz. Body in Dante MT, designed by Giovanni Mardersteig and Charles Malin in 1957, digitized by Ron Carpenter in 1993. Titles in Interstate, designed by Tobias Frere-Jones in 1993–4. Thanks to Nathan Matteson.

FOR
ALL
AMERICANS

1
_____

LIGHTNING STRIKES A JUNIPER ON THE RIDGE ABOVE ANDREW WRIGHT. Thunder claps, and the scudding clouds open. Hailstones the size of marbles—*shooters,* he thinks—pummel him as he clambers up the red sandstone boulders toward an overhang. At five-foot-ten and 170 pounds, he doesn't quite fit under the outcropping, and so he hunches there, the hail splatting and careening around his cross-trainers.

The hail turns to rain, large cool drops driven by the wind. Steam rises from nearby boulders. It's mid-afternoon in August in the Mojave, the temperature 108 on the desert floor and ninety-seven, even in the shade, at this altitude in Red Rock Canyon. Rushing water stains the canyon's sandstone and limestone walls deep red and dark gray. Almost instantly waterfalls, some five hundred feet high, spew silver and red torrents toward the canyon floor. Below him, the gravel washes are already filling. The pungent odor of wet desert rock and creosote permeates the air. And the rain douses him, soaking his khaki shorts and Yankees T-shirt.

The storm has come on suddenly, a wall of black advancing from the west, obliterating the sky. Wright is alone, high on the far side of the canyon, a good three miles from the pine tree where he left the motorcycle he'd rented on the Strip in Las Vegas. He wanted to get away from the glitz—the grandiose architecture, the garish video billboards and jacked-up music, the stench of cigarette smoke in the casinos, and the constant electronic chitter and occasional siren-ching of the slots. And he certainly has escaped. His producer and his camera crew knew about the motorcycle, but they hadn't a clue about where he was headed. Nor, really, had he. And now, though he is fit enough to have hiked up the dry creek bed far beyond the trail, he's not absolutely certain he's ready to slip-slide, drenched and dehydrated, along the treacherous, flooded wash back to the picnic area.

He notices a shadowy indentation above him to his left and in his mind traces a path toward it. Though he waits a couple of minutes for the storm to slacken, stronger gusts blow hail and rain at him horizontally. He scrambles over a boulder the size of a pickup truck, slipping twice and scraping his knee. He eyes the cleft in the rock still eight feet above him, nudges the toe of his shoe into a slot in a sheer limestone block, and stretches to grab for any purchase at the top. His fingers find a handhold exactly where he needs it, and he clutches tight, pulls himself up, turns on his stomach, and slides backward into the narrow three-foot-high mouth of a cave.

Lightning arcs and slashes from the blue-black clouds. Thunder roars. Water cascades down limestone and sandstone cliffs. Murky water roils down the wash. He takes a deep breath and inches farther into the mouth of the cave. On the wall to his right, a strange petro-glyph, far different from any he's seen before, depicts a fierce beast like a winged lion with pointed fangs and extended claws. Above the etching are three concentric circles, and below it is a line like an arrow. He runs his hand across the rock. The carving doesn't look all that goddamned old. *What is this place?* he wonders. Glancing over his shoulder, he can see only a dark shaft angling downward into the rock. This spot can't be seen from the trail or the creek bed, and, if he's wrong about the age of the petroglyph, he might well be the first human to see it in centuries.

Would this place make a story? A counterpoint and, frankly, an antidote to the stuff he's been putting out the last couple of days? The last eleven years, really. It's not that *The Wright Stuff,* his three-minute feature on ABC's *Good Morning America,* is all that bad. In fact, it's pretty goddamned good, having improved a lot over the years. Won an Emmy two years ago. But does any of it really matter?

Take these four stories in the series the New York suits are calling *The Fight to Save Vegas.* First, the already aired pre-bout promo on the upcoming Championship Fight ballyhooed as the super-event that will revitalize the city's failing economy. Except that it's not exactly clear that anyone cares about heavyweight boxing anymore. Then, today's story, *Ghost Hulks on the Strip*, about the bankrupt and deserted 63-story Fountainbleau, the scratched second Trump Tower, the struggling Sands Corporation's stalled St. Regis, Caesars Palace's suspended Octavius Tower, and the seriously scaled down CityCenter. The piece was visually terrific—the crew got just the right shots of all the abandoned construction cranes hovering atop the unfinished bulidings. But after Maggie cut his line about the cranes looking like raptors stripping flesh from the skulls of ruminants, there wasn't really all that much of him left in the script.

Tomorrow's story features Benjamin Kupferberg, the owner of The Tahitian, the newest, most expensive hotel-casino in Vegas and an underfunded gamble that the world will, despite the recession, throng to a dazzling and excessive psuedo-paradise here in the American desert. Wright has a say only on the fourth piece. And this spot might just be it, except that all those network suits won't get it. He can already hear them: "A red rock canyon, Andy? A sandstone cliff? That's not fucking Vegas! And who gives a rat's ass about petroglyphs, anyway?"

A cool, almost dank, breeze rises from the darkness behind him, sending a chill through him despite the afternoon heat. He takes another deep breath, exhales slowly, and cranes his neck. Is that a faint glimmer deep in the shaft? As he wriggles farther out of the rain onto the interior slope, another shiver ripples between his shoulders. He hears—or thinks he hears—a hum, something mechanical, above the drumming of the rain. Squatting on his drenched crosstrainers, he shifts his weight and leans away from the outside light. *What the hell is this place?*

Suddenly, he's sliding down the slope, plummeting into the darkness, his fingernails raking the loose rocks tumbling with him. The shaft steepens, and when he tries to slow his descent by jamming his left foot against the side wall, his ankle twists and his right shoulder and head bang against the other wall. And then he's sprawled at the bottom on a heap of stones, breathless, the taste of blood in his mouth. He lies there for a time before muttering, "Shit. God-fucking-damn-it!"

Sitting up, he catches his breath and takes stock. He's in a cavern, mostly dark, light filtering forty or so feet along the shaft he's just skittered down. His nose is bleeding, and his upper lip is cut. He runs his tongue across his teeth, relieved that none has been knocked out. His forehead is warm and damp, but he isn't sure whether it's blood, sweat, or rain. His head aches, his elbows and knees sting, and his ankle throbs. He tilts his head back to slow the bleeding from his nose.

All in all, though, he's not seriously injured. In fact, despite his utter solitude, he feels more embarrassed than hurt. He's just biffed, goddamn it. Miguel and Arnuz will be doubled over in hysterics, and Maggie—he doesn't even want to think about her reaction. Sniffling and coughing, he pulls his iPhone from his pocket. The phone is dead, its face shattered. Not that it matters. There'd be no reception anyway, none at all in this part of the canyon much less under a god-damned mountain. As he stows the broken phone, he spits blood into the darkness.

He rolls off the pile of stones and stands tentatively. Dizzy and disoriented, he holds his arms out. The luminescent dial of his watch, a Timex that has despite the rock-ride actually kept on ticking, seems to hover in space. Although he turns a full circle, he touches only the wall below the shaft. Stooping and craning, he looks back up the shaft and mumbles, "Shit!" It's a goddamned chimney. The first thirty feet rise at close to a seventy degree angle. It'll be a slippery, difficult, even excruciating climb back up.

As his eyes adjust to the darkness, he looks for the shimmer he first noticed. Off to the right, a yellow stain spreads from a crack in the rock. And the mechanical thrum echoes, though he can't tell its source. Maybe there's another, easier way out. He creeps carefully, hands ahead and waving slowly so that the watch's dial cuts figure-eights in the darkness. Fearful of slipping down another drop he can't see, he scuffs his feet along the cavern floor, edging toward the pale smear. He turns once, to make sure he can still make out the shaft

4

opening, and continues until the toe of his cross-trainer stubs a wall. His hand grasps a rough, cool corner. When he slinks farther, following the contour of the wall, there's more light ahead. And that sound, too—the rumble of a motor?

He shuffles through the dimness, the passageway narrowing around him. The light emanates from a slit in the rock, and there's definitely a mechanical drone. He has to turn sideways and stoop to continue inching forward, anxiety beginning to well in his chest, stealing his breath. He leans toward the illuminated crack in the wall. Then, sensing something, he turns his head abruptly—but there's only darkness behind him. When he peers through the bright slit, he sees another cavern lit by three hanging bulbs. Five metallic canisters, each a little bigger than a fifth of scotch, line a table covered with bright red material.

He crouches lower and gapes through the crack to make sure he isn't imagining the scene. Three of the canisters are set parallel to the back edge of the table, and the other two form a perpendicular line from the middle canister toward the table's front. Each canister has a series of stenciled yellow letters and numbers—some sort of earmark. Below the ID, painted in glossy white, is the image of a human fist, the fingers clearly delineated. Hanging from a hook driven into the cavern wall behind the table is something that looks a lot like a NASA spacesuit.

And then he again senses movement behind him. Something brushing down his neck. The petroglyph of the beast flashes in his mind. His upper arm stings. A bite? Spider? Snake? He swipes his shoulder, rises, begins to turn, and stumbles backward. Swirling dizziness spins him about. And darkness.

2

LIGHT, IMPOSSIBLY BRIGHT. AND A SHADOW, A MOVING SHADOW. THOUGH his eyes blink open, Andrew Wright can see nothing but shapes in this deluge of light. The shadow speaks, the words unclear. And then the shadow, bending over him, blocks much of the light. A woman. He's lying on his side looking up, and behind her is a vast emptiness.

The woman's words begin to take form. "I have water. Lie still, but lift your head." Her voice is calm, firm, authoritative without any hint of imperiousness. Her English, though clear, has an odd lilt, a subtle difference in inflection. "Here. Drink."

His lips sting, but the water's cool in his parched throat. As he drinks greedily from the half-gallon plastic bottle, he breaks abruptly into a sweat.

"Not too much at once." She takes the bottle, pours water onto a white cloth, and returns the bottle. She mops his forehead, dabs his cheeks and chin. He guzzles more water as she wipes his neck.

When she lifts the cloth, it's brown with grime and dried blood. There's a metallic taste in his mouth. And an acrid smell. Himself? His memory suddenly returns—the storm, the petroglyph, the shaft, the dark cavern…the second cavern and the canisters. "What…?" he croaks. Coughing, he clutches her wrist. "Where the hell…?"

"Slow down," she says as she pries his hand from her arm. "You're going to be okay." He tries to get up, but she presses firmly on his shoulder. "I'm a doctor."

When he rises on his elbows, two flies whirl around his head. His T-shirt, shorts, and shoes look like he's been mud wrestling, but the ground around him is dry, hard-packed, as though it rained hours ago. He's in the partial shade of a scrawny piñon pine next to a narrow road. He squints at a dusty black Land Rover Discovery standing ten yards away. Beyond the dirt road, the sun is low over barren hills that stretch to the horizon. In the other direction, the nearby Joshua trees and sandstone shards are suffused with light. Off in the distance, gray and red stone walls rise toward North Peak.

"What's your name?" she asks as she shoos the flies away with the white cloth.

"Andy," he answers. "Andrew Wright." She's wearing a blue work shirt, wheat jeans, and brown hiking boots. She's around five-foot-six, nicely built, if a little wide in the hips, in her late-thirties, perhaps forty.

"Were you caught in the storm?" she asks as she brushes loose strands of black hair behind her ear.

"Yes." Guzzling more water, he thinks of the cavern. "No. Not really."

"Hiking?" One of the flies returns, and she snaps the cloth at it, striking it in midair.

"Yes." Nodding back toward North Peak, he realizes he's down the *other* side, the western slope beyond the canyon.

She rips open a cellophane bag and swabs his forehead, lip, and nose with a gauzy tissue that smells of disinfectant. Both the odor and the tingling help clear his head. Her hair is black, naturally wavy, and her face is pale, oval, pretty. A prominent nose and a radiant smile. Her eyes are worlds unto themselves, darkly bright and deep.

"With friends?" she asks. There is nothing judgmental in her voice. She seems as though she's simply taking a medical history.

"No. Alone." Those eyes: What did the poet say, windows into the soul?—he can't quite remember.

"Without water?" Perhaps, now, there's just a suggestion in her voice that she understands all too well that Innate Male Idiocy—IMI, he muses—might be the primary symptom, if not the disease. When he doesn't answer, she adds, "You're a long way from any hiking trail."

"I guess." He doesn't, in truth, have the foggiest goddamned notion how he got to this piñon pine. The last thing he remembers is… the sting. He reaches over and feels his arm, but there's little sore-

7

ness and no swelling. In fact, it's no more sore than the rest of his body, which feels like, well, he's fallen down a chimney. Did all that really happen? he wonders. He almost tells her about the cavern and the canisters, but it all seems so strange. Maybe he was hit by lightning, and he's been wandering, dumbstruck and stupefied, through the desert. He peels the dried blood and dirt from his lower lip and says nothing.

As she screws the cap on the water bottle, she asks, "Do you think you can walk?"

Taking her free hand, he gets to one knee before he tastes bile. The desert undulates for a moment, then settles. He takes three deep breaths and hobbles to his feet. His left ankle won't bear much weight, so he lays his arm over her shoulder as she wraps her arm around his waist. With her support, he limps over to the Land Rover. She opens the passenger door for him, hands him the water bottle, and helps him into the seat. As she walks around the front of the Land Rover, he looks up and down the road and then back at North Peak—and he's still pretty perplexed by what's happened to him. He's on the goddamned *other* side of the mountain.

In stark contrast to its dusty exterior, the Land Rover's interior is spotless. The back seat is down, and the cargo bay is filled with five more water bottles lined next to a series of blue plastic tubs containing neatly labeled and arranged medical supplies under clear plastic lids.

"I've got a bike…a motorcycle," he says, "the other side of…" He points back toward North Peak and Red Rock Canyon.

She laughs, her teeth stunningly white and her eyes aglow. Still laughing and shaking her head, she reaches back into the cargo bay and slips the cloth, tissue, and cellophane bag into a ziplock garbage container. As she puts the Land Rover into gear, she says finally, "You have a choice, Andrew Wright—your hotel or my clinic. Or, if you want to risk public humiliation, I suppose I could drop you back at the Bureau of Land Management visitors' center. But I'm not sure your viewing public would be amused to see you in your current condition."

"But…" He knows she's right. He's going to have a tough enough time trying to explain things to his crew, much less anyone else. "You know who I am?" He's not really surprised; it's been years since he's been able to go anywhere without being recognized, even if the gray creeping along his temples gets brushed out each morning in the make-up chair. He's had to keep that youthful blond hair and adventurous good looks for the camera even as the crow's feet and the gray have begun their inevitable encroachment.

As she drives along the dirt track, the Land Rover trails a plume of dust. The stereo is on low—playing Chopin, the second piano concerto. "I get up early, Andy," she says. "And though I don't often watch the tube, I occasionally turn it on just in time for *The Wright Stuff.*"

He can't quite tell if there is a note of irony in her voice; it seems as though she might again merely be stating a fact without any judgment. The western sun is hot, even through the tinted windows, and he takes a long swig of water. After nestling the bottle on the floor between his foot and the gear box, he wipes his damp hands on his grimy shorts and asks, "What are you doing way out here?"

"On West Canyon Road?" She gestures with her thumb over her shoulder. "I was checking on someone. A special case I see regularly." Still smiling, she adds, "And you're more than a little lucky I spotted you." She taps his watch band. "The glint caught my eye."

He looks more closely at her profile. She is, he thinks, in some way he's not used to, beautiful—the exact antithesis of a brassy Vegas showgirl. Her chin is firm, her lips full, her nose long, and her eyelashes lush; her hair, spilling over her neck, is luxuriant, so deeply black it seems almost gold in the sunlight. "Thanks," he says. The more he thinks about the cavern and the canisters, the more uneasy he is. Something happened up in that canyon, something that doesn't make sense and definitely isn't right. Not the goddamned *Wright Stuff* at all. But he's still genuinely thankful she found him, and he doesn't even know her name. "Thank you so much," he says. "I really mean it, Doctor…"

She glances at him, smiling. "Raisani," she says, "Fereshteh Raisani. It's Persian…Iranian."

He rolls the name over in his mind, likes the rhythm, the sound of it.

"Most of my patients mutilate it," she adds. "Something like *Fresh and Raisiny.*"

He squints out the passenger window at the bright, arid expanse of rough hills and valleys flowing toward the setting sun. Maybe he'll feature her in one of *The Wright Stuff* segments. The Persian doctor wandering the Mojave.

"Don't even think it," she says, as though he spoke his thoughts aloud or she is telepathic. "I value what little privacy I have." She's still smiling, but with her head tilted, ironically.

He glances down at his hands, which, though he wasn't aware of it, are trembling. His mind returns to the cavern and the canisters; he feels suddenly as though the painted fists are clenched, ready to strike.

3

WHEN ANDREW WRIGHT HEARS THE KNOCK ON HIS HOTEL ROOM DOOR, he grimaces. He's looking in the bathroom mirror at the mess that used to be his face, and he knows he'll have some explaining to do. In fact, Maggie will undoubtedly hurl some serious shit his way. He's already forty minutes late for her nine PM production meeting, and he's wearing only a towel. Doctor Raisani was nice enough to drop him at The Tahitian's back parking garage entrance so that he was able to slink past the coconut palms lining the periphery of the new hotel-casino's posh tropical lobby without drawing much attention. A long shower and a fistful of ibuprofen have revived him, but he still can't get the goddamned canisters out of his mind.

As he limps across the room past the king-size teak four-poster bed, he shouts, "Who is it?"—even though he knows. Only Maggie would come fetch him rather than call.

"Open the damn door, Andy," she answers.

When he does so, Marguerite McNamara has her hands on her hips. She is petite, barely five feet, and pretty, with green eyes and black hair cut short in a perky, no-nonsense style. Her black skirt fits tightly over her slender hips, and her emerald blouse complements her eyes. Her black ABC computer bag is under her arm. She gasps—not for affect but because she's genuinely taken aback by his face. His chin is the color of a plum, his upper lip and nose are swollen to the point of caricature, and his blond hair does nothing to hide the welt that's beginning to scab on his forehead.

"Don't ask," he says.

"Don't ask!" she exclaims, her eyes flashing. "You look like you did a nosedive off that friggin' bike I warned you not to rent, and I'm not supposed to ask. Jesus, Andy!" She has been his producer for five years, and she's done a terrific job. Indeed, her nickname at the network is *Tank,* after the coach in the comic strip, because, despite her diminutive size and angelic appearance, she gleefully runs over anyone or anything in her way. She is also nine years younger than he is, and they would, he's sure, have become lovers if it weren't for her consummate and sometimes distracting professionalism.

As she brushes by him into the room, she says, "Get some clothes on, Andy." She sits in one of the two bamboo chairs by the window and takes her phone from her computer bag.

Pulling on a red sportshirt in the bathroom, he can hear her talking to Miguel, their camera man, about changes in the morning shoot they'll need to make to keep his face off-camera. "New cover shot… No walk-and-talk…Definitely no stand-up at all, even if the suits demand it…And lots more b-roll…" When he returns still barefoot but wearing slacks and the shirt, she flicks off her phone, slips it back into her bag, and sighs. The sigh, he knows, is strictly for affect.

"Shit, Andy," she says, "I've got Benjamin Kupferberg primed to show you just how much of a paradise The Tahitian really is tomorrow morning, and you look like you went duck hunting with Dick Cheney."

He slumps into the other bamboo chair and gazes across the room at the print of Gauguin's *Two Tahitian Women* on the wall above the teak dresser. Both women are bare chested; one holds a platter of red flowers, the other a bouquet. "Maggie," he says, "something happened this afternoon." She's the only one he can tell—he knows that, but he's still unsure how to begin.

"Yeah," she answers, "you took a header off a motorcycle you shouldn't have been riding." She pauses, looking at his face. "We're lucky it isn't worse."

The plural pronoun, he realizes, is good news. She's buying in, though she doesn't yet have any idea what she's purchasing. He goes over to the mini-bar's refrigerator, with its teak sides decorated with images of Polynesian gods, and pulls out a seltzer water for himself and a ginger ale for her.

When he hands her the ginger ale, she points to the seltzer and says, "Yikes, Andy, something really is bothering you."

Smiling, he says, "And I didn't take a dive off the bike, either." He sits, twists the cap off the bottle of seltzer, lets the carbonated water soothe his throat, which is still dry, and launches into the story. He leaves out nothing, telling her every detail he can remember. As he talks, she leans forward, her hands cradling the ginger ale, her elbows on her knees, and her eyes on him.

After he finishes, she sits back, sips the soft drink, taps the chair's arm with her free hand, and asks, "And you're sure this isn't a hallucinogenic flashback?" When he doesn't laugh, she adds, "Okay, Andy, you saw these canisters. But you have no idea what they are?"

"None."

"Did it look military?" she asks.

"Sort of. The yellow lettering wasn't words. More of a serial number." He shakes his head. "But it was kind of religious…or psuedo-religious, too. The red material covering the table was like an altar cloth or something."

She nods, stands, and approaches his chair. "Which arm?" she asks. When he pulls up his right sleeve, she runs her index and middle fingers over his triceps and says, "You could've been injected. But if the canisters are something…sinister, why not simply kill you? No offense."

"I thought about that," he says. "You, Miguel, Arnuz, even Charles knew I blew out of town on a bike. The rangers at the visitors' center greeted me by name…"

"And a manhunt," she finishes his thought, "especially for a celebrity like you, might uncover the cache."

He smiles at her again. She's constantly amused by his fame, which, she periodically reminds him, might be as much notoriety as anything else. In fact, only a month ago when a talk show pundit remarked that *The Wright Stuff* was a national treasure, she pointed out that televised gabfests invariably proclaim at least one darling du jour and suggested to him, as kindly and as gently as she could, that he might simply have become a media jester, America's Favorite Fool.

"I don't know, Andy. Not to diminish your status as a celeb, but if somebody wanted you dead out there, you'd be dead. And from what you said, dumping your body in that cave would've been no problem." She sits in her chair and curls her legs under herself. "People disappear in the desert. Fall off cliffs. Die of exposure. Practically every day. Hell, a day before we arrived some hiker vanished out in Red Rock Canyon."

He nods, though he doesn't like the sound of any of it.

"And if they recognized you, they'd never leave you alive." She smiles. "They'd know you'd be back to investigate."

"Yeah." She's right. A lot of his stories over the years have been, literally, ones he'd tripped over.

"Could it've been somebody else, not whoever stored the canisters?"

He shakes his head. "I hadn't seen anybody for over an hour."

She drinks the ginger ale and asks, "Have you thought about talking to the cops?"

He knows the question's loaded, looks for a smile, but doesn't find one. He's had more than his share of run-ins with local gendarmes over the years. He's told her before that it's the nature of *The Wright Stuff,* but they both know he's got a thing about authority. As the daughter of a Kankakee, Illinois, cop, she's got a certain respect for the law and government agencies—but he's never had much use for rules or for those who enforce them. "And tell them what?"

She shrugs, but he can finally see the smile in her eyes.

He laughs for the first time that evening. "In this town, they must get some lamebrained, crackpot, or lunatic story every two minutes."

"Just asking, Andy," she says. "The doctor…?"

"Raisani. What about her?"

She slides her glass onto the bamboo and Capiz coffee table. "Her just happening to find you there by that deserted road. That's quite the coincidence. Do you think she's involved?"

"No." Leaning forward, he shakes his head again. "Not directly, anyway. You could eat off the interior of her Land Rover. There'd have been some mud or sand or something if I'd been transported in it." He scrapes the empty seltzer bottle's label with his thumbnail. "I checked for tracks. The Land Rover had swerved to the side, as though she'd suddenly seen something. There were other tire tracks, but nothing that looked like another vehicle had pulled over or stopped there after the rain. And there was only one set of boot-prints—hers—approaching the spot where she found me."

"And?"

"That's just it." He peals off the seltzer bottle's label. "There weren't any other tracks at all."

"Not even yours?"

"None." He wads up the label and tosses it across the room into a wastebasket near the dresser. "It was like I dropped out of the sky."

She smiles again. "I've always pictured you as an overgrown Cabbage Patch Kid." As she takes her reporter's notebook from her bag, she says, "You're going back out there, aren't you?"

"I've got to pick up the motorcycle."

"But only after the morning shoot. And it'll take time. With that face of yours, we're going to have to shoot more b-roll," She starts writing in the narrow spiral notebook. "We've got to finish the *Fight to Save Vegas* stories. Got to focus on business, right, Andy?"

"Deal," he says.

Still taking notes, she asks, "Can you find the spot?"

"Where Doctor Raisani found me, yes," he answers. "I triangulated it. But I don't know if I can locate the petroglyphs, find my way back to the caverns. I was deep in the canyon, way up the eastern slope. And I got turned around a little in the rain. I wasn't really…"—he'll use her favorite word—"*focused* to begin with."

She gazes at him as if to say, *No shit, Sherlock!* But the look fades, and she begins to jot in her notebook again. "Once we've finished up with Kupferberg tomorrow, I'll check any records of petroglyphs in Red Rock Canyon," she says. "The one you saw sounds…unique."

He knows she means *bizarre*.

"And I'll run a background check on your friend, the doctor," she continues. "And see if there's any scoop in the military about lost or stolen canisters of…what? Anthrax?"

They look at each other for a moment in silence, and then he says,

"My mind went there, too. But I don't think...I don't know..." He shakes his head. "You might turn up something on the symbols on the canisters. Maybe, check out the local fire-and-brimstone scene."

"Got it," she says. "Draw me a picture of the fist, okay? And one of the petroglyph, too."

"Sure thing." He stands and touches her shoulder. "Thanks, Maggie." Limping over to the teak desk for a piece of the hotel letterhead, he's not sure he feels better—but at least they're starting to do something.

4

JOSEPH WENGELT SITS ALONE IN HIS PRIVATE CHAPEL. HIS BACK IS ONLY slightly hunched and his head is held high, his eyes on the solid gold *crux commissa,* the authentic cross, hanging on the gold chain before him. He is a large man, almost six-foot-four, and, though he is past sixty, he has not become soft like so many others. True, his legs and waist and neck may thicken, but his spirit remains lean. His hair may have thinned and turned, but his blue eyes retain the gleam of eternal youth and boundless faith. He is communing with his Lord, praying alone, apart from the Elders, the acolytes, and his far-flung congregation.

With maple floors, stone walls, and a ventilation system that circulates and purifies the air, the windowless chapel is monastic—sparsely furnished with only his seat, the crux, and, low against the far wall, the End Times Vessels he recently had installed. The golden fist, his icon for the Day of the Lord, lies on the hand-woven red cloth covering the Vessels. No, nothing in this chapel is ostentatious. Nothing is at all like those ornate and gilded tabernacles in those infernal Jewish and Papist synagogues and cathedrals. This is his refuge, his sanctuary. He comes here when he needs to confer with the Lord Almighty, to make critical decisions, decisions that will alter the lives of all of the Lord's children during these End Times.

It is not so much that he can talk to his Lord here in this chapel, or that his Lord talks to him. What transpires in this sanctum sanctorum goes beyond words. The Lord's Will resides in him, lives with him, suffuses through him. And the certainty that he is the Vessel of Truth is obvious not merely to those who know and follow him, but to all those others—those that bear witness, that see it exude in the grandeur of his visage and hear it resonate in the timber of his voice.

He is pondering a most momentous decision, indeed, the alpha and omega of his ministry. As always, he is allowing the Lord's Will to imbue his thoughts—but then the door behind him opens. He is not to be interrupted when he is in chapel, and he does not turn. A hand, a soft hand, touches his shoulder, and he knows by that contact and by her scent that it is Christine, his favorite acolyte, the first among equals. The Elders have sent her because they know that by doing so they will not have to endure his wrath.

He tilts his head toward her, and her hand gently caresses his ear and neck. Although she has celebrated her nineteenth birthday, she still retains a sweetness and innocence that invariably soothes. She is a voluptuous woman, her endowments obvious even in the standard long white cotton nightgown she is wearing, and her blonde hair is cut short like Joan of Arc's. She is now in her sixth month, beginning to fully show. The Lord demands that he be fruitful and multiply, and he always heeds the Will of the Lord.

"Mr. Smith is here, Prophet," she whispers.

"He's come *here?*" he hisses, clenching the arms of the chair with both hands.

"Yes, Prophet," she says as she strokes his neck. "Even at this hour. He waits for you in the Commons."

This intrusion is maddening. He is preaching, spreading News of the End Times, on air in less than an hour, but he forces the facade of peace to fall over his features. He loosens his grasp on the chair and stands stiffly, his knees cracking in the silence. He is spotless in his starched blue shirt with silver Divine Eagle bolo, his pressed denims, his tooled leather belt, and his snakeskin boots—and he needs only to pull at the cuffs of his shirt to gird himself.

"Thank you, Sister," he says to her as he places a hand on each of her shoulders. They are the large, rough hands of a man who has labored long in the Fields of the Lord, and, as she looks up into his eyes, he allows his hands to meander for a moment before saying, "Please, Sister, extinguish the lights."

She steps back, gazes with her pale enchanting eyes at the cloth covering the Vessels, and asks, "Mr. Smith has come about the Day of the Lord?"

"Yes," he answers. He does not explain further. Christine understands full well that because he alone communes directly with the Lord he never needs to justify any of his decisions to *any* member of his flock. She has been his acolyte for four years, except for a brief, sad period concerning her apostate mother and infidel father twenty months ago. Since her return to the fold, he has taken an ever-increasing interest in her progress in the Lord. And her ministrations have certainly provided great succor. But she would never question his authority. Never.

She averts her eyes and, her voice again a whisper, says, "The Lord's will be done, Prophet."

5

The Commons, the main building's large front room in which
Prophet Joseph Wengelt meets those who do not dwell with him,
is, like the rest of the sprawling Divine Eagle Institute, built and
fitted out entirely with Western materials. Every stone and board
is indigenous, if not locally, at least to the Western Frontier of this
Great Nation. The furniture is comfortable without any trappings
of the effete East Coast Elitist Conspiracy. When the Prophet—as
he always thinks of himself when dealing with his flock or the public
—enters the room from the corridor, Mr. Gary Smith is hunched
over fingering, almost fondling, the Frederic Remington bronze of
the Bronco Buster.

Smith straightens quickly and extends his hand, saying, "Evenin',
Mr. Wengelt."

The Prophet shakes the philistine's hand, but his eyes fix him hard.
The man is unkempt. He is barely six feet, with stooped shoulders
that make him seem even shorter. His unruly graying hair—though
he is more than a decade the Prophet's junior—curls over his ears
and down the nape of his neck. His wrinkled brown shirt is loosely
tucked in, his pronounced paunch hangs over his baggy jeans, and
his black boots—Doc Martens, is that what they're called?—haven't
been polished in weeks. Worse yet, the man invariably acts as though
they are equals—just because he can trace his pedigree back to James-
town. Or so he says. Yet...The Prophet lets his eyes soften. Yet, the
man has for the previous six years been and will again be useful—
a Tool of the Lord. "We have agreed that you not come here," the
Prophet says, his voice even.

Smith grins, the crooked teeth of his overbite stained by decades of smoking. "No, Mr. Wengelt," he says, "*you* agreed that I don't come here."

"You know I am to preach within the hour," the Prophet says. "Why have you come at this time?"

Smirking, Smith gazes around the room at the large stone fireplace in the canted wall set with local stone, the other three pine-paneled walls, the rough-hewn roof beams, even the tiled floor.

"What is your business?" An edge creeps into the Prophet's voice despite his resolve.

"*Our* business, Mr. Wengelt," Smith answers, "is Der Tag."

The Prophet nods. Reining in a philistine, even a useful philistine like Smith, is an irksome task. "I have told you," he says, "that the Day of the Lord is at hand."

"Yes, Mr. Wengelt, you have. Repeatedly." Smith scratches his chin. "But the mud people are swampin' the Strip. Slime everywhere. Making millions for the Man this very fuckin' minute. The fact is, the whole fuckin' country's in the crapper, and the Man just keeps gettin' richer and richer. Plus, the fight's only a coupla fuckin' nights away. My Protective Security Force is just itchin' for a boot party, if you know what I mean."

The Prophet knows all too well. And this is just like the lout: gratuitous profanity, but no imagination and no foresight, and certainly no inkling whatever of the Lord's Will. He walks over to the wall where his collection of vibrantly painted wooden snakes hangs, artfully arranged so that they swarm over the paneling. He chooses a brown and gold rattler shaped like a lightning bolt, removes it from its brackets, turns, and sighs. "Mr. Smith," he says finally, "I have told you that your boys will have your day." He raises the snake, almost but not quite brandishing it. "All will be revealed very soon."

Smith stuffs his hands in his jeans pockets, cocks his head, chews his lower lip, and says, his eyes now fixed on the Prophet, "That ain't fuckin' good enough, Wengelt. Not for me or my Protective Security Force neither."

Taking a deep breath, the Prophet runs his thumb and forefinger over the snake's gilded rattle. His own newly formed Guardian

Angels, led by Michael the Archangel himself, are strong and self-disciplined, but certain unsavory tasks are beneath the Angels' dignity—hence these continuing dealings with Smith and his so-called Protective Security Force. They're mostly a bunch of tattooed skinheads, the spawn of boozers and drug addicts, from broken homes, unemployed and for the most part unemployable, almost beyond salvation. But, as with all of God's children, they will serve the Lord's ends. And the Lord, it is true, does, indeed, work in strange ways.

Though the Prophet's inclination at this moment is to personally kick Smith's sorry ass from the Institute, that won't serve the Greater Purpose. He exhales slowly, squares his shoulders, raises himself to his full height so his dominance becomes palpable, meets the man's gaze, and holds it. "All right," he says. "In three night's time, Authentic Israel will triumph beyond your dreams. Water will turn to blood. Babylon's idolators and whoremongers will be struck down and driven out on a scale you have not ever considered. And you, Mr. Smith, and your Protective Security Force will be the instruments. You will pour out the Vessels of the Wrath of the Lord. Through you, the New Jerusalem will arise in the desert."

Pausing to let that idea sink in, the Prophet taps the snake against the palm of his hand. "I will meet you tomorrow," he continues, "at 16:00 sharp in the designated place. You will arrive with exactly eight members of your Protective Security Force, your eight most trustworthy men. At that time, Mr. Smith, all will be revealed to you."

Smith pulls his hands from his pockets, nods slowly, smiles, and says, "Now, that's more like it, Reverend. We'll be seein' a whiter and brighter world."

Watching the yahoo lick his lips, the Prophet cannot let him have the last word. "But the scope of this *Apocalypse...*" he adds; he was not going to use the term, but it is justified now, "...demands that your Protective Security Force does nothing, and I mean absolutely nothing, in the interim to draw the attention of government agents. You must understand that." These are the End Times. The Day of Reckoning is nigh. The Lord is at hand! The Alien Usurper and his Aborters may pay lip service to the Lord, but they are all, by their very nature, Godless. The secular government's minions inevitably fail, at every turn, to serve the Lord their God. The ignorant fools are wholly incapable of comprehending the Truth: The Lord's Will must be done on earth as it is in Heaven. In their blasphemous belligerence, they promote the ludicrous illusion that Church and State are separate.

Even in those years in which God-fearing men ruled the nation, their efforts were inadequate. Their feeble attempts to construct a New Jerusalem did not suffice. And now the mongrelists and traitors within who threaten this Great Nation must be destroyed so that the New Order will be ushered in. The *liberals*—the word itself makes his skin crawl—must be crushed immediately. Their lies must be denounced, and their shame must be exposed before Heaven. Any government run by an Alien Usurper—and overrun with elitists and internationalists and women—must be eliminated. That last abomination of an election was a sham perpetrated on this Great Nation by the mainstream media's manipulation. Indeed, there shall be no elections whatever in the New Jerusalem—the Prophet is making absolutely sure of that. All of this is beyond Smith's meager powers of comprehension, however, and so the Prophet concludes simply, "And now I must prepare to spread the Word of the Lord." He turns, replaces the snake in its proper bracket, and struts from the room without a handshake or another word.

Smith stands for a moment, again surveying the room, his smile broadening into a grin. Wengelt is one pompous fuckin' dickhead, that's for sure, but he, like so many other stuck-up assholes, can be handled pretty fuckin' easily. He saunters to the polished, petrified-wood coffee table, opens the humidor, and removes all seven cigars. He just finishes slipping them under his brown shirt when the two squeaky clean hulks in their white shirts and silver-eagle bolos arrive to escort him out.

6

STARS FADE. BIRDS CHITTER AND CALL. TO THE EAST, THE CREST OF THE dark ridge glows. Nick Larson sits alone, as he does each morning, cross-legged on the boulder. His back is straight, and he rests his wrists on his knees. His breathing is slow, deep, and even. To his left, the trickling creek, falling thirty feet along its sandstone bed, rings like small chimes. In this spot, the Strip, only twenty miles away, and the ever-encroaching Vegas sprawl are never visible. It is still cool in this moment before dawn, and Larson wears a gray long-sleeved cotton T-shirt, cotton pants, and scuffed chukkas. A woven strap looped over his shoulder and across his chest holds a canvas satchel under his right arm. Another bag, like a large recyclable lunch bag, hangs from his belt next to his stainless steel canteen.

More white than yellow, the sun glides above the ridge. The wind rises with the sun. Light sparks the rock, sears the water. The sun, too bright to gaze at, ignites the creosote bushes and the juniper— and shadows Larson. The canyon is, suddenly, an illuminated manuscript. And Larson prays:

> *Glory be to the Creator*
> *And to the Created*
> *And to the Spirit that binds us,*
> *As it was in the beginning,*
> *Is now,*
> *And ever shall be,*
> *Eternally,*
> *Amen.*

A vestige of his upbringing and a bridge from past to present, it is the only prayer he still says. He will repeat it intermittently, almost subconsciously, throughout the day.

As the sun climbs, Larson remains seated. There is no bobcat or mountain lion this particular morning, but a coyote, nose pointed and bushy tail twitching, lopes along the rocks toward its den. Collared lizards skitter; ground squirrels scramble from bush to bush. A desert cottontail skirts the creosote. In the distance, four Desert Bighorn sheep clamber, their hooves clacking, up the steep, rocky canyon wall.

A Mojave rattlesnake, almost four feet long, emerges from a crag in the rock across the creek from Larson. Its dark tongue flicking constantly, it slithers into sunshine and halts. The snake is brown; dark diamonds surrounded by pale borders run down its back to its segmented rattle. The snake eyes Larson for a moment, then ignores him, basking in the sun and waiting for its warmth to prepare it for the day's hunting. Despite its potent venom and natural belligerence, the snake made a truce with Larson. And now, he is simply another element in the snake's domain.

Larson sits for another ten minutes sorting out his day. It will be full: the pinnacle first, a few moments with his wife, and then vigilant research and reconnaissance followed by a sojourn back in this canyon. What he'll do after that likely depends on what occurs during his reconnaissance. He's close, he knows, to the missing canisters; at least one, he's sure, is still there, and others may be nearby as well. Time is the issue. Though he himself has on rare occasions dwelled out of time, he's acutely aware that at this juncture time's arrow is very much in flight. But in this moment, he will, before all else, reside at this still point and let his mind empty. Let it give up all personal concerns, even the heart of the matter—a rendering that is both voluntary and necessary each morning. He raises his right arm, opens his hand, and spreads his fingers as though he is slowly releasing the day itself.

Finally, he uncrosses his legs, rises fluidly, stretches, and begins to follow the creek bed down into the canyon. He is agile and, at five-foot-eight and 155 pounds, lean and strong. His skin is deeply tan, his brown hair short, his face shaven the day before. Cutting back and forth across the water, bounding from boulder to boulder, he descends quickly. He fully understands personal gain and loss, the weight of the world, the swoop and scud of societal events, but his expression is fresh as well as worn, exuberant as well as weary. The lines around his gray eyes suggest his age—fifty-three—but in these moments he is far younger and far older. His life, as he well knows, is paradox.

After a few minutes, he stops near a large boulder, rolls his neck, scuttles up the rock without slipping, sticks his boot into a toehold, and flings himself upward. Catching the hidden handhold, he pulls himself up until he can see the cave mouth and the petroglyph. The rain, as he suspected, has rinsed away any sign of another human. He pushes away from the wall, drops to the boulder below, and leaps to the ground. Using dead creosote branches, he brushes away his tracks all the way back to the wash.

He keeps moving nimbly downstream, pausing occasionally to snag a candy wrapper or other bit of trash and place it in the bag on his belt. There is less garbage than usual, though; the previous day's storm not only drove off the tourists but washed their refuse down toward the picnic area.

He finally finds the motorcycle pitched against a juniper three-fifths of a mile above the trailhead marker. It's dented and scratched from its ride with the torrent, but it looks like it might still run. As he rights the motorcycle, he scans the wash below him. The Bureau of Land Management rangers have been too busy cleaning up after the flashflood to look for the motorcycle, even if the TV guy reported it. The front wheel is locked over so he lifts the handlebars and rolls the motorcycle on its back wheel to a small stand of piñon pine fifty yards away. Swinging it back around, he drops it where it can't be seen from the wash. He crouches, fiddles with the muddy engine for a few seconds, stands, and stretches again. Then he takes a deep breath, gulps water from the bottle, and starts to clean his tracks before heading back up along the trickling creek.

7

The morning shoot at The Tahitian starts well, mostly, Wright knows, because Maggie has everything organized and his crew works well together. The interview with Benjamin Kupferberg takes place in his plush and tastefully appointed office. There's wood throughout, and the only concession to the hotel's South Seas theme, Gauguin's *The House of Song*—the goddamned original, not a print—hangs on the wall opposite the Brazilian rosewood desk. Wright and Kupferberg sit in two wine-red leather armchairs angled toward each other near a paneled wall adorned with artfully framed photographs of the casino owner hobnobbing with the rich and famous. A small man, five-seven at most, Kupferberg is tan and fit. His Armani suit is impeccable, his auburn hair perfectly coifed, his smile brilliant. He looks a little dwarfed, though, in the armchair, so Miguel Ramirez keeps the Sony tight, varying close-ups with head-and-shoulder shots. It helps, of course, that the camera loves Kupferberg, who, at fifty-nine, is still a superlative showman.

Wright opens with the standard stuff that fits the goddamned network format, but it all works because Kupferberg speaks in quick sound bites, modulating his voice just so for each answer. "Started with a buck-twenty and a case of Jim Beam," he tells Wright. He parlayed a twenty percent interest in a cousin's liquor distributorship into a third-rate resort, then a chain of second-rate motels, and finally a first-rate hotel-casino operation worth four billion and change until he bet everything, all in, on the construction of The Tahitian. When Wright asks about the financing, Kupferberg drums his fingers on the arm of the chair and admits, "Of course the debt's an issue. Expanding when money is tight is always a risk." His smile isn't forced or the least bit ironic. "Like the rest of the market, my stock's taken a hit. And, sure, guys are going belly up all around me." He shrugs. "But life, Andy, is *always* risk."

Kupferberg looks directly into the camera and raises his voice. "The Tahitian is my crown jewel, Andy," he says. "The finest hotel anywhere—ever! I've stolen my staff..." his laugh's loud and genuinely friendly, "from the best hotels around the world. My general manager is Swiss, and my loss-prevention chief's German. It's loss prevention now, Andy. Not *security* anymore. *Loss Prevention!*" He waves expansively. His energy—even seated, he can't stop moving —is making Miguel's job tricky. "My director of engineering's Japanese, and my executive chef's French-Polynesian. Would you believe, Andy, I'm serving the best food in the world right here under my roof! It's true. People are coming here to eat. To Las Vegas, Andy, to *eat!*"

When Wright asks about the tributes and trophies that stand on the shelves of the custom-built, rotary-cut rosewood bookcases, he sees just how tightly wound and deeply competitive Kupferberg really is. Despite creeping arthritis, he's a scratch golfer, an avid skier, and a champion sailor. "Ocean racing's just like business, Andy," he says, "hand-picking your crew and whipping 'em into shape's the key!" He's also hugely amused by Wright's face. At one point, he stops extolling his Gold Mountain Properties, Inc. just long enough to chortle, "Andy, my boy, you look like you skied a double black diamond face first!"

During the grand tour following the interview, Wright sees that the thirty-five story, 3,550-room Tahitian is, in fact, a gem. "Makes Wynn and Encore look like No-tell Motels!" Kupferberg crows. "Had a few cost overruns," he then admits with another shrug. "And play is down everywhere. But even with the market's collapse, I didn't scale back or cut corners at all. Didn't skimp on anything—ever! And my investors, the first foreign, ah, *international,* group ever sanctioned by the Nevada Gaming Commission, have stuck with me. So far, anyway. Got to think positive, right, Andy?"

The main lobby, designed around a seventy-five-foot waterfall, re-creates a tropical paradise in precise detail. Miguel, despite the usual snafus with lighting, gets the camera angles exactly right, and Arnuz Jones is able to adjust sound levels to keep most of the hotel's incessant background noise to a minimum. "Orchids, hibiscus, gardenias, frangipani—every flower's imported from Polynesia," Kupferberg points out. "Even the dirt!" And, with a knowing smile, he adds, "The water is All-American!"

Indeed, a grand and conspicuous display of water is, though this is one of the few things Kupferberg doesn't say, The Tahitian's real theme. At this hotel in the stark Mojave Desert, water is omnipresent —even to the small streams winding through the spacious casino. The gaming parlors, neither as dark nor as cramped as those in other casinos, emerge like an exotic and tumultuous jungle from beneath the tiered ceiling of the lobby opposite the waterfall. Bamboo and vegetation set off the high-stakes tables from the rest of the casino— and water wends and babbles through it all.

Outside, in front of the hotel, the mammoth lagoon features double-hulled canoe races eight times daily for the hotel's guests and the general public. And within the hotel's lush confines, a second, private lagoon, separated from the hotel's main pool by a soft blue palm-lined wall, includes, for the exclusive pleasures of the whales—"The high rollers, Andy, willing to drop a million a night at the tables!"— and the glitterati, a dozen *fares,* personal thatched-roof bungalows set on stilts in the water just like those at the most upscale Polynesian resorts. "You want room service? We deliver in an outrigger canoe!"

All is tropical here at the inner lagoon. A boardwalk skirts the water under a row of palm trees, and finger piers run across the water to each of the *fares.* A dark volcanic-sand beach gleams at the far end of the lagoon. And, even more of a rarity in Vegas, it's quiet here, almost tranquil—in every respect perfect, even to the bare-breasted Tahitian beauties sun-bathing on the beach. The cover shot, Wright decides, will show Kupferberg laughing and chatting with a captivating young wahine in profile to the camera, the traditional gardenia behind her ear and her long black hair covering just enough of her bare skin, while the voice-over asks, "Why is this man, who's billions of dollars in debt, smiling through the recession?"

8

DRIVING WEST OUT INTO THE DESERT ALONG ROUTE 160, WRIGHT TRIES to script the morning's piece in his mind, arranging and rearranging sound bites—but he has difficulty concentrating. The cavern and the canisters keep intruding on his thoughts. The crew shot three hours of video, which they'll edit down to three minutes of *The Wright Stuff.* And, Maggie, no doubt, is already screening tape.

A mile after Wright turns onto Lost Canyon Road, he sees three mustangs, a sorrel and two grays, galloping across the open range kicking up dust. Not as much dust, though, as the red Hummer he's driving, the only vehicle available, according to the rental agency manager, large enough to carry a motorcycle. Wright's wearing his crosstrainers, blue jeans, the sport shirt he wore the previous night, and a floppy khaki hat he bought for an exorbitant price at The Tahitian Store. Kupferberg wanted to comp the hat and everything else including the rooms, but network policy prohibits any special treatment.

Wright stops first at the spot where Raisani found him. Other vehicles have since used the dirt road, but he can still make out Raisani's and his prints. Carrying one of the two plastic water bottles he purchased, he follows the prints back to the piñon. His ankle is swollen and sore, but he can hobble, just as he did during The Tahitian tour, at a pretty good clip. He stands by the piñon for a few minutes, sipping water and scanning the hills and canyon walls, hoping he'll notice something that will key a memory, any memory, of what happened after he saw the canisters. But nothing at all registers.

Using the road as a baseline, he turns increasingly large semicircles around the piñon, inspecting the ground for a trail or any other sign to suggest he didn't plummet from heaven to the foot of that tree. Though thunderheads rise over the vast hills and valleys to the west, he treks under a clear sky and scorching sun. If anything, it's even hotter than it was prior to the goddamned storm yesterday. His lip stings whenever the sun hits it, and he's soon sweating through his shirt. A white Cadillac Seville with tinted windows roars down the road heading out toward Route 160. There's so little wind that the car's dust tail hangs in the air like a brown cloud before settling. He hears another sound, a muffled whine, but doesn't see another vehicle.

He is about to give up when he finds a knot of boot prints that looks like someone got out of a vehicle or stepped up toward a passing vehicle—he's not sure which. But the prints, disappearing at the edge of the road, lead nowhere. He removes his hat, wipes his face with his forearm, and squints up and down the road.

He pulls on his hat, limps directly to the Hummer, and drives farther north along the road. The grade steepens through starkly beautiful terrain—sandy soil and pale, stunted shrubs that gradually give way to stands of scrub pines. Telephone wires strung from pole to pole on the east side of the road provide the only trappings of civilization. Five-and-a-half miles later in a higher, partially forested area, he slows for a red and white sign with WARNING printed in large block letters above

NO TRESPASSING

VIOLATORS WILL BE PROSECUTED

One hundred yards farther on, a rough wagon track forks to the west. Another three hundred yards beyond the fork, high wrought-iron gates block the road. In the center of each gate, painted gold, is an insignia of an eagle striking a coiled snake. He lets the Hummer idle but doesn't get out. An eight-foot chain link fence topped with spirals of razor wire stretches from both gate posts across the barren terrain into thick stands of pine. On the other side of the gates, the road, covered with a fresh layer of blacktop, angles behind more trees. Other than the fence and road, there's no sign of human habitation.

He backs the Hummer to the fork, turns, and drives slowly over the rutted wagon track up into the hills. He passes a couple of old campsites and a broken down, rusted horse trailer before stopping at a narrow turnaround. When he climbs out of the Hummer, he can see on the wooded hill across the rocky valley a large cistern, a flag pole flying an American flag above a gold flag with a red emblem, a white wooden or steel "T" even taller than the flag pole, and seven roofs fitted with solar cells—enough cells, it seems to him, to generate electricity for a small town.

Wishing he had binoculars—or, at least, sunglasses—he hikes up the track a quarter mile until he finds a better vantage point. Even with his hat on, he uses both hands to shade his eyes from the glare. Squinting again, he's able to trace the fence and razor wire around a compound that must be forty acres or more. In addition to the seven buildings with the solar cells, a half-dozen other buildings nestle among the trees. The front building is a sprawling L-shaped ranch house facing the end of the paved driveway. A wide patio separates the house from the tall white T and a semi-circular stone churchlike building. The three buildings behind the church, connected by covered walkways, look from his angle like a bird in flight. The middle building, the body, is thick and square. The other two, which spread like wings in either direction, are long and thin. Dormitories, he suspects, or barracks.

Six dark jeeps ranging from a dusty, stripped-down Wrangler to a freshly washed Grand Cherokee are parked downhill from the central area in front of a mammoth garage with eight bays and three gas pumps. A cellular phone tower rises behind the garage. Up the hill, set a little away from the larger buildings, is a rectangular, windowless building with two television dishes beside it and a microwave broadcast antenna behind it. *That,* Wright thinks, *is pretty goddamned interesting.* The compound looks like a cross between a religious school and a military outpost. And whatever the hell it is, somebody's poured a shitload of cash into this desolate spot at the dead end of an almost deserted road.

He watches the compound for fifteen minutes before a blond man leaves the main building by a back door. Wearing a khaki shirt and khaki pants, the man looks, even at that distance, as though he's in uniform. His posture erect, he stands stiffly for a moment, surveying the grounds, and then marches briskly past the buildings and the cistern into the trees. The man doesn't return, and, though Wright observes the compound for another ten minutes, no one else exits any of the buildings. Finally, he shakes his head slowly and smiles ironically, aware that only mad dogs, Englishmen, and demented reporters venture out in sun and heat like this.

9

Driving along Route 159 east of the mountains toward the Red Rock Canyon entrance to pick up the motorcycle, Andrew Wright slows when he sees a sign for Red Sapphire. He shakes his head. Even by Nevada's standards, the name is odd—red sapphires are rubies, not sapphires. He glances to his left at the dozen or so houses, mostly upper-bracket, set into the side of the mountain. Below the houses, a smattering of one-story buildings spreads among the trees. And a black Land Rover is parked in front of one of the buildings.

He stomps on the brakes, swerves, and fishtails the Hummer onto the two-lane access road. Recently paved, the road leads past a red and white sign at the town limit:

RED SAPPHIRE NV

POPULATION LOW

ELEVATION HIGH

WILD BURROS WELCOME

He passes the adobe library, the Sapphire Church of God (painted bright red, of course), a double-wide trailer that serves as the United States Post Office, a cinderblock school surrounded by a chain-link fence, and a public pool in which a gaggle of children are splashing. The Land Rover has been washed and detailed, but the license plate matches. Parking next to the vehicle, he gazes at the hand-painted sign nailed to the porch roof over the entrance to the low-slung building: Red Sapphire Market & Sheriff's Office.

When he enters the market, he nods to the obese woman seated behind the counter and then spots Raisani, midway down one of the two aisles, taking a roll of black electrical tape from the shelf. Her hair is pulled back loosely, and she's wearing a dark, sleeveless cotton

34

dress with a pattern of red, green, and yellow symbols that look like Anasazi pictographs. The only other customer in the store, a stooped, blue-haired woman, plays one of the old-fashioned nickel slot machines lining the wall by the door. Just which part of this single large room is the sheriff's office isn't entirely clear to Wright.

As he walks down the aisle, he says, "Dr. Raisani, I presume."

She wheels quickly, recognizes him despite the hat pulled low over his face, and says, "Traveling incognito, are you, Mr. Wright?"

"Andy," he says.

She puts the tape back on the shelf and inspects his face, doing, it seems, a damage assessment. She smiles. "Andy," she asks, "what brings you back out here?"

"Returning to the scene of the crime." He shrugs. "And you?"

"I live here, Andy," she says. "My clinic is here." She seems preoccupied. Her eyes are wide and deep, as though she has been pondering something he couldn't possibly grasp.

The slot machine up front rings loudly, the old woman lets out a whoop, and coins spill across metal.

"I saw the Land Rover outside, hoped it was yours," Wright says, brushing his fingers across his bruised chin. "Wondered if you might want to have dinner tonight."

She hesitates before saying, "That sounds nice, Andy, but I'm busy this evening."

The lilt's in her voice, and he's not sure if he's being brushed off or if there's genuine regret. "How about a coke or something now?" he asks.

Sliding the tape so that it's snug against the others, she hesitates again. "I've got to…Yes, okay," she says, "a lemonade would be nice."

"Good," he answers. "I'll meet you on the porch."

When he exits with the two twenty-ounce bottles of lemonade, she is seated in one of the two white plastic chairs set in the shade of a ponderosa pine fifteen yards from the porch. He hands her one of the bottles, takes a seat in the other chair, and taps her bottle with his. "Cheers," he says.

She smiles again.

"I came back out here," he says as she sips her drink, "because I'm still confused about what happened yesterday."

She nods but doesn't say anything. It's hot in the shade of the tree, but not oppressive. Across the road from them, an open lean-to with a corrugated metal roof is filled with junk. An airplane propeller is fixed to the front right support pillar, and a dart board hangs from the front left pillar.

"Did you notice anything odd?" he asks.

She laughs. "You mean other than an American television personality lying by the side of the road? No, Andy, I didn't. But I was mostly concerned with whether you were okay."

"There were no tracks."

Concern, or perhaps alarm, shows fleetingly in her eyes. "You mean, other than yours?"

"No," he answers, looking into her eyes. "I mean, not even mine."

She looks over at two young boys peddling bicycles from the pool. They are shirtless, and the towels over their shoulders flap like wings. "I did wonder," she says, "how you wandered so far from the hiking trails."

He holds her gaze. "I drove up the road today, till it ends."

She looks away at the two boys, now gliding no-handed downhill, their laughter trailing after them.

"You said you'd been seeing a patient up that road," he says.

She turns and meets his stare, her long lashes unblinking. "Actually, Andy, I said I needed to check on someone."

A special case, he thinks, but he says, "I saw the compound. What the hell is going on, Fereshteh?" He knows he didn't quite pronounce her name right, but he wants to step inside whatever reserve she has.

She still looks directly at him. "Andy," she says, "this is beginning to sound like an interro…an interview. And I don't appreciate it." Her voice has that same firm but not authoritarian tone he noticed the day before.

"All right," he says, "but I did see the compound, and it's the only place up that road you could've been."

She puts her lemonade on the ground next to her chair, reaches over, touches the back of his hand, and then grips his fingers. Her eyes take on an even greater depth. She is about to say something, he can tell, something important, but then the depth recedes and she looks over at the propeller before turning to him again. "Andy," she says, "please stay away from that compound, at least for a couple of days." Her voice remains firm, not plaintive at all, as though she's stating a fact, not asking a favor. "The people who live in these hills do so because they value their sec…their privacy. They go their own way. And some of them don't take to strangers at all." Letting go of his hand, she looks back at the propeller.

"I understand," he says. And he does. But he's spent most of his adult life accosting people, some of whom really didn't want to talk to him at all. He'll get Maggie on it as soon as he's back at the hotel, and he'll know about that compound by midnight. "But I can't promise you I'll stay away," he adds.

She continues to stare at the propeller. "Andy," she says, "I was born in Tehran, but I'm an American now. I fled Iran, and I came here. I *chose* to be an American." The light fades from her eyes for a moment. "There are things about this country most Americans take for granted. I don't. Things like the freedom to come and go, to ride through the streets without looking over your shoulder. Equal education for women. Separation of church and state." She turns, lifts her hand, and with her forefinger traces a vein on the back of his hand. "Three days, Andy," she adds. "Please." She smiles that wonderful smile. "Then we'll have dinner, and I'll tell you my story."

I'll be gone in three days, he thinks, and she knows it, goddamn it. He's about to bring up the canisters, but he stops himself, just as she did earlier. If she knows about the canisters, she's already involved; if she doesn't, involving her is pointless. "Thanks, that would be nice," he says simply. "But no promises. I can't make any promises."

10

JOSEPH WENGELT IS THE LAST TO LEAVE THE SMALL WAREHOUSE ALONG the back street between Highland and Interstate 15. As he opens the door, the heat radiating from the pavement blasts him. It's surely a sign. There will, according to prophecy, be fire next time—and certainly in this inferno that is Las Vegas, he can well believe it. Yet the Prophet has divined the deeper truth: the Apocalypse is both fire and water, conflagration and flood. This time, however, the deluge will not take forty days and forty nights. No, forty seconds will suffice to bring the idolaters and whoremongers to their knees. In the torrent's aftermath, *all* will understand that the End Times are at hand...that Authentic Israel must triumph...that the New Jerusalem shall rise. And that he who keeps the Lord's word will have power over nations.

Perspiration already beading on his forehead, he locks the warehouse door and looks around to make sure that Mr. Smith and his Protective Security Force have departed. Across the street, shimmering heat waves rise above the air-conditioning vents and ducts stockpiled behind the chain-link fence topped with barbed wire. The shattered wooden skids look like they're about to spontaneously combust, and the overflowing dumpster, wavering in the heat, seems about to ignite. Smith and his minions have already gone, praise the Lord. And nobody else is out in this scorcher of an afternoon—not even the woebegone illegal aliens that pick through the dumpsters and steal the shattered skids along this back street. Only one old Chevy junkster rolls slowly by using a knotted rope to tow another rusted hulk. Neither of the drivers even glances in his direction.

That philistine Smith and his boys were late for the meeting. Still, all went well. Once those skinheads comprehended the import of their mission, the Prophet held them rapt, just as he does his far-flung congregation. Charisma is the key to molding others to the Will of the Lord. And he could feel his charisma, the force of the Lord, working through him. Yes, those disaffected youth, sinners all, will now readily do his and the Lord's bidding without question. Indeed, they eagerly formed three strike forces, each with its assigned sacred sorties after the rendezvous two nights hence.

As he walks toward the Cadillac, he uses his remote to unlock the doors. Though he parked in what little shade the warehouse wall provides, the car will still not be suitable until the air conditioning cools it sufficiently. Sweating profusely, he opens each car door, starts the engine, and escapes back into the shade of the mansard roof over the warehouse's black double-door. He is, like most large men, gravely affected by the heat, and his breathing is shallow. At the meeting, only Smith seemed untouched by his charisma. And that is exactly why the Prophet assigned the lout the leading role—the Fire Bearer at the Arena. The philistine will revel in his meteoric flash in the night, his light-blasted moment of glory. It is a role so filled with fame that Smith, as the Prophet well knew, could not refuse it, especially in front of his underlings. That the acclaim will be fleeting, as Smith so clearly does not comprehend, is absolutely justified. Smith is, fundamentally, nothing more than a two-bit thief. But no, the theft of those fine rum-soaked cigars is not the sole issue. Smith's coming to the Institute was, in and of itself, a flagrant error, one in a long series, one for which justice is inevitably demanded. But with Smith, you always have to weigh his usefulness against his vulgarity.

The Prophet slams the three passenger doors, slides into the driver's seat, feels the blessed blast of cool air from the vents, and shuts the door. He should, he realizes, return directly to the Institute. And he feels the need for Christine's ministrations, her soft hands, full lips, and deep throat. And yet, he's drawn toward the sin-besotted Strip instead. He winds along the back streets he knows so well until he can cut onto Tropicana right below the looping highway ramps. As he approaches Las Vegas Boulevard, the scantily clad strollers, even in this scalding sultriness, flock along the walkways in their folly and decadence. The crowds are not as plentiful as they were before the damnable recession caused by the Alien Usurper and his doctrines. The Prophet must reap the Lord's fields now before the liberals can further their takeover of this Great Nation. And here is the throng whose fate the Lord places in his hands. He needs to view them in all their flesh-and-blood humanity. Traffic is heavy and slow, but the fully-loaded Caddy is cool now and comfortable, with its leather seats and trim, and he can gaze at this sweltering assemblage from on high. Clearly, this rabble has no idea that the Tribulations have begun and the End Times are at hand.

At the intersection, the multitude is more abundant, the sidewalks brimming and the overpasses teeming. The Statue of Liberty in front of New York New York beckons the masses not toward freedom but to sin. And, across the Boulevard, MGM's massive electronic video screens herald the Championship Bout, the fight that will be, as the Prophet knows but the barbarians do not, the sight of Authentic Israel's first conquest. Indeed, here it is, practically ground zero, and all of these mortals are completely oblivious to the fate that awaits them. A few are the filthy rich Jewish Papists and the super-fly gangsta' rappers already in town for the ill-fated fisticuffs, and some are mud people, the Arabs and Asians and Hispanics and other aliens formed from the leftover mud after the Lord created whites. But many—indeed, most—appear to be middle-Americans, perhaps even lapsed members of his own congregation. There is no exact outward measure of a sinner or saint, at least among whites. Yet all of these souls certainly have come to the Strip to sin in some manner or other. Vegas is, after all, Babylon, Sin City, Sodom and Gomorrah rolled into one—and this Strip is the Serpent's black heart. The Lord's retribution must befall all of these lost souls! Their bodies must litter the streets! Let the Lord alone recognize his own and decide who shall enter the Kingdom and who shall be banished to Eternal Damnation!

He finally makes the turn onto the Strip itself and drives the heathen corridor between all these graven images—the phony New York skyline with its rollercoaster, the phallic Coca-Cola bottle, the Hard Rock Café's oversized, pulsing gutar, the Monte Carlo billboard touting the foppish entertainers, and the dark jutting towers of the vacant CityCenter, that almost fully erected megalith to Greed, a sin he has known and conquered. He runs this gauntlet of all these seductive idols until he becomes stuck in traffic near the so-called Grand Cluster—on the right, Paris and Planet Hollywood, and on the left, Bellagio and The Tahitian, that newest, most decadent shrine to the false gods of extravagance and excess. The holy city, the New Jerusalem, must supplant these temples. The idolators most certainly must be held accountable for their profligacy—before the Lord, if not before man. And this time the Lord will show no mercy. Only eternal darkness, not the Father's feast, will welcome all of these prodigal sons and daughters.

He gazes out the Caddy's windshield at the Eiffel Tower, that priapic emblem of Parisian porn. Then, he turns his gaze out the tinted driver's window toward The Tahitian where a cheering crowd encircles the vast lagoon—probably for one of those canoe races featuring those strapping young heathens, almost naked, performing for the hordes. It's unfortunate that, like the good shepherd, he must essentially work alone. Only Michael, his Archangel, most trusted Michael, can be privy to this aspect of his ministry. Only Michael even knows about the Grotto. Christine has glimpsed two of the Vessels, of course, and has some inkling that an event of great import and magnitude is imminent. But Michael has insisted, quite rightly, that, because she is a woman, she must be excluded from *all* logistical considerations. And no one else, not his acolytes and certainly not the four and twenty Elders, must know of the mission until the Day of the Lord is at hand. Only then can he proclaim it! And even then, not as his own but as the Lord Almighty's divine retribution, the Terrible Swift Sword of the Apocalypse!

11

GARY B. SMITH CLOSES THE GATE TO THE FENCE THAT SURROUNDS HIS
single-story clapboard ranch house. As he sidles along the cracked
cement sidewalk toward the back, he steps over a partly coiled hose
and around the bowed plywood sheets leaning against the wall. His
Protective Security Force boys stopped for shots and beers after the
meeting, but he wants to check his e-mail, fax, and phone messages.
The house is paid for, his mother having buried the mortgage before
she passed on. In fact, the house is perfectly free and clear except for
the fuckin' taxes.

But the neighborhood has gone all to hell—bean-eaters everywhere, chattering their feeble fuckin' brains out. The loser next door
has three derelict cars parked right on the front lawn, all of them rust-
ing under tarps held down by roofing tiles. None of the shitheaps has
so much as moved in over a year. And the dirtball on the other side
has this shit-brown pickup with a black hood and bare fuckin' sheet
metal for one of the door panels. The whole neighborhood's just
as fuckin' bad. And the music blaring from everywhere—hell, the
beaners wouldn't know a good country tune if it ran 'em over!

When he reaches the war room's entrance, he unlocks the dead-
bolt. His mother had this back room added to the place when he was
a teenager, but it was never finished. He finally got the chance to put
up the drywall a couple of years ago, and he's still gonna put in a
ceiling sometime when he's not so fuckin' busy. For security reasons,
he also boarded up the interior doorway a year before his mother
passed on. This is now the only entrance, and he's got the only key.

As he enters his war room, he wipes his feet on the Israeli flag covering the cement floor, flicks on the overhead light, and punches on the

air conditioner he rehabbed and installed himself. Steel shelves filled with fliers, pamphlets, cartridge boxes, and other assorted patriotic publications and war materials line one wall. The more serious munitions his PSF boys have been able to liberate from construction sites are stored in the three bottom drawers of the metal file cabinet in the corner. A black swastika gleams on the deep red wall behind his metal desk and swivel armchair. Two card tables and assorted folding chairs stand along the other wall where his PSF boys have marked their slogans below the photographs of Adolf Hitler and Heinrich Himmler—*kill a fuckin raghead TODAY! Death to jews & papists! Stomp a mudhead for your Mother! Aliens—Go Home!!! Fuck women—that's all they're good for! Today's Der Tag!* and other ones just as good. It's cooler here in the war room, and maybe a little musty, like a bunker.

There are no fax or phone messages, and none of the five e-mail messages requires his immediate attention, so he opens the top drawer of the file cabinet, removes one of Reverend Dickhead's cigars, unwraps it, and tosses the cellophane into the waste basket. Using the commando knife he always keeps on the desk, he severs the butt so it'll draw easier. He then passes the cigar back and forth under his nose, savoring the smell of rum for a moment before firing it up. The meeting went pretty good except that the Dickhead tried to hypnotize the PSF with all that high-sounding shit about the End Times and the Lord's Will. Of course, God is on the side of the white race, but they're the one's that've gotta get the fuckin' job done. He'll straighten that out when the boys stop by the war room in ones and twos like they always do.

He blows smoke rings toward the bare joists and roof beams. It's truly one fine fuckin' cigar. He cut back on cigarettes after his mother died, she being a pack-and-a-half Marlboro lady until the day the cancer got her, but a man should still be able to enjoy a rum-soaked cigar on occasion. Surprisingly, the Dickhead's plan for Der Tag, or what little he really shared of it, isn't complete shit. Offing the high rollers and mud scum at the fight'll send the perfect fuckin' message. And making it look like a fuckin' terrorist attack is right on. And so is escape-goating the fuckin' A-rabs! But he's sure as hell not gonna be the one to fuck around with the transformers like the Dickhead said. No fuckin' way. One of his PSF boys'll be only too happy to take on that job.

He tries to blow smoke rings inside of smoke rings, but he can't quite get it, probably because the air conditioner's not running smooth again. The part of the plan about the hotels isn't bad neither. The MGM's the biggest fuckin' hotel in the country, The Tahitian's practically the most expensive one ever built anywhere in the world, and all the other ones cater to rich fuckin' mud people, too. They'll take out a swamp full of foreigners, screw the fuckin' ragheads, and secure the future of the white homeland all at once.

If only the Dickhead would've explained what's in the containers he's gonna distribute to the strike forces at the rendezvous. All he said was you wouldn't need protective clothing or special precautions, but that could be a pile of crap, too. It's gotta be bacteria or chemicals. Not Anthrax, though. It's impossible to get that shit anymore. It's sodium cyanide, maybe, or botulin toxin. Or maybe even sarin or ricin. What the fuck did that one website say? Ricin's 6,000 times more toxic than cyanide, and there's no fuckin' antidote. Where the hell did the Dickhead get his hands on whatever the shit is?

Both ashtrays are over on the card tables so he taps the ash into the wastebasket. Just because the plan's not bad doesn't mean it can't fuckin' be improved on. He balances the cigar on the rim of his plastic NRA coffee cup, cracks his knuckles, and roots through the piles on his desk until he finds the white pad and the red rolling writer. It sure as shit seems like the Dickhead's not quite telling the whole fuckin' story. But whatever the hell the deal is, the mud people all gotta pay big time so Der Tag makes the history books as the day everybody finally fuckin' woke up! The country's finally gonna rid itself of the alien scum…that mudmutt President, all his commie buddies, and those whore-bitches—the Speaker's even worse then the fuckin' Secretary! There's really gonna be a whiter and brighter world! He sets the cigar between his teeth and begins to scribble notes.

12

ANDREW WRIGHT PARKS THE HUMMER NEAR THE PICNIC AREA IN RED Rock Canyon. The conversation with Raisani ended awkwardly. She remained pleasant, and he was amiable enough, but they were clearly at an impasse. And, just as clearly, neither was going to give in to the other. His chat with the ranger at the makeshift visitor center—like almost everything else, the new center is only half built—was no more productive. They had not, the tall young woman with freckles and a wry smile told him, found the motorcycle—primarily because they had not, given the flood damage, had the time to look for it. But, if it wasn't carried all the way down to West Las Vegas, he would likely find it somewhere along the wash he should *never* have been riding up.

He locks the Hummer and, with his second water bottle in hand, limps along the hiking trail toward the wash. He's been on his ankle too much already, and it throbs with each step. The sun, flaming above the ridge line, paints the canyon's walls—the red deeper and the gray almost silver. There's no wind at all, and the phrase "goddamned oven" repeats in his mind like a mantra. Nothing that's happened this afternoon has made him feel the least bit better about what occurred yesterday. In fact, both seeing the compound and talking with Raisani have made him even more unsettled. The good doctor was definitely less than candid with him, but he still can't believe she's involved in…he doesn't know what. All he really knows is that he can't shake a nagging sense that something's not right out here in the Mojave.

By the time he reaches the wash, his leg muscles ache and he's sweated through his shirt again. A hundred yards up the wash, he sees a young guy off to his right seated on a rock in the scant shade of a juniper, writing or drawing in a hardcover notebook. They wave to each other, but Wright presses on, thinking that when he finds the motorcycle he'll at least have something to show for an otherwise wasted afternoon. As he climbs, a narrow stream trickles down the wash, the last remnant of the flood. He has been scanning the periphery of the wash, and he's unsure when he passed the stream's vanishing point, its silent return to the earth.

Sweating and winded, he stops when he finally finds the pine. Though he's certain, despite the altered landscape, it's the tree under which he left the motorcycle, there's no sign of the bike anywhere. *Shit,* he thinks, the afternoon *is* a total goddamned bust. He takes off his hat and wipes his head and neck with his arm. The hat has no sweatband, and the crown's already discolored. He drinks the last of his water, stares at the empty bottle for a moment, and then flings it hard against the pine. It bounces back to his feet, and, though he feels like leaving it there, he picks it up. Looking up the wash, he wonders if he has any chance at all of finding the mouth of the cave. Everything looks familiar—but different. He didn't mark the cave's location at the time, his goddamned slide down the shaft having nullified any chance of that, and the flood must've both washed away any tracks and altered the landscape enough to confuse his already jumbled memory.

He's still standing there gazing up at North Peak when the guy he saw earlier comes up the wash behind him. He seems to be trotting up through the gravel, barely sweating, zipping right along. He isn't whistling, but he might as well be. He wears a long-billed baseball cap without a logo, a plain T-shirt, khaki shorts, high gray hiking socks, and lightweight boots. He has a canvas satchel under his arm and a cylindrical metal canteen and nylon bag clipped with carabiners to his belt. As the guy approaches, Wright realizes he's not all that young. He's wiry and short, only a little taller than Benjamin Kupferberg, with not, it appears, an ounce of fat. His eyes are pale gray, very much like the color of the limestone glowing in the sunlight.

"Hey," the guy says.

46

"Hi," Wright answers, though he's not in the mood for small talk.

"You okay?" the guy asks. "You don't look so good."

Wright's not sure whether the guy's referring to his face or his sweaty, disheveled appearance in general. Smiling, he says, "I've been better."

"Here," the guy says, unclipping the canteen and handing it to him.

Wright accepts the canteen, tilts his head back, and lets the luke-warm water stream down his throat.

After Wright hands the canteen back, the guy points to the empty plastic bottle and says, "I'll take that for you. Recycle it later." He crushes the bottle with one hand and slips it into the nylon bag. "What're you doing up here?"

Though he's not really wary of the friendliness, Wright hesitates.

The guy cocks his head and smiles. "I mean, you're not exactly dressed for a hike to North Peak."

Wright shakes his head and returns the smile. "I'm looking for a motorcycle."

The guy acts like that's not, despite the locale, a grossly absurd statement. "A yellow dirt bike?" he asks. "Yamaha?"

"Yeah." *Exactly,* goddamn it, Wright thinks. "You saw it?"

Nodding, the guy turns and points with his thumb over his shoulder. "Half a mile back down." He smiles again. "I'll show you if you want."

Wright shrugs. "Yeah," he says, "that'd be great. Thanks."

The guy turns and starts scrambling back down the wash. He seems preternaturally surefooted, as though he knows each step without having to look. Wright follows, but the pain in his ankle is sharper going downhill. He begins to zigzag back and forth across the stream, creating his own set of mini-cutbacks to lessen the angle of descent.

The guy stands completely still on a boulder. Breathing rhythmi-cally and murmuring something, he gazes at the sunlight playing over the ridges. The colors shimmer, changing constantly. When Wright finally catches up to him, the guy asks, "Are you that TV reporter? *The Wright Stuff?*"

Wright nods. "Guilty as charged."

"Nick Larson," the guy says as he extends his hand.

"Andy."

They shake hands, and Larson starts off again, but much more slowly this time so that Wright can keep up with him.

As he hobbles beside Larson, Wright asks, "Do you come out here often?"

Larson's smile is quick and full. "As often as I can."

"Were you here yesterday?"

"Not here, but in another part of the canyon." Larson stoops, snatches a bottle cap from among the stones, and drops it into the nylon bag. "What a magnificent storm that was!"

Wright isn't sure he'd use that exact word, but he understands what Larson means. "Yeah," he says. "I had to leave the bike here." He's beginning to forget the pain in his ankle. "Had to sit out the storm in a little cave." He points back up the wash but doesn't mention the cavern or the canisters. "You know the one?"

"Hundreds of caves and old mine shafts in these canyons, Andy." Larson shrugs good-naturedly. "Thousands."

"This one had petroglyhs at its mouth."

"Really?" Larson's pale eyes gleam. "Hunting icon?"

"No, at least, I don't think so. An animal—a mountain lion, maybe, but winged—and some sort of symbols."

"Lots of petroglyphs around here," Larson says, tugging at the bill of his cap. "Some pictographs, too."

Wright changes his tack. "Do you live around here? In Red Sapphire, maybe? Or over by Lost Canyon Road?"

"Farther out," Larson says as he gestures vaguely westward.

"Know anything about a large fenced-in tract of land—the road dead-ends into it?"

"With big gates and concertina wire?" Larson climbs out of the wash.

"Yeah. Exactly." Wright slips on the gravel as he follows Larson.

"It's some sort of religious community, I think. Why?" Larson takes off, seeming to glide through heavy underbrush and over scattered boulders.

48

Wright wonders what somebody dressed like the blond man he saw would be doing in a religious commune. "Just curious," he answers. "Saw the gate and wondered." He hurries after Larson toward a stand of piñon pine.

"Some minister with a television show, if I remember right," Larson calls back to him. "You're more likely to have heard of him than I am."

Wright only knows the names of the famous and the infamous televangelists—Pat Robertson, Oral Roberts, Jerry Falwell, Jim Bakker, Jimmy Swaggart, and the like. Thinking about how none of them would ever live in close proximity to a hotbed of vice and corruption like Las Vegas, he's practically in among the trees before he spots the motorcycle. It lies on its side, its front wheel tilted up. Both fenders are scratched, and dried mud covers the frame and engine.

"Dinged up pretty good," Larson says.

Staring down at the bike, Wright wipes the back of his neck and then fishes the key from his pocket.

Larson takes the handlebars and stands the bike up, and Wright inserts the key—but neither man can get the engine to cough, much less run. Wright finally turns the bike and walks it out of the trees.

"Here, let me do that," Larson says when they reach the wash. "You're a little dinged up yourself."

"Yeah," Wright admits. "Thanks." Sweat is running down his back, and he's again aware of the throbbing in his ankle.

Larson straddles the motorcycle, guides it down into the wash, and lets it roll slowly down among the boulders. He looks like he's melded with the bike as it seems to skim along the wash, a quiet, effortless ride.

13

WRIGHT IS AGAIN LATE FOR HIS MEETING WITH MAGGIE, AND THIS TIME he hasn't even showered. He and Larson muscled the motorcycle into the Hummer quickly enough, but he got bogged down in traffic along the Strip. Vegas may be running on empty, but the streets and sidewalks are still pretty clogged. He was then delayed even longer at the rental agency haggling with the manager over the preposterously exorbitant late fee and the deductible on the insurance. When he finally got back to his room, he found a sumptuous fruit and cheese basket, a flower arrangement the color of the blossoms in *Two Tahitian Women,* and a bottle of 1996 Silver Oaks Cabernet resting on the dresser.

He's seated on the edge of his bed taking off his cross-trainers when the knock comes at the door—and he wonders if Maggie has spies in the hotel lobby. He kicks off his second shoe, yanks off his sweaty socks, and limps to the door. Wearing a yellow sun dress with spaghetti straps, she looks more cute than sensual. Her green eyes glint, but the skin under them is puffy—a sign she's starting to wear down.

He knows that she routinely functions on little or no sleep, so he says simply, "Hello there, Marguerite," goes over to the refrigerator, and takes out a chilled demi-bottle of pinot grigio for her and both a seltzer and a Heineken for himself.

Her laptop bag slung over her shoulder and an accordion file tucked under her arm, she accepts the wine and a glass. Gesturing toward the dresser, she says, "I see Ben's little perks awaited you, too." She sits in the bamboo chair she sat in the night before, and, tilting her head, stares at him as he guzzles the entire bottle of seltzer. "The swelling's down some, which is good," she says, "but you've got to ditch that friggin' hat, Andy."

Smiling, he removes the hat, which looks like it's been worn for years, and tosses it onto the floor near his shoes and socks. He feels clammy; his shirt and jeans are sticking to his skin. "What'd you find out?" he asks.

"Lots," she answers. "But let's focus on business first, okay?"

"Okay," he says as he sits down. He slides the empty seltzer bottle onto the coffee table and then rolls the Heineken bottle back and forth across his forehead.

She puts the wine and the glass on the table next to the seltzer bottle, slips the bag from her shoulder, and sets the bag next to her chair. Opening the accordion file, she pulls out four pieces of paper. "I wrote the Kupferberg story," she says. "You seemed distracted, and I, uh, thought maybe it'd help if I…"

He nods as she hands him the paper. He always writes his own scripts—the feature segment is, after all, *The Wright Stuff.* But she often edits for him, and her suggestions are invariably on target. While he reads, she pours the wine and sips it. Her eyes stay on him, gauging his reaction. After skimming the piece, he rereads it. Her writing is damn good, in spots brilliant—even better, he admits to himself, than he could've done in the time she had. And, he won't have to be on camera at all. Smiling, he says, "It's really good, Maggie. Excellent, in fact." He shrugs. "I may want to tweak it a bit."

"Of course," she answers, sitting back and grinning. "I can get the guys going on the editing tonight, if you want."

He nods, looking at her large eyes and her pretty, almost girlish, face.

"You can track your narration in their room," she says. "It's quiet. You may not even have to talk into a suitcase."

"Good." As he leans toward her to return the paper, he asks, "Am I a tad ripe?"

Grimacing, she admits, "Maybe a little."

"Hold on," he says. He goes into the bathroom, pulls off his shirt, and splashes cold water on his face, neck, and chest. He's in pretty good shape, but no one, he knows, would use terms like "washboard" or "six-pack" to describe his stomach. His muscles are stiff, and he has trouble peeling off his jeans and boxers, which he leaves in a heap on the floor. As he puts on the plush terry-cloth robe that was hanging on the back of the door, he wonders if it's another of Kupferberg's not-so-subtle goddamned gifts.

When he returns to his chair, she has sheets of yellow legal paper filled with notes lying across the top of the accordion file on her lap. "How was your afternoon?" she asks.

"Not so good," he answers. He drinks half the beer and then tells her about the compound, his chat with Raisani, and his recovery of the motorcycle. He again leaves out nothing—except his invitation to Raisani and her refusal.

When he finishes, she asks, "Did this Larson guy seem a little too friendly?"

"Like he was coming on to me?"

"No!" she scoffs. "Like he was waiting for you."

"Why?" he asks. Then, shaking his head, he adds, "No. He said he's out there a lot." He drinks the rest of his beer, stifles a burp, and gazes at the green bottle. "He acted like the canyon was his home, and I was a guest. I mean, he was...I don't know...natural. Like he and the canyon were somehow entwined." He smiles. "I know it sounds weird." He stands, tightens the belt on the robe, and fetches another Heineken from the refrigerator. "So what did you find out, Ms. McNamara?"

"Okay," she says, sifting through the yellow sheets of paper. "There's a wealth of info on petroglyphs. Too much, really. Lots of glyphs in the canyon, and many more in the area. But I faxed your drawing to a guy at UNLV, who's got a computer database." She glances at the sheet. "Dr. Nieman, the local glyph guru. He'll try to match it, or at least translate the images. In fact, he's already called back, but I couldn't reach him again before he left his office."

That's not much of a start, Wright thinks. "What about Dr. Raisani?" he asks.

She shuffles the papers. "Born in Tehran in sixty-nine. Immigrated to the U.S. with her mother in eighty-three. Los Angeles. Is that the

U.S.?" She laughs. "Berkeley undergrad, and UCLA med school. Moved here a year ago with her baby. A daughter."

"Husband?" he asks.

She smiles ironically. "No mention of one. Her house…everything is in her name. But she's fast becoming a pillar of the community. Her practice is hooked into two Vegas hospitals. And she's well thought of professionally. Already sits on a couple of philanthropic boards."

He nods. "And?" Tank invariably rolls over him with personal stuff about whomever's life they're digging into.

"And she has the clinic in Red Sapphire. Which, as you discovered today, is where she lives. She keeps to herself a lot. Has a live-in Costa Rican nanny."

"And?" he repeats.

She does an innocent Bambi thing with her eyes. "Your Doctor Raisani's mother came for a visit two weeks ago. Five days ago, grandma, the bambino, and the nanny vamoosed. To points unknown. Nobody at the clinic or either hospital seems to know where or why."

"Interesting timing."

"Exactly."

"But not," he says, "something that would link the doctor to a secret cache of…whatever the hell is in those canisters."

"I did some digging on those canisters, too." She pulls out another sheet of yellow paper. "Didn't come up with anything, but had a couple of interesting conversations with Air Force personnel at Area 51."

He rolls his eyes. "Not that extraterrestrial bullshit?"

"Same area," she answers, "but not that crap." She gives him a hand-drawn map of Nevada, a large polygon with two bright asterisks appearing next to the words *Papoose* and *Groom* in the upper right corner. "Andy," she says, "Nellis Air Force Range is 3.5 million acres, and, whatever happens there—rumors range from the testing of captured UFOs to the creation of chemical weapons—the government denies that the Papoose Lake and Groom Lake sites even exist. This, despite the fact that employees who worked at the sites are suing over what they say were toxic accidents."

"Yeah," he says, "but you're not buying into some government conspiracy theory here, are you, Mags?" He's been holding the beer without drinking it, and the condensation is dripping off the bottle onto the robe.

She winks at him. "You know me better than that, Andy." She pauses for a moment. "And, from what I gathered, nothing's missing."

Wright feels a tingling along his spine. "What do you mean?"

"Naturally, the military's touchy about *anything* that's unaccounted for. But both guys I talked to…" She pauses again. "I kept giving them openings to get defensive or disavow something or lapse into jargon, a lot of insert-foot-in-mouth opportunities."

It's been his experience—both of theirs, really—that whenever somebody makes a denial or disclaimer before an accusation is made, he's hiding something—and, most often, you've got him by the short hairs. He rubs the back of his hand across his mouth, looks into her eyes, and says, "Nothing?"

"Nothing. They never missed a beat," she says. "You sure those canisters aren't a hallucinogenic flashback?"

14

ANDREW WRIGHT PUTS THE HEINEKEN BOTTLE ON THE COFFEE TABLE, sits back, and brushes his hand through his hair. The canisters could've come from lots of other places. There are many explanations—in fact, *too* many goddamned possibilities. But one, he has to admit to himself, is that he's losing it, coming unhinged, going out of his gourd.

McNamara laughs suddenly. "I've saved the best for last," she says, "but you're going to have to cover your guys, Andy."

He sits up abruptly, pulls the bathrobe closed, and crosses his legs. He's slightly embarrassed, but the fact that she wrote the Kupferberg script and found out all of this while he was wandering in the desert disconcerts him far more. "Shoot," he says.

"I looked into the local fire and brimstone scene like you asked." She glances at her notes. "The most active local pulpit-thumper is one self-ordained Reverend Joseph Wengelt. And he has an...*interesting*...midnight cable TV show, *Will of the Lord,* that he produces in his own studio..."

"At the end of Lost Canyon Road," he finishes her sentence. "Shit."

"That compound you saw is Wengelt's Divine Eagle Institute—DEI. Get it?"

He looks blankly at her.

"It's Latin, Andy," she says, "meaning *of God.*"

He shakes his head. "Do you think I stumbled onto his property?"

Letting him answer his own question, she puts the file on the floor and then pulls her laptop from her bag.

"No," he says. "I've looked at maps of Red Rock Canyon. I had to be on the other side of the ridge line. And I was too high up. But there might be a connection." And, if there is, maybe he isn't losing his goddamned marbles.

Opening the laptop, she nods. "It's circumstantial," she says, "but, probably, yeah. The guy was a ranch hand and a Chrysler salesman before the Lord spoke to him and saved him." She grins. "He lives pretty friggin' well now. His ministry has been very, very good to him." Her fingers whir on the laptop's keyboard. "I've already screened one of his shows. Want to see the lowlights?"

Nodding, he leans forward. That Wengelt could be connected to the canisters makes sense, but that doesn't help him understand any more about what they are or where and why they're hidden.

She clears a space on the table and sets the computer on it. "It's a simple two-camera operation," she says, "broadcast live three nights a week and on Sunday morning. The production values are nothing spectacular, but not bad. And Reverend Joe sure fills up the screen."

"What's the format?" he asks.

"A mixed bag," she says as she clicks on an icon. "He starts with the typical bully-pulpit shtick, but the longest segment is a gabfest with a special guest. And I do mean *special!*" She turns the laptop toward him. "He makes a plug for contributions every six minutes, ten times in the hour. Oh, and I can't wait for your take on the show's finale."

She adjusts the angle of the screen so Wright can see better. The man who appears is large and fleshy, his thin gray hair combed over to hide his receding hairline. Wearing a blue denim shirt with a bolo, he stands at a gilded pulpit, his big, meaty hands folded before him. A gold T hangs behind him, and red fabric covers the backdrop.

"That's a tau," McNamara says, pointing over the man's shoulder. "Also called a *crux commissa* or Saint Anthony's cross. It's what you saw by the flagpole in his compound." She smiles ironically. "Some people, apparently including our Reverend Joe, believe it's the real cross."

And, the goddamned canisters were arranged that way, Wright thinks.

"Brothers and sisters," the man on the screen begins, "repent! The End Times are at hand. I say unto thee, repent!" His expression is solemn, his voice resonant, with that oily sincerity Wright associates with televangelists. The man unfolds his hands and grips the sides of the pulpit. "The day of the Lord is nigh! The final battle for the holy city, Jerusalem, has begun!" His voice rises to a shout as the camera cuts to a close up. "Let no one doubt that Satan is behind the attacks on the Holy Land. During these days of Tribulation, Israel's fate hangs in the balance. But doubt not, brothers and sisters, that the New Jerusalem shall rise. The great day of the Lord's wrath is near. Thunder shall roar, and lightning shall fire the sky. The Earth itself shall quake. Death and hell shall be cast into the lake of fire." The man's bolo features a stylized silver tau, and the intensity in his blue eyes surprises Wright. It's as though the guy really believes what he's saying. "Sinners, repent! Fear the Lord! Give glory to the Lord for His retribution is nigh! The hour of His judgment is come. The Lord shall visit saint and sinner alike…" The camera switches back to a medium shot. "Taking his own unto himself…" The man claps his chest. "And sending the rest to eternal damnation!" He raises his fist. "I am the Prophet of the Lord! Repent, I say, for in these End Times, the Lord's Will must…"

McNamara clicks pause. "You get about five more minutes of this before he hits you up for cash. It's mostly closet racist crap about separating wheat from chaff and true Israel from mud people."

Wright's heard it all before, the idiocy about the white race alone descending from Adam and everyone else being beasts of the earth made from the leftover mud—and he really doesn't want to hear it again from this clown.

"The Rev's staunchly pro-Israel," McNamara says, "but only—and here's the political and theological leap—so he himself can create the New Jerusalem."

"Skip to the guest, Mags," Wright says.

Nodding, she fast-forwards. At speed, the preacher's gesticulations look exaggerated, even histrionic. "Tonight's topic, for your viewing pleasure," she says, "is massive and deeply meaningful pyramids on Mars. I wasn't smart enough to follow the logic, but maybe you'll have better luck." When the address:

www.willofthelord.org

OR

Will of the Lord

PO Box 459

Red Sapphire, NV 89103

appears on screen, she taps the keyboard. "As you can imagine," she adds, "the website is extremely donor friendly."

Cutting to the address, Wright knows, gives the preacher time to hightail it to a different set. This must, he muses, occasionally provide some comedic moments.

The next shot is of the preacher seated in a hickory armchair with an enlarged color photo of Red Rock Canyon as a backdrop. A shriveled woman who looks about a third the preacher's size perches next to him in a matching chair. Her face is pinched, her silver-blue hair falls in a long braid across her shoulder, and her tiny hands flutter in her lap.

"We are pleased to have with us again tonight," the preacher says, "Ms. Rhonda Spellman, this great nation's foremost authority on planetary phenomena. A trained mathematician, Miss Spellman has been studying signs of intelligent planetary life for more than thirty-three years, and tonight she will share with us her discoveries about Mars. Miss Spelllman."

"Thank you, Reverend Wengelt," she says. "I'm pleased to be back on *Will of the Lord.*" Her voice squeaks, as though it's at the upper threshold of human hearing.

"Yikes, Mags," Wright says, "she's going to shatter the windows."

"I knew you'd love her," McNamara says as she fast-forwards again.

"Does Wengelt skewer her?" he asks.

"Actually, no." She glances at him. "He puts an apocalyptic spin on everything. Her Martian discoveries are yet another sign of the End Times." She continues to jump forward through the interminable discussion and the periodic pitches for donations to support the Lord's work at the Divine Eagle Institute. Each successive pitch for cash becomes more edgy, almost desperate. "This is what I really wanted you to see," she says as she pauses on a head-and-shoulder shot of the preacher again standing alone at the pulpit.

"The Lord is omnipotent," the preacher begins. "Fear the Lord in these times of Tribulation! Give glory to the Lord!" His eyes are even more intense, and his voice is again unctuous. There's a rattling noise in the background. "I am the Lord's sole living Prophet, and I say unto you that the hour of the Lord's judgment is come!"

The camera cuts to a wide shot of the preacher holding a writhing four-foot brown rattlesnake at arm's length. The dark diamonds with pale borders running along its back seem to enlarge and contract with each gyration. Gripping the snake just below its head, the preacher steps around in front of the pulpit. His silver belt buckle features the embossed profile of an eagle, and his boots look like they're made from the rattler's cousin. "The Will of the Lord is beyond your powers of understanding," he intones. "But I commune with the Lord. I know beyond a shadow of a doubt that if you obey my Word, you have nothing to fear!"

The snake's tail shakes belligerently.

"The Serpent is evil incarnate, a mighty and formidable foe capable of destroying us all! Never underestimate the Serpent's potent evil."

The snake's tongue flicks madly; its tail rattles fiercely.

"But I say unto you that when you obey the Will of the Lord, you shall fear no evil!" A chorus of trumpets rises in the background, and the camera cuts to a close-up of the preacher's face. "Heed my call!" he shouts over the music. "Obey the Will of the Lord!" He glances sideways for a second, and then his eyes blink rapidly. "Fear no evil!"

A quick cut back to a wide shot reveals that the snake has vanished, replaced by a gilded shepherd's staff. "The End is nigh!" He grasps the staff more tightly and thumps its base three times against the floor. "In these Times, live in the Lord!"

McNamara taps the keyboard, and the preacher vanishes. "So, Andy," she asks, "what do you think of Reverend Joe, now?"

Wright shakes his head slowly. The guy is mostly a goddamned huckster, but there were those moments of genuine—and frightening

—zealotry mixed in. At times, both his words and his eyes suggested fanaticism. "The out's a cheap trick," he answers, "but it probably flies just fine with his flock."

"He apparently varies it," she says. "But there's always a snake— and always some video-miracle. Some televised triumph of good over evil."

Yeah, Wright thinks, and there's probably a *Wright Stuff* story here somewhere, but he's sure as hell not going to be the one to give the preacher and his twisted theology any publicity.

15

ANDREW WRIGHT IS CAUGHT UNDER WATER, LOST IN AN AQUATIC CAVE. Flames spread toward him in furling waves, sparks like spindrift. He swims fast, eyes burning, looking for something…anything. Eels and sea snakes swarm around him. Occasionally, one brushes against him, slick and cold. Though he knows they're not all lethal, he can't tell the innocuous from the venomous. He's not yet out of air; his brain is still clear—but he's aware he has little time. Snakes with eyes like lasers thrash, impervious, in the fire. The sense of urgency peaks as his air supply dwindles. Time is running out. He has to act fast, make his discovery in this very moment—or not at all. A ringing assaults his ears. Flames glint, streak, whirl. Even as he surfaces from the dream, the ringing persists.

Awake and sweating, he swats the travel alarm—but the ringing continues. His heart races, and he's panting as though he really was submerged. His eyes open wide in the darkness. It's the goddamned phone. Not his iPhone, which Maggie has had replaced but he has shut off. The hotel phone. He fumbles for the receiver. "What?" he croaks.

"Andrew Wright?" a calm voice asks. He's heard it before, but he can't place it.

"What?" he repeats.

"This is Nick Larson," the voice says. "We need to talk."

The guy from the canyon? Wright looks at the glowing digits of the travel alarm, which has landed face up on the floor. It's 1:45—he's been asleep less than an hour.

"I'm outside your room, at your door," Larson says.

Shit, Wright thinks. He's about to ask what's so goddamned important, but he can still feel that strange sense of urgency from his dream. Shielding his eyes against the brightness, he turns on the lamp. "I'll be right there," he says, swinging his feet out of bed. He hangs up the phone, stands, and squats back onto the bed. He forgot the ankle, and pain shoots up his leg. He rises, throws on the terry-cloth robe, and hobbles to the door.

Larson is standing in the hall, just as he said, the woven strap across his chest, his satchel under his arm, but no phone in sight. He wears a long-sleeved shirt, tan pants, and low leather boots. He smells like the desert. "Thanks," he says as he walks past Wright into the room. He scans it quickly, heads to one of the bamboo chairs, and sits. The low light on that side of the room seems to suit him fine. He pushes back the satchel so that it rests on the arm of the chair.

Scratching his scalp, Wright follows him and then sinks into the other chair. He's still groggy, still sweating, the dream still very much in his mind.

"It's about Joseph Wengelt," Larson says. He's staring at Wright with those pale, clear eyes, as though the need for sleep is superfluous, something perhaps necessary for others.

"What about him?" Wright grumbles. His mind's muddled, and all he can focus on is the Tahitian women, who look even more exotic in the half-light.

"You and your producer," Larson says, his voice still utterly calm, "have gotten his attention. Your visit in the Hummer and your producer's prying."

"So what?" Wright rubs his eyes and rolls his neck. His head is clearing. What the hell's this guy doing here? And what's he got to do with Wengelt?

"You need to lay off," Larson says.

Wright stifles the anger rising in his belly. He's got to stay cool, got to somehow find out what this guy's up to. "Why?" he asks.

"Wengelt is dangerous. It's imperative that you have no more contact with him."

"Who the...?" Wright leans forward, almost in the guy's face.

62

"Where the hell...?" Shit, he thinks, focus! Get a goddamned grip! He sits back and takes a deep breath. "Are you *telling* me what to do?"

Larson crosses his legs and folds his hands in his lap. He's even more placid than before, if that's possible. "Andrew," he says, "both you and your producer need to stay away from Wengelt and the Divine Eagle Institute."

Wait just a goddamned minute, Wright thinks, you pretended like you didn't even know who Wengelt was this...yesterday afternoon. "What's going on here, Nick?" he asks. He forces himself to take another deep breath. "Is this a threat? Do you work for Wengelt?"

Larson brushes something—a dead bug, maybe—off the cuff of his shirt. "You don't understand what's happening, Andrew," he says. "You and your producer are in harm's way...but it's not just yourselves you're endangering."

Larson, Wright realizes, hasn't answered any of his questions. "No," he says as matter of factly as he can, given the fire spreading up through his chest. "I'm not laying off Wengelt. Not unless you tell me *why.*" He's not going to lay off in any case now, and definitely not because some guy he's barely met orders him to. There's got to be an even bigger story here than he thought.

Larson exhales. Keeping his eyes on Wright, he says nothing for a moment. "It has to do with the canisters," he says finally.

Wright swipes his mouth with the back of his hand. Jesus, he thinks, the goddamned canisters. "You...you were waiting for me yesterday."

Larson nods.

"You were trying to find out what I knew, what I remembered. And I thought I was the one pumping you for information."

Larson shrugs.

"Do you work for Wengelt? Is this some goddamned threat?"

"No, I don't. And no, it's advice. Advice for the common good."

Thoughts race through Wright's mind. He's not going nuts. The goddamned canisters exist. And Reverend Joe is involved. But who the hell is Larson? "Are you...do you work for the milit...the government?" he asks.

"No."

Then what the hell business is it of yours? Wright thinks. His anger is finally receding, at least a little, but he feels even more in the dark than ever. With Maggie working her *Wright Stuff* magic, he's used to knowing a lot more than he lets on, but here he knows a hell of a lot less. In fact, next to nothing. "What's in the canisters?"

"That isn't the issue."

Anger flares behind Wright's eyes, but he keeps it out of his voice. "Of course, it's the issue, Nick. You wouldn't be here otherwise."

"You're going to have to trust me, Andrew," Larson says, as though it's a done deal. "The canisters you saw in that cavern are *not* the issue. But there is an issue—a catastrophic issue. And, as I said, your nosing around Wengelt's property will only cause problems for you and imperil other people. I'm already worried about…your producer."

Larson's acting like he's doing Wright a favor. But basically the guy is still ordering him around, and that doesn't sit well. Not at all, goddamn it. He's never been any good at taking orders. How does Larson know about Maggie's inquiries if he doesn't work for Wengelt? And how the hell does the guy know he saw the canisters? He's got too many questions at once. And then he thinks about how Raisani told him almost the same thing yesterday. Fully awake now, he's starting to feel like he's in a dream—somebody else's dream. He limps over to the refrigerator, takes out a seltzer, and asks, "You want something, Nick?" But he doesn't even know if that's his real name. He knows absolutely nothing about this guy, zilch—and finding out is going to be Maggie's first task in the morning.

"No, thanks," Larson answers, his tone polite.

Smiling, Wright shakes his head. This guy probably doesn't eat, drink, or sleep. When he sits down again, he asks, "How did you know about my producer's inquiries?"

Larson waves his hand. "It doesn't matter."

Wright almost slams the unopened seltzer bottle onto the coffee table but instead sets it down carefully. "Shit, Nick," he laughs, "or whatever the hell your name is. You want me to do—or not do—certain things, but you haven't leveled with me at all. Not once, goddamn it. Why should I trust you?"

64

Larson doesn't answer at first. He seems to inspect the satchel's strap, which looks hand-woven. Then, he cocks his head; his eyes bore into Wright's. When he speaks, his voice is low, but his tone is clear and forceful. "Because, Andy," he says, "I'm the one that got you out of that cavern. If you'd been found bungling around in there, you'd be dead. And we wouldn't be having this conversation."

Wright sits back as though he's been shoved.

"I sedated you," Larson says, tapping the satchel with his middle finger. "I hauled you out of there." He shakes his head and smiles to himself. "You were a load."

Wright grabs the seltzer bottle, twists off the cap, and drinks. The guy saved his life, or so he says. And, it rings true, somehow. How the hell else would he know about it? But what was Larson doing in the cavern? How'd he get him out undetected? How'd he transport him to the other side of the ridge? And, most basically, *why?*

"We're all at risk here, Andy," Larson says. "I am, and others I care about. Thousands…countless other people, too. And your stumbling into the situation at this point has complicated matters. Wengelt's radar was already up, and, frankly, I think he has you in his sights."

Wright thinks about that. Larson may be right. It kind of makes sense. Still, Wright doesn't yet have any real idea what he's dealing with. The risks aren't at all clear. "If what you say is true, Nick," he says, feeling himself becoming almost as calm as Larson looks, "then if Maggie and I suddenly stop looking into his business, Wengelt will get even more suspicious."

Larson brushes his fingers along the satchel's strap.

"Maybe I can help," Wright adds. There's some goddamned story here. A big one. And he's not going to just walk away from it. No way in hell. He's been doing network fluff far too long. He doesn't, of course, know what's really going on. But that's never stopped him before—and he'll take his proverbial shot. "I could do a *Wright Stuff* piece on Wengelt." He's fully aware that the piece, however it turns out, isn't going to be about the televangelist—he's already decided not to give the guy any airtime. "Or, at least seem like we're doing one." It might just get him into the loop. Larson would need to let him know *something* about what's happening. "You know, how people turn to religion when times are hard. Saving Vegas through the Lord."

Larson nods but doesn't answer. He looks over at the *Two Tahitian Women,* then swings the satchel around so that it's on his lap.

"Maybe we need to work together here, Nick." Wright leans forward, waiting for an answer, but Larson only strums the satchel's strap as though he's searching for some lost chord or playing out the future—or a series of possible futures.

16

THOUGH HE HAS SLEPT ONLY TWO HOURS, NICK LARSON SITS ON THE BOULder near the creek as the sun limns the ridge with gold. He has his canteen but neither his satchel nor his garbage bag because he can only stay a moment. He murmurs his prayer, but he has far too much on his mind this morning to fully settle, to become wholly empty. He rode his black modified and muffled Suzuki out of Las Vegas the instant he finished with Andrew Wright. He has misgivings about involving Wright, even to a limited extent, but both Wright and his producer had already engaged Wengelt's attention, so there really was no choice. He told the reporter little, avoiding issues concerning the canisters and how he knows what he knows. And, there's certainly not enough for Wright to build a story on, not even a three-minute ditty. Wright's still unaware of entire pieces, vital pieces.

Larson's ambivalent, too, about having Wright follow up with an interview, but he knew even before his meeting with the reporter that it would likely go that way. Wright wasn't about to desist, so he might as well let the guy bluster on, thereby allowing Larson some freedom of movement, which has been hindered by Wengelt's security chief stalking him.

Larson can feel the security chief's presence, even now. He doesn't turn or scan the ridge, but the man was perched along the upper trail earlier in the week, and he's there now—the watcher watching the watcher. The security chief has a martial perspective that makes it easy to predict his moves. But Larson wonders if Wengelt, so close to his goal, might become more volatile, more panicky—and send the security chief out to dispatch him. It's a possibility that shouldn't be ignored.

He stands and stretches even before the Mojave rattler appears. He's more worried about others than he is about himself. The stakes are too high to go it alone, but risking the lives of others, especially of people he loves as much as life itself, gnaws at him. Wright and his producer are even more problematic because he doesn't know how much he can trust their instincts once time's arrow strikes.

17

MICHAEL GRANT SMILES AS HE SURVEYS THE PERIMETER AROUND THE Grotto. The terrain is wooded and rocky, the location so remote and inaccessible that the Prophet himself has only visited the site twice. You can't even see the entrance when you're five feet away. Still, Grant has set his trip wires and his booby traps—and nobody's going to gain access to the Grotto without his knowing it. He's so adept at this task because his training prepared him to solve *all* security problems. He's got the brawn, the brain, and the background. He's exactly six feet and 180 pounds with only five percent body fat, thanks to a vigorous ninety-minute workout six days a week. He graduated third in his class at the South Tulsa Evangelical Academy. After his first year at Oral Roberts University, he enlisted in the United States Army because all that sitting around and talking in college was for wussies. His first three military tours of duty in mechanized cavalry should have led to Special Ops, but he was passed over for lesser soldiers and sent stateside instead.

His tours as an MP prepared him for his high-level security work in Area 51 and for this current position with Reverend Wengelt, but he missed all of the *real* action in Iraq and Afghanistan. The armed forces, even the military police, were being feminized, and so he took retirement—and with it the means to save this Great Republic. The conspiracy to elect a foreigner to the office of Commander in Chief fortified his resolve. Finally, the hostile takeover of the government by the corrupt and cowardly powers in Congress necessitated immediate action. He must fight for nothing less than the survival of the Constitutional Republic that is every natural-born American's birthright. He is the ulitimate Minuteman—and this is his call to arms.

In leading the New American Revolution, he will save his beloved Constitution and prove to the brass not only that devaluing his skills and abilities was a strategic error but also that homeland security is a joke. The civilian leadership have never risked their lives for God and country. They are overeducated wimps who have never once tested their mettle in battle. He has no respect whatever for the Stupid Homeland Idiot Turds—the SHIT, an acronym he himself devised. The SHIT are about to hit the fan.

His incorporation of *American Security* soon after his retirement led directly to his contact with Reverend Wengelt. His subsequent work as Security Chief of Divine Eagle Institute the last eighteen months has been rewarding, both tactically and financially. He has secured the Institute's perimeter, improved security immeasurably, and established and commanded Reverend Wengelt's Guardian Angels. Though he was presented with barely enough able men for one combat team, he has armed them fully and trained them rigorously.

Not even Reverend Wengelt will ever know his specific assignment in Area 51 or his real name—Michael Grant having such a nice ring for the DEI faithful. He believes strongly in Reverend Wengelt's just and mighty Lord, and the plan he and the Prophet devised for the Day of the Lord will commence the Revolution. Yet, he is aware that the Institute has already outlived its usefulness. So many of the DEI congregation are soft and weak, people whose adherence to the Prophet's mandates comes only from fear of damnation. He himself has necessarily meted out punishments to young and old alike.

Though there have been a number of vehicles intermittently parked on land near the Institute, mostly riders with horse trailers looking for free range and occasionally a black Land Rover owned by some alien doctor with an unpronounceable name, only the caveman has ever ventured near the Grotto. Last week's test subject, the Asian hiker, was detained a full four kilometers from the site and was transferred here simply because a guinea pig was needed. The results were even more interesting than anticipated: the writhing was expected as was the initial gasping, but not the subsequent massive

70

bleeding from every orifice, even the eye sockets. The search parties never even got close to the Grotto.

The caveman is another story. Indeed, still wearing fatigues and combat boots, Grant has just come back from tracking him. The caveman apparently lives in the area, though Grant has never been able to follow him all the way back to his lair. He keeps losing him in the rocky tracts west of the Institute, never in the same place, always along outcroppings over which the caveman scampers like a mountain goat. The caveman appears each morning by the stream and scuttles around for an hour collecting garbage like he's some work-release inmate doing community service. He never encroaches on Institute property and never wanders *too* near the Grotto—and that's what's finally, in these last critical hours before the Day of the Lord operation, gotten Grant's attention. Random chance would dictate that the caveman would periodically skirt the Grotto; it's almost as if he purposely avoids the immediate area. Significantly, the caveman also didn't stay long in the canyon this morning or carry his usual equipment—both of which deviate from his routine. Still, Grant in his tracking has found nothing overt in the caveman's behavior to suggest he's not what he appears to be—an odd, rustic, environmentally quirky desert doofus.

Crouching, Grant passes through the entrance, counts the fifteen paces in the darkness, avoids two trip wires, bears right for twelve paces toward the increasing light, and, circumventing the booby traps, turns into the Grotto. The generator hums, but one of the light bulbs is out. He's not sure, though, that he'll need to replace it. Tomorrow night is the night, after all. The whole set-up here—the lighting and altar and crimson cloth and painted Fist of the Lord and especially the arrangement of the five canisters in the shape of a Tau—is unnecessary, but it is the Prophet's will. And, though the Prophet is more closely in touch with the Lord than any other man Grant has met, the Prophet has still paid a premium for these arrangements in the Grotto. Because of its incomparable potency, the price charged for the Virin was also stiff, even though Grant already possessed it.

Even with one bulb out, the canisters gleam in the Grotto's light. The five of them. The Prophet insisted on hoarding two himself, but even the Prophet doesn't know about the eighth canister. Procuring the Virin was dangerous, certainly, but far easier than his associates in the Level Seven laboratory would have imagined. The mortal danger was in the transfer, not in the chance he would be discovered. Virin was developed in the heat of the Cold War, but even the chemical warfare geeks that contrived it came to fear it as too volatile, too uncontrollable, and *too lethal*. At the end of the Reagan administration, the Virin was decommissioned but never destroyed. The truth is that the generals never had the balls to use it. He, however, understands that events in Washington now dictate its dipersal—and his valor is manifest.

In the final ten months before his retirement, Grant had full security clearance in Area 51, but his ruse when commandeering the Virin was too simple for any of the other MPs to see it anyway. All you had to do, if you had the cojones, was transfer the Level Seven materials to outmoded containers and leave the originals, filled with inert materials, to be counted during inventory. The surveillance videos were readily manipulated. And it wasn't like anybody was ever going to test the stuff on himself to find out if it was every bit as lethal as the rumors suggested. True, one inept move during the transfer would have cost you your life. You would've melted down just like that Asian hiker. But Grant has never been careless.

It has been almost two years since he completed the transfers, and no scuttlebutt whatever about a possible theft has ever surfaced in Area 51. In the intervening months, hundreds of military officers and civilian technicians accessed the Level Seven laboratory. In any case, if an investigation ever occurred, he planted an evidence trail that would cause one of the techies to take the fall. The dweeb was expendable, a wog—born in the United States, it's true, but a wog is always a wog just as a woman is only a woman. Grant himself, now safely retired and gainfully employed in the private sector, would, of course, remain above suspicion.

Grant walks to the altar and gazes at the canisters without touching them. He is satisfied with his work but feels no vanity. He is, after all, the New Minuteman, the first of innumerable brothers-in-arms ready and able to liberate the Constitutional Republic from the cowards and conspirators in Washington. The Virin is, because of its special qualities that no one fully comprehends, the most dangerous entity ever synthesized by humans. In terrorists' hands, its use would be calamitous. However, his deliverance of the Virin has essentially been a matter of patriotic duty, something which he has always taken seriously. He served his country for eighteen years, and he was passed over for lesser men—and even *women*. The cancer—the aliens, legal and illegal—must be eradicated, and the infidels must take the fall. The SHIT and other fools must be taught a lesson, a hard lesson, about vigilance. The Prophet's Day of the Lord crusade has lofty, unattainable goals, but Reverend Wengelt at least understands that this first shot heard round the world must *not* kill the Alien in Chief. Another martyr like the Kennedys would only bolster the cowardly conspirators. No, the initial volley that will save this Great Republic must *shame* the President and the Elites, expose the SHIT's incompetence, and destroy the credibility of all those weak sisters stealing the Constitution from true Americans.

18

THE PROPHET PACES THE FLOOR OF THE COMMONS. HE IS HOLDING A color photo of Andrew Wright that one of the acolytes just downloaded from the ABC website. His palms are sweating. He needs to think, and his sanctuary would be more suitable—but he needs to keep moving, too. He could go for a walk in the woods, but, even though it's only 9:15, it's already scorching outside.

That ABC lady, the one that was calling around yesterday asking all those questions, phoned at 9:00 sharp. On the button. First thing in the morning. Wiping first one hand and then the other on the back of his jeans, he gazes at the photo of the pretty-boy reporter. This same reporter Michael spotted yesterday snooping around the Institute wants to do a piece for *Good Morning America*. National network exposure. Huge coup for *Will of the Lord*. And Lord knows, the influx of cash would be a Godsend. Even with that legal windfall involving Christine, expenditures have exceeded contributions five-fold the last two years—and the Institute's coffers are depleted, utterly empty.

Although the recession and the Alien Usurper's liberal policies are certainly to blame for the lack of donations, the core of the issue has been the extreme cost of enhancing the Divine Eagle Institute's security. Just when the problem of security seemed insurmountable, the Lord delivered Michael Grant to the Prophet. And, thankfully, Michael's reforms and upgrades have been both indispensable and topnotch. Still, the price, especially for the Day of the Lord logistics and materials, has been extraordinarily steep.

The Prophet stops and stares at his wooden snakes slithering up the wall. Those filthy network liberals always have an angle, a Godless agenda. Plus, they spent at least a day checking everything out before they made the call. He glances again at the photo. This *Wright Stuff* patsy must be up to something. They're all snakes in the grass. New Yawkers. Dissolute backsliders.

He starts pacing again. The timing is suspicious, too. Why the sudden interest? *Will of the Lord* has been on the air for six years, and the network slime haven't so much as acknowledged the show, much less admitted the Truth of its message. But now, thirty-six hours before the Day of the Lord, the most significant moment in the millennium, Mr. Wright Stuff suddenly comes calling. Something, as those New Yawkers would say, isn't kosher.

The Prophet is playing along, though. Readily agreed to the lady-producer's proposal. Told her to have the pretty boy call to firm up details. And, he just might go through with the interview, too. The exposure would certainly begin to refill the coffers, which is critical —an absolute necessity. And, if the timing is just right, the interview would provide the perfect alibi. Nothing's more airtight than praising the Lord for a national television audience at the exact moment that the Terrible Swift Sword falls on all those idolaters.

But the network liberals can never be trusted. Never. He should get Michael on it, see what the pretty boy's real agenda is. But Michael's already too busy. So much has already been laid on Michael's shoulders. Michael's shoulders are certainly strong enough, but there's so little time, and Michael still has so much preparation to do for the Day of the Lord. Not to mention the surveillance he insists on doing on that caveman. It's a waste of time. He himself has never seen the caveman, but the dipshit is certainly just some dimwitted tree-hugger. Still, Michael thinks something might be going on. And it's Michael's business to know. He should probably have Michael do away with the caveman, use him as one final test subject, so they can both concentrate on the more important matters at hand. It's not like anybody's going to miss the hermit anyway.

The Prophet looks at the burled walnut humidor. Involving the philistine and his PSF skinheads may be necessary. Not desirable— they're always messy—but necessary. If the liberal swine have caught even the slightest whiff of the plans for the Day of the Lord—though that doesn't, given Michael's masterful security precautions, seem possible—then the pretty boy is going to have to have an accident. He scans the photo a third time. The pretty boy's probably an airhead. His blond good looks must've gotten him the job in the first place. The lady producer must be the brains of the outfit. If something is amiss, she'll have the accident. Yes, that's the way to go on this. As he well knows, if you cut off the Serpent's head, the body dies. He crumples the photo, walks to the fireplace, and tosses it onto the grate.

19

Andrew Wright logs off Maggie's laptop after viewing the final cut of the Kupferberg story one last time. Maggie made sure they finished the piece before she called Wengelt. "Focus on our job for one hour when the guys get here for the final edit, okay?" she pleaded when he told her about Larson's visit. And the Kupferberg story turned out extremely well, even though he didn't have all that much to do with it. Maggie's signature, more than his, is really on the piece. Now, she's gone off with the rest of the team to grab something to eat. They promised to bring back some exotic Tahitian fare, but he's not really hungry. In the meantime, he's supposed to be making calls to the white shirts in New York proposing that the final *Fight to Save Vegas* story be about some obscure televangelist with an apocalyptic bent. They won't like the idea any more than they'd like a piece on petroglyphs, and he can't tell them that the Divine Eagle Institute isn't the real story. The network honchos would have the hard news guys out here in a second, bulldozing everything—and that's exactly, Larson told him, what can't happen. Sure, much of what Wright does is inconsequential, but that doesn't mean he can't do something worthwhile, something tough. He has a sense of this story. And a lot of those hard news guys suffer from Innate Male Idiocy a hell of a lot worse than he does. In any case, everything, as Larson emphasized, has to seem exactly like business as usual.

Larson told Wright what to do if and when they got inside Reverend Joe's compound, but he didn't tell Wright much of anything else. And Maggie, in the hour or so she had before the final edit, came up with exactly nothing on the guy. She located dozens of Nicholas

Larsons, but the only match in the Las Vegas area was a seventeen-year-old place-kicker at Bishop Gorman Catholic High School. A couple of matches on out-of-state guys might be worth pursuing, but there are no local records at all on the Nick Larson whom Wright's met. It's as though the guy doesn't exist. Which reminds him—the petroglyphs he saw supposedly don't exist either. The glyph guru at UNLV, unable to find anything resembling a match in his computer database, told Maggie that either Wright's mistaken or the glyphs are recent ripoffs of the authentic item. In any case, they're not, Professor Nieman insisted, Native American. But they do exist, goddamn it. Wright saw them. And he's not mistaken: he can still picture them clearly.

Wright slides Maggie's laptop onto the coffee table and stretches. Arnuz and Miguel and Charles Paglia, the editor they use when they're out in the field, cleaned up but left equipment boxes lined along the wall. Still feeling a little slow from his lack of sleep, he takes a can of Coke from the refrigerator, lifts from the nightstand the phone Maggie got him, winks at *The Tahitian Women,* sits on the edge of the bed, and drinks half the Coke. He starts to call the white shirts but instead drinks the rest of the Coke and belches. He has to get in touch with Reverend Joe, too. He's supposed to smooth the preacher's feathers, keep the subterfuge going. But not yet, not right away—he doesn't want to seem *too* eager to interview Reverend Joe.

He calls information and asks for Dr. Fereshteh Raisani's number. When he reaches the office, the receptionist informs him that Dr. Raisani is out of the office for the next forty-eight hours. Though he pumps the receptionist a bit, she doesn't seem to know anything other than, yes, Doctor Raisani's leave was a little abrupt. The timing's pretty goddamned interesting, to say the least, so he next tries her home number. When he gets only voice mail, he turns the phone off and leans back against the teak headboard. He wants to ask Raisani again why she just happened to be out in that remote area where she found him and why she warned him off Reverend Joe. But there's more to it, he admits to himself. He wants to talk with her again regardless of her involvement—and now she's unavailable. He glances around the room at the South Sea furnishings and the bare-breasted girls in the print. It may only be fatigue, only a trough before the sugar and caffeine kick in, but a sense of separateness, of isolation—he can't quite find the right word—is running deep. *Dissociation* is close, but not exact. *Dislocation,* maybe that's it.

The Wright Stuff's been wildly successful in lots of ways, but he's paid a price. He's got a condo overlooking the Park but no real home. Friends, even good friends, from work—but only sporadic contact with high school and college buddies. An ex-wife and no children. Women, yes, but nobody, except maybe Maggie, with whom he'd ever share his thoughts. And nothing about *The Wright Stuff* requires any real thought, anyway. Something deeper, far deeper than a story, is at work in him now. Something he was unaware of—or, perhaps, only vaguely aware of—until he slid down into that cavern. It has something to do with Innate Male Idiocy. Or, perhaps, that's the issue—maybe the idiocy is more cultural than innate. And maybe, just maybe, he's been a contributor to it. He's had these sorts of thoughts before, but here in Vegas he's had more trouble pushing them from his mind. He knows that the idiocy isn't really innate, that it's far more cultural than inborn. It's just getting too hard to ignore that TV and the Internet contribute to the selfish, slipshod, slapdash, self-aggrandizing approach to life that he sees not just here in Vegas, where it's pandemic, but almost everywhere as he crisscrosses the country. He can't rid himself of the feeling that the culture, and particularly TV, glorify and reward the rudest exhibitionists and the most obnoxious carnival barkers.

The dream wells in his mind—water and fire and snakes and the compelling sense that he has to act fast. Maybe his uneasiness is partly the residue of the dream, but, as Larson's visit confirms, something *is* happening in the desert and perhaps here on the Strip, too. He's never really been forced to take a stand—he just did stories, features, human interest pieces to entertain people and, once in a while, pro-vide a minor insight or two into the human condition. He was in

LA on 9/11, and he didn't personally know any of the victims. A co-worker's nephew. An acquaintance's cousin. And the network had him do nothing—no *Wright Stuff* at all—for close to a month afterward. And in the following years, he definitely got better at what he did—or, at least, more comfortable, more slick. Perhaps, more glib. But he's not really sure, after all, what he actually *did*—other than fill air in a sometimes wry and amusing way. Now, suddenly, he has this weird inkling that he's got a crucial role to play in some battle he doesn't understand.

20

GARY B. SMITH PLAYS THE QUARTER SLOTS CLOSEST TO THE GUEST ELEVA-
tors at The Tahitian. His gray hair spilling out under his black NRA
baseball cap, he's hunched over, smoking a Marlboro, yanking the
bandit's arm, one eye on the elevators. He hates the new machines
with their fuckin' electronic buttons and video-arcade sound effects—
slip in your cash, punch a button, and wave good-bye to your dough.
At least this slot's got an arm. Most of the new ones are fuckin' amputees.

He likes to crank the bandit's arm for his money. Gets a kick out
of that old metallic clang. Plus, this place isn't like the casinos downtown. It's way fuckin' fancier. Actually has a lobby without any slots
in it, a big fuckin' area with vines and flowers everywhere, even a
fuckin' waterfall. It's almost like you're not on the Strip, not in the
desert at all. It seems like some tropical fuckin' island, though he's
never actually been to an island.

He had to have a clear view to recon the elevators so it took him
awhile to figure out which was the best slot. And, he's not even sure
they're the right elevators, the place is so big. The place is so fuckin'
snobby, too. It's all too much, really. There's actually this little river
running over there and palm trees, real ones, mixed in with the slots.
It's like he's sitting on the edge of some fuckin' jungle. And the people! Most of 'em are mudheads, naturally, but *rich* fuckin' mudheads.
Or, they're dressed like it, anyhow. There's bright silky sport shirts
everywhere, and some of the rimmers are actually wearing suits
and ties. None of those high-rolling superfly pimp rappers in town
for the fight are prancing around yet—those lazy asses'll be lying in
bed for another coupla hours—but he still doesn't feel comfortable.

In fact, he's feeling more than a little like he's a sore thumb here in his Doc Martens, jeans, and black NRA T-shirt with matching cap —and, no matter who's sitting his sorry alien ass in the White House, it's his fuckin' country, not theirs. His father's family's been here for almost four hundred years, and these mudheads just got here—and they're all sauntering around like they got Jags and Beemers and Range Rovers in their driveways back home. And they probably do, too. These fuckin' mudheads probably own whole countries. It's enough to make a man puke. There should be a fuckin' law. There will be, too, real soon. None of 'em will even be allowed in the white homeland. Hell, let these fuckin' mudheads strut their stuff, bet their millions. They're all doomed anyway. Tomorrow's Der Tag, and they haven't got a fuckin' clue. There's a whiter and brighter day coming, all right!

He hotfooted it over here right after Reverend Dickhead's call. He got the email with the attachments, the photos of the reporter and his cutesy producer, and hauled ass. He's got both pics tucked under his shirt now. The Dickhead's paying him a thousand bucks, one large, just to keep an eye on these two, check their comings and goings. Plus, the Dickhead said that his PSF guys might get their boot party tonight after all. That'd be good, too, because they're straining for some kick-ass action. You can smell the fuckin' testosterone in the war room.

He stubs out the Marlboro in the ashtray on top of the one-armed bandit. He knows he shouldn't be smoking, promised his late mother he'd stop, and he has, kind of—but he can't help it in a fuckin' place like this. Smoking has been outlawed every-fuckin'-where else, like it's a crime or something. Allowing these mudheads to prance around like they belong here, that's the real fuckin' crime. Plus, the knockers on the cigarette girl dressed in that grass skirt and almost nothing else were just so luscious. He couldn't keep his eyes off 'em, would have bought fuckin' cancer itself just to keep her there for another minute, for Christsake. He's playing slowly, winning a little, losing a little more, only down about twelve bucks so far, a small expense against the grand the Dickhead's promised.

He's pulling the bandit's arm, first quick then slow at the last second, when there she is, the cutesy producer. She's heading toward the elevators, sashaying between two guys, one a skinny jungle bunny and the other a stocky beaner. The reporter—the *pretty boy,* the Dickhead called him—is nowhere in sight. She's carrying a white paper bag with a palm tree on it and smiling at both the mudheads like they'll all have one fine fuckin' time together when they get upstairs. That's the worst sin of all, a white woman consorting with mudheads, the lesser races. The worst fuckin' sin of all!

The red light atop the bandit starts flashing and whirling, and the machine sounds like a fuckin' car alarm's going off. Triple fuckin' cherries! He's winning big, sirens whooping and hollering—hell on horseback, as his mother used to say. Everybody's looking his way, even the cutesy producer and her mudhead flunkies. He pulls his cap lower and squints at her out of the corner of his eye. Damn, she's a pretty little thing in her capri pants and white tank-top hiding nothing. Pixie haircut, slim but not skinny, tight little ass! No longer looking his way, she keeps talking to the mudheads and then hands the beaner the white paper bag.

The bandit keeps making one hell of a racket as the two mudheads step into the elevator. But she's not. She's turning, beginning to get away. He stands and starts dancing like he's got to whiz until the bandit finally shuts up. He hammers the CASH OUT button, rips the chit from the bandit, stuffs it in his pocket, and goes after her. She's winding her way through all the tropical vines and shit, moving that sweet can of hers real nice. He follows at a distance, trying to be sneaky, but a big guy like him doesn't really have a fuckin' chance.

She heads into this long marble-like hall full of fancy shops, Gucci and Armani and all that overpriced shit. Almost nobody else is in the fuckin' hallway or any of the stores, what with the recession and all, so he halts, slouches against the dark wood entranceway, and watches her as she window-shops. He's breathing hard from the sudden exertion, and a hard-on's pressing bigtime against his jeans. She doesn't look back, not once, just meanders along, and then, finally, turns into one of the stores. He straightens his cap, looks around to make sure nobody's gaping at him, and pulls the photos from under his shirt. They're a little damp with sweat, but he unfolds them, and, chewing his lower lip, studies the one of her. It's cute, all right, but the pic really doesn't fuckin' do her justice. Not at all.

21

As the rented van passes the red and white Divine Eagle Institute warning sign, Arnuz Jones, who's driving, says, "Whatchu doin' to us, man? This cracker's got to be completely paranoid."

Miguel Ramirez sits in front with Arnuz; Maggie McNamara and Andrew Wright are in the back seat, and the equipment is stowed in the aluminum cases behind them. The van's been laboring up the incline stirring dust, and it's warm in the backseat even with the air conditioning blowing full blast. Though Wright's had a tedious last couple of hours, he's feeling fairly calm—not exactly tranquil, but... focused. His conversations with the white shirts in New York went even worse than he expected. *Livid* isn't too strong a word to describe their reaction to his pitch. The Kupferberg piece was top drawer, but there's got to be a thousand better stories in Vegas than some fruitcake televangelist. Ten fucking thousand! Finally, he simply lied to them, told them he'd have a better idea by mid-afternoon, something they'd like a lot. He won't lose his job over moving ahead with this Reverend Joe charade, but there'll be a major shitstorm. Still, he doesn't much give a damn. This is what he needs to do.

Wright's little chat with Reverend Joe wasn't much better. Tomorrow, they agreed, would work well for the interview, but the preacher balked over their shooting a couple hours of b-roll—all the voice-over, background, and local color shots—today at the Institute. Reverend Joe only relented, granting a guided tour, when Wright informed him that without the b-roll there'd be no interview. They were both polite on the phone, but Wright could feel the undercurrent of antagonism, and so, he was sure, could Reverend Joe.

Wright's instructions to Arnuz and Miguel on the way out here weren't much of a success, either. "Make sure you get a lot of interior shots," he told them. "Get everything, even the most mundane stuff. *Everything.*" Arnuz and Miguel glanced at each other, expressions dubious, before Miguel asked, "Just what the hell is going down here, Boss?" Wright knew that Miguel only used the word *boss* when he was contemplating mutiny, so he told them they were to get all of the footage not for a *Wright Stuff* piece but for a story that was going to break soon—which could well be the goddamned truth.

When the van approaches the wrought-iron gate, Arnuz points to the gold insignia of the eagle clawing the snake and says, "And folks tell me African religions are primitive!"

Nodding toward the fence, Miguel says, "Concertina wire. Just shouts, *Hola! Good to see ya, America! Come on in!* Right, Boss?"

Maggie, who has been uncharacteristically silent since they left Las Vegas, says nothing. When she asked earlier how the honchos reacted, he told her not to worry—but her job, not his, is more likely on the line.

Hoping the mutiny won't occur until after the shoot, when, as per Larson's instructions, he'll drop the BluRay Disc in a sealed bag at the rusted horse trailer he'd noticed along the westward wagon track, Wright shrugs and says, "Okay, guys. Let's pretend like we're professionals for a few minutes here—no matter how much of a lunatic the Reverend is."

They wait three minutes in sight of the security camera at the gate before a green Jeep Cherokee with tinted windows pulls up. The blond man Wright saw the day before steps out of the Cherokee and strides toward the gate. He's again wearing faux uniform khaki pants and a khaki shirt with epaulets. The afternoon sun glints from his reflective silver wrap-around glasses.

"Shit, man," Arnuz says, "we've got us a real live Nazi here."

"Will you look at those shades, Boss!" Miguel exclaims. "This dude's been watchin' too much TV."

The blond man punches a series of numbers on the key pad, and the gates swing slowly open. As the van pulls through, he raises a hand for them to halt, steps forward to the window Arnuz lowers, and turns his head toward each of them as though sizing them up individually. Facing Wright, he says, "Proceed directly to the front of the main building and wait for further instructions." There is no inflection whatever in his voice, but his accent has a Southwestern twang.

While Arnuz and Miguel unload the equipment under the blond man's expressionless supervision, Maggie and Wright enter the large front room of the main building. Holding a white ten-gallon hat in his left hand, Reverend Joe greets them with an almost ceremonious formality. He wears a starched white shirt with silver eagle bolo and pressed jeans. Only when he shakes Maggie's hand, leaning his bulk down close to her, does the affected propriety vanish. It takes Wright a moment to draw his eyes from the guy's snakeskin boots.

The initial shot, a close-up of a Remington bronze, is pretty ordinary, but then Miguel gets a low angle on the wooden snakes swarming one wall and a nice wide shot of a fireplace set in a canted wall. Arnuz follows along, helping with the lights and getting all the sound, anything anybody says. All the while, Wright's asking Reverend Joe a slew of innocuous questions about the obvious craftsmanship of the place, softening him up. And, Reverend Joe, it turns out, has a bit of a presence. It's far different from Kupferberg's tightly wound energy, but there's something there the camera would like—were they really going to focus the piece on him. In fact, Reverend Joe's comments only cause Arnuz to roll his eyes once during the first ten minutes —when the guy refers to himself in the third person as *The Prophet*. Maggie takes notes, and the blond man, though never introduced, hovers in the background. Once, when Miguel pans the Sony in his direction, the blond man raises his arm and shakes his head sternly.

Everyone else, it seems, has been instructed to stay out of sight. Near the main building's back door, Wright glimpses a young woman with short blond hair peering at them from around the hallway corner, but as soon as Reverend Joe spots her she vanishes. The church, which Reverend Joe calls *The House of the Lord,* features a large gilded *crux commissa* suspended from the ceiling and a raised pulpit centered in a semi-circle of oak pews. "In addition to my full Sunday and

Wednesday worship services," Reverend Joe says, "I hold two services here every day, Matins and Vespers. Attendance is mandatory, and all of the Lord's Disciples congregate for all services and all meals."

The two sample rooms they view in the barracks—the *cloister*, Reverend Joe calls them—are spartan and tidy. "The Divine Eagle Institute," he points out, "currently has one hundred and sixty-two Lord's Disciples. Those under my care range from infants to Elders in their eighties. Some of the Elders have praised the Lord with their Prophet since the founding of the Institute twelve years ago."

"Men in one cloister, and women in the other?" Wright asks.

"Indeed!" Reverend Joe replies. "This is a religious community fully dedicated to the Will of the Lord. It is a known fact that conjugal cohabitation diminishes the ardor of worship." He takes off the ten-gallon hat and runs his hand through his thinning hair. "Men and women carry out duties and are accorded privileges appropriate to their sexes."

Wright nods but does not follow up with a question about race because Maggie told him earlier that, although both the *Will of the Lord* and the DEI website encourage everyone to donate generously, all of the Institute's residents happen, in fact, to be white. And now is not yet the time to point out that odd little discrepancy.

The cafeteria—the *refectory*—is large and clean, almost sterile. A lone high table, like that at a wedding reception, faces twenty rectangular tables, each surrounded by eight molded plastic chairs. "The Institute," Reverend Joe says, "is self-sufficient. All members of my congregation work at one task or another. Private, outside enterprises do provide food, durable goods, and a few services, but I take nothing from the State. Absolutely nothing." His tone becomes strident for a moment. "I see to it that we at the Divine Eagle Institute, we who have dedicated our lives solely to the Will of the Lord, are beholding only unto Him. We pump and purify our own water from the well and cistern, and we generate all our own electricity from solar power." He raises his large hands toward the ceiling. "We depend on the Lord for all of our needs."

22

THE DIVINE EAGLE INSTITUTE'S TELEVISION STUDIO IS SURPRISINGLY sophisticated, the equipment a bit out of date but first-rate and perfectly serviceable. Andrew Wright has Reverend Joe talk about how he got started on cable, the best and worst moments on the live set, and the show's future. As they're leaving the studio, Wright says, as though he's just thought of it, "You know, I watched your show, and the ending, the use of the snake and the staff, intrigued me."

At ease now and talking freely, Reverend Joe says, "You were impressed?" He puts his ten-gallon hat back on and taps the silver eagle bolo with his thick index and middle fingers. "The idea developed over time, and it's all highly symbolic. I was looking for a powerful, an exceptionally powerful, image to demonstrate to my far-flung congregation and to the unbelievers alike that we all, each and every one of us, have within us the Lord's power. We can all overcome our fear of Satan, of any evil, if we only trust completely, five hundred percent, in the Lord. We must all live in the Will of the Lord."

If Reverend Joe is kidding in any way, Wright can't see it in his eyes. The guy, at least in this moment, believes deeply in what he's saying.

The blond man glances at Reverend Joe as if to ask if he should be mentioning this, but Reverend Joe adds, "I end every program with the transformation of the Serpent, evil incarnate, into the crosier, the Lord's Truth and Power." He brushes Wright's arm with the tips of his fingers. "And I do so even though I, myself—and Andy, this is strictly off the record—have had to overcome a personal fear of snakes. A deathly terror of snakes."

"Really?" Wright says. "That's amazing." It's a good sign that the guy is starting to call him by his first name. "How do you get…are they rattlesnakes?"

"Yes," the preacher says, *"Crotalus atrox,* the western diamondback." He takes a deep breath, pulls himself up to his full height, shoulders thrown back, and exhales slowly. "Would you like to see our herpetology lab, Andy?" he asks.

"Yes," Wright answers. "Yes, I would, Reverend."

A brief smile flickers across Maggie's lips. This, she has mentioned to him before, may be what he does best—make instant friends with people who, if they had any sense at all, would not be talking to him in the first place. And as the group heads toward a small white building hidden among the trees, she whispers to Wright, "Whatever this lunatic's selling, Andy, it's not Christianity."

When they enter the one-room herpetology lab, the blond man sidles away. Once they're inside, Reverend Joe lays his meaty hand on Wright's shoulder and confesses, "Sometimes this place still gives me the heebie-jeebies, Andy."

The twelve-by-fifteen-foot room is well lit but warm, with an unpleasant mixture of chemical and fecal odors; a low but distinct rattling permeates the area. A ferret-faced young man, who is slipping a white mouse into one of the stacked cages that line two of the walls, nods to Reverend Joe and says, "The Lord's Will be done, Prophet." Plastic bottles of chemicals, labeled vials in wooden racks, and aluminum bins fill the shelves below hanging snakeskins along the third wall. Two spotlessly clean stainless steel tables stand in the center of the room above drains in the tile floor.

"Crotalus atrox," Reverend Joe says, "is a member of the pit viper family." He sucks in his breath, takes off his hat, wipes his forehead with a red paisley bandana, and replaces the hat.

As Arnuz and Miguel hurriedly set up, the young man puts on a padded leather glove.

"They've got heat receptor pits," Reverend Joe says, "between their eyes and nostrils so that, even in the dark, they can strike warm-blooded prey."

Though there's a loop-pole set in brackets on the wall, the young man simply opens one of the upper cages, waits a few seconds until the rattlesnake buries its fangs in the glove, grabs the snake behind its head, and pulls it from the cage. The snake, just over three feet in length, twists in the man's grip, and its rattle shakes violently. As the snake releases its fangs from the glove and turns its head, the young man smirks. He runs his gloved hand down the snake's swaying body. Reverend Joe wraps the bandana around his hand and takes a half-step backward. Wright steps back, too, bumping into Maggie who's staring at the snake's flicking tongue. Miguel zooms in to get a close-up of the snake's head, but Arnuz remains crouched behind the portable light stand.

"It certainly is warm in here," Reverend Joe says, sweat dripping down his temples below his hat. "I'm going to step outside for a minute, but if any of you would like to handle the serpent, Brother David will be glad to assist you."

Wright follows Reverend Joe out into the shade of the pines. They stop beyond the cistern near a shed humming with equipment. It's even hotter outside, but Wright doesn't mention that to the preacher. Instead, he says, "It was a little close in there."

Breathing hard, Reverend Joe twists the bandana with both hands, and Wright suspects that the snakes he uses in the show have been defanged or otherwise rendered harmless. He wants to know more about the snakes, but that's not why he's here. "Reverend," he says, "the knock against some televangelists, the Bakkers and the Swaggarts, was that they were simply TV personalities on the make."

Nodding, Reverend Joe wipes his forehead with the wrinkled bandana.

Wright scuffs fallen pine needles with his shoe. "I sense a spiritual side to you," he continues, "that's different."

Reverend Joe touches Wright's arm again, letting his big hand linger there for a few seconds, and says, "Agnostics may scoff, Andy, but I really do live in the Lord. I am an instrument of the Lord. The Lord's Will resides in me." His voice grows stronger, not the oily preaching voice from his TV show, but a deeper voice emanating from his gut. "I *am* the Lord's Will."

Speechless for a moment, Wright only nods. The others are still in the lab, and these words, he knows, are meant only for him. "Uh, how…where do you feel closest to the Lord?" he asks finally.

"Come," Reverend Joe says as he takes Wright by the elbow. "I'll show you."

Wright glances back at the building among the trees. He needs all this on video, but his team must still be charmed by the goddamned rattlesnakes.

When they reach the end of a long corridor in the main building, Reverend Joe says, "This, Andy, is my private chapel." He pulls from his pants pocket an oversized key with dappled bumps and sharply delineated teeth. "My chapel's the one spot on earth where I can most deeply feel the Lord's presence in me. Here, Andy, I can, on blessed occasions, feel the Lord's Will coursing through me."

"It's a sanctuary?" Wright asks.

"Yes. Exactly." His hand trembling, the preacher touches Wright's forearm. "It is the sanctum sanctorum."

Wright nods as Reverend Joe inserts the key in the lock, turns the key, and opens the door. The room is cool, almost dark, with no odor at all, the only sound a soft purring. A single ceiling light shines on a gold *crux commissa* hanging from a gilded chain.

As Wright is about to step into the chapel, the blond man marches down the hall toward them saying, "Excuse me, Prophet. I need to speak to you at once."

"In just a moment," Reverend Joe answers as he ushers Wright into the room.

The cross commissa seems to levitate in the half light, a glowing, mesmerizing presence. An oak armchair stands in front of the cross. Against the far wall in the shadow behind the cross, a deep red cloth covers an object about the size of two scotch bottles. A single gold amulet shaped like a human fist rests on the cloth.

23

JOSEPH WENGELT STANDS WITH MICHAEL GRANT BY THE FRONT DOOR OF the Commons. His heart races, and he's gulping air, trying to stifle his rage. Unaware of what he's doing, he crushes the crown of his ten-gallon hat with his hand. "Flat out rejected?" he asks, speaking low so that none of the Elders or acolytes can hear him. Michael has just rid the Institute of that fiend, Andy Wright, and his motley crew. Didn't toss them out on their asses, but stopped that mongrel cameraman from shooting and abruptly cut short the tour—and the message, though nothing was said, should have been abundantly clear.

"That's what my source at ABC tells me, Prophet," Michael answers. Standing close to Wengelt, he can feel the large man's breath on his hair and neck. "The word is that your cute little buddy made the proposal and was apparently serious about it, but his boss shot him down. Refused to even consider the idea."

The Prophet continues to crumple the hat. "Maybe Andy got them to change…" he sputters. "Your source…"

"My source," Michael interrupts, his tone suggesting that he should not be questioned on such matters, "is more trustworthy than any twenty network newsmen."

The Prophet's face is florid. "Damn him!" he mutters. "Damn all the media to hell!" The network liberals' outright rejection of him as worthy of a story angers him, but it's nothing compared to the depth of burning ire, the furious enmity he feels for Andy Wright. Though he knew better, he trusted the reporter, genuinely liked him, found him friendly and open, very attractive—and it was all some heinous, diabolic sham. But in the Lord's name, why?

He should have known. Easy-going friendliness like that is always

Satan's mask, the Serpent incarnate. Still, the Prophet's charisma, which he felt sure was glowing brightly, must have had some effect on Andy. It could not have been to no avail. It never is. And now Michael, his archangel, who warned him against the television crew's visit, has taken on an arrogant, self-righteous attitude that borders on the sin of Pride.

"Perhaps, Prophet," Michael says, "no real harm was done. It may simply serve as a lesson to us."

The Prophet knows that his security chief does not really mean *us*, that he's deliberately twisting the knife. But, yes, it will be a lesson the Prophet will not soon forget. And, yes, to his recollection, the crew shot nothing that could be incriminating in any way. But that impious Andy Wright even wheedled his way into the chapel. Acolytes often go a full year without seeing the inner sanctum, and Andy conned him on their first meeting. The Lord's retribution must befall the reporter. He must be punished. And his demonic crew must not escape unscathed either. To deceive the Prophet in his own sanctuary is anathema. He must discover *why* he was deceived—and then have Michael inflict an austere punishment. It's difficult, but he finally gains control of his breathing. "An…Wright must know something!" he says.

"My conclusion as well, Prophet," Michael answers. "But he can't." He looks the older man in the eye. "It's impossible. There's simply no way he can know…unless there's a leak in Smith's organization."

The Prophet notices Michael's thin smile. His archangel is consciously giving the knife another twist. Michael has never approved of Mr. Smith or his Protective Security Force—with good reason. They are volatile and messy, two things Michael never is. Indeed, Michael has wanted Smith shunned since he first took over responsibilty for the Institute's security. The problem is that Michael has never understood their usefulness either. The Prophet's ire still burns deeply, but he can feel a smile almost cross his lips as well. Gazing down, he sees what he has done to his favorite hat. But rather than becoming angrier, he gently pushes the crown back out and carefully reshapes it with both hands. If Smith's PSF can deliver Andy Wright to him this very day—bloody and battered, if necessary—he can exact the Lord's just retribtution *and* be far more certain that someone in Smith's organization has not betrayed what little they know of the plan for the Day of the Lord. If the PSF fails, or, worse yet, Smith refuses, then the plan will change significantly without their knowledge. Trust in the Lord, and the Lord will always provide—and a single call now will demonstrate just how well the Will of the Lord works. "Michael," he says, able now to return his security chief's penetrating gaze, "please get Mr. Smith on the phone for me."

24

FERESHTEH RAISANI PULLS THE LAND ROVER OFF THE DIRT TRACK INTO a narrow clearing near an old campsite. The sky is clear, the temperature outside ninety-eight. Coming here in daylight always involves risk, but this afternoon the potential for peril is exponentially greater. Yet she must deliver the information her husband requested. And she has brought a gift of her own. She runs her hands down the legs of her loose-fitting black pants. Because this may well be her last visit, she is wearing the gold earrings that were her maternal grandmother's and the gold rope and diamond necklace her father gave to her on her tenth birthday in Tehran.

She gets out of the Land Rover, pulls a black garbage bag from the passenger seat, locks the vehicle, and, carrying the bag over her shoulder, begins to make her way through the pine trees toward the sandstone outcroppings. The bag with the gift is heavy, and her shoulder slumps as she climbs the sandstone boulders. Taking a circuitous route as always despite the heat, she perspires freely. As she passes a dilapidated shack and an abandoned mine shaft partially covered by a landslide, she looks back over her shoulder. She has never been followed here, but anything seems possible today.

When she reaches her husband's dwelling, he is working at the console in his lab, fully focused on the electronic array. He knows she's here, of course—and has been aware of her coming every step of the way. She leaves the heavy bag by the lab's entrance but carries the disc to him and places it on the console. He turns and gazes at her, his hands reaching for her hips and his eyes telling her of his love but also of his concern, his apprehensiveness. His smile lets her know that he, too, perhaps even more than she, knows that after this visit worlds will clash and their lives will inevitably be altered.

Leaning down, she kisses his forehead, his eyes, his cheeks, and, finally, his lips. She is aware of how much work they both must do and cognizant, too, that neither of them will sleep this night. They may never again lie in each other's arms—and she wants him always to remember her like this, wearing her family's jewelry.

He stands and kisses her hard, their mouths open, tongues swirling. Her lips tingle. He leans back, and his hands, rough from so much time spent in the desert highlands, cup her chin and caress her hair. His calloused index and middle fingers trace gently along the back of her neck. Her skin tickles, the perspiration drying in the cool of the lab.

Her eyes close and her neck arches as they kiss even harder. They both, she knows, want deeply to make love; they both need the fling and flare that has been their refuge beyond time and place. But when she opens her eyes, he is looking into her. She returns his gaze, fixing him in this moment. "I talked with Maya," she says. "Gave her your love. She is well…and safe."

"Good," he says. "There are complications here."

Still holding him, she rests her head on his shoulders. Her lips touch his neck.

"Wengelt and his security chief know that Wright's visit was a sham," he says. "He and his crew are in danger."

She clings to him a second longer, takes a deep breath, lifts her head, and looks again into his eyes. There is no need for him to say anything more.

25

GARY B. SMITH LOUNGES IN A BAMBOO ARMCHAIR RECONNING THE TAHI-tian's front desk and main entrance. People are absolutely flooding the lobby—a real fuckin' mudslide—and it's making it hard for him to keep his eyes on the prize. Plus a lot of these mudheads are sporting silky shirts and other gaudy garb. The fuckin' idiots are dressed like they're actually strolling the beach in Tahiti or they're at some carnival or something. There's one young blonde, though, probably Swedish, swinging out of the elevator wearing some long silky blue and gold gown wrapped so tightly around her that you can see every curve, but none of these mudheads gaping at her have a clue how to dress.

Still, he feels like he sticks out much less now that he's put on new black Nikes, clean black denims, and a blue and white striped shirt with a button-down collar. He's got a silver and black walkie-talkie, one of three newfangled ones he just bought with the six hundred bucks he scored off the bandit this morning. It's concealed in his lap under the copy of *After Dark* he picked up from some mudhead hawker outside—and it's way cooler even than the one he always wanted when he was a kid. He's mobilized his Protective Security Force, gotten the guys organized into two squads, Alpha and Charlie, and the walkie-talkies are working pretty fuckin' good. Keeping one eye on the entrance, he checks out the photo of the redhot redhead on *After Dark's* back page.

When Reverend Dickhead called, you could hear the piss through the phone. The Dickhead wants him to round up the TV people so fuckin' bad he's offered another three grand—one for the special delivery of the pretty boy reporter, one for that hot little producer, and one for the mudhead camera crew—the jungle bunny and the beaner. He's got his two squads, four men in each, stationed outside —Alpha the other side of that big lagoon in front of the hotel and Charlie hidden near where the TV fag's rented van is parked out back in the garage. The Dickhead gave him the license number, and locating the van was no problem. Both squads are set so you won't notice them much—but they're ready to strike fast.

You can't snatch people inside a place like this. For one thing, there's all the fuckin' security cameras—but it's more than that. It just doesn't feel right. The whole Tahitian's a palace, but this lobby is way fuckin' over the top. You can't help staring at this waterfall that tumbles down over real rocks from who the shit knows how high up, dark wood everywhere, paint this deep, dark red color on the walls, thick carpeting, and the flowers—more fuckin' flowers probably than in the whole State of Nevada. And they all smell like perfume, too. But, like everything else the Man gets his mitts on, it's way the fuck too much. He probably hired half the fuckin' fairies in San Francisco to decorate the place. Like this huge brass planter next to his chair overflowing with tropical flowers—hibiscus, maybe, who knows? His mother would of loved 'em, but they're so perfect they don't even look real—and the smell's overwhelming, almost enough to make you puke.

He rubs his thumb and forefinger together, wanting a Marlboro bad but not wanting to lose his seat. Anyway, you can't smoke here neither, only in the casino or outside away from the doors. He's given Alpha and Charlie careful orders. They're not to act until they get the word from him. He's not planning to bother with the mudhead camera crew at all unless he has to. He'll lose out on that grand, but they're a two-for-one deal that's no good anyway. Plus they look kind of tough for mudheads, like they could give the PSF a pretty good fight. And he can't have his guys banged up with the Der Tag operation just twenty-four hours away.

Both squads, though, have been given free boot on the pretty boy reporter whether he leaves front or back. And the guys are more than ready for that fuckin' party—they can kick the shit out of him, kick those perfect fuckin' teeth of his down his throat. The hot little producer's a different story, though. The Dickhead didn't give him any special instructions about her, but he's ordered both Alpha and Charlie to avoid damaging the goods in any way, not even to mess up that cute pixie hairdo she's got. And, he's not real sure he's going to deliver her to the Dickhead immediately. He's getting a hard-on just picturing again that tight little ass of hers twitching down that hallway with all those fancy stores, and he thinks that maybe he'll stash her back at the house until after Der Tag. When all hell breaks loose, nobody's gonna be looking for one little TV producer, and he'll have no trouble convincing her, one way or the other, that putting out is good for her fuckin' health.

Some fuckin' posse storming through the lobby wrenches his mind from the fun he's going to have with pretty Miss New York TV Producer. All these people are dressed up nice, but the little man they're following looks like he just stepped out of a fuckin' foreign movie or some snobby BMW ad. The guy's very tan, with not a single reddish hair out of place, and his suit, tie, and shoes just sneer, "I've got more money than you can imagine, sucker!" In fact, he's just the perfect sort of little bastard that his mother would of swooned over. She was a big woman, but she had this thing about small, good-looking rich guys. Practically threw herself at 'em. Couldn't fuckin' help herself.

This little bastard's acting like he owns the fuckin' place, ordering everybody around like he's Napoleon or somebody. And when the bastard stops at the registration desk, he starts chatting up one of the clerks—the sexiest one, naturally, a dark woman who must be Tahitian, a real, what-do-you-call-it, *wahine*. No wonder all those fuckin' sailors jumped ship. She may be a mudhead, but she's one prime example of the lesser races. And, it's no real sin for a white man to have his way with a woman like her.

Meanwhile, the little bastard's flock just hovers around him trying to look like they're doing important crap. One tall shithead is pecking away on some little gizmo, and some Chink is punching something into a hand-computer like the ones the guys in the Lucky's use when they're gonna restock the shelves. And, the *wahine's* making eyes at the little bastard like she's gonna leap over the counter and go down on him right there. It all makes you more than glad that The Tahitian's high up on the fuckin' list for Der Tag.

Smith is so busy watching the little bastard's show that he almost misses the pretty boy reporter getting off the elevator. The guy's wearing running shoes, blue shorts, a T-shirt, and some stupid looking floppy hat like he might just be nuts enough to go jogging in this heat. Sure, it's past six, but it's not like the fuckin' broiler out there has cooled down any. And the pretty boy's limping toward the big front entrance like he'll be lucky to make it to the lagoon before he falls on his face. Smith fumbles with the walkie-talkie, raises it close to his mouth, pushes the call button, and says, "Alpha, Alpha, the pretty boy's proceedin' out the front door. He's wearin' dark runnin' shorts and a fuckin' faggoty flophat. As soon as he gets past the lagoon and all those fuckin' mudhead tourists, hit him." He hasn't thought about what he himself should do, go or wait, but then he realizes that the hot little producer might be coming out of the elevator next—and there's really no decision at all. His PSF guys'll have no trouble taking care of one gimpy reporter.

26

ANDREW WRIGHT REACHES THE TAHITIAN'S PUBLIC LAGOON JUST AS ONE of the canoe races is finishing. Hundreds of people are leaning on the railing, yelling and clapping. Some are slapping each other high-fives, and others are swearing under their breath and pulling out their wallets. A rotund guy in bluejeans the size of a studio backdrop is jiggling unbelievably as he kicks the railing. A lot of cash, Wright figures, is changing hands.

He's not a hundred yards from the entrance, and he's already sweating—but he had to get out, walk somewhere, even on his bad wheel, to sort things through in his mind. The image of the golden fist lying on the red cloth keeps welling. The same goddamned fist he saw on the canisters. And the snakes, the goddamned snakes—he can't get them out of his head either. He dropped the BluRay Disc at the trailer, but he hasn't heard word one from Larson. And, there's no way to let the guy know about the goddamned fist.

Good Morning America's executive producer, however, phoned Maggie to inform Wright that, insubordinate son of a bitch that he is, he's on the verge of being canned and his crew banished to the graveyard shift in Albany. The only conceivable way to redeem himself and return his crew from exile is to have a finished piece—and a damned fine one, every bit as good as the Kupferberg piece—in New York by six tomorrow night.

Arnuz and Miguel are in open revolt because they know they've got a better chance of winning the MEGABUCKS slot lotto. Maggie has been able to placate them, at least in the short run, but she's on the warpath herself. Ever since they got booted from Reverend Joe's compound, she's been pushing to get the goddamned disc back and actually do the piece. Now, she's even more sure than he is that Reverend Joe's cooking up something with those canisters, and she wants to cobble a story together even without the interview—and scoop the world about the country's next biochemical threat. She's been Googling, gleaning material from Reverend Joe's site and related apocalyptic and televangelist sites. He asked her to follow up on her earlier Larson inquiries, but she's so focused on Reverend Joe that she hasn't had the chance.

Everything was going so well during the shoot, too, goddamn it. Reverend Joe was ready to stick his tongue in Wright's ear until that brownshirt bastard shunted everybody out. How did the guy get on to them so fast? And how does he fit into whatever's happening? Wright feels as though he's got enough of the puzzle pieces now, but he's still too obtuse to see the pattern. He's spent far too long playing the goddamned fool.

Wright limps away from the lagoon and the crowd. When he reaches the corner, he notices a couple of burnouts glancing his way. He turns on the side street to avoid the throngs milling along the Strip. It's hot and his ankle aches, but he's still happy to be outside. He needs air and open space to think clearly, and the sweat running down his neck from under his Tahitian hat feels good. The hat's not exactly a fashion statement, but he's sort of becoming attached to it.

As he heads farther from the Strip, the blare of piped music subsides. And there's suddenly no traffic. None at all. He walks along next to the plywood and chain-link barrier of a derelict construction site strewn with rubble and equipment. On the other side of the fencing, a dozen unplanted thirty-foot pine trees stand in crates, each the size of a Hummer. Pine cones hang from the branches of the trees and lie in the hardscrabble among the waste. And there are birds. Birds are singing in the goddamned trees.

Glancing over his shoulder, he spots the same two burnouts trailing him. Or, they seem to be anyway. As he limps across the street and toward a vacant lot behind the row of hotels, he wonders if he's becoming paranoid. He knows that, if he's really being followed, he should turn around and mingle in the crowd on the Strip. But he wants to know for sure—and so he heads toward two yellow construction cranes parked inside a rectangle of temporary cyclone fencing.

Two more burnouts are lumbering around the corner ahead of him. And it's definitely not his imagination. They're all going to meet along the cyclone fence near a telephone pole and an orange portable light generator, and he doesn't like the odds. It's too late to turn back, but he could outrun them in their Doc Martens—except for his ankle. A call to 911 would be good idea, but he left his new phone in the room partly because he doesn't have any pockets but mostly because he didn't really want to hear from anybody back in New York or anywhere else.

All four of the burnouts look like they belong to some Deviants 'R' Us club—the heavy boots with red laces, jeans with studded belts, black T-shirts, buzz cuts, pierced eyebrows, and tattoos, lots of tattoos. Trying to negotiate with burnouts like this is useless. And staying and fighting might be noble, but it's stupid, too, even for someone suffering from Male Idiocy. He's just not that much of a fool.

Wright slows near the fence, waiting for the burnouts to converge on him and feeling like he's being treed by dogs. He glances up the telephone pole at the wires that look more like power lines than phone lines. There's no goddamned way he's shinnying up there even to save his ass. The crowd along the Strip two-and-a-half blocks away isn't looking in this direction at all and probably couldn't hear anything over the music and the traffic. The burnouts seem to be in no hurry—but it's going to get ugly soon enough. One of the two ahead of him is yanking his belt free, wrapping it around his hand so the heavy buckle protrudes. The other one is pulling a thick metal key ring from his pocket. The original duo is closing in from the other side, and one of those two losers has a swastika tattooed in the middle of his forehead—not a particularly good sign at all. The rushing in Wright's ears drowns out the birds.

When the burnouts are about fifteen feet away and just starting to circle, Wright bolts away from the fence into the street. He makes it to the middle of the street, tooling fast, when his ankle gives out, just goddamn gives out, and he skids across the pavement on his shoulder. He's pushing himself up and shaking out the cobwebs when they reach him. The belt buckle gets him the first time just behind his ear. The second time, it tears into his cheek. He rolls and flails, the only thing he can do, trying at least to remain a moving target. Something sharp—the keys maybe—smack the side of his head, and he thinks with clarity, objectivity even, that it's going to be a long time before he's on camera again. Somewhere near him, an amplified radio voice is saying, "Charlie, Charlie, the producer's headin' to the back. To the parking lot. I'm on my way. Remember, don't fuckin' damage the goods."

The world is fading to black when Wright hears the squealing of tires. He feels a rush of air and hears the dull thud of metal against flesh. Someone, not him, is screaming in pain. And then a voice shouts, "Shit, it's just some fuckin' bitch! Get her!"

He looks up through a gray haze at the black Land Rover, its door swung open, and Raisani stepping out. "No, don't," he wants to shout to her, but he's breathing in erratic fits, and his voice won't work. Someone is on the ground near him, writhing and shrieking, and only three of the burnouts are circling her.

Raisani looks pretty and diminutive in her loose black cotton pants and blouse. Her eyes are bright, her expression calm. With the detachment of a triage doctor, she looks down at the man her Land Rover struck and then at the others. "Get in the car," she shouts to Wright. "The car, Andy! Now!"

As she raises her right arm, one of the burnouts yells, "She's got a fuckin' piece."

Flicking a switchblade open, Swastika Forehead steps toward her. When she fires the black and yellow gun, there's a soft pop rather than a sharp report. The guy collapses instantly, crumbling onto his knife just before his nose and forehead slap the concrete. He convulses, face down, smearing his swastika with the blood spreading from his broken nose. Raisani adeptly changes the TASER's cartidge, but the other burnouts are already running, their Doc Martens clapping the pavement.

Swastika Forehead continues to shudder and twitch, and the other guy, his leg protruding at a strange angle from his hip, goes on yelping. A hand-held radio lies between the downed men and Wright. The same amplified voice Wright heard before is shouting, "Alpha, Alpha! Come in, Alpha! What the fuck's happenin' out there?"

Raisani stoops, cups her hand under Wright's arm, and says, "Come on, Andy. We've got to get you out of here fast."

27

IN THE FAR CORNER OF THE SEVENTH LEVEL OF THE MIRAGE'S GARAGE, Fereshteh Raisani bandages Andrew Wright's face and head. He messed up the Land Rover's pristine interior again—no mud this time, but plenty of blood. She backed the Land Rover in so the light's better, but she's still wearing a headlamp. The vehicle's tailgate is open, and he's seated by the tubs filled with medical supplies. Over her shoulder he can see Rio's curved blue tower, the roofs of warehouses, the tops of spindly pine trees, and, in the distance, the red and gray mountains of Red Rock Canyon.

He's nauseated and dizzy; his head hurts, his shoulder stings where he slid across the pavement, his ribs burn every time he takes a breath—and he will, he expects, be pissing blood for the foreseeable future. She's given him only ibuprofen, telling him he can't take anything stronger that might cloud his thinking. She has also let him know he'll need plastic surgery later, but the steristrips are going to have to do for now. There's no time for the hospital, and there would be too many questions anyway, even if she were the admitting physician.

While she works, she talks to him. Her smile isn't forced, but it's tinged with sadness. She tells him that her father was a surgeon who taught at Tehran University. Although he was a Muslim and well-respected, he was more secular than devout. In the winter of 1979, shortly after Ayatollah Khomeini seized power, the Revolutionary Guards arrested and jailed him. He had loathed SAVAK, the shah's secret police, but he had once operated on the shah's wife. He had also been educated in England and often wore ties, both of which, though not technically crimes, were affronts to Khomeini's regime. She became afraid to leave the family's apartment, and, in any case, her school, a French Lycée, was soon shut down.

As she dabs his head wounds with disinfectant, he winces. He's not exactly sure why she's talking about all this, other than to take his mind off the pain, but he knows that it has something to do with her rescuing him. She goes on to tell him that her father was released only after Saddam Hussein's invasion of the oil-rich Khuzestan province started the Iran-Iraq War in 1980. Given that the Iranian *Martyrs,* as all the young soldiers were called, were engaged in human wave attacks, his surgical skills became indispensible. He was rotated to the front for six months, and later, when the Iraqi bombing of civilian targets in Tehran began, he called in all his old markers to get Fereshteh and her mother safely out of the country. When he was recalled to the front after Hussein's poison gas attacks began, she and her mother left him and most of what they owned, fleeing through Turkey and Europe to the United States.

"Thanks," he says as she steps back to examine her job. He was watching her eyes as she worked, the depth of sadness but also the wellspring of strength. "Thanks," he repeats, meaning for attending to his injuries but even more for saving him. "Wh...what were you doing here this time?" Once may have been fortuitous, though he knows it wasn't—but saving him twice in two separate places has more to do with who she is than with any laws of probability.

She picks up a roll of white surgical tape and stares at it as she turns it in her hand. "I never saw him, my father, again," she whispers. When she looks up, her welling eyes are bright even in the half-light of the garage. "The Iraqis gassed the field hospitals."

He takes a breath cut short by pain. "I'm sor..." he chokes. Shaking his head only stirs the burning. "Thanks," he says again. "Thank you, Fereshteh." He's not exactly sure about all he's thanking her for now —aid and first aid and something deeper—but gratitude is suffusing through the pain.

As she tears a strip of surgical tape from the roll, she smiles. "I was on my way to pick you up," she says. "I saw you leaving The Tahitian, but I was stuck in traffic. Sorry I didn't get to you sooner."

The image of her facing the burnouts flashes in his mind. His skin tingles somehere beyond pain. "You were picking me up?" he asks.

"Yes, I need to take you somewhere." She wipes her eyes with the back of her hand.

"Where?"

Without answering, she begins to clean up the bloody compresses and torn bandage wrappers she's piled on one of the tub's clear plastic lids.

"Where, Fereshteh?" he repeats. And then he remembers the hand-held radio squawking on the pavement. "Oh, shi…god…" he mutters. "Can I borrow your…" As he stands, the garage walls shimmy around him, and the cement tries to leap up and slam him one more time. The distant mountains waver and quake.

One hand on his shoulder and the other on his chest, she guides him back down on the Land Rover. "Slowly," she says, the lilt returning to her voice. "Take everything very slowly, Andy."

He nods, his breath stuck again and pain stabbing his chest. "Can… I need your phone."

"Hold still, Andy," she says, leaving her hand on his shoulder a moment longer. "Please."

As she retrieves the phone from the charger in the Land Rover's console, he swallows the bile rising in his throat and tries to regulate his breathing. When she hands him the phone, he punches Maggie's number, and then, as he raises the phone to his ear, feels pain race across his chest. There's no answer so he tries Miguel's number.

As soon as Miguel answers, Wright asks, "Hey, is Maggie there?"

"No," Miguel says. "She went out to get a notebook she left in the van. She should…"

"When did she leave?"

"Not sure. But she should be back any min…"

"Where's Arnuz?" Wright interrupts again. His eyes are burning, and he has trouble raising his other hand to rub them.

"Down in the Bora Bora Bistro, celebrating the loss of our…"

"Get him," Wright shouts. "Get out to the van fast. She's in trouble."

"But…" Miguel begins.

"Go, goddamn it!"

Raisani takes the phone from Wright and turns it off. When he starts to stand, she presses her hand on his shoulder and says, "There's nothing you can do right now, Andy."

He looks at her, those eyes telling him to trust her despite what she's saying. "You have to come with me, Andy," she adds. Her voice has that same authoritative tone he's heard in it before.

28

GARY B. SMITH STARES AT THE TELEPHONE ON HIS DESK IN THE WAR ROOM. He knows he has to make the call, but he really doesn't want to listen to any fuckin' whining when he tells the Dickhead that the pretty boy reporter got away. Wiggling the tip of his forefinger in his ear does nothing to stop the buzzing in his head so he pulls off the NRA cap and scratches his scalp until it tingles. At least he's got that hot little producer, Maggie Mac, stashed away in his bedroom. She's tied to the bed and gagged, but it could be a lot worse for her. It's the only air conditioned room in the house, the bed's sort of new, and he's cleared out all his PSF guys—didn't let any of 'em so much as cop a feel.

Nothing's gone right, though, not even snatching Maggie Mac. She scratched the living shit out of Bobby's face and kicked Sam in the nuts so hard he's gonna be singing fuckin' falsetto for a week. And that's nothing compared to the casualties in the Wright mess. He lost two men, both of 'em from the Der Tag strike teams. They're still in the fuckin' hospital, Larry in intensive care with internal bleeding from a smashed up hip and leg. Tommy's in Emergency with his smushed nose and a concussion and his brains scrambled even more from getting fuckin' tasered. Tommy wasn't too bright to begin with, and the doctors said they were holding him for observation.

The guys couldn't tell the paramedics or the fuckin' cops the truth, had to say they got jumped by a rival gang. And the pigs weren't buying any of it, 'specially with Larry looking like he was fuckin' run over—which he was. The fuckin' pigs even confiscated the new walkie-talkie, like it was evidence that something more than a gang fight was going down.

Smith pulls on his hat and pats his pockets, but there's still no fuckin' Marlboros, no miracle like the loaves and fishes. He stands, opens the file cabinet's top drawer, and stares at Reverend Dickhead's last cigar. He's saving it to celebrate Der Tag, but he needs a couple of deep drags right now to settle his nerves. He sure as shit can't tell the Dickhead the truth, either. How do you explain that a woman— a fuckin' *woman*—took out two of your best men? You don't, that's how. You make up some shit about a bunch of paramilitary types piling out of this black Land Rover. And who the fuck was she anyway?

He slams the drawer shut, slips back into his chair, stares at the commando knife, and chews his lower lip until he can taste blood. He promised each of his PSF guys a c-note when the job was done, and the only way he can make good on it is to deliver the producer. And he doesn't want to do that, at least not yet. She's right in his bedroom now, her blouse already torn from her fuckin' struggling—and he's gotta get her out of his mind and make the fuckin' call to Reverend Dickhead. He wraps his fingers around the commando knife's haft, gazes at the blade, kicks back his chair, stands, reaches up, and buries the knife's point deep in the joist above the desk.

29

HIS BLUE EYES BRIGHT WITH THE WRATH OF THE LORD, THE PROPHET SITS heavily in the oak armchair and shuts off the phone in his quavering hand. He has come here to his sanctuary quite without realizing it. He was speaking to Mr. Smith, that philistivne, and came down the hallway unaware of where he was going. He is still so livid he doesn't even remember unlocking the chapel's door. The audacity of that lout! The cretin has screwed up beyond belief, absolutely beyond belief, and he's still demanding $2,000. Says he won't bring Andy Wright's producer to the Institute unless the cash is delivered to him first. Who is this moron kidding? He needs to make atonement, seek absolution, indeed, beg for the Prophet's and the Lord's forgiveness —not arrogantly demand money. After what's happened, Smith will burn in hell before he'll see a cent of that two grand.

It's bad enough that Andy got away—though, at least according to Smith, not unscathed—but it's worse, far worse, that the police swarmed the scene. Didn't he warn the lout not to draw attention? It may well be true, as Smith said, that the Las Vegas cops are too dense to figure anything out. There is, most likely, no immediate danger. The Day of the Lord is still imminent. But that isn't the point. The point is that Smith bungled the job horribly and then did not so much as offer an apology.

The Prophet taps the phone against the chair's arm. Even as he was berating the philistine, Smith tried to divert attention from his atrocious stupidity, blaming some paramilitary force. But that excuse doesn't wash. Not at all. The Lord is omniscient, and the Prophet holds deep within himself the sure sense that that the only truth in Smith's ramblings is that Andy got away and the producer did not.

And the philistine's fiasco will inevitably alter the plan for the Day of the Lord yet again. In the eyes of the Prophet, and, certainly, in the eyes of the Lord as well, Smith has lost his last shred of credibility.

At first, the Prophet does not hear the knocking on the door that's producing a counterbeat to his own tapping of the phone on the chair. Then, when he becomes aware of it, he hopes—he almost prays— it's Christine. He needs her ministrations to calm his nerves. His face feels flushed, and blood pulses in his temples; he must regain control, measure his breathing once more. But ever since Andy Wright first made contact, the Serpent has been slithering around the Institute like some pestilence visited upon his house. He must, absolutely must, overcome his anxiety and grind the Serpent into the earth with the heel of his boot. "Enter in the name of the Lord," he says.

Michael, not Christine, opens the door, and the Prophet hopes his disappointment doesn't show. After all, Michael must be informed of these abominable new developments—and his archangel had better not be sanctimonious about the news.

"Excuse the inter…" Michael begins, but he stops when he notices the Prophet's florid face. "What's the matter, Reverend?" he asks.

The Prophet shakes his head and raises the phone. Knowing he must seize the high ground before Michael can, he says, "Our worst fears about Mr. Smith have been realized."

"He's been arrested?"

The Prophet begins to tap the phone on the armchair again. Michael's hair is wet, and he's wearing an army green T-shirt stretched over his sculpted muscles. He must have just showered after completing one of those spectacular workouts of his. The man truly is a specimen, a marvel of the Lord's handiwork. "Not arrested, no," he says, "but Andy Wright escaped, and two of Mr. Smith's PSF misfits are in the hospital."

Standing ramrod straight, Michael smacks his palm with his fist. "I told…" he begins, but then, catching himself, stops. "How? What happened?"

The Prophet stands so that he is not looking up at his security chief. He sucks in his stomach and exhales slowly. "According to Mr.

Smith, just as his PSF team was softening Wright up, a black Land Rover pulled up, and five men in fatigues leapt out and attacked the team and rescued Wright."

"If there was a squad in the area," Michael says flatly, "I would know about it."

"We both would." The Prophet grimaces at the phone before slipping it into his pocket. "There's no way to know what really happened. Perhaps, though, you can verify that two of his PSF boys have been hospitalized." Given the circumstances, he is careful to avoid making it sound like an order.

"I will," Michael answers, the shadow of a smile crossing his face. "I can also ensure that those in the hospital don't talk."

"That's not necessary," the Prophet says, noting Michael's smile. "They have no reason to say anything. They appear to be the victims of a crime. And, anyway, they know nothing but that they are to serve the Lord."

Michael scratches his ear for a moment. "Did Smith tell you it was a black Land Rover?"

"Yes," the Prophet says. "He made a point of it."

"Our perimeter surveillance system picked up a black Land Rover twice today."

Surprised by the news, the Prophet cocks his head. "Do the tapes show who was driving?"

Michael shrugs. "I haven't checked, but I've tracked the vehicle before. The owner is an *Iranian* doctor. A woman."

"An Arab...female?"

Michael stares into the Prophet's eyes. "The doctor must be a courier for the caveman."

The Prophet sinks back into his armchair. Michael's voice is flat, but the Prophet knows that his archangel is excited, that he has wanted an excuse to terminate that tree-hugger. And Michael now expects to earn the Lord's blessing. Maybe Michael's right, and the caveman isn't the harmless environmentalist fool he seems to be. Andy Wright was first spotted yesterday in the direction the caveman apparently disappears. Maybe the woman doctor really is the caveman's courier.

Maybe she lent the vehicle to whoever broke up—what did that philistine call it?—the boot party. The Prophet grasps the arm of the chair. Maybe the caveman is at the root of the evil that's plaguing his plans for the Day of the Lord. He looks up at Michael, whose gaze has remained fixed on him. "Yes," he says, "perhaps you should tend to the caveman."

"The Lord's will be done," Michael answers.

"Yes," the Prophet says, "it is the Will of the Lord. But, Michael, remember you have far more grave responsibilities that take priority. Given Mr. Smith's bungling, we will have to modify our plans for the Day of the Lord. You will need to take on additional logistical tasks." He looks into his archangel's eyes. "You'll need to become involved in the distribution of materials and the implementation of the Lord's plan. You'll have to be both hand and fist."

"Yes, Prophet," Michael answers, still standing as though he is at dress parade. "I've already thought of that. I can deal with the caveman in the morning without neglecting my other duties."

30

THE BLINDFOLD IRRITATES ANDREW WRIGHT, PARTICULARLY BECAUSE HE and Raisani are crossing rocky terrain that, he guesses, would prove tricky even if he could see. After parking the Land Rover at a defunct campsite about a mile up the dirt track from Reverend Joe's compound, she insisted in that no-nonsense tone of hers that he wear the blindfold. And his protests were useless, of course. The upside is that as they move slowly from boulder to boulder, she holds her right arm around his waist and her left hand on his arm. Her right breast and hip press against him with each awkward step. Still, the blindfold seems to him both excessive and amateurish.

Finally, after too much goddamned climbing, they pass from heat and light into cooler darkness. After they turn twice at sharp angles, first right and then left, she removes the blindfold. When his eyes adjust, he can see yellow electric light ahead. The walls around him are hewn stone, the ground beneath him solid rock. They're obviously underground, but the air smells fresh. He can hear, too, the soft hum of an exhaust fan—and he feels suddenly apprehensive. They aren't anywhere near the cavern with the canisters, but is she somehow involved in whatever goddamned scheme Reverend Joe and his cohorts are concocting? She takes her arm from around him but leaves a hand on his elbow. Though he doesn't feel like her prisoner, fear or the aftereffects of the beating gnaw at his stomach.

The lighted area, about the size of Reverend Joe's snake house, has rough sandstone walls and a russet rock floor. A Rube Goldberg conglomerate of connected electric batteries stands on his left. Above it, three shovels, a pick, an axe, nylon ropes, and other climbing paraphernalia hang on hooks driven into the wall. A row of plastic five-gallon water drums, a portable toilet, and an inflatable camping shower line the wall ahead of him. To the right, a Suzuki dual sport motorcycle, painted a dull black, leans against the wall next to labeled stacks of plastic tubs and molded plastic storage boxes. Whoever lives here sure as hell hasn't skimped on supplies. And the guy is pretty goddamned anal about everything.

Raisani ducks into an opening at the far left corner of the area. His uneasiness increasing, Wright crouches and follows her through a low, narrow tunnel. His sore shoulder bumps repeatedly into the wall, and he's still sweating despite the cool, dry air. As images of the cavern form again in his mind, his breath becomes short. He tries to keep up with her, but she disappears into a splash of light to his left. When he reaches the spot, he brushes through a barrier of clear hanging plastic strips and emerges into a brightly lit twenty-by-thirty-foot cavern with a high stone ceiling. A clean gray tarp stretches across the entire floor—and he feels like he should be wiping his shoes.

Her hands cupped at her waist, Raisani stands next to Nick Larson on the other side of the cavern. Wearing lightweight black hiking boots, dark socks, black cotton pants, and a long-sleeved black shirt, Larson sits in a forest-green folding armchair. Even more jarring, a long white console running along the wall behind Larson is laden with audio and video equipment every bit as sophisticated as the stuff in some of ABC's smaller New York studio control rooms. Among the images on the ten television monitors are live feeds of Reverend Joe's front gate, the large room with the fireplace in the main building, and the cavern with the five canisters set on the red cloth. Though an exhaust fan purrs somewhere nearby, there's no generator, no smell of fuel—only the dry tang of the desert.

"Thanks for coming, Andrew," Larson says, as though Wright were an invited guest. "But you still don't look so good."

Removing his hat, Wright glances quickly around the cavern. He's standing near a small galley with a microwave, mini-refrigerator, cooler, and metal pantry. Two green nylon camp chairs, long pine shelves crammed with books, a camp bench that matches the chairs, the console with its electronic array, and more shelves filled with supplies form three sides of a square. Lights with metal reflective shades jut at intervals from a steel conduit grid overhead. An American flag hangs on the wall above the bookcase, and Hopi pots line the top of the supply shelves. He can see above and behind the pots the curved peak of a tent that must serve as a bedroom. Larson's some goddamned Twenty-first Century caveman, absolutely isolated but still electronically connected.

Wright's eyes return to a silver-framed photographic triptych on the shelf above the console. The shot on the left is of a blonde child riding a red and yellow Big Wheels. Her head is turned, and she is looking up at the camera with a half-smile that suggests equal parts excitement and stubbornness—as though she has just gotten the tricycle and no one is going to take it from her. The central photograph is a formal shot of Larson and Raisani. He wears a tuxedo, and she has on a long white dress with gold embroidery. Her hair is parted and pinned up with a small diamond pendant. Wisps of hair frame her face, and an ornate gold necklace arcs above her breasts. The portrait on the right is of a toddler with curly black hair, pale skin, a sweet smile, and her mother's beautiful eyes. At least one small mystery begins to make sense, but he can't say he's altogether happy to discover the source of Fereshteh's reluctance to have dinner.

"I suppose an explanation is in order," Larson says. He stands and gestures toward the camp chairs.

As Wright sits down, Larson takes a plain manila envelope from the console. He then goes to the galley, pulls a squeeze bottle from the cooler, hands the bottle to Wright, and takes the other chair.

"Thanks," Wright says. He's still queasy, and the cool water makes him feel a little better.

Raisani sits on the bench in the corner between the bookcase and the console and gazes silently across the cavern at the two men.

Larson leans forward, his forearms on his thighs, and taps the edge of the envelope against his palm. "Andrew," he says, "you've fallen upon…we've both come across something that's…" He stops, gazes at the envelope's clasp for a moment, and raises his eyes to Wright.

"You need to look at these." He glances at Raisani and then hands the envelope to Wright.

Wright puts the squeeze bottle on the floor, drops his hat in his lap, opens the envelope, and pulls out half a dozen computer print-outs of color photographs. When he glimpses the first, his stomach turns and sweat beads his forehead. He tastes bile but holds down the vomit. He's seen death before, of course, and numerous photos of the dead, but this close-up is truly gruesome. The face seems to have imploded around the skull, the eyes sunken and the lips contorted. A dark gooey scum oozes from the eye sockets, nostrils, lips, and ears. His hands trembling, Wright glances at the next photograph, a longer shot of a man in hiking clothes lying in an open body bag on sandy dirt. His limbs look spasmodically rigid, and his neck's sharp-ly angled toward his left shoulder as though he hurled his head side-ways at the moment of his death. Wright turns over the whole set of photographs without looking at the others.

"My thought exactly, Andrew," Larson says.

Wright slides the photographs back into the envelope, bends the clasp, and drops the envelope onto the tarp. Feeling as though even the photographs might somehow be contaminated, he keeps wiping his hands on his jogging shorts.

31

ANDREW WRIGHT IS TOO STUNNED TO THINK, MUCH LESS SPEAK. HIS
whole body is sweating, and there's still a real chance he'll puke. Drawing his legs under the chair, he continues to scrub his hands.

"Thanks for the disc, Andrew," Larson says. "But unfortunately I
didn't find what we were looking for. And we're going to need your
continued help."

Wright thinks of the golden fist, but he still can't find his voice.

"Fereshteh and I," Larson says, glancing again at Raisani, "didn't
take those photographs, but we did locate the grave in another part
of that cave two days before you tumbled onto those canisters. Had
you been found there, that would have been your fate, too."

Wright shudders. When he looks over at Raisani, she's staring at
him, her eyes seeming to look deeply into him. He sucks in a great
mouthful of air and asks, "What the hell is in the canisters?"

"We don't really know," Larson says. "Wengelt's security chief refers to it as Virin."

Raisani stands, roots through a neat stack of papers on the console, and takes out a file folder. She walks over to the two men and
hands Wright the folder. "The security officer at The Divine Eagle
Institute," she says, "is a retired military policeman at the Nellis Air
Force Range Area 51 lab. The photos are from a personal file on his
computer at the Institute."

"Area 51," Larson says, "is near Harrison Lake. According to the
government, the site doesn't exist."

Wright remembers Maggie's conversations with the military
spokesmen and her certainty that nothing was missing—or at least

that the authorities believed nothing was. Then, he recalls what he heard on the hand-held radio just as Raisani arrived at the back lot where the burnouts were kicking the crap out of him. He's got to find out if Maggie's okay. Scanning the cavern for a phone, he asks, "The blond guy?"

"Yes," Larson answers, pointing to the folder.

Wright opens the folder and gazes at the photograph of the man in uniform staring without expression at the camera.

"You probably weren't introduced," Larson says. "His name—or his alias—is Michael Grant. He also serves as Wengelt's chief enforcer."

"Grant," Raisani says as she rests a hand on Larson's shoulder, "began to appear at the Institute about a year and a half ago." She glances down at Larson. "Wengelt was jittery about security breaches at DEI. Ten months ago, Grant moved into the compound—though, unlike Wengelt's disciples, he comes and goes as he pleases."

"So Grant stole the Virin from Area 51?" Wright asks.

"We don't really…" Raisani says. "We assume that he did."

"He could've obtained it elsewhere," Larson says as he stands and gives his chair to Raisani. "Wengelt doesn't even know where it originated."

"Though we don't know what it is," Raisani continues, "we're reasonably certain, based on Grant's computer notes, his conversations with Wengelt, and the photographic evidence you saw that if one so much as touches Virin, one's body bleeds out."

"Turns to mush," Larson says.

Wright closes the folder, looks hard at Larson, and asks, "How the hell do you know all this?"

Larson shrugs. "I've built this place out here over the last couple of years." Apparently unaware of what he's doing, he reaches over and traces his forefinger along the back of Raisani's neck. "I cracked the DEI system six months ago because I…I was worried by Grant's movements and Wengelt's increasingly messianic tone."

Nodding toward the console, Raisani says, "Nick's very adept with computers."

And video surveillance, Wright thinks. And who the hell knows what else. Maybe the guy's some fringe anti-government lunatic himself.

"I've recently enhanced our monitoring," Larson says. "We just learned that Wengelt plans to deploy the Virin in Las Vegas tomorrow night."

Wright wrings his hat. "If Virin's so goddamned lethal," he asks, "why the hell haven't you gone to the cops? Or the FBI?"

"We're only a few days ahead of you," Larson says.

"We've talked about that a lot, Andy," Raisani says, glancing at Larson, "and we concluded that we couldn't."

"Why not, goddamn it?" Wright feels himself getting angry at their calmness and their—he can't quite pinpoint it—but it seems like composure bordering on arrogance.

"We don't know enough yet," Larson says.

"Don't know enough yet?" Wright picks up the squeeze bottle, swigs the water, and licks his lips. "You just told me that the goddamned world's going to end *tomorrow.*"

"Andrew, it's not just that cavern you saw. It's more complex than that." Larson's tone is curt for the first time. "There are more than five canisters."

Wright drops the bottle next to the folder and looks at Raisani.

"There are at least seven," she says, as if she's reading his mind. "Probably eight. And we don't know where all of the others are."

"But they must be somewhere in the compound," Wright insists.

"*Must?*" Larson asks. "The five canisters you saw aren't within a mile of that compound." He pauses, letting that fact sink in. "But Grant does have a large cache of automatic weapons stored in one of the compound's out-buildings."

"The gov…" Wright begins.

"Andy," Raisani says, again as if she's reading his mind, "there's nothing that links Wengelt to the cavern. What would happen if the government swept in and confiscated those canisters? Or arrested Grant?"

Wright gets the point. "Whoever has the other canisters, Reverend Joe or somebody else, will use the rest of the Virin."

"That's been our thinking," Raisani says. "We aren't even sure if we know everyone who's involved."

"But…" Wright understands the point that two or three of the canisters aren't accounted for, but he's still mad. And though he himself probably wouldn't do it either, their reason for not contacting the goddamned authorities still seems lame. There's got to be more to it. Larson's some outcast vigilante who *wants* to go it alone.

"Andy, would you be willing to assault Wengelt's Institute?" Raisani asks. "Risk another Waco?"

"And torch all Wengelt's disciples," Larson says, "none of whom knows what's really going on."

"And endanger the lives of tens of thousands of people if the Virin were used?" Raisani asks.

Wright isn't sure. He'd need to give it some serious thought, and both time restraints and his physical condition preclude that. But what, he still wonders, can these two people possibly do that the government can't?

"Andrew," Larson says, "I need to know about anything unusual you saw in that compound. Especially anything you noticed after you left the herpetology lab."

Straightening out his hat, Wright glances at the bloodstains. "You mean," he asks, "when…what's his name…kicked us out?" He has a pretty good memory for details, at least when his head's right, but the guy's name is already escaping him.

"No," Larson answers, "before that."

"Okay," Wright says, thinking again of the golden fist in the chapel. Abruptly, though, his mind races ahead. "Why aren't you interested in why we left so suddenly?" he asks.

"Grant," Larson answers, "cut off the interview because he found out from someone at ABC that your story idea had been rejected, that your interview wasn't authorized."

Wright looks at Raisani, who says, "I told you he's good with computers. Phone-intercepts, too."

"Wait a second," Wright says, his anger returning. He looks from

Larson to Raisani. "You knew those burnouts were coming after me. Reverend Joe sent them."

Raisani avoids his eyes.

"You knew, goddamn it, didn't you!"

She shifts in her chair and gazes at him. "We knew," she admits. "I planned to pick you up before they attacked…tried to time it so we seemed to bump into each other *before* you left the hotel grounds. I told you I got stuck in traffic, Andy."

"Shit!" Wright shouts. He stands quickly, the cavern spinning and turning gray. Larson catches him as he begins to fall and guides him back into the chair.

"Get your goddamned hands off me," Wright mutters. Icy sweat snakes down his back. As Larson steps away from him, he asks, "Maggie—what happened to Maggie?" When neither of them answers, he yells, "I need a goddamned phone, *now!*"

"That's not an option at this point," Larson says.

"Fuck you!" Wright shouts, standing again, but more slowly this time. "I need to talk to Maggie."

Raisani stands too.

Glancing at her, Larson says to Wright, "One of Wengelt's contacts, a neo-nazi named Gary Babington Smith, kidnapped her shortly after you were beaten. We know where she is, and we'll deal with her situation once we…"

Wright swings at Larson, but Larson deflects his fist with his forearm, sweeps behind Wright, and pins his arms against his chest in some excruciating goddamned wrestling hold. Wright can't breathe; pain shoots back and forth across his chest and shoulder.

As Raisani walks across the cavern toward the supply shelves, Larson whispers sharply into Wright's ear. "Andrew," he says, "we couldn't notify you or your producer without jeopardizing what we're doing, giving the whole thing away. Fereshteh tried to get there, but we realized we might have to allow it to happen."

Wright gasps, the pain wracking his chest.

"We'll do whatever's required to stop Wengelt, Grant, and Smith,"

Larson says, loosening his grip and turning Wright so they face each other at an angle. "We're risking everything here, Andrew. Every-thing." His pale eyes fire. "We want your help. If you refuse, we'll…" His eyes bore into Wright, and his voice becomes lower so that not even Raisani fifteen feet away can hear him. "This isn't some TV show or media event, Andrew. I don't want to…" He locks his wrists and tightens his hold so that Wright can't catch his breath. His strength—or, rather, the concentration of his strength in his hands and arms —is daunting. "But I'll kill you, if have to."

32

ANDREW WRIGHT SLUMPS IN THE CAMP CHAIR, HIS HAND ON HIS FORE-head. Larson exacerbated his bruised ribs and shoulder, and he's feel-ing at the moment like unadulterated shit. Larson's working at the console, but Raisani stands next to Wright. Having just checked his vital signs, she says, "Andy, please help us. We really need to know what you saw at Reverend Wengelt's Institute."

Wright nods. He's breathing okay, and none of the pain is getting worse. He finds, to his surprise, that he still trusts Raisani—but Lar-son's another matter. The guy seems, in his own way, to be as much a fanatic as Wengelt. Leaving Maggie at the mercy of some burnout skinhead is frightening, goddamn it, but not as much as that fleet-ing burning in Larson's eyes. His dispassionate objectivity masks an underlying ferocity. Wright understands that Larson is weighing Maggie's well-being against, what?—possibly thousands of lives. But the guy still seems too ready to sacrifice her. It's all too logical, too goddamned mathematical.

Turning, Raisani says, "Nick, Andy's ready…if you want to find out what he saw."

Larson waves to her over his shoulder, taps one of the console's three keyboards half a dozen times, and hops to his feet. As he crosses the tarp, his face is placid, providing no indication whatever that he just threatened Wright's life. "Go ahead, Andrew," he says after he sits in the other camp chair. "What have you got?"

Wright lowers his head and, nodding toward the console, says, "You must have tapes you could send to the government." He waves painfully at the monitors displaying the compound's gate, the main building's front room, the TV studio, and the snake house. "Surveillance shots, audio clips of phone conversations..."

Larson shakes his head slowly. "Andrew," he says, his voice even, "we need you to focus on what happened at that compound. It's vital."

Raisani lays her hand gently on Larson's shoulder.

"Okay," Larson murmurs as though she has said something to him. "I've made tapes, Andrew, both audio and video. They'll be delivered to government and media sources should we fail tonight."

"Why haven't...?" Wright begins.

Larson raises his hand as if to silence him. "The tapes, Andrew," he says, "are not our first option."

Wright wipes his mouth with the back of his hand. There's got to be more to it. "But..."

"But nothing," Larson says, his words clipped. As he leans closer to Wright, his eyes flare for a second. "We have nothing concrete. Nothing."

"Andy," Raisani says, lifting her hand and stepping away from Larson toward Wright, "Reverend Wengelt is a zealot. He speaks to his associates, even to Grant, in religious metaphors...phrases like *the time of Tribulation, the day of the Lord,* and *the Lord's retribution.* We know what he's saying because we know about the Virin, but he'd sound to most people just like any overzealous preacher."

"We have no smoking gun," Larson says. "If there's a protracted legal battle without all the Virin having already been destroyed, there'd..." He sits back and brushes his hand through his short hair. "Hell, Andy, you figure it out."

Wright knows what would happen. The democratic process, especially in the judiciary branch, moves maddeningly slowly. The catastrophic use of *any* Virin is almost a foregone conclusion. The more he thinks about it, the more he's aware that legal action won't work. But he's still adverse to Larson's vigilantism. Though he's not big on rules himself, the rule of law has, historically, shaped—and perhaps saved—the country. And too many people who want to take the law into their own hands have personal agendas that are anything but beneficial to the country as a whole. It's true that Larson appears to have no agenda, except maybe the common good, but Wright's still suspicious that something emotional, even obsessive, lies beneath the orderliness. He takes a deep breath, pain pinballing around his chest. "Yeah, I get it," he says, "but if you've got all this surveillance going, what can I tell you?"

Raisani steps back, clasps her hands, and knits her fingers in front of her.

"Andrew," Larson says, "I've entered that compound half a dozen times…to set or replace mics and cameras. It's always been risky, and I've never made it into the more private areas, Wengelt's bedroom or his so-called sanctuary." He leans forward, keeping his gaze on Wright. "I know the general layout, but I don't know exactly what's there."

Wright finds himself almost smiling. It's nice in a perverse sort of way to actually know something Larson doesn't. "You've never been in Reverend Joe's chapel?" he asks.

Larson shakes his head. "I've only been in the main building twice, and the chapel has a special lock that would take time to pick. It's off limits even to Wengelt's disciples."

"In the chapel," Wright says, "there is something covered by a red cloth and a gold figurine—a fist."

Larson glances over his shoulder at Raisani who stares at Wright. There's light in her eyes, and she looks like she's almost smiling, too.

33

At dusk, Gary B. Smith cracks the bedroom door and peeks in at Maggie Mac. She's lying on the quilt, each hand and foot bound to a bedpost. She's not stretched, though, not splayed, and she's turned a little on her side away from him. That sweet ass of hers in those white shorts is angled right at him. The tear in the neck of that light blue sleeveless pullover shows her collarbone, the powder blue bra strap, and the curve of her tit. Her head is turned away, too, and her black pixie hair is tangled above the gag's tape across the back of her neck.

Maggie Mac does something special for Little Gar, who's already pressing hard against his jeans, that's for fuckin' sure. He's been with his share of women, hotter looking women than her, dealers and dancers with spectacular tits—but he's never been with a woman of her caliber. And he hasn't been with anybody but whores in the last two or three fuckin' years. It's like she's traveled all over the world, seen and done everything, eaten in fancy fuckin' restaurants like all the ones in the new casinos. It's the way she carries herself, that twitch of her ass that says with so much fuckin' confidence that she's just got *it*—that something special to drive a man wild.

He gapes at that tight little ass of hers on the quilt—that same quilt his mother gave him back in the '82 when he got married the first time. Susan, that fuckin' tramp, ran off to Tahoe with a pit boss from the Golden Nugget, but he's kept the quilt all these years anyway. His mother made it, a genuine American quilt with a wedding ring design. She was good at sewing anything, grew up outside of North Platte, didn't come to Nevada until she was pregnant with him. Never did say who his father was, except that he was some fuckin' hotshot cornhusker politico descended from the fuckin' pilgrims.

She got money in the mail once in awhile, but that was it. Never even one fuckin' word to him from the shithead!

He's still got all his mother's stuff in the house, too. Didn't throw out anything or change the place at all when she passed away, just moved the air conditioner from her room into his. And fixed up the war room. Sort of let the rest of the place run down a little, which didn't fuckin' matter, at least not until…

Maggie Mac shifts her body, turns her head, and stares straight at him peeking into the room. The fire's gone from those green eyes, but there's no fear there neither. She's just looking straight into him, like she's reading a book or something. He pushes the door farther open but keeps the Colt Automatic in his right hand out of sight behind the door. It's the standard Army issue .45, but it's the best combat pistol ever made, the only souvenir he took when he was discharged, and easily his favorite weapon. Sucking in his stomach, he steps into the room, the Colt at his side. He's showered, shaved, slicked down his hair, and put on a clean denim shirt, no hat. He doesn't expect her to fuckin' like him, but it's weird—he still wants to make a good impression.

Maggie Mac nods at him, and he shuffles across the rag rug closer to the bed—glad that he got all his dirty clothes out of there before the boys strapped her in. Her skin is pale and her eyes shiny in the overhead light. The shade on the window is pulled, and the air conditioning's running high so the fuckin' beaner neighbors won't notice nothing. And anyway, they've learned to leave him the hell alone.

She nods again, and he circles between the dresser and the side of the bed. Those eyes—green-eyed lady, lovely lady—aren't telling him nothing. Nothing at all. Even when he raises the Colt, there's not so much as a flicker of fear. But no anger or hatred neither. Keeping the Colt trained on her, he says, "If I take off the gag, don't make no loud noises." And he's thinking, Please don't fuckin' scream because a pistol whipping would mess up that pretty face—and that'd be a shame.

She nods a third time.

"Okay," he says, brandishing the Colt, "but don't make no mistakes, little lady." He leans down, the fingers of his left hand shaking for a second as they touch the perfect skin of her cheek above the tape. He yanks as gently as he can, peeling down the tape under her nose so that he can get at the white handkerchief in her mouth. He found the handkerchief, clean and folded, in his mother's bottom dresser drawer. There was sort of a cache of stuff there left by her boyfriends, including a silver lighter and a gold-plated money clip with the initial 'S'.

The handkerchief's wet in his hand as he pulls it out—wet with the saliva from those pouty lips—and he balls it in his palm.

"Thanks," she says, her voice muted by the tape that's still partly across her mouth. "I have to pee."

His ears and neck tingle. He's thought of a lot of things, but he didn't think of this. There's only the one bathroom with the one small window which even a little lady like her couldn't squeeze through—but there's no way in hell he's gonna fuckin' unstrap her. He remembers all too fuckin' well what she did to Bobby and Sam. Slipping the wet handkerchief into the back pocket of his jeans, he says, "I'll get something, a pan."

"Thanks," she says again.

Because her voice is muffled, he can't tell for sure, but it sounds like she's just talking to him normal—not like she's his prisoner. And that confuses him. As he heads toward the kitchen, he flicks on the Colt's safety, thinking maybe he won't be needing the gun. He's got a lot to do—checking on the guys in the hospital, reorganizing the Der Tag squads, making sure Reverend Dickhead hasn't changed the plan on him after that mix-up with the pretty-boy reporter—but the thought of Maggie Mac wiggling out of those shorts to whiz has Little Gar fuckin' bulging.

When he returns with a circular cake pan, the closest thing he could find to what might work, she hasn't made a sound. She just lies there, those green eyes wide, looking at him. "I'm gonna untie one arm," he says, his mouth getting dry, "then turn around. You'll have exactly one minute." He tries to sound business-like, tries to keep the excitement out of his voice. He could take her easy right now, and Little Gar's fuckin' ready, but it's that weirdness again—he wants her to want it, too.

He unties the knot on the bedpost but leaves the other end bound to her wrist so he can grab it fast if he has to. Raising the Colt, he turns his back to her. The Colt's sight points at the ceiling so it looks like he could spin and shoot quick. Over the dresser, there's a framed copy of some famous painting of a cowboy riding in a snowstorm that his mother got him at a garage sale a long time ago, and he tries to focus on the horse bowing into the wind. She seems to be taking too long, rustling around too much, but then he hears the trickling onto the tin—and he thinks Little Gar's gonna explode. He stops himself from looking right away, waits until the sound stops, and then counts to twenty-five. When he turns, she has the cake pan next to her and her zipper's stuck half way up.

"I'm thirsty," she says, looking him in the eye.

Her belly is flat, her navel small and perfect, her cream-colored panties silky with little puckers of material—and he stifles a groan as Little Gar loses it completely.

34

Andrew Wright hobbles over to the console just after Larson and Raisani have left the cavern. They carried night goggles and large backpacks—but no weapons other than her TASER. Before they left, Larson told Wright to stay put, and Raisani suggested he get some rest. Neither explained to him where they were going or what they were doing, but he suspects they're attempting to confiscate—steal back?—the goddamned Virin. How many canisters they'll even be able to locate is unclear. And, what, he wonders, is their real chance of success against Wengelt and Grant and their Divine Eagle Institute lackeys?

Wright shakes his head. Larson stressed that they still had things they needed him to do, which they'd explain when they returned. *If they return,* he thinks. He has no doubt about their resolve, but their black clothing and cumbersome gear reminded him all too clearly that they're a doctor and a...*what*—he still isn't sure what to make of Larson—two amateurs heading off on a deadly mission. And though they're absolutely focused, they are likely, he knows, totally out of their depth.

He lifts a leather-bound portfolio lying on the shelf to his left, opens it, and pages through the hundreds of intricate hand-drawn maps of tunnels and air shafts. A glyph, an animal and a series of symbols, marks the entrance of each—a private, idiosyncratic key created by a guy who's more than a little obsessive. When he finds the glyph that marks the shaft he slid down, he stares at it for a moment. The trail from that cavern to this one has been both sinuous and straight as an arrow. He has never, though, been a fan of paradoxes, and the sense that he's caught in some maze as intricate as these hand-drawn maps boils up through the pain in his chest.

He puts the folio back, sits in Larson's armchair, and scans the console. There's got to be a cell phone around, but he doesn't see one. Larson seems anal enough that he'd have a particular spot for the phone. And if he took one with him, which is likely, he'd still have a back-up somewhere. He's that sort of guy.

Movement on one of the video monitors catches Wright's eye. Lights are on in much of Reverend Joe's compound, including the herpetology lab and the studio. No one is in the main building's front room, but a man and two women are walking from the main building toward the studio. And, on yet another screen, a vehicle, a dark jeep, is pulling out of the garage. Wright watches the monitor of the compound's front entrance, waiting until the vehicle appears on the screen. When the jeep stops, Michael Grant steps out, salutes someone hidden in the trees, strides to the gatepost, and taps out a code on the key pad. As the gates open, Wright squints at the image of the jeep—it's not the same one Grant used when the crew was at the Institute to shoot the Reverend Joe b-roll. This one's a Wrangler, green with a dark brown canvas top and oversized, all-terrain tires. He can't tell if anyone else is in the Wrangler, and he wonders if Larson and Raisani are aware that security at the compound has been increased.

When the jeep leaves, Wright quickly surveys the other monitors. There's a bit of activity around the compound but nothing noteworthy. He stares for a moment at the upper right screen that shows the canisters he glimpsed after sliding into the cavern. They rest on that red altar, a twisted offering to some perverse misconception of God. He turns his gaze to the console again—the keyboards, modems, audio and video recorders, discs and tapes neatly labeled and stacked—but there's no phone. When he nudges the mouse by the nearest keyboard, the screen message asks for the password. Not surprised that Larson logged out before he left, he stares for a moment at the photographic triptych in the silver frames. The password must be some cryptic combination of names, but there's no way of knowing.

He stands, waits a moment for the pain to ebb, and limps over to the bookshelves. The books are mostly hardcover and, not surprisingly, neatly arranged by category—science and technology running the gamut from nuclear medicine to astrophysics; philosophy, much of it Eastern; and natural history, with an abundance of Abbey, Eiseley, Hoagland and other Western writers. Thoreau is there, and Merton and Campbell, but there's no fiction at all. Not one goddamned novel.

He turns around and shuffles past the supply shelves to the sleeping alcove. Goosebumps line his arms; either it's becoming too cool in the cavern for shorts and a t-shirt or his body's reacting to the effects of his injuries. A set of free weights and a lifting bench stand near the entrance to the green and beige nylon tent. He peers inside the tent at the covered double camper mattress and moon blanket, glances at the bare stone walls, takes a deep, painful breath, and tries to focus. Maggie first, he thinks, I've got to get to Maggie first. *But where's the goddamned phone?*

Returning to the living area, he notices Larson's canvas satchel resting on the supply shelf at waist level closest to the entrance. He yanks the bag from the shelf and opens it. The phone's there, of course, along with an emergency medical kit, a hardcover notebook, a ziplock bag of trail mix, a small carved stone fox, and a single motorcycle key. He takes the phone and key, reshelves the bag, turns toward the cavern's entrance, and stops. Turning back, he grabs the bag and the headlamp lying on the shelf above the bag. He punches 911 before the phone's screen informs him that he's out of the service area, and he figures that Larson must have rigged a separate, specialized antenna for his console's electronics.

And what's Wright going to tell the police anyway? Even if they believe him—and that's a big goddamned if—they'll go into their hostage negotiation mode. It'll take too long and probably, if the cops are dealing with burnouts like those that kicked the shit out of him, end badly for Maggie—a risk he won't take. He grabs the manila envelope that still lies on the tarp near the camp chairs, takes his bloodstained hat from the seat, and heads for the tunnel. As he crouches and pushes through the hanging plastic sheets, he knows what he needs to do.

35

THE HEADLAMP GIVES ANDREW WRIGHT PLENTY OF LIGHT IN THE NAR-
row tunnel, but rolling the black Suzuki up the incline quickens the
throbbing in his ankle and the excruciating pulsing across his chest.
He's no longer cold, and by the time he breaks into open air, he realizes that bringing along a water bottle would've been a good idea. He
stands on a ledge facing the wide, hilly expanse of desert he's seen to
the west each time he's driven on West Canyon Road. Turning off the
headlamp and stowing it in the bag he's slung over his shoulder, he
lets his eyes adjust to the darkness. A thin line of ambient blue light
shimmers on the western horizon, but the sky above him is a dark
field strewn with stars. Sandstone outcroppings on either side of him
conceal the ledge, and a sheer rock wall rises behind him. Though
he knows he's got to be within a mile or two of Reverend Joe's compound, from this ledge there's no sign of human habitation.

He checks the phone again, but there's still no service. Back-up
might be crucial, but if he can't reach the guys when he arrives in
Vegas, he'll simply go it alone. Time's the critical factor. Looking down
through the shadows, he can't find the covert trail Larson must take.
Even if he weren't injured, he couldn't carry the goddamned bike
down from the ledge. Hoping he won't attract attention if there's
some watcher out there, he mentally traces a path down the boulders, trying to reverse what little he remembers of Raisani's leading
him blindfolded to the cavern.

He shakes his head, takes the Suzuki by its handlebars, smiles, and
steps toward the first boulder. He makes it about half way down
before he rolls his bad ankle, loses his grip on the handlebars, and

tumbles hard on his right hip. The bike careens down along the boulders and wedges between two rocks near a path he couldn't see from the ledge. He's more goddamned angry than hurt, but there's a burning along his hip. He picks himself up—slowly, as Raisani suggested —and slides awkwardly on his ass to the bike. It takes all his strength to pull the bike out and get it righted on the path. He leans panting against a sandstone boulder and licks his lips. His running shorts are torn, and his hip, damp with blood, stings. He wonders if there's one goddamned spot on his body that doesn't hurt.

Deciding that his left forearm feels okay, he pushes himself away from the boulder, takes the handlebars again, and trudges along the trail. It seems more like a labyrinth than a path, and he loses his way a couple of times before he rounds a bend and sees the lights of Reverend Joe's compound in the distance. He chooses an angle away from the compound that should intersect the road. Sweating and breathing hard, he heads past stands of scrub pines. Intermittently, he moves through patches of cool air settling in the night, the scent of piñon strong. Thinking he's somehow made a wrong turn, he gazes at the crescent moon beginning to rise above the ridgeline, finds the Big Dipper, traces it to the North Star, and stumbles on.

When he finally hits the road, he climbs on the bike and guns the engine. The bike has been modified, the exhaust system muffled so that it's amazingly quiet for a motorcycle. Shifting gears hurts like hell, but he's thankful to be riding the bike rather than pushing the goddamned thing. Despite his growing sense of urgency, he rides at only twenty-five miles an hour, the headlight off so that if he needs to he can ditch the road before he's seen by Grant returning in the jeep or anyone else coming up the road. When he reaches Route 160, he finally switches on the headlight and picks up speed. The chin strap, pulled tight, keeps his hat on despite the rush of arid wind.

On the outskirts of Vegas, he stops at Terrible's Chevron station. The phone works this time, but neither Arnuz nor Miguel answers. When he calls directory assistance, he messes with the phone's keys until a human being finally comes on the line. He chats her up, eventually sweet-talking her into giving him Gary Babington Smith's address as well as the phone number.

The only other customer in Terrible's is a burly man in a satin *Collision Service* jacket and blue cap who's playing video poker. At first, the sallow-faced attendant with long, stringy blond hair looks at Wright as though he's auditioning for *Night of the Living Dead*. Then, the attendant cocks his head, seeming to recognize Wright but unable to believe that this battered twit with the canvas satchel and the bloodstained hat is the news dude he's seen on TV. And Wright realizes that, with his cuts and swollen bruises and bandaged face, he must look almost as bad as he feels. The attendant's skinny arms dangle from his short-sleeved white shirt with patches of the American flag and *Terrible's* above the dual front pockets. Speaking slowly as though to a foreigner or a dolt, he gives Wright very specific directions. As he's about to leave, Wright takes three packs of matches from the box on the counter. Back outside of the Chevron station, he tries Arnuz and Miguel again without any luck.

The neighborhood's more run down than he expected—not squalid exactly, but worn out. It's not that far from downtown Vegas, and in the distance the stunningly phallic Stratosphere juts above the roofs of the small ranch houses and bungalows—but nothing's glitzy here except for a couple of the jacked-up cars with garish customized detailing. Stunted trees and unruly bushes mark the meager front yards choked with weeds and clods of sandy dirt. Window air conditioners rumble, fans whirl in the open windows, and Latin music beats in the night. People slouch on front stoops and lean on car hoods. Only the young boys shooting hoops on a paved but unlighted playground seem to have enough energy to laugh and shout. Maybe, Wright thinks, everything associated with Vegas falls apart faster, decays more quickly, a sort of cultural Progeria.

The ranch house he's looking for appears more neglected than most. In fact, it's pretty goddamned dilapidated—its wood frame sagging slightly, its off-white paint peeling from the clapboard siding, and its small cement front porch ruptured. Yellowed shades cover poorly lit front windows. A picket fence encloses the yard, but there's no lock on the front gate. The place is basically a dump—but close to perfect for his plan. He rides by slowly a couple of times, scanning the property but not seeing anyone, and then cruises the neighborhood for five minutes before he finds what he needs in a carport two blocks away.

36

GARY B. SMITH BENDS THE BLUE PLASTIC TRAY SO THAT THE ICE CUBES crack and pop. The water's running in the sink, and the plastic *Viva Las Vegas* tumbler with the dice in the bottom sits on the counter. It's been almost an hour since he retied Maggie Mac's wrist and beat feet out of the bedroom. He's been busy, calling a mandatory emergency meeting of his Protective Security Force—or what's left of it—for 23:30 hours. And he has tried repeatedly to reach Reverend Dickhead, but some stuck-up prick at the Institute keeps feeding him bullshit about Wengelt being in a meeting that can't be interrupted. He's going to give the Dickhead about another two hours and then he's heading out there for a fuckin' face-to-face chat. He's got to get the PSF organized first because Der Tag's tomorrow come hell or high fuckin' water. Dropping the cubes into the glass, he smiles. Der Tag's going to *deliver* hell and high water to all the fuckin' mudheads and aliens!

He holds the tumbler under the spigot until its almost full, turns off the tap, and wipes his hands on his jeans. The Colt's tucked into his belt at his hip. He's changed his jockeys just in case something happens when he brings Maggie Mac the water. He doesn't have to use the good glass or the ice, but he wants to. He remembers a special he saw on the tube a while back about how kidnapped people often bond with their captors. Like—what the fuck was that rich bitch's name?—Patti Hearst. Changed her name to Tanya. Sometimes they even fuckin' fall in love. And he can kind of feel something already happening between Maggie Mac and him. Little Gar is definitely getting excited again about the possibilities.

When he enters the bedroom, she's got her head turned away again. Her shorts are still part way unzipped, and the tear in her shirt looks almost like it was arranged to flash him some skin. His breath catches in his throat, and the glass is slippery in his left hand. He wipes his right hand again, pulls the Colt from his belt, and slides it onto the dresser.

As he goes around to the other side of the bed, she looks at the glass. Her eyes are only half open, like she's been sleeping. Leaning over, he tucks his forefinger under the tape and tugs it tenderly from her lips. He didn't stuff the handkerchief back in her mouth. Instead, he folded it, feeling the moisture, and put it by the phone in the war room.

"Thanks," she says. Her voice is muffled, almost a purr.

He cups the back of her head, his fingers in the pixie-do, but he can still tell that the water's gonna spill. Lifting one knee onto the bed and hunching farther over her, off balance—almost like he's ready to gently mount her—he tilts her head forward and lifts the glass to her lips. Her eyes lock on him, the brightness suddenly back, like some fire's starting. Those beautiful green eyes…But she's coiling, her whole body flowing with energy.

Her knee rips into his nuts.

He lurches backward, slams against the wall, and staggers, unable to breathe, his eyes bulging and fuckin' pain exploding through him. Water splatters every-fuckin'-where as the tumbler crashes against the wall and clatters to the floor. He sinks and rolls onto his back, the pain clawing at him all the way to his throat, choking him so bad that he can't even groan.

She's already standing over him, shorts zipped, the ropes still dangling from her wrists, the Colt big in her hand, the barrel pointing at his face, not fuckin' shaking at all. Her eyes gleam like she's gonna blow his face off with his own fuckin' Colt, and he can't even raise his arms. "You stupid goddamned prick," she hisses. "I ought to…"

He pulls his knees up but can't even roll over. Tears cloud his eyes. He gasps, trying to cough, but can't. Saying anything, getting even one fuckin' word out, is impossible. A long moan finally rolls from his throat.

"You goddamned son of a bitch," she says as she cocks her leg. She steps forward, getting her whole body into it, and kicks him so fuckin' hard between his legs that his left nut actually jams right up into his body. Air squeals from his lungs, and tears roll down his cheeks into his sideburns. The room reels like the fuckin' night sky —and she's gone. Gone with the fuckin' Colt.

37

ANDREW WRIGHT SPLASHES THE LAST OF THE GASOLINE OVER THE PLY-wood sheets piled against the side of the house and then pitches the can underhand to the base of the fence. He takes one of the match-books and the phone from the satchel. He strikes a match, lights the whole book, and sticks it between two split clapboard slats. The matchbook flares for a moment—an ephemeral blue flame—and then clear flames flash and surge along the siding toward the roof. A sound like wind gusting through an open window follows the fire. As he steps away from the flames already puckering the peeling paint, he taps 911 on the phone, waits until he hears the dispatcher's voice, and says, "There's a fire at 1631 Harold. The whole house! Spread-ing fast! Hurry!"

He hobbles around to the front, takes a deep breath, and lowers his good shoulder. As he shifts his weight to hurl himself through the window, the front door bursts open. He ducks instinctively, and Maggie pivots, swinging a handgun toward him. She's got cords hang-ing from both her wrists and a look in her eyes that could kill.

"Maggie," he shouts, "don't shoot, goddamn it!" He stands straight again, slowly raising his arms. "It's me!"

"Andy!" she exclaims, clambering from the cement stoop. "Andy, what the…"

When she throws her arms around him, he wants to hug her back, hold her tight—but it hurts too goddamned much. "Are you okay, Maggie?" he whispers.

Her head against his chest, she nods.

"Did they…?"

"No," she says, looking up into his eyes. "Nothing happened. Everything's okay."

"Thank God," he whispers, and he lets her hold him for a moment despite the pangs in his ribs and back.

She takes a deep breath, as if to purge whatever happened, gags on the smoke curling toward them, and coughs. Stepping back, she yells, "Shit, Andy! What...?"

"Where's Smith?"

"The guy?" She shakes her head, the glint back in her eyes. "He's preoccupied right now. Has some male-oriented health issues he's struggling with. But he'll be...Let's get the hell out of here!"

Smoke's billowing now, and sirens scream only a few blocks away.

"Yeah," he answers, shifting the satchel and taking her hand. "Good idea."

38

GARY B. SMITH KNEELS, HIS FACE BURIED IN THE QUILT AND HIS RIGHT hand clawing the fuckin' stitching. He still can't stand, still can't cough, still can't really breathe. But he smells something—fuckin' fumes or smoke. Maggie Mac's burning his mother's house down... No, it's much too quick for that. It must be something else. But something's definitely fuckin' burning. And smoke's sure as shit starting to roll into his room, curling through the doorway, spreading across the fuckin' ceiling.

He pulls at the quilt, trying to rise—but it just keeps slipping off the bed on top of him. A long moan escapes from his throat, and he's finally able to cough. He crawls around the bed under the smoke, the fuckin' anger building with each gasp. That little bitch tricked him, probably untied her other arm when he had his back turned waiting for her to piss. Then she laid there, patient as hell, until he brought the fuckin' water. Planned the whole thing, counting on him to do exactly what he did, the goddamned fuckin' bitch. And then she fuckin' stole his Colt, the only thing he ever really got out of the fuckin' army. Those eyes of hers, those lying fuckin' eyes.

He slumps in the doorway, still unable to catch his breath. Sweat mixing with the tears, he stares down at the grime stuck between the floorboards. It's like fuckin' toe jam. He'll get that little bitch and whatever fuckin' asshole started the fire, too, even if it's the last fuckin' thing he ever does. Now, though, he can't even get to his feet. There's sirens outside somewhere, coming closer. As he pushes himself up off his belly, his left nut finally dislodges, sending a new wave of pain through his stomach, chest, and lower back.

When he crawls toward the kitchen, a wall of fuckin' smoke stops him. Sirens are blaring everywhere as he finally makes it up to one knee. It's hell in the hallway. The fuckin' heat's unreal. *The war room,* he thinks, *the munitions stashed in the fuckin' file cabinet!* The cartridges and the powder and the nitro the boys liberated from construction sites! Everything's gonna fuckin' blow. Bracing his shoulder against the wall, he staggers to his feet and then stumbles blindly through the suffocating smoke toward the front door. He smashes his fuckin' knee against his mother's favorite end table, veers to his left, and plows through the front door onto the porch. His hair, shirt, and jeans smoking, he teeters into the yard and collapses onto the walkway just as the first firemen demolish his front fence.

39

As Andrew Wright climbs painfully off the back of the Suzuki, the sixth level of The Tahitian's eight-story parking garage trembles. A distant rumbling echoes among the concrete pillars.

"What was that?" Maggie McNamara asks. She rolls the motorcycle behind a pillar so that it'll be out of sight of anyone driving up the ramp. The garage's first four floors were full, but only a few vehicles were parked on the next floor—and none on this level.

"Don't know," Wright says. "An explosion, maybe." He takes the phone from the satchel and punches Miguel's number again. When there's no answer, he calls a second and then a third time. When Miguel finally answers, Wright shouts, "Hey, is Arnuz there with you?"

"Boss?"

"Yeah, Miguel."

"What the fuck phone're you on?"

Wright shakes his head and leans against the pillar. "We need you. The parking garage, level six. Now."

"Boss, Maggie's gone. We can't find her nowhere. And the New York suits've been layin' shit on us about whatever you've been doin'. Or not doin'. We finally just fuckin' stopped answerin' any number we didn't recognize."

Maggie huddles close to Wright as he says, "Miguel, level six. Maggie's here. With me. We'll talk when you get here. And answer your goddamned phone next time."

"Yeah...okay," Miguel says, but he doesn't sound too sure about it.

Wright stows the phone next to the Colt pistol in the satchel.

"You were really going to burn down that house with me in it?" Maggie asks, placing her hand on Wright's forearm.

"Yeah," he answers, "and burn out the burnouts." Now that the rush to find her is over, he feels like hell again. It's not just the injuries, but a weariness that's seeping deep into his bones. He's starting to shiver, too, which doesn't make any sense with the temperature still above eighty along the Strip. "The idea was to set the house on fire, call the LVFD, rescue you while Smith and his goddamned skinheads tried to deal with the fire, and then trot out into the arms of the firemen."

"It might've worked," she says, smiling ironically. "But didn't it seem *risky*, Andy?"

He knows she means half-witted or lame-brained—a prime example of Male Idiocy, probably of the cultural sort brought on by, among other things, TV cop shows. And now, after the fact, the plan doesn't sound all that bright, even to him. But he still feels as though *not* attempting to rescue her would have been the real risk. "I couldn't call the cops," he says. "Couldn't have some extended stand off...No time." The incessant buzz of the traffic along the Strip six stories below numbs his mind. He's becoming so tired he can barely stand. "The same skinheads that got you came after me, but..." His voice trails off as he remembers lying helplessly on the pavement, unable to do anything but squirm.

"But what, Andy?"

"But I don't think they were going to kidnap me." He shakes his head. "Raisani saved me." Fatigue washes over him, and he rubs his forehead below the bandage. "Maggie, we've got to...We've..." He's having trouble concentrating, has to sit down somewhere fast, needs to figure out what's next. Time, he reminds himself, is crucial. He glances at his Timex, but the hands are blurry. Sucking in his breath, he pulls the strap over his head and lets the satchel slip onto the concrete at their feet. "Maggie," he says, "I know what's going on... Sort of, anyway...I've been in Larson's...I've been to see Nick and Fereshteh...They're..."

"Shit, Andy," she says, grabbing his wrist. "His name's not Nick."

"Huh?" He slumps next to the satchel and leans back against the pillar. His ribs and shoulder hurt worse but otherwise sitting is a definite improvement.

"It's Gerard Nichols Larson. That's why no match came up my first time through the database." She shakes her head. "Nick's his nickname."

Nick's a goddamned nickname! Wright thinks.

"He's a doctor. An inventor. A techie wunderkind." She crouches, takes his hand again, and looks into his eyes, excited. "He's got patents on a series of surgical…on stents and miniature medical cameras and other state-of-the-art surgical stuff. UCLA Medical Center. Lived in Brentwood. Lots of money."

He gazes at the dried blood on his leg. His running shorts are stuck to his hip where he was bleeding after his fall on the rocks. His ankle looks bloated under his white sock. It makes sense—the console in the cavern, the other equipment, even the modifications to the Suzuki. "But what the hell's he doing out…?" he asks.

She lets go of his hand and leans back, examining his most recent injuries. "Two years ago he was arrested for attempted kidnapping."

"What?"

She smiles. "His own daughter. Previous marriage. He didn't actually kidnap her. He hired deprogrammers to…"

The image of the girl on the Big Wheels crosses Wright's mind. He can sustain thought as long as the topic's specific. It's the bigger questions about what to do that are stumping him. "The Divine Eagle Institute?"

"Exactly," she says. "She was—*is*—one of Reverend Joe's devotees."

Wright feels as though the floor beneath him is shifting. The location of the guy's cave, his motives, his attitude toward the government, the fire beneath the calm—It's all lurching toward a certain clarity. "And, he got caught?"

"Yep. The deprogrammers botched the kidnapping. The daughter—her name's Christine—apparently pressed charges only because Reverend Joe put her up to it." She stands, needing to move as she sometimes does when she gets on a roll. "The case never went to trial. Nick got himself a good lawyer, adept at both plea bargaining and at keeping the lurid details away from the media." Looking down at him, she takes a deep breath. "The lawyer cited mitigating circumstances. Bitter estrangement from the wife who bolted with the daughter to some religious commune in Arkansas when the kid was eleven. She gave the Arkansas preacher a major chunk of Nick's money after the divorce, but she still flew that particular coop after seeing Reverend Joe on the tube. Liked the show so much she dragged the kid out here. When the mom's sojourn at DEI ended badly three years ago, the kid, almost a woman herself but still understandably confused by her mom's machinations, stayed on. Apparently Wengelt took an, ah, *personal* interest in her. He himself convinced her to continue Living in the Lord."

Wright nods, wondering whether the birth of Nick's second daughter fueled guilt about the first. "The settlement?" he asks. "What were the plea bargain's terms?" he asks.

"Serious money changed hands. Both as restitution and to stave off a civil suit." She smiles ironically. "And Nick had to cease and desist. Absolutely no contact at all with the daughter or DEI. Mandatory prison sentence for any violation." She stoops next to him. "Nick vanished. Sold his practice and his tech company and disappeared." She sits down and crosses her legs so that her knee is touching his thigh. "Tell me what you found out from the guy."

He's not sure where to begin. "It's worse, Maggie…" A helicopter flies low over the garage, the beat of its rotors pounding inside Wright's head. "Where are Arnuz and Miguel? Shouldn't they be here?"

"They'll be along," she answers. "What's worse?"

He unzips the satchel and pulls out the envelope with the photographs. "It's worse than we thought."

40

THE PROPHET SITS NAKED AT THE FOOT OF HIS KING-SIZED BED WITH THE wild stallion bedspread. Christine, also naked, crouches behind him, her arms around his chest, her chin on his right shoulder, and her breasts and belly pressed against his back. They are both staring at the fifty-inch high-definition flat-screen plasma TV, where the news reporter, a well-endowed brunette with hair only a little longer than Christine's, stands in front of a fire engine.

"...Disaster would have been far greater," the reporter is saying, "except that firefighters apprehended the owner of the house as he fled the scene. Though he has not been officially identified, sources have informed WNTS that he is..."—she glances quickly at her notepad—"Gary Babington Smith, a longtime resident of Las Vegas."

The Prophet slams his hands against the side of the mattress. Bouncing against him, Christine clings more tightly. He clenches his fists and mutters, "That stupid..." He almost calls Smith a "fucking son of a bitch" in front of Christine but catches himself. "That imbecile. He only had to avoid attention for one more day! Twenty-four hours!"

"Smith allegedly admitted that there were explosives on the property," the reporter continues, raising the microphone closer to her mouth as shouting off-screen grows louder. "Smith's neighbors and most firefighters were evacuated before the blast that was felt along the Strip and as far away as McCarran International Airport."

The Prophet wipes his sweating hands on the bedspread. He's already completely eliminated Smith and his PSF louts from the plans for the Day of the Lord, but the moron, it appears, is in police custody. And the blithering idiot will probably blurt something inflammatory, if not outright incriminating.

"The speculation is that Smith, an avowed racist, was making bombs in his house." The reporter is becoming more animated as she talks, nodding at the camera to emphasize her point. "For more on this tragedy, here is my WNTS colleague, Daniel Mitchell, at the UMC Trauma Center."

The Prophet pulls away from Christine, stands, runs both hands through his hair, and turns around. That producer had to still be in that hovel when it blew. Little bits of her must have scattered all over the city, and there will be hell to pay when the cops discover that the fucking dolt had a woman, a network producer no less, incarcerated in the house! He raises his arms in exasperation. "How could that philistine screw up so miserably?"

Christine looks up expectantly, though the question is directed not at her but to the Lord.

The Prophet ignores the knock on the door because the limp-wristed reporter in the green polo shirt is gazing intently at the camera and saying, "More than a dozen victims of the explosion have been brought here." The reporter turns slightly and points up at the TRAUMA CENTER sign in blue block letters above him. A blue and white American Medical Response ambulance stands with its lights off just to his right. "There's no word yet from hospital spokespersons, but two of the victims, both LVFD veterans, are said to be in critical condition with third-degree burns." Almost smiling, the guy shows his capped teeth. "One firefighter who accompanied his fallen comrade here…"

There's a second knock on the door, and the Prophet shouts imperiously, "Who is it?"

"Michael," he hears, the tone not entirely respectful. "We need to talk."

The Prophet seizes the clicker but does not turn off the TV or mute the sound. "Come in," he barks.

No one has ever been allowed into his private quarters when he and Christine are sowing the Lord's seed, and a quizzical look crosses her face. She scrambles to conceal her nakedness under the sheets.

Michael struts into the room and briskly shuts the door. "You've been watching this?" he asks, pointing at the reporter. A vein in his neck is pulsing. He's wearing black combat boots, camouflage fatigues, and a sleeveless olive T-shirt that reveals every muscle.

"You called five minutes ago, Michael," the Prophet answers in a tight but cordial voice. He pulls in his stomach and expands his chest, making every effort to enhance his manhood. Questioning the Prophet's authority in front of his select acolyte is going too far, even for Michael. "I've been watching."

Christine's eyes move back and forth from one man to the other, but, despite the Prophet's nakedness, they linger each time on Michael's upper body.

Michael turns and stares at the TV.

"...Cannot be confirmed," the reporter says, "but two youths known to be associates of Smith's were admitted to this same hospital earlier this evening." He shifts so that the camera catches the TRAUMA CENTER sign again. "They were apparently victims of a gang beating or a struggle for power within Smith's loosely knit hate group."

"Bullshit!" Michael yells at the screen. The vein in his neck bulges. "It's the fucking caveman."

Christine starts, pulls the sheet a little higher, and gapes at Michael.

"Michael, do not..." the Prophet begins.

"Prophet," Michael interrupts, "when I got back from doing your... the Lord's work in town, the guardians I'd posted beyond our gates reported a black Land Rover parked less than a mile away along the westward track. I ordered the fucking vehicle disabled, and..."

"Michael!" the Prophet says sharply. His eyes lock on his archangel.

Michael meets the Prophet's gaze, his look coldly fierce. "At first light, I'll track the caveman and..." he says, his voice more dutiful but his eyes mutinous.

"The caveman?" Christine asks. "What...are you talking about?"

She never speaks when the Prophet and Michael are having words, and, though neither man answers, both look at her for a moment before facing off again.

"You will take whatever measures you deem necessary," the Prophet says, his voice even. "With my permission."

"Of course," Michael answers, but there's nothing at all, no respect or disrespect, in his voice.

41

Nick Larson and Fereshteh Raisani work well together, antici-
pating each other's actions almost as though they share a single mind.
He holds the special thermos he designed while she pours the Virin
from the last canister. Her hand absolutely steady, she waits to ensure
that every drop falls from the canister. Only one light bulb still burns
in the cavern, and their headlamps carve sharp arcs of light and cast
clear shadows in the dimness. As she wipes the canister's interior
with an absorbent cloth, he seals the hermetic lid of the thermos. She
double-bags the cloth, and he refills the canister with water. Closing the canister, he remembers something in Grant's computer files
about one drop of Virin, diluted in two hundred gallons of water,
proving lethal.

The rhythmic hiss of their biohazard suits' ventilators is barely audible over the hum of the generator. Their wearing of the bright blue
suits with clear faceplates, thick rubber boots, and rubber gloves over
latex surgical gloves might seem overly cautious, even extreme, to
others, but Larson's meticulous about protective equipment. In his
work, attention to detail has been every bit as important as imagination. He has personally checked everything; not knowing that something's shoddy is, at least in his mind, no excuse. And, he has learned
not to trust anyone else with any matter that's vital to him.

Larson and Raisani have waited until this moment to remove the
Virin because they worried that Grant would test it again and discover the water they're substituting. Without the other canisters
accounted for, they would not risk a premature intervention. They
entered the cavern through a narrow back shaft, squeezing the backpacks that hold their gear through a cleft not visible from the floor

of the cavern. Grant's elaborate electronic surveillance and intricate explosive trip-wires more than protect the cavern's front entrance, itself hidden from view. But Grant did not fully explore, much less secure, the mountain's labyrinthine defunct mine tunnels and abandoned air shafts.

Larson places the thermos with the others in his backpack. While Raisani makes sure that the canisters are arranged in the exact configuration that the digital photograph she took earlier shows, he brushes clean their tracks around the back of the altar. They double-check that they've had no detectable impact whatever on Wengelt's iniquitous shrine and retreat to the crevice near where Wright first viewed the canisters through the slit in the stone wall. As Raisani crawls through the cramped tunnel, pushing her backpack ahead of her, Larson pauses to look back one last time at what he's heard Wengelt refer to as the *Grotto*. He surveys the altar covered with the red cloth, the canisters with their yellow and white markings, and the spacesuit with its international biohazard symbol. There's nothing sacred here in any sense of the word as he understands it, nothing that benefits humans or the earth, nothing that preserves life, nothing that honors God in any way. Though he feels bound to the Creator and to the world, this place, within the mountain he loves, is profane.

He follows Raisani's route until he reunites with her in their staging area, yet another subterranean cavern, two hundred yards away. There's no airlock here, of course, but they still take precautions, bagging their suits and even stripping off the surgical scrubs and caps they wear underneath. Without needing to speak, they dress again in their black clothing and put on their night goggles. Their next task—to infiltrate the DEI compound and recover the Virin from Wengelt's private chapel—will, he knows, be even more difficult and more dangerous. Despite what his heart dictates, he'll complete this greater task first. If all the Virin's there, if and only if they can locate *all* of it, he'll make the rescue.

42

"But, Andy," Maggie McNamara says, "we've got to go to the police." She still sits next to Wright; their backs rest against the pillar, and their shoulders touch.

"Yeah," Wright says. "I know that." He's just finished telling her everything he knows about the situation, and he's shivering with exhaustion, as though he has been wandering awake for nights in some desolate desert. "We'll do it when Nick and Fereshteh get back…" *If,* he thinks again. "Then we'll know what…"

He and Maggie have also hashed over Larson's reasons—stated and unstated—for not contacting the government. The guy's daughter might well be killed in any confrontation. And he'd likely go to prison himself for violating the court order, something that would hurt both Raisani and his younger daughter. Maggie gets it all, even the idea that the evidence linking Wengelt to the Virin is too goddamned nebulous. But she's still not willing to leave everything to Larson and Raisani.

"What the hell can we do now?" she asks.

Turning toward her until the pain stabs his shoulder, he says, "I'm thinking we should talk to Kupferberg."

"Huh?" Her eyes shine with surprise. "Why Kupferberg?"

He straightens his neck so that the pain subsides some. "The bastards have got to be going after the big hotels. So he, or at least his hotel, must be one of the targets." He fingers the tear in his jogging shorts, not quite wanting to yank the material stuck to the dried blood. "And, anyway, he's well connected. If he believes us, we can at least get the hotels to be more…to increase security."

She pulls her knees toward her chest and wraps her arms across her shins. "You think tomorrow's the day?"

He nods. "That's what Larson thinks. And he's been watching Reverend Joe's compound pretty goddamned closely."

Taking a deep breath, she rests her chin on her knees. "The fight," she says. "The fight's the main target."

He turns to look at her again.

"If tomorrow's the day, the arena *must* be the main target." She looks into his eyes. "Think about it, Andy. It can't be coincidence. All the media coverage. The arena's going to be overrun with…"

The elevator door across the garage opens, a bright rectangle framing two backlit figures.

Wright flinches, turns, and reaches for the motorcycle's handlebars to pull himself up.

Craning her neck to see in the direction of the elevator, Maggie grabs his forearm and murmurs, "It's okay."

Arnuz Jones and Miguel Ramirez step from the elevator, glance around, and, noticing the motorcycle's fender jutting from behind the pillar, trot toward it. Arnuz, the taller of the two by six inches, lopes easily, and Miguel, at five-nine and stocky, runs with a much tighter gait, his thick arms held close to his body.

"Hey, Bro," Arnuz says as they approach. He stops abruptly, gaping at Wright, who's hobbling to his feet.

"Holy fuckin' shit, Boss!" Miguel says. "You look like you been dragged behind a pick-up!"

Wright shrugs. "Something like that."

Arnuz turns from Wright to Maggie, who has also risen. "You okay, Tank?" he asks her. "You had us worried, disappearing like that. Specially after…You don't look so good, either."

"I'm all right," she answers, "but we're going to need…"

"New York called, Boss," Miguel says. He unzips his blue jogging suit jacket. A gold crucifix hangs on a gold chain over the black T-shirt stretching across his barrel chest.

"That's what took us so long," Arnuz adds. "We got to do a shoot right away. Like, ten minutes ago."

"We gotta do it if we want to keep our jobs," Miguel says, surveying Wright from head to toe. "But we sure as hell can't put you on camera."

"Some damn house blew up," Arnuz says.

Wright glances at Maggie.

"CNN," Miguel says, "and some local boys are already there, but we…"

"A house exploded?" Wright asks. His mind races, and he begins to sink into a darkness somewhere beyond fatigue.

"Yeah, Boss," Miguel says. "A coupla firemen got blown up."

As Wright leans back against the pillar to stop the gray spinning that's widening around him, Maggie asks, "Where?"

Arnuz fishes a yellow post-it note from his jeans' pocket. "Sixteenth and Harold," he says.

"No. Shit, goddamn, no," Wright mutters more to himself than to the others. As the gray gyre widens around him, he presses against the pillar, the pain ricocheting between his chest and shoulder. "No," he repeats. "No."

43

ARNUZ JONES FLASHES HIS PRESS BADGE AT THE BURLY COP MANNING the barricade. As the cop shakes his head, his jowls wiggle. "No way," he says, his voice strangely high. "No vee-hicles beyond this point." Behind him, half a block beyond the intersection, firetrucks, patrol cars, and ambulances stand in a web of flashing lights. Smith's ranch house is gone without a trace—not so much as a chimney standing. The houses on either side are demolished—hoved in and charred. Walls and roofs across the street are collapsed, and windows are shattered all along the block. Three helicopters hover in the sky, their rotors thwacking the night. The fires are out, but the acrid smell of smoke remains.

Still dazed, Wright sits in the back seat of the van with Maggie. Both of them washed up, changed clothes, and fetched their press credentials while Arnuz and Miguel loaded the van with the equipment. Wright wears a blue sport shirt, khakis, and cordovan loafers, the only shoes that'll fit with his swollen ankle. He's got the hat on again, too. He wants to wear it, despite the bloodstains, and it's not like he's going to have his unshaven, battered mug on camera anyway. Larson's satchel, with the Colt inside, rests on the seat beside him.

The scene outside the windshield seems distant, as though on video from some remote feed. He's covered disasters before, of course, but never one he caused. On the way over, the radio's all-news station— he can't remember the goddamned call letters—reported that one fireman was dead and a second was fighting for his life in the University Medical Center burn unit. Another dozen victims had been taken to UMC or Sunrise. A couple of neighbors are still missing. It was not a bomb that obliterated the house, sources have verified, but apparently an explosives factory in the owner's backroom set off by a fire. Still unconfirmed is a report that an arsonist started the fire.

Wright's thoughts are jumbled, but he's perfectly clear on one thing: He has himself become a terrorist. Unwittingly, maybe—suffering an ultimate moment of idiocy—but a terrorist nonetheless. Vigilantism—isn't that what all terrorists consider the atrocities they commit? Guys outside the law—above the law—fighting for their just causes, their higher goals. He's responsible for the fireman's death —and any subsequent fatalities. That's inescapable. And he'll take responsibility. He loathes the current tendency, especially among the politicians and celebrities he's interviewed, to refuse responsibility for their actions, to blame others for their own problems. For the most part throughout his career, he's assumed responsibility for what he and his crew did, and, in the long run, it's paid off for him with his colleagues and the white shirts.

But there's no way he can go to the police immediately; he can't yet approach them with the truth. The military isn't an option either. He's personally responsible, and he himself has to do something to deal with what's happened, goddamn it. And, anyway, there's nothing he can tell anybody yet. If he mentions the beating he took at the hands and boots of the skinheads, the fire would look like simple revenge rather than an attempt at a rescue. There's certainly no goddamned evidence left to prove Maggie was a hostage in that house. Hell, there's no goddamned house. He'd have to implicate Raisani, too—and perhaps destroy Larson's efforts to stop Wengelt. Ironically, though the explosion has deepened his confusion, it's also rejuvenated him, at least physically. He no longer feels like pond scum; with his worries about what he's done and what he may still need to do, his own injuries, though still painful, have faded into insignificance. That even climbing into the van was excruciating doesn't matter much anymore.

Arnuz parks the van a block off Sixteenth Street. While he and Miguel take out the equipment, Wright limps with Maggie toward the disaster scene. They're silent at first, but after they pass the outer police cordon, he glimpses between the fire trucks the remnants left by the destruction—the blackened nub of a fence post at the corner of the lot, the ruptured chunks of the sidewalk that led to the front stoop, and the jagged slabs of concrete that were the house's foundation. Adjusting the satchel's strap so it doesn't dig into his shoulder, he says, "I can't do this, Maggie." He thought he'd work through the piece and then bolt for The Tahitian, but it's going to take too long— and his report doesn't really matter anyway.

Mistaking his statement for a failure of will, she answers, "You'll be all right, Andy, once we get going." She sucks in her breath for a moment and adds, "I don't exactly have fond memories of this place either."

As they approach the neighbor's wrecked ranch house, wisps of smoke curl from the charred two-by-fours laid bare by the blast. Four TV crews are shooting video, and another crew is setting up. Cameramen perch in the bays of the helicopters hovering above the rescue vehicles.

Despite his dry throat, Wright coughs phlegm that tastes of blood. "No," he says, "I can't cover this, can't stand here and talk about this when there's a goddamned worse disaster that's about…that I've got to prevent."

She stops by a squad car parked at an angle, its front left tire hard against the curb. Though there's nobody in the car, its engine is running and its lights whirl in a quick, rhythmic pattern. "What the…" she begins. What're…?" She gazes up at the helicopters. "You okay?"

"No," he admits, shaking his head. "I can't get that fireman out of my mind." He stares at the rubble and smoldering wood. "I've still got to…"

"To do something?" she finishes his thought. "What the hell can you…can we…do?"

"I've got to…" he repeats. He's got to make amends, but he has no goddamned idea how.

"Kupferberg?" she asks, taking up the thread of their earlier conversation.

"Yeah…yeah," He nods. "It's a start. Then back to Raisani and Larson. They said there's more they need me to do."

"What about our guys, Andy? What're you going to tell them?"

He shifts the satchel and pulls out the phone. "Don't know. This is more important…" He punches 714-543-2100, the number he saw on the side of a cab on their way over.

"They're…" she says, "…we've got to do the shoot."

He smiles ironically. "Maggie," he says, "the goddamn fork's already in me. My career's over. I can't think about *reporting*…" He glances around at the carnage. "…any of this." He pauses, looking into her eyes, an idea welling. "You do it."

"What…? No." Her eyes reflect the swarming lights. "I'm going with you. Like you said, it's more imp…"

"You do the shoot, Maggie," he repeats. No one is answering the goddamned phone. "You're every bit as good…better than I am."

Squeezing his arm, she shakes her head. "I'm going…"

"No," he interrupts, his voice barely audible over the helicopters' thundering, the cops barking orders, the TV crews spewing, and the firemen coiling hoses. "Do the piece. Arnuz and…"

"Andy!" Her voice is fierce, and she's not letting go of his arm. "I…"

"No," he says again, his voice even softer. "I'll…We can meet at the hotel in an hour. In the garage, by the bike."

She shakes her head, but he knows she'll agree. Her loyalty is to him—but also to Arnuz and Miguel, if not the network. A blasé voice finally answers the phone, and he shouts directions for a cab. Though Maggie still clamps his arm, she's already surveying the scene, looking for the best camera angles.

44

As a voluptuous young Polynesian woman ushers Wright past an angular fiftyish woman outside Benjamin Kupferberg's office, the older woman looks askance at Wright. Kupferberg sits at his rosewood desk squinting at the screen of a laptop computer lying near the communications console. He glances up when Wright enters the office, does a double-take, and types quickly for a moment. Then, he looks up again and says, "You sky-diving without a chute now, Andy? Skiing face first wasn't enough?"

Wright pulls off his hat as though he's a goddamned supplicant, which, in some way, he is. "Thanks for seeing me, Ben," he says.

Kupferberg stands up, pulls at the cuff of his charcoal Armani suit, and gestures toward the two dark leather armchairs by the bookcase. "I saw the piece," he says. "Excellent work."

"Thanks," Wright answers. "You're working late?"

Kupferberg smiles as he passes Wright. "Got to keep the customers satisfied, Andy." Taking the armchair angled to face Gauguin's *House of Songs,* he adds, "Got to service the debt, too. Keep the creditors sailing on tack while everybody else is scuttling."

Wright limps after him, sits in the other chair, pulls the strap around so that the satchel rests in his lap, and rolls up his hat. He doesn't mention that the *Wright Stuff* story was mostly Maggie's doing.

Kupferberg crosses his legs and gazes at Wright. "What the hell did you do this time, Andy?" he asks.

Wright kneads the hat as though it's dough. "That's what I want to talk with you about, Ben."

Kupferberg's eyes narrow. "Somebody roughed you up," he says, "I'll take care of it."

Shaking his head, Wright thinks, *Good, there's the fighter.* During the interview, he glimpsed the tough competitor lurking just below that suave public veneer—and he was hoping he'd reappear. "I got the shit kicked out of me," he says, "but it's more complex than that."

Kupferberg uncrosses his legs and leans forward. "So, shoot, Andy," he says. "We don't have all night."

Kupferberg has no idea how true his words ring. Nodding, Wright says, "I stumbled onto evidence of a..."—there's really no better word—"...*plot* to kill, to poison people in Las Vegas." He doesn't use the term Virin because neither Kupferberg nor anybody else would've heard of it. "I think..."

"Andy..." Kupferberg interrupts. He sits back and cocks his head.

Wright holds up his hand. He realizes that, in some sense, he's got to pitch what he's saying as though it's a *Wright Stuff* story concept. "Hear me out, Ben," he says. "This hotel of yours is, I think, one of the targets." Though Kupferberg's gaze remains skeptical, Wright plunges on. "The primary target's the arena, the fight crowd tomorrow night."

"Andy," Kupferberg says, not quite scoffing, "we get bizarre threats regularly around here. It's part of the territory." Smiling, he shrugs. "Or it's the drinking water." He brushes his hand through his auburn hair. "What's this evidence you think you've found?"

Avoiding Raisani's and Larson's and even Wengelt's names, Wright describes the canisters in the cavern, the private chapel with its covered contents, the beating, the surveillance of the compound, and his rescue of Maggie—but not the fire or explosion.

Kupferberg gazes for a time at the Gauguin, as though he's studying the people and the foliage around the house on stilts—and Wright suspects he knows whose compound it is.

"It's not that I think you're bullshitting me here, Andy," Kupferberg says finally. "Times are bad. And I'm the first to admit we've got more than our share of lunatics. But I can't..."

As Kupferberg speaks, Wright opens the satchel, pulls out the manila envelope, and hands it to him.

"What's this?" Kupferberg asks, raising the envelope.

"It's what thousands of those satisfied customers of yours are going to look like tomorrow night." He lets Kupferberg shuffle through the whole stack of photographs before adding, "That's why I'm here, Ben."

Kupferberg replaces the photographs but doesn't hand back the envelope. When he looks up, disgust and anger, but not fear, burn in his eyes. "Where'd you get these pictures?" he asks.

"A source," Wright answers, "a guy I met here."

"And you're sure they're real?"

"My source is betting his life." Wright yanks at his hat. "And me, too. I am, too."

"Can I meet this source?"

"I don't know." Wright shrugs. "Probably not." He doubts that Larson would meet with a casino owner. In any case, there's no time.

"And the stuff you're talking about..." Kupferberg taps the edge of the envelope on his knee. "...you're sure that's what did this?"

"Yes."

"Who else knows about this?" Kupferberg asks.

Wright points to the envelope. "My source's..." He hesitates for a moment, choosing his word. "...associate, a doctor here in town. And Maggie, my producer."

"What about your crew?"

Wright shakes his head.

Kupferberg raises the envelope. "Why haven't you gone to the police with these?"

"I needed your advice first." Wright realizes he's kowtowing, but he doesn't want to talk about either Larson's reasons or his own.

"Good," Kupferberg says. "If rumors of this make the street, we'll have wholesale panic." He takes a deep breath, exhales slowly, and gazes again at the Gauguin. He then stands abruptly, crosses to the desk, and presses a key on the communications console. "Marge," he says, "we have a code five here. Alert Gunter. Have him call me immediately." His tone, though conversational, leaves no doubt that what he's saying must be done *now.* "Have Alex contact all security personnel, on and off duty. I need everyone in on this. No exceptions."

He pauses for a moment, scratches his eyebrow and then glances at his gold Rolex. "And Marge, contact the Inner Circle. We need a video conference, *everyone* involved, ASAP. Let me know as soon as we've got a go."

"Right away, Mr. Kupferberg," a nasal voice replies.

Stepping away from the desk, Kupferberg pulls a phone, only a little larger than a cigarette lighter, from the inside pocket of his suit-coat. "The Inner Circle," he says to Wright, "is my friendly competition along the Strip. It's a loose, sometimes antagonistic group. But I should get some agreement—and action—on this. Like you say, they may be targets, too. And they all know a disaster at any hotel hurts everybody's business. Hell, after that explosion over on Harold, a couple of my whales are already beached." He lifts the envelope. "Can I hold on to these for awhile to show the Circle? Just in case any of them balk when I explain things."

Wright nods. "Yeah, sure," he says, his mind leaping back and forth between the dead fireman and what he should do next.

45

NICK LARSON INSERTS THE ELECTRONIC PICK INTO THE CHAPEL'S LOCK. Crouching on one knee, he breathes slowly and deeply, unhurried despite the risk of being caught this deep in Wengelt's territory. He has modified the pick so that it will work in this particular type of lock, and he has to wait only five seconds before he hears the click. Removing and stowing the pick in his black hip-pack, he stands and glances back along the empty hallway. Getting to this chapel was easier than he expected. The route among the buildings he had worked out for earlier visits was still serviceable despite the additional surveillance cameras set up in the compound. More significantly, something's happening that's got everyone except the sentries at the main gate glued to the compound's few television sets. He caught a glimpse of a disaster scene on a big-screen TV as he passed the cafeteria's windows, but he has no idea why whatever's going on is so compelling to the DEI populace.

He slides the door open, slips into the cool, dark room, and shuts the door. He pauses for a moment, his back against the wall, before pulling down his night goggles. Whatever's happening, it's fortuitously providing him with the cover he needs, but he still won't risk the room's light showing under the door. He left Fereshteh with their packs in a wooded area outside the compound's back fence near the tunnel he excavated a month before to allow himself easy access to—and escape from—the compound. Together he and Fereshteh had sealed the Grotto's Virin in a steel box he built to fit the five thermoses. The box is safe now, buried so deep in one of the mountain's treacherously labyrinthine shafts that not even somebody like Andy

Wright could blunder onto it. But his business here remains unfinished until he retrieves these canisters, disposes of them, and then completes the rescue.

He begins to scan the room through his goggles, stopping almost immediately at a cross shaped like a T. It seems an apparition, suspended as it is from that finely wrought gold-link chain. And it dominates this cell to which Wengelt retires alone to concoct his diabolic schemes. Ironically, the cross provides silent testament to the fact that Wengelt really does believe at least some of the tripe he espouses and that he really does imagine that he communes with his Lord. Wengelt's insane—the Creator has been throughout time, is now, and always will be silent on all human matters. But this cross suspended here in the darkness is no prop. The man who sits before it *must* derive some sort of meaning here, no matter how misguided.

He finally shifts his gaze from the cross to the wall beyond. But nothing's there—no gold amulet, no red cloth, and definitely no canisters. "Damn," he whispers to the darkness. Taking a step forward and placing his gloved hands on the back of the oak armchair, he surveys the rest of the room. The irony touches him again: it's bare, almost stark, a place well designed for meditation. Glancing down at the armchair's seat, he sees the golden fist resting on a neatly folded red cloth. Andy Wright wasn't mistaken about what he saw. The Virin, or some of it, was here, but it's been recently moved. He's still got to check Wengelt's and Grant's quarters and scout the rest of the compound as thoroughly as time and circumstances will allow, but he has a strong sense that the Virin's been transported from the compound—and this exacerbates the situation immensely. If it's not in Wengelt's warehouse in town, the problem becomes exponentially more complex.

46

GARY B. SMITH SHUFFLES ALONG THE SNOT-GREEN HALLWAY AWAY FROM the holding cell. He still can't walk right, and he feels like complete crap. His fuckin' nuts still hurt like hell. He got a good look while he took a leak, and he's swelling up like a bag of rotten cherries. That little pixie bitch is gonna pay. He wasn't gonna hurt her, and she fuckin' knew it. His hair and eyebrows are singed, and he smells like fuckin' smoke and sweat, too. Plus, three of the buttons ripped off his shirt, the only fuckin' shirt he still owns, and his belly's hanging out. He can't hold it in—the pain's too fuckin' bad whenever he takes a deep breath.

The fuckin' pigs stomped him pretty hard when he tore out of his yard yelling that the munitions were gonna blow. He tried to get away, but he couldn't do much with his nuts still in his throat, and they kept jamming his face in the dirt. One of them was boog-scum, but even the two white pigs joined in—the fuckin' traitors. And if he hadn't kept screaming at them about the TNT and the Nitro, they'd all of been fuckin' smithereens! He fuckin' saved their asses, that's what he did!

When they got him down here to the station, the bastards grilled him about the munitions. But it hasn't been all that bad. No KGB tactics, or nothing like that. He's becoming famous, and the sons of bitches know it. He's on the map now, and they can't rough him up like they did during the arrest. And sure, they read him his rights and offered him a public defender, but he told them he'd fuckin' speak for himself. Always has, always will. He kept insisting he was just storing some guns and ammo in the back room. There wasn't really any TNT—or Nitro, neither. But the bastards didn't believe one fuckin' word. Plus, they seemed to totally fuckin' forget that some asshole torched *his* place, that's why he's here to begin with. They threatened him with all this felony shit, but the evidence is all blown to hell, and they know it.

They wouldn't listen to word one about him being the victim in all this, which he sure as shit is. And they still fuckin' booked him for resisting arrest. Just so they could hold him in that fuckin' cell while they scrambled their stupid asses off looking for something bigger to nail him with. But they got absolutely nothing so far, not one fuckin' thing, and now he's finally being sprung. It's about fuckin' time, too —past midnight. Der Tag's beginning. A whiter, brighter day's dawning. And he's still gonna make the plan work. Snuff all those fuckin' mudheads! True, things haven't gone so good yet. Shit, the fact is that so far everything's gone all to hell. But that just makes Der Tag all that much more important. All those mudheads got to pay for what they've done to him. They're gonna fuckin' pay, all right. Big time.

The uniform guarding him on the way out, a tall guy with lots of acne scars, isn't so bad for a cop. Tipped him that some reporters were waiting for him out in the lobby and there was a side entrance he could use once he got back his personal items at the desk. But so fuckin' what if the media vultures are ready to pounce on him. Let 'em. He didn't do nothing. He's the fuckin' victim, after all, and they need to know that. Those dumbass reporters are gonna get one fuckin' earful. He needs a cigarette first, that's all, just one fuckin' Marlboro.

Some shithead burned down his mother's house, that's the main thing that's happened. Destroyed every fuckin' thing he owned except the Buick. And it's just dumb luck that when he got back yesterday afternoon—or whenever the hell it was, time's all fucked up—he couldn't find a space in front of the house with all those rusted-out shitheaps around. Had to park the Buick way the fuck up the street. Really pissed him off back then, but now the Buick's all he's got left. It's fuckin' weird. There's a word for everything turning out backasswards. It's on the tip of his tongue, but he can't fuckin' remember it.

When he and the uniform round the corner to the lobby, he sees the flock of vultures with their cameras and lights. They're gonna find out in just a minute if they can handle the truth. But sitting over away from the reporters are two young guys, big fuckers, in white shirts and silver eagle bolos. There's no expressions on their faces, but they're sure as shit both staring straight at him. And it's not just because his shirt's torn and his belly button's showing. He grabs the uniform's arm just before they reach the desk. "You told me two of my guys bailed me out," he whispers, his voice cracking. His head's suddenly pounding, and there's this burning in his chest.

"Yeah," the uniform says, looking confused.

"Those guys?" He nods toward Reverend Dickhead's two holy fuckin' hulks.

"Yeah," the uniform answers as he picks up a clipboard with some form for him to sign.

He wipes his mouth with the back of his hand. This is no good, no fuckin' good at all. He figured his Protective Security Force guys were springing him. Not the Dickhead's goons. And where the fuck are his PSF guys when he needs 'em? They gotta know what's going down. Even if they missed it on the tube, which, judging by the vultures circling the lobby, is fuckin' impossible, they still would of gotten the picture when they came to the emergency meeting and found a fuckin' hole in the ground where the war room should of been. He scribbles his name on the form, and, taking the brown envelope, says to the uniform, "Where's that side entrance you mentioned?"

"Follow me," the uniform says, thinking he's worried about the media vultures. "I'll show you." Seems like this pig hates those vultures even more than he does.

As he bends back the envelope's clasp, he glances over his shoulder at the holy hulks. One of 'em is already standing, looking like he's a tree or something. He's got to take another piss—there was no blood last time, but he needs to check again—and then get the fuck out of here fast. It's not like he doesn't want to talk to Reverend Dickhead. They need to have a fuckin' man-to-man real bad. But it's got to be on his terms. Nobody's gonna drag his ass out to that fuckin' Institute. And, he wants no part of these holy hulks. Grant, that fuckin' robot, probably sent 'em. And it's just possible, what with the house getting torched after that pretty boy reporter got away, that Reverend Dickhead and the Robot are beginning to view him as—what would those two arrogant fuckin' shits call it?—a *liability* that needs to be eliminated. Reverend Dickhead might even be seeing it as the Lord's fuckin' will.

47

BENJAMIN KUPFERBERG'S PERSONAL BODYGUARD, A POWERFULLY BUILT German with light hair and cold blue eyes, steps out of the elevator first. Though he immediately spots Maggie waiting by the Suzuki, he paces back and forth glowering into the shadows. With each step, he taps his forefinger on the middle button of his navy blue suitcoat as though he's making tabulations. Finally, he signals his boss and Andrew Wright to step into the garage.

As Kupferberg strides briskly toward Maggie, Wright limps after him, the satchel slung over his shoulder. Kupferberg's video conference with the Inner Circle begins in fifteen minutes. His security teams, under the direction of Gunter Beckmann, head of Loss Prevention, are already combing the hotel and setting up unobtrusive checkpoints at all of the entrances. Still, Wright knows, as Kupferberg must, that finding a single small canister among all the luggage, supplies, and other goods transported into The Tahitian is improbable. Trying to also police the crowded periphery of the lagoon out front is simply absurd.

Shaking Maggie's hand, Kupferberg says, "I'd hoped to see you again, Ms. McNamara. But in more pleasant circumstances."

She nods, flashes Wright a quick, quizzical glance, and looks over at the German bodyguard, who stands on the other side of Kupferberg facing the ramp, his thick hands clasped behind his back.

"I've filled in Mr. Kupferberg," Wright says, "and he's organizing the casino owners." The sudden dry heat, after the hotel's air conditioning, causes him to hack painfully.

Turning to Kupferberg, she asks, "What about the arena?"

"It's owned by SportsWest in LA," he says, smiling at her. "But I know the GM. And, yes, I'm bringing him into the loop right away, too." He pulls the flip phone from his coat and then, looking into her eyes, asks, "What else should we have thought of, Ms. McNamara?"

The German, whom Wright's beginning to think of as *Hans,* shifts his weight and takes a half-step toward the ramp.

"The police?" she asks.

"Andy and I discussed that," Kupferberg says.

"And?" she says.

"We're going to give the owners six hours to secure their facilities. In any case, a police or military intervention would be too heavy-handed at this point," Kupferberg says. "Excessive."

She glances again at Wright. "You mean you'd have to evacuate."

Kupferberg nods. "I know the owners. They won't call in the LVPD. Not without something tangible."

"Bad for business," she says, her voice taking on its Tank tone.

"Trust me on this, Ms. McNamara," Kupferberg says, "the casinos' security teams are highly trained. And well equipped for situations like this. For crises within the hotels, better than the LVPD."

"You're sure of that?" she asks, the edge in her voice even stronger.

Hans glares over his shoulder at her.

"Maggie," Wright says, "let's let Mr. Kupferberg go about his business." Feeling as though he's going to start hyperventilating, he takes off his hat and wipes the sweat suddenly beading on his forehead.

"Ms. McNamara," Kupferberg says, "your point's well taken. Thanks."

Maggie nods to Kupferberg and then looks again at Wright, her eyes saying, *This conversation isn't over.*

"We've got to get going, Mags," Wright says. As he trailed after Kupferberg, watching him direct his employees as though he were rallying troops, he became more and more anxious. He feels like he hasn't done anything himself, and he needs to find out what's happened to Larson and Raisani. At one point, he overheard a customer tell a blackjack dealer that a second fireman died. It may only be a rumor, but the thought that he still somehow has to make up for the harm he's caused is driving him into some nervous state, beyond pain and exhaustion, that he's never experienced before. There just isn't any ironic goddamned laid back *Wright Stuff* left in him.

Maggie's stares at him, no doubt noticing the sweat and the shortness of breath. "Okay, Andy," she says after a moment, "but I'm driving. You're too beat up to do anything but hold on."

"I offered Andy the use of one of the hotel's Hummers, but he refused." Kupferberg says.

She nods a second time, seeming to know that Wright has to return Larson's motorcycle despite the pain of riding on the back like he's some battered, cumbersome package that's got to be delivered.

48

Away from the city, the desert air feels cool. As Wright and McNamara head up West Canyon Road on Larson's Suzuki, they run at thirty miles an hour with the headlight off. Wright has his arms around Maggie just above her waist, and his head is turned to the side so that neither blowing sand nor bugs get in his eyes. The chin strap holds his hat on, and the satchel, pulled around behind him, presses against his ribcage. He has stopped sweating, but his breathing, whether because of his injuries or apprehension, still isn't right.

On his way into Vegas earlier, he marked the spot at which he hit the dirt road, and they turn off into the desert just beyond that point. When she stops next to a squat juniper, he climbs awkwardly off the seat and gazes at the sky. The crescent moon is already setting to the west, and the stars are glimmering—the same stars he saw earlier, but changed now like everything else. They've shifted around the North Star, the one still point. He uses it to choose a route leading away from the road. "This way," he whispers to her as she hops off the bike.

Taking off the sunglasses she was using as goggles, she asks, "Are you going to be able to find Larson again?" Her voice is low, too, barely carrying to him in the dark stillness. Though there's enough light to discern the outlines of bushes and stunted trees, she seems to have concluded that they're about to get lost.

"I don't think so," he answers.

She takes the handlebars, begins to push the bike, stops, and says, "Andy, what the…"

"Larson and Raisani will find us," he says. And he's sure they will —if they haven't failed in their mission.

"Yeah," she says as she begins to push again, "if somebody else doesn't first."

After the first hundred yards, he takes the motorcycle from her.

"Thanks," she says. "Kupferberg's almost as friggin' pigheaded as you are, huh?"

"It's different," he says, his breath catching in his throat. "If he brings in the cops or the military, he loses control of The Tahitian. He can't accept losing. He'll bring them in if necessary, but only as a last resort. Same with the other owners. But for me, it's…" He doesn't finish. For him, it's a chance at redemption, but he doesn't quite know how to say that to her.

They walk on for a while in silence before she says, "The shoot went pretty well."

At first, he's not sure what she means, but then, realizing she's talking about the disaster scene, he asks, "No problems?"

"None," she answers, skirting a bush that lies in their path. "The feed…everything looked good."

"That's fine," he says. His life as a television correspondent seems remote, something he did long ago in some distant place—not yesterday in the city he just left. His life is, he knows, irrevocably altered. Assuming he lives through the next day, he still can't return to the life he led. He has already wandered too deeply into the desert to return unchanged. He sees, up the slope they're climbing, the dark shape of the Land Rover, a wide, squared-off mass among the smattering of spindly shadows. "Come on," he says to Maggie as he pushes the motorcycle up the incline.

Just as the shadow begins to materialize into an object with glass and chrome, Maggie grabs his arm. "Wait," she whispers, "something's…It doesn't look right."

When he stops and stares at her, she nods in the direction of the Land Rover.

Something is wrong. The shadow is skewed, listing to starboard, sunk into the desert. And then he understands. "Here," he says, giving her the motorcycle's handlebars. "I'll be back." He pulls the strap over his head and hands her the satchel.

He hobbles off, staying low among the creosote bushes, and circles around the Land Rover so that he comes at it from his right, the passenger side. If someone's watching—but doesn't have a night scope —he won't be seen. When he's within ten yards, he drops to his belly, crawls forward, and runs his hand over the slashed front tire. The back tire is also slashed. Not punctured, shredded—as though the slasher couldn't get enough of the tire. Even if one tire were changed, the remaining wheel's rim would, in this terrain, dig into the grit and bury itself up to the axle.

As he squirms backward, he can feel a dampness spreading along his hip where the abrasion is bleeding again. He turns, crawls another twenty yards, and then scuttles awkwardly, like some maimed crab, back toward Maggie. She has leaned the motorcycle against the trunk of a piñon, and the satchel lies by her feet. As he approaches, she spins around and aims the Colt at him. Both hands hold the gun steady, the barrel pointing directly at his face.

"Shit, Andy!" she hisses. "I was about to blow your head off."

He stares at the Colt until she flicks the safety on and lowers the barrel. She has looked comfortable with the gun twice now, and he wonders for a moment if she's been trained, something she has never mentioned. He knows, of course, that her father was a cop, that she was a scholarship student at Medill where she earned honors and the nickname Tank, and that she worked at ABC affiliates in the Midwest for three years before coming to New York—but he has no clue where she learned to handle a goddamned gun.

"I heard something," she whispers. Starshine lights her eyes.

He signals for her to crouch with him by the bike. Then, putting a hand on her shoulder, he whispers in her ear, "Both passenger-side tires are slashed. Somebody's…"

A hand sweeps between them, snatches the Colt, and shoves the pistol's butt against Wright's shoulder, toppling him into the bike. Another hand loops around Maggie's head and covers her mouth, preventing her from screaming. As she starts to kick with her heel, she's spun sideways. The hand holding the gun flashes across her torso, striking her in the pit of her stomach. Grunting, she doubles over.

His back against the motorcycle's wheel, Wright tries to rise. The Colt's barrel nudges the bandage behind his ear. "Andy," a voice whispers, "sit there and keep your mouth shut." It's Larson's goddamned voice, but there's only a quick shadow stooping now by Maggie, who's gasping for air. The shadow, propping her gently, says, "Sorry, Ms. McNamara. I couldn't have you pulling the trigger. Here, place your hands on your knees."

Wright can make out Larson now, dressed in black, with some bulky outer garment. His face is covered by a dark ski mask, but the pale eyes are unmistakable. "What the..." he begins.

"Andy!" Larson's voice, though a whisper, is sharp. The eyes turn from Wright, and the shadow takes Maggie by the shoulders. "Slow, deep breaths," he says.

Wright rolls to his knees and wobbles like a drunk toward his feet. Larson's free hand snaps out, its heel smashing into Wright's injured shoulder.

Sprawling on the ground, Wright mutters through the pain, "Nick, you goddamned son..."

"Andy!" Larson's tone is fierce. "Not *now.*" As he turns, Maggie swings her elbow at his face. Deflecting the blow with his wrist, he laughs quietly. "You two do make a good team," he says. "But you both need to stop." His hand shoots forward and grabs Maggie's wrist. Their eyes lock, the bright and the pale. "Just listen for a minute, Ms. McNamara," he whispers close to her face. "Please." When her shoulders sag, he turns to Wright. "Smith's house," he says, "was that your doing?" There's little recrimination in his voice, more just a frank need to establish facts.

Wright rises to one knee. "Yes," he answers. He wants to ask Nick about his daughter, how he deals with the knowledge that she's close by but lost to him, and how he's able to go about his business now knowing the danger. But he simply repeats, "Yes."

Larson turns to Maggie, who's still gasping for air. "Rescuing you," he says, "was part of the sequence. But other things necessarily took priority." Still looking into her eyes, he spins the Colt once and returns it to her handle first. "Andy apparently didn't see it that way. Disagreed with our priorities." He stoops, lifts the satchel by its strap, and brushes off the sandy dirt. "I understand. Believe me." He takes a deep breath. "But it was still wrongheaded."

"Nick," Wright says, hobbling to his feet again, "what about your…?"

"Stay low, Andy," Larson interrupts. "You make less of a target." As he rummages through the satchel, he adds, "Wengelt's security chief left the compound on foot forty-five minutes ago. Had a rifle with him." He pulls out the headlamp and tosses it to Wright. "Though I think I know what he's doing, I can't be sure."

Wright hunches under the piñon.

"We still haven't located all of the canisters," Larson adds, peering into the satchel. "I'm heading into Vegas to check…Where are the photos?"

"I gave them to Benjamin Kupferberg, The Tahitian's owner," Wright answers. He's finding himself needing to be as direct, even blunt, as Larson is. "Kupferberg's organizing the casino managers to search for canisters. They won't leak any information. It's not in their best interest."

Larson pauses as he slings the satchel over his shoulder. "All right," he says after a moment, "at this point, that might do more good than harm." He adjusts the satchel's strap and then touches Maggie's elbow. "You okay?" he asks.

Though her chest is still heaving, she nods.

"Keep the North Star at your right shoulder," he says to her. "Stay low, and stay away from the trail." Taking the handlebars and wheeling the motorcycle around, he says to Wright, "Fereshteh will rendezvous with you. And this time, Andy, do what she says." And then he's pushing the bike away from them, fading with it into the desert.

49

As Andrew Wright and Maggie McNamara make their way west-northwest among the boulders, he's sweating hard, his body still fluctuating between overheating and becoming chilled—and he's having difficulty keeping up. Maggie stops suddenly, waits for him, nudges his shoulder, and points at a sandstone outcropping no more than twenty-five feet ahead. Fereshteh Raisani sits there, legs crossed, silent, unmoving, a shadow framed by stars. Like Larson, she's dressed in black, but her cotton pullover isn't bulky—and she wears no mask.

"Fereshteh?" Wright calls softly.

Without answering, she slides from the outcropping, gazes at them a moment, turns, and begins to walk away into the darkness.

"What...?" Maggie begins.

"Follow her," Wright says. He understands that she's ticked off at him, probably deeply.

He doesn't recognize the entrance to the cave until they're climbing the boulder he fell down on the way out with the motorcycle. Raisani has led them on a roundabout trek over more difficult, rocky terrain—probably so that they won't be tracked. When they enter the alcove with the russet stone walls, Maggie glances around at all the equipment stored there. And, when they reach Larson's home, she gapes across the tarp at the communications console. She then turns slowly, taking in everything about the place.

"Andy," Raisani says as she removes a black scrunchie that's holding her hair back in a tight ponytail, "get Ms. McNamara some water." She shakes her head, then runs her fingers through her hair. "Get yourself some, too. You both look dehydrated." Her voice is flat, with no lilt at all.

As Maggie checks the console out, he pulls two squeeze bottles from the cooler.

"Have a seat," Raisani says, waving toward the camp chairs. She sits in Larson's chair, scans the video monitors, and opens a file on the computer screen.

He hands Maggie one of the squeeze bottles and then drinks from the other. His body is plunging into one of its frigid phases, but the cool water still tastes good.

Raisani turns in her chair. "Andy," she says, "consequences." She taps the chair's arms. "When you left, you didn't think of the consequences."

He pulls off his hat and exhales. He's starting to shiver again, and he doesn't want to get into this with her. He's sure she's got a point—but he feels bad enough about what happened without her rehashing it.

Maggie places the Colt on the seat of the other camp chair, crosses to the console, extends her hand, and says, "Doctor Raisani, I'm Maggie McNamara, Andy's producer."

Raisani shakes her hand but says only, "I know, Maggie."

"Andy was trying to save me," Maggie says.

"Yes, Maggie," Raisani answers. "I understand that." She stands up, her face close to Maggie's. "But at what cost?"

Maggie doesn't answer but doesn't step back either.

"Two firemen are dead," Raisani says, meeting Maggie's gaze. "Three people are missing. Another twenty people are injured, some severely. And, because we had no vehicle, we may have lost our best chance of locating the missing Virin. We spent too much time both trying to cover Andy's tracks and waiting for him to reappear with the bike." She scratches her scalp. "It may already be too late."

"Andy could not have known that Smith had a friggin' arsenal in his house." Maggie's tone is furious—she's going back into her Tank mode. "Or that your tires would be slashed."

"He could have…" Raisani begins.

"Stop it," Wright shouts. "Both of you." He flings his hat down on the tarp and limps toward them. Looking first at Maggie, he says, "Thanks." He touches her shoulder lightly. "But it's not necessary." Turning to Raisani, he adds, "I understand the consequences of what I did. I put personal loyalty ahead of good sense. And it didn't work out." He doesn't mention that Maggie was able to free herself without his help. "It's done. I can't undo it." He doesn't expect forgiveness, doesn't ask for it, maybe doesn't even want it.

"Andy," Raisani says. "I understand personal loyalty. I do. But I also understand duty. The greater good. As does Nick. And we…"

"His daughter's still in that compound," Maggie interrupts.

Raisani turns her dark eyes back to Maggie, as if she's being forced to recalculate some equation. "You've done your homework," she says. "He's driven by the need to save her. I thought that the birth of *our* daughter would salve…" She turns to Wright. "But Nick knows that we must locate all the Virin *first.*"

Maggie glances at the computer screen and the video monitors. "He set up all of this to spy on her?"

"No." Raisani shakes her head. "Yes…At first…He couldn't legally have any contact with her." Biting her lip, she sits back in the chair and gazes at the photograph of her daughter. "He felt he failed her twice. With the divorce…"

"And the botched reprogramming," Maggie says.

Grimacing, Raisani stares at her for a moment. "Recently, when Nick became aware that Reverend Wengelt was planning some… catastrophic event, he added…" she turns toward the console, "cameras and microphones."

"Grant's involvement with DEI?" Maggie asks. "Is that *because* of the reprogramming fiasco?"

Raisani flinches. "No. Yes. Perhaps, not directly…"

"But?" Maggie says.

Raisani takes a deep breath and turns toward her. "But Reverend Wengelt was attempting to improve security when he and Mr. Grant met…That's why Mr. Grant started working at DEI…"

"And the money, the funding for Reverend Joe's apocalyptic event?" Maggie presses. "Is it from Nick's legal settlement?"

"I don't know," Raisani answers, but she nods as she adds, "Nick thinks so. It's part of what drives…"

"So Nick feels responsible for the Virin? For whatever…"

"Maggie!" Wright shouts. His shivering is worsening. "Enough."

Maggie's eyes glint, but then she shrugs. "Right, Andy," she says. "Right."

"Fereshteh," Wright says, "Can we focus on what needs to be done…on what Maggie and I can do…?"

Turning back toward him, she says, "It depends on what Nick finds. And what happens when he returns."

Wright isn't sure what she means. Suddenly, sitting again, painful though it is, seems like a good idea.

"What did you want Andy to do?" Maggie asks, her tone less sharp.

"Originally?" Raisani smiles ironically. "If we disposed of all the Virin, Nick hoped Andy would take what evidence we've gathered, do a story, and then give the evidence to the authorities."

"Exactly how much Virin is there?" Maggie asks.

"That's one of the problems." Raisani sighs. "It's impossible…I don't have a definitive answer."

"What's your best guess?" Maggie asks.

Staring at Maggie, Raisani shakes her head before answering. "There were originally," she says, "seven canisters in the Grotto. But Mr. Wengelt moved two…" She glances at Wright. "Apparently, to his chapel. He seemed to need them close by." She stands, goes into the sleeping alcove, and returns with a hooded camouflage jacket. "Put this on, Andy," she says and then turns again to Maggie. "Those two canisters are no longer there."

Wright slides his arms into the jacket's sleeves, holds his breath, and grimaces as he rolls his shoulders and pulls the coat on.

"Nick also found a reference in Grant's files to…" Raisani pauses for a second, her smile again ironic. "…a private…a personal canister. We don't know for sure, but I suspect it's not one of the original seven. It's separate, an eighth canister."

Maggie tugs the hood out from where it's stuck inside the camouflage jacket. "Having Andy do a story's obviously not going to work now," she says.

"No, it's not," Raisani admits.

"And if you *failed*, what was the plan for Andy?" Maggie asks.

"He was to make some grand public gesture—on TV—to cause the boxing match to be postponed and the casinos evacuated." Raisani shakes her head, the lilt momentarily back in her voice. "We figured Andy would think of something suitably grandiose."

"And now?" Maggie asks.

Raisani's eyes darken, and the lilt disappears. "Now, we wait for Nick."

Wright's not sure, but it seems almost like he can hear her thinking, "And hope that he makes it."

50

Michael Grant flips the latches and turns the lock on the black leather carrying case. Though it and its twin resting on the crimson cloth look like salesmen's sample cases, each is lined with aluminum —and each contains, within a plastic foam mold, three canisters. To balance the load, he's added his *personal* container to the cache stored here in the Grotto. He adjusts the shoulder strap of his .30 caliber Remington hunting rifle, lifts the leather cases, and glances around. Another bulb has burned out, but the cloth remains bright, even in the scant light. He'll return here at least once more to dispose of his prey, but this site has already served him well. The Prophet's Day of the Lord is at hand. And with it, the coming of the New American Revolution, the Minuteman's time, and the salvation of the Constitution.

He squares his shoulders and turns. He'll leave the site's defenses intact as well—the trip-wires and the booby traps. As he marches toward the dark tunnel he senses that something's wrong. He halts and turns about. At first, he isn't sure. Nothing is out of place. But there is something, an odor—human, the scent of a woman? He raises his chin, sniffs, turns his head from side to side. A mere trace, the scent of a woman?

But that's impossible. It must be Christine's ripe fragrance. She exudes carnality. The Prophet's quarters reeked of her, and he's still wearing the boots, camouflage fatigues, and T-shirt he had on when he was there. He must be carrying her lustful odor with him. He cocks his head. Yes, definitely, the faint aroma of a female. They're necessary for procreation and, sometimes, for pleasure. But they're otherwise useless—weak and emotional and untrustworthy. That the military now routinely accepts them for combat, promotes them, and permits them to give orders is a travesty. And the scent of one of them has followed him even here to the Grotto. A strong smell for the weak sex.

He paces through the dark tunnel, knowing his way so well that he need not hesitate even in the darkness. When he emerges into the night, the odor dissipates with the cool desert air. The moon has set, and there is some truth in the saying that it is darkest before dawn. The going is treacherous, especially with the two leather cases, but he doesn't stumble. He may not be as nimble as that caveman, but he's absolutely sure-footed. He will not permit himself to fall.

This is the dawn he has awaited. He is able-bodied and clear-headed, the best of the best, the American Patriot. In order for the Great Republic to rise again, the liberal conspirators must fall. Especially now with that Alien-in-Chief and those pathetic compromisers, all weak as women, emasculating the nation. All of those conciliators, the very antithesis of true patriots, must be drummed out. And he is just the man to bring those wimps to their knees, show them for the impotent sissies they are, and demonstrate, absolutely and conclusively, that the Republic's security is riddled and unsound, all maggot-infested dry rot. At the end of the day, there will inevitably be fallout in the military as well as in the civilian sector. But there will remain enough good men, strong and God-fearing brothers-in-arms, that the military will survive, even thrive, once the chaff is blown from the wheat. And he will, as this day dawns, raise the wind that will blow away those who are not worthy.

A lesser man would be breathless and sweating by the time he reached the Institute's perimeter defenses, but he is neither. He sets down the cases and the rifle, crouches, and slips through the concealed slit he cut in the fence so that he could go to and from the Grotto undetected even by his own sentries. Pulling the rifle and cases through the cut, he is invigorated—not at all daunted by all he has to do. First he must load the jeep with the second and third waves of the Virin. Then he must eliminate the caveman and, if time permits, the Arab woman doctor—though the Prophet has not, technically, ordered her elimination. Then there's the transportation and deployment of the remaining Virin, a complex logistical task made far more complicated by that moron Smith and the mainstream media attention following the destruction of his house. Though the Prophet still wavers concerning what should be done about Smith, the solution is abundantly clear. He slings the rifle over his shoulder and takes the cases. He must seize the high ground before dawn so that he's in a strategic position to take out the caveman.

51

GARY B. SMITH WAKES WITH A START WHEN HIS FOREHEAD BANGS THE TOP of the Buick's steering wheel. At first, he doesn't know where he is, what time it is, or what the fuck he's doing in the Buick. Then, looking out the window over there at the lights of the Golden Nugget, he remembers every fuckin' detail—the pixie bitch kicking him in the balls *twice,* the fire spewing smoke, his mother's house disappearin' in the goddamned explosion, sittin' in the pigs' holding cell—everything. He had to take a fuckin' cab back to Harold to get the Buick. Didn't tip the mudhead hack a fuckin' nickel neither.

He drove downtown with the wad of cash and the piece—a Luger, the real German deal—he'd stashed under the spare tire in the Buick's trunk. He bought the Luger at Big Richard's Gun Shop a few months back when he had some extra cash after doing a job for Reverend Dickhead. It was a messy little job that the arrogant shit didn't want any of his own holy hulks doing. The Luger doesn't have the sentimental value of the Colt that pixie bitch stole, but it's almost mint—and it'll stop a mudhead cold. He's been keeping the piece and the cash in the Buick ever since the Der Tag planning got heavy—and it's paying off now. Being able to pack the piece and the cash this morning's made all the fuckin' planning worth it.

And it is fuckin' morning. The sky out toward the east above that fuckin' big assed garage is already blue-white. He must've slept at least a little bit because it was still totally dark when he bought his smokes. He was fuckin' exhausted after all the shit he'd been dragged through, but there was no time to really sleep—and no more fuckin' bed anyway. He rubs his forehead where it smacked the wheel. His whole fuckin' body hurts, especially his knee, which feels all fucked up. He must've smashed it during the fire, but he can't remember. He's sweating big time, too, and he's feeling skanky as hell. Fuckin' filthy. He's gone a long time without a shower before, but this is different. And it's not just the smell of smoke and the singed hair. It's a lot of bad feelings all mixed up together and oozing out his skin like some fuckin' poison.

He hears whistling and looks out at some dude strutting along the sidewalk with that fuckin' hiphop walk of theirs. The dude's carrying a quart bottle of Colt 45, looking like he's got panhandling or worse on his peabrain, but the bastard stops at the steel vending boxes to gape at copies of *Showgirls, Young Blondes, Little Darlings,* and *Slut.* The boxes look like they've been treated to a fuckin' boot party, but there's still plenty of literature in them—and the dude keeps whistling that same high-pitched note over and over. Nothing but mudheads and beaners out this early, acting like they got exactly nothing to fuckin' do. And nothing's all that those worthless scum ever do anyway.

This was supposed to be the best day of his life, and now everything's fucked up. He thought about getting the hell out of Dodge while the getting's still good. The pigs, the Dickhead's holy hulks, and a bunch of other sons of bitches are all trying to tear him a new asshole. And his PSF isn't worth snake shit. Those guys talk big, but some mudhead bitch TASERS one of 'em, and the rest act like fuckin' rats leaving a sinking ship. It sure looks like time to fuckin' pull up stakes, all right. But Las Vegas is *his* town. He was born here, fuckin' grew up here. He was here before the fuckin' mudhead invasion. He's a Vegas old-timer, and he's not goin' to blow town for nobody. Hell, he was here *before* the Strip. Plus, he's got scores to settle. And if the dude doesn't stop with the whistling pretty fuckin' soon, he's gonna start by grabbing the fuckin' Luger and blowing him to hell.

Remembering again that he bought himself a pack of smokes, he pats his pockets. The wad of cash is in his jeans, but there's no smokes. He reaches over along the seat next to him and pushes aside the Lucky's bag with the Luger in it, but the smokes aren't there neither. And then he remembers he was about to light up before. He must've fallen asleep when…He can't see the fuckin' floorboards over his belly hanging out of his ripped shirt, but he reaches down and around, straining, and his fingertips touch the corner of the hard-pack. He bends forward and, pressing his face against the steering wheel, finally wraps his fingers around the pack. "God fuckin' damn it!" he mutters aloud. But at least Whistlin' Willie's finally got his fill of white women and is hip-fuckin'-hopping off down the sidewalk.

His hands shake as he fires up the Marlboro, but that first puff's worth it. He holds the smoke in, stifling a cough, and then lets go slowly, the smoke curling out his nostrils. Rolling down the window, he can finally think clearly about which score to settle first. He'd like to go after that tight-assed pixie bitch, but he can't be heading into The Tahitian looking like this. He fondles the wad of cash in his pocket. Maybe he should get cleaned up some, but there's really no fuckin' time. No, he's gonna have that little talk with Reverend Dickhead first. But not out there at that Institute. No fuckin' way. Yeah, that's it. That's why he came downtown in the first place—to make the fuckin' call from the public phones at Binion's. He'd put his phone on the kitchen counter with his wallet because he didn't want nothin' else bulging in his pants when he brought the fuckin' water to that pixie bitch, and it got blowed up along with everything in the house. His whole fuckin' body starts shaking again at the memory of all that shit, and he needs to take an even deeper drag. Yeah. First he's gotta lure that pompous Dickhead away from Michael fuckin' Grant and his holy hulks.

52

CHRISTINE SLEEPS FITFULLY, HER BODY TURNED AWAY FROM REVEREND Joseph Wengelt, her blooming belly, holding the future, almost at the edge of the bed. Generally, he does not permit Christine to stay the night in his bed, but she was upset, wrestling some internal demon, asking questions, which she never has before, and running hot and cold during her ministrations—almost as though she was no longer willing to perform them. And her ministrations were an absolute necessity so that he could sleep even the three hours he caught before he woke in the darkness. He stares at the ceiling now, still straining, as he has the last two hours, to hear the Word of the Lord, to receive one final epiphany. But the Communion he lives for has not occurred. The Lord has been uncharacteristically silent. Not a single Word.

He *needs* a Sign. The Day of the Lord is commencing, the Day he has labored so assiduously and paid so dearly for. And yet he must act as though it is an ordinary day, go about his ministry as though nothing momentous is happening, tend to his flock as though the Lord's Judgment is not at hand. He's done everything humanly possible to prepare for this Day. Now, the implementation is in Michael's strong, capable hands. Michael suffers from the sin of Pride, a sin that becomes more egregious each day, but he otherwise serves the Lord admirably. He is so completely task-oriented, so utterly single-minded, that he will not allow himself to fail. And, if necessary, he shall willingly, if not gladly, sacrifice his life for the Prophet and for the Lord.

It was preordained that Gary Smith would become that particular sacrifice, but that's not feasible now. The media morons are already paying Smith too much attention. And, because of that bumpkin, all has not gone smoothly. Logistics have had to change with each new mishap of Smith's. Perhaps, the Prophet did err, as Michael in his arrogance has twice suggested, in allying himself with the heathen. Yet, on earlier, less significant projects, Smith performed more than adequately. But the philistine was incapable of serving the Lord in an undertaking of this magnitude. To err is human, it's true, and the Lord may yet forgive Smith. Michael, however, is less benevolent, suggesting in his bloodlust that the Prophet has gone soft because he will not condemn Smith even after the latest transgression, will not order him immediately banished to eternal hellfire.

As the Prophet slips from the bed, a spasm passes through Christine's body. A muffled cry escapes from her mouth. She does not awaken, but she seems to sense that something of import is about to occur. He sucks in his stomach, throws back his shoulders, and paces naked to the sliding glass doors to greet the dawn on this Day of the Lord. His joints crackle with each step, but he pays no attention. He has not gone soft, will never go soft. In accordance with the Lord's Will, he is ushering in the Apocalypse this very day, pouring out the seven vials of the seven last plagues, ordering the demise of those who have not the seal of the Lord upon them. He has masterminded the Lord's retribution, leaving the Lord alone to sort the faithful from the infidel. No, he has not gone soft. Michael simply does not understand the weight of the Lord's Will, the responsibility of being the Lord's sole living Vessel of the Truth.

He pulls aside the doors' curtains and looks out from his quarters' personal, private entrance across the patio at the Crux Commissa, The House of the Lord and the corner of the Women's Cloister. Beyond them rise the transmitters and the water tower. He has, with the Lord's direction, built the Divine Eagle Institute as a living testament to the Truth. The Lord resides in him, speaks through him alone. And no one, not Michael or the Council of Elders, understands the enormity of his burden. He gazes at the pale sky, watching a curve-billed thrasher swoop down and settle on the branch of the juniper at the edge of the patio. The thrasher's grayish wings shiver with light. Even at this hour, it is not too late to call off the Day of the Lord, to grant pardon to the tens of thousands that will be sacrificed. But he will not. He has not grown soft. Looking for a sign, he lifts his eyes again to the pale sky and to heaven beyond. This is the Day that the Lord's Will be done.

53

THE SUN, RISING ABOVE THE RIDGE LINE, FLOODS THE CANYON. LIGHT flows along the creek, washes over rock and gravel, bathes the creosote and juniper. Lost in thought, Nick Larson scrambles upward over the boulders. He left the Suzuki hidden in a stand of scrub pines, put Fereshteh's gift on again beneath his turtleneck, took up his satchel, and headed here to the creek for his morning prayer. This diurnal ritual, this moment in and out of time, has helped keep him in balance the past year and especially the last few weeks. Fereshteh's apprehensions have validity, but there's certainly no inevitability to her vision. It's not sensible for Wengelt to make that sort of decision; it would take time and energy from his essential task, and that defies logic.

The sky is bright, the air still and clean without even a murmur of wind, the rough luminous slopes an intimation of time beyond human understanding. The world neither affirms nor denies human folly. Whatever Wengelt may wreak upon the city and the nation today, the Mojave will have no comment. Humans can defile the world, of course, with poison as baleful even as Virin, but these rocks, this creek, this canyon will remain mute—the silence itself beyond comprehension.

The warehouse concealed no Virin. Circumventing the alarms and gaining access wasn't problematic, but his lack of discovery is. Three containers remain unaccounted for, and today is the day for which Smith and Wengelt have longed—Smith's Der Tag and Wengelt's Day of the Lord. Grant must have transferred the remaining canisters from the Divine Eagle Institute, but the likely interim storage depot, the warehouse, is empty except for thousands of copies of *The Will of the Lord,* Wengelt's apocalyptic diatribe. And none of the boxes is a dummy containing the Virin; each and every box weighs the same.

Perhaps, the meeting originally scheduled with Smith this afternoon has been canceled, Smith's role having been curtailed in the aftermath of Andy's wrongheaded rescue attempt. But this turn of events will reduce rather than enhance the chances of locating the Virin. At least some of the Virin was to have been distributed to Smith at the meeting. And now Grant is the only link, the only person to have left the Institute in more than twenty-four hours. To locate the Virin, Larson must think like Grant—logically, sequentially, maniacally—which he will once he clears his mind and acclaims the day.

He settles on the boulder, shifts his satchel to his side, straightens his back, and rests his wrists on his knees. He begins to breathe slowly, deeply, evenly. *Maya.* His younger daughter's name resonates within him. *Maya.* She, at least, is safe with her maternal grandmother. He has not seen her in two weeks, misses her terribly, may not see her for…A father can never really protect a child. One can only…He shuts his eyes, listens to the creek, and tries to pray:

Glory Be to the Creator…

Thoughts of his older daughter intrude: *Christine.* His sense of loss is different, not as acute, but no less deep, an ache that can't be assuaged. *Christine.* One can find the still point, open oneself to the world, and breathe the morning—but one can never truly, as the sages would suggest, become wholly detached. *Christine. Maya.* He may never again see either of them.

And to the Created…

He opens his eyes and watches the coruscating water dance down the creek bed, ringing in the new day as it always does. Whatever happens today, light will pour into this canyon tomorrow and each morning after—just as it did when the area was covered with sand dunes 180 million years ago or when it was a shallow sea 420 million years before that.

And to the Spirit that Binds us…

A desert cottontail approaches the creek, pausing beneath a creosote bush. The cottontail's ears twitch, and its fur pulses with each quick breath.

As it was in the beginning…

Its tongue flicking, the Mojave rattlesnake sticks its brown head from the crag.

Is now…

The cottontail skitters to the creek and lowers its head to drink. *Maya,* Larson thinks, *Christine.* He is never quite whole without them or Fereshteh. *Fereshteh.*

Its rattle silent, the snake slithers across the sandstone.

And ever shall be…

54

Michael Grant rubs his right forefinger against his right thumb. His left hand cradles the Remington's forestock, steadying the rifle. The Remington's well-balanced, a truly fine weapon, its California mesquite stock custom-made for him, engraved, and inlaid with an ivory American flag. The Zeiss scope is, quite simply, the finest available. And, he has maintained the rifle impeccably in the four years he's owned it, cleaning and oiling it and polishing the stock regularly.

He lies prone on a sandstone outcropping in the crook between two of the ridge line's boulders that both conceal him and shade the rifle's sight so that there's no telltale glint of sunlight. The black body bag he's going to use to dispose of the target is folded on the rock next to him. The Grotto already holds one corpse, and soon there will be another buried there. He could leave the target as carrion, but that would not only be messy but also draw attention. He's not worried about witnesses. Those at the Institute will be at Matins. The park rangers are never this deep in the canyon this early—which is probably why the caveman comes here—and any hikers would still be miles away down near the trailhead. He'll carry away the corpse solely because he can't stand loose ends.

He shuts his eyes for a second, takes a deep breath, and peers through the scope. He's finally got the target in his sights. The caveman was late this morning, of all mornings, so late that Grant may not have time to trace the trail back to the Arab woman. Eliminating her may have to wait until after the Prophet's work is done today. Anyway, she's a peripheral player at best, a nuisance he can rid himself of later.

At least the primary target now sits on his perch, oblivious to his fate. And, it's a fate the caveman deeply deserves. Whatever else he is, the life he leads—solitary and isolated with only an occasional visit from the Arab woman—defies belief in both God and country. And the Land Rover, now incapacitated, provides the evidence that the caveman knows something—probably too little and definitely too late—about Gary Smith's connection to DEI and the Day of the Lord.

Grant rolls his neck, relaxes his muscles, adjusts for the steep downhill shot of approximately three hundred and fifty meters, and resights his target. He's aiming for the heart. A head shot would be messy. Though he's loaded three .300 magnum bullets into the Remington's magazine, a single shot is all it will take, even with the tricky angle. He brushes his finger along the trigger, draws in his breath, exhales, and squeezes. The rifle recoils, and the target lurches backward and lies still even before the report stops echoing around the canyon. Grant ejects the casing, picks it up, rises to one knee, and runs his hand along the inlaid flag on the stock.

55

THOUGH PAIN SEARS HIS LEFT SHOULDER, NICK LARSON LIES STILL, PLAY-ing possum, until he reaches the count of thirty. This shooting is something that could've happened at any time in recent days, but the wound's electric burning's still not something he could have possibly prepared for. Fereshteh saw the shooting coming despite his protests that it was in no way inevitable, that there was no logical reason for Wengelt and Grant to kill him. She gave him the bullet-proof vest only yesterday, telling him in that firm, uncompromising way of hers to wear it whenever he was in the canyon.

He opens his eyes to the azure sky, bites through his lip because of the pain, turns his head, and looks at his shattered shoulder. The vest has worked—except that Grant isn't a good enough shot. The bullet grazed the edge of the vest and ripped through his shoulder. Though the bleeding's profuse, soaking the satchel's strap and pooling on the sandstone, no artery has been cut. He'll live if he can survive the next half hour, but he's got to get out of here fast before Grant arrives to apply the coup de grace. He's got to throw off Grant's timing, delay him from returning to the Institute, and keep him from his business. He's also got to somehow lead the maniac away from Fereshteh and the others.

He rolls onto his knees, coughs with pain, and crawls away from the creek into a crevice to the right of his boulder. He's safe for the moment, out of sight of the ridge line, but he's dizzy. The canyon is blurring, the sandstone going gray and darkness closing in. Figuring he has maybe five minutes before Grant makes it down from the escarpment, he slumps with his back against the boulder. He pulls the satchel's strap over his head with his right hand and then takes his Swiss Army knife from his pocket. Unable to use his left arm at all, he opens the knife with his teeth, bloodying the blade with his gnawed lip.

Sawing through the satchel's strap requires all the concentration he can muster. The pain is terrible, but he knows that if he feels it that deeply he's not yet going into shock. He has to staunch the blood, avoid shock, and lead Grant astray. Though it's probably a waste of time, he closes the knife when he's finished and puts it back in his pocket. Looping the slip-knot with one hand doesn't work, so he uses his teeth again to hold the strap fast. Once he's got the knot set, he pulls the strap up his left arm to the crown of his shoulder above the wound. The world spins, and he tastes bile and blood. He yanks the strap. His breath seizes in his throat, and gray darkness swarms over him.

Blinded by sunlight, he has no way of knowing how long he blacked out—but it can't have been long. The bleeding has slowed but not stopped. He takes a deep breath, pushes himself upward against the boulder, and scans the terrain for Grant. He's got to get going—first down and then up. Pulling the tourniquet tight, he teeters toward the creek, then heads downstream, twice crossing the creek but otherwise avoiding the wet, slippery rocks. His balance is off, and his breathing's short and quick; the canyon's askew, listing first to one side and then the other. He stumbles, lets go of the strap to reach out with his good arm to regain his balance, and then yanks the tourniquet tight again. Blood runs down his arm and drips intermittently on the ground.

After he's past the point at which the creek sinks underground, he pauses, trying unsuccessfully to make the canyon settle itself. Looking back over his shoulder, he still does not see Grant. He trots another ten yards, deliberately brushes his bloody shoulder against a boulder, turns so that his boots mark the sandy soil as he faces the boulder, and steps backward onto a flat rock at the bank of the dry creekbed. Leaping from one rock to the next, he backtracks upward parallel to the trail he's left. The canyon around him fades in and out, the sky darkens and lightens, the sun and the escarpment shift at strange, irregular angles. When he locates the right spot, he begins to climb the boulders. He's already blacking out again when, reaching the last ledge, he has to leap for the handhold and pull himself up with his right hand. Gasping, he expends his remaining strength.

56

Sweating hard, Michael Grant reaches the target area. He has climbed down from the ridge line with all deliberate speed, but there's no fast route. And now, having lost valuable time, he's got to quickly...But the target's gone. There's no fucking body to bag. Jerking the Remington around at an angle across his chest, he's ready, in a split-second, to wheel and fire.

This can't be. That shot was dead on. He saw the body blown back, lying there. A direct fucking hit. Crouching on the boulder, he discovers fresh blood. He removes his sunglasses, dabs his forefinger in the drying blood, and notices the crevice into which the target disappeared. A rattling startles him, and he leaps to his feet, turning fast. A diamondback's nearby but out of sight. It won't strike, he knows, unless provoked, but he inspects the crevice carefully before clambering down into it.

There's a good deal of blood on the ground. He crouches again. A lot of blood. The target is, he suspects, mortally wounded, already dying. Still, the canvas bag the caveman used lies against the rock wall, its strap cut off. A field dressing? He replays the shot in his mind. He's a first class marksman, having almost won a trophy in bootcamp so many years ago. He hit the chest, he's sure, if not the heart directly, and bandages would be useless. The caveman's got to be sucking blood into his lungs, drowning in his own fucking blood. Got to be.

Grant will not, however, take credit for the kill without confirmation. He stands, raises the Remington, and surveys the area. This time the rattling has no effect on him. Just the same, he steps out of the crevice into more open terrain. He's not worried about a counterattack—the target's too badly wounded—but he's naturally vigilant.

He follows the bootprints in the granulated soil back toward the creek and then down along it. Between the prints and the periodic splotches of blood, tracking the target's almost too easy. The caveman is in full flight, just like a wounded deer. But this better be quick. It's getting hot, he's thirsty, and he's got the Prophet's work pressing. A loose end, though, is a loose end, and it's got to be dealt with.

The creek narrows to a trickle and then disappears completely. By the time he sees the blood smeared on the boulder, he's growing frustrated. He should already be carting the body bag to the Grotto. The fucking caveman, even in his dying moments, is messing up the schedule. He glances down at the bootprints, takes off his glasses again, and looks at the face of the rocks. It's a difficult climb for a healthy man, much less a guy gurgling blood. Stepping back, he squints hard. There's no more bloody smears. None. He kneels on one knee, traces the edge of the right bootprint with his finger. The heel is deeper than the toe, which is all wrong. The caveman's trying to play games.

He paces twenty yards farther down the slope, inspecting the boulders and the creekbed. There are no additional marks anywhere. The son of a bitch has doubled back, could be anywhere up the canyon. He gazes at his black military watch. It almost oh-seven-hundred; he can continue to track the son of a bitch, and he'll find him all right, and finish him off if he's not already dead. But he doesn't have the time. He'll let the prey drown in his blood, come back when he can to bag the body. Most days, no one makes it this far up the canyon. And even if a ranger or a hiker does discover the body, there's no link to the Institute—and no connection whatever to him.

57

FERESHTEH RAISANI PATS WRIGHT'S FOREARM, WAKING HIM FROM A dream in which he's lost in a subterranean cavern, a dark maze from which there's no escape. Every turn he takes, he passes a cage containing a dead canary. Thousands of bones scattered along the sinuous shafts cause him to stumble every few steps. The air becomes more noxious with each passing second...

"Something's wrong," Raisani says, her eyes wide with alarm.

Disoriented, he shifts painfully in the camp chair. A shiver runs through him, and it takes him a moment to place himself in Larson's cave.

"It's after seven," she says, "and Nick's not back. He hasn't checked in."

He gazes over at Maggie curled up asleep on the camp bench, her hands tucked between her thighs. She's petite enough that she actually looks comfortable.

"What?" he asks Raisani.

"Nick should've been back by now." She clutches his elbow; her tone is somber, laced with foreboding.

"Where is...was he?" He rises slowly to his feet, putting as little weight as he can on his injured ankle.

"He went to Wengelt's warehouse near the Strip." She bites her lower lip. "He probably stopped in the canyon at dawn to...But he still should've been here by now."

Wright limps over to the camp bench and gently shakes Maggie's shoulder. She wakes with a start, swatting away his hand and sitting up abruptly. "Oh! Andy..." she murmurs. "I thought..."

"Nick's missing," he says to her. Then, turning to Raisani, he asks, "What can we do?"

"I've got to find him." Glancing at the video monitors, Raisani wrings her hands.

"What about the Virin?" Maggie asks. "Is finding him a priority? Part of the plan?" Her eyes are bleary, but Wright knows Tank's already starting to kick into gear.

Raisani's eyes fire. "No, Ms. McNamara," she says, "it's not part…"

"What about the consequences?" Maggie interrupts.

"The consequences…" Raisani hesitates. "Without Nick…We don't know if he has located the other canisters. I've got to…"

"Then, I'll go, too," Maggie says, glancing up at Wright.

"I don't…" Raisani begins, but then she pauses again. It's the first time he's seen her unsure of herself. "Yes, okay," she says. "We can cover more ground. But it might be…dangerous."

Wright stares at the lower right monitor where a dark green Jeep Wrangler with a brown canvas top is approaching the compound's front gate. Two heavily muscled young men in khakis and white T-shirts with black eagle insignias approach the jeep from the cover of the trees and speak to the driver for a moment. One of the men punches the keypad and, as the gates open, waves the jeep out. "Maggie," Wright says, "what's the license?" He can make out letters, but it looks like the goddamned next line on the eye chart—and her eyes have always been better.

"D-E-one-G," Maggie says, squinting at the screen. "No, DEI-G. Who is it?"

"It's Mr. Grant," Raisani says. "That's his personal vehicle."

"He may already be starting to distribute the Virin," Wright says.

Raisani gnaws again at her lip and shakes her head as if to rid her mind of some thought. "Let's get going," she says to Maggie. Then, turning so that she can look Wright in the eye, she adds, "With your ankle, you may be more of a liability than…"

"I'm coming, Fereshteh," he says.

As Raisani fills a knapsack with a first aid kit and other medical supplies, Wright pulls the remaining two squeeze bottles from the cooler. When Maggie returns from the portable toilet in the antechamber, she goes over to the second camp chair, picks up the Colt automatic, checks the safety, and tucks it into her belt.

58

In the cave's antechamber, Raisani pulls a folded index card from her pocket. Handing it to Wright, she says, "Here, Andy. These are the serial numbers for the five canisters Nick and I exchanged. At some point, you may need to differentiate these from others." She then turns to Maggie and says, "Let's go!"

Outside, the light's blinding, the sky free of clouds, and the sun radiant. The terrain rises steeply, and Wright has a hard time keeping up with the two women. At Raisani's insistence, they're spaced twenty yards apart. Carrying the knapsack with the medical supplies, she takes point; Maggie's in the middle, and Wright has the rear. Seeming to know exactly where she's headed, Raisani climbs swiftly. Maggie moves quickly, too, and he struggles along behind. Breathing hard and sweating freely, he keeps his eyes on each boulder and crevice ahead of him. Only when Raisani stops, waiting for them in the shade of an outcropping, does he begin to sense that he's in familiar territory. The sandstone and limestone strata run along the ridge at an angle he's seen before.

Raisani's not winded, but sweat lines her forehead. "Around the bend," she says, "there's a creek Nick...visits...each morning. Her voice cracks twice, and she seems fearful of what they'll find. "I'll go first. Follow me at thirty-second intervals...unless you hear something..."

Nodding, Maggie lifts the squeeze bottle hooked to her belt. She tilts her head back and drinks deeply. She then hands the bottle to Raisani, who takes three quick sips and passes it to Wright. Already drained by the hike, he gulps the water.

"Thirty seconds," Raisani repeats, glancing at each of them, a mixture of hope and apprehension in her eyes.

As Wright returns the bottle to Maggie, Raisani begins to climb toward the creek. Thirty seconds later, Maggie follows her. Alone for a few seconds, he takes off his hat, wipes his face, and gazes across the narrow canyon at a scrawny juniper growing—*tenaciously,* he thinks —from a cleft in the rock. Light washes the canyon, but here and there high up the walls he can make out traces of the vertical stains the storm's run-off made...the other day...or a century...a millennium ago. He knows he's been here, but it seems ages before...sometime in the distant past. A different life. And then he, too, starts to climb, heading around the goddamned bend.

Raisani is hunched on a boulder, either collapsed or inspecting something closely. Maggie stands by her, leaning over, too. As he approaches them, first Raisani, then Maggie disappear. When he reaches the top of the boulder, he sees the two women crouching in a crevice. Larson's satchel lies by their feet, but something's different about it. The creek running nearby gurgles as Wright climbs down into the crevice. Blood has smeared the rock, soaked the sandy soil. Staring at the bloodstains, Raisani weeps silently. Tears streak her face.

Wright gazes for a moment at the satchel and then says, "Nick's alive...Or he was when he left here."

Maggie gapes at him, and Raisani shakes her head. Her eyes glimmering, she murmurs, "No...Nick...no."

"The strap," he says, pointing to the satchel. "He cut off the strap. He was conscious..." He picks up the satchel, takes the phone from it, slips the phone into his pocket, and places the satchel neatly on the edge of the boulder.

"I knew that man would kill him," Raisani moans.

Wright looks at the markings in the soft ground. "Fereshteh," he says, "listen to me." When he puts his hand on her shoulder, she pulls away. "Other than ours, there are two set of prints, one partially covering the other."

She stares at the ground.

"Nick," he says, "left here on his own."

Raisani nods, but she doesn't stop crying.

"Doctor Raisani," Maggie says, "Andy's got a point."

Still nodding, Raisani follows the bootprints out of the crevice and over toward the creek. She paces fifteen feet and stops, staring again at the ground. When Wright reaches her, he sees what she has noticed—two clear sets of bootprints. She looks up, scans the escarpment, and turns slowly in a full circle. Her eyes are brimming, but she has stopped crying.

"The guy in the jeep?" Maggie, who has followed them, asks. "Are you sure it was Grant?"

Wright nods. "I couldn't tell, but...yeah, probably."

Maggie offers Wright the squeeze bottle.

"This way," Raisani says, pointing upstream away from the tracks.

He takes the bottle but doesn't drink. "Fereshteh," he says, "the bootprints..."

The thought that Larson could be alive seems to be reinvigorating Raisani. She stands straighter, brushes the sweat from her hairline, and says, "Nick would never leave a trail like this, except to throw a stalker off."

Wright gazes at the bootprints. They're obvious, even blatant, marking the soil where he could have, even wounded, moved undetected from rock formation to rock formation. "Yeah, he wanted to be followed," he says, handing the bottle back to Maggie even though he hasn't taken a sip.

Raisani looks at the tracks along the creek, turns, and gazes upward again. The terrain above them is rugged—stark rock, sharply angled overhangs, and immense boulders heaved there by deep time. "He's this way," she says. "Up here somewhere."

Wright trails the women up the creek. The heat rises with the sun. His hat and shirt are damp with sweat, and his saliva's gummy. He's so intent on keeping up with them that he almost doesn't notice the boulder. Stopping, he gazes up at the narrow outcropping. With his eyes, he retraces the path he took to the shadowy cleft. He climbs over the boulders and reaches the overhang where he crouched in a futile attempt to stay dry. There's no shoe-prints under the outcropping, but the rain would've washed them out. The view's the same, only it's sundrenched rather than storm-blasted.

"Andy!" Maggie calls. "What the…" She and Raisani are another forty yards upstream. She's turned toward him, one hand on her hip and the other shading her eyes. "What the hell are you doing?"

He doesn't answer her. He's right—he knows it. It makes perfect sense, especially in Larsonian logic—lead the predator away from the nest *and* find cover *and* conceal yourself where only one particular guy would be able to locate you. But the next part was difficult even before the skinheads kicked him around. He climbs the truck-sized boulder and scans the sheer limestone wall. There are a couple of scrapes, one recent—and, yes, three feet to his left and just above shoulder level, there's a dark stain, small but distinct. Farther up, there's a narrow smudge.

He sticks his shoe in the toehold and raises his arm, his breath catching as he stretches his ribcage. He squeezes his eyes closed and lunges upward. His fingers catch the handhold, but he doesn't have the strength to pull himself up. He simply can't do it—and he drops back to the boulder.

He turns and squints up at the sun.

"Andy!" Raisani's voice is even more insistent than Maggie's. She has made her way back along the creek, and she's looking up at him as though he's a madman.

Inserting his shoe again, he sucks in his breath, flings himself up, and clutches the handhold. His arm trembles with the strain of his weight, and it feels like a rib is piercing his lung. The toes of his shoes scrape against the limestone as though, if he moved his feet fast enough, he could run up the goddamned wall. Incandescent spots weave before his eyes like soap bubbles. If he misses, he's going to splat hard. As he's losing his grip, he swings his leg up, hooks his calf and ankle, and rolls.

Willing the pain in his chest away, he gulps air, rises on his elbow, and turns toward the cave. Nick Larson lies there, curled, unmoving, in the mouth of the cave. His left shoulder is mangled, a mess of torn cotton and clotted blood. The strap is knotted tightly above the wound; his hand below the turtleneck's sleeve is blue-gray. Larson's other hand holds a Swiss Army knife. Scratched below the petroglyph of the fierce animal are the letters DEI-G.

59

ANDREW WRIGHT PRESSES TWO FINGERS TO NICK LARSON'S NECK AND feels the faint pulse. Larson's ashen; his skin's clammy, and his breathing's so shallow that there seems to be no movement beneath the bulletproof vest. Something's got to be done immediately. Turning, Wright shouts, "Fereshteh!" The word echoes back to him. *"Rr-ash-ta!"*

Maggie and Raisani climb the boulders almost to the level of the outcropping and look up at him.

"He's alive!" he yells. "He's breathing!" As he stands, the canyon yaws around him, and he has to grab the rock above the petroglyph to keep from pitching forward. Crouching next to Larson again, he takes the Swiss Army knife, folds in the blade, and puts the knife in his own pocket. Larson seems to have gone into shock, and he remembers something about keeping a shock victim warm. But he can't imagine that Larson's cold. Though Larson lies out of the sun, heat's radiating from the rocks below—and the vest and turtleneck —must be keeping his core warm.

They have trouble getting Raisani up to the mouth of the cave. She's not tall enough to reach the handhold even when she leaps. And, Maggie can't boost her enough on her own. Finally, Wright takes off his belt, sticks the end through the buckle to form a loop, and wraps the free end around his hand. Raisani hurls up her knapsack and then jumps three times before she snares the loop. He pulls her up as Maggie pushes her dangling feet from below. And then Raisani is sprawled on top of him—but staring past him at Larson.

She crawls to her knees, cup's Larson's head with her hand, and inspects the wound. As she moves her fingers down his arm toward

his discolored hand, she begins to shake her head. She weeps silently again, tears running down her face. "Open the knapsack, Andy,"
she says over her shoulder. "Please." She seems like she's trying, in
vain, to retain her medical objectivity, to snap herself into some sort
of physician's autopilot.

As she rolls Larson gently onto his back, Wright glances down at
Maggie, who has set herself low behind a rock and pulled out the
Colt. Turning back, he asks Raisani, "What do you need?"

"A dressing for the wound," she says, stroking Larson's forehead,
"and the scissors."

Wright opens the knapsack and finds the surgical scissors and the
packages of sterile gauze bandages. His hand trembles as he nudges
her elbow.

Taking the scissors and bandages without looking at him, she
says, "Thanks. Lift his feet onto the knapsack." She begins cutting
the sweater at its neckline, angling down toward Larson's wounded
shoulder. "We've got to keep his feet elevated, keep the blood flowing to his brain." She loosens the tourniquet, cuts the sweater around
the shoulder, and pulls away the material, fully exposing the wound.
The shoulder's wounded just at the edge of the thick vest.

Wright bunches up the knapsack and props Larson's feet.

Using the scissors' blunt tip, she picks at the material stuck to the
wound. "He's lost a lot of blood," she says to herself, "a lot of blood."
She lays the scissors on Larson's chest, tears open two of the packages,
and covers the wound with the sterile dressing. "Nick," she murmurs,
patting Larson's cheek. "Nick."

Larson doesn't open his eyes.

"Nick!" she says more loudly. "Nick!"

When he still doesn't respond, she looks over her shoulder and says
to Wright, "He needs…We've got to get help…He's never…He's got
no chance otherwise."

The wound doesn't look life-threatening to Wright so he asks,
"The loss of blood?"

"Shock," she says. "Short-term, the shoulder's the least of his problems." She stares for a moment at the petroglyph and at the letters DEI-G that Larson scratched into the rock. Then, biting her lip, she gazes again at Larson's face.

As he looks at her kneeling beside Larson, her hand on the guy's cheek, he begins to comprehend the depth of her dilemma. "Fereshteh," he says softly, "I'll call. I'll make the call."

She's crying again. "He'd tell me not to," she whispers through her tears. "He'd tell me that the mission is much more important." She turns to face Wright. Sobbing, she begins to shake her head again. "But he'd call for help if he found me like this. He would never let Maya grow up without a mother. He knows…"

"We'll work that stuff out later," Wright says. He's not sure they will, or even if they can, once the authorities and the media guys find out there's been a near-fatal shooting and an air-evacuation in Red Rock Canyon. There'll be a shitstorm out here for sure. The god-damned TV helicopters may even get here before the rescue team. And once the information has been splashed on TV, there's no telling what Wengelt will do. Hell, the choppers coming into the canyon'll catch the goddamned Institute's attention.

"I can't let…" she murmurs. "I took an oath to…He'll die if…"

Wright leans toward her.

"The phone won't…" she says. "You've got to go farther down the canyon to get reception." Her eyes, with all of their depth, meet his. "Fast, Andy. Every second matters." She turns back to Larson, puts one hand on his chest, and strokes his forehead with the other. "Nick," she whispers. "Please, Nick…" And then she lapses into a foreign tongue, Farsi, maybe.

60

THE THUMPING OF THE ORANGE AND BLACK FLIGHT FOR LIFE RESCUE helicopter's rotors numbs Andrew Wright's already muddled mind. The sandy dust swirls like a cyclone. His hat pulled low over his eyes and the camouflage jacket tied around his waist, he stands on a boulder by the creek waiting his turn in the chopper that's perched about fifty yards downstream in the only spot flat enough for it to land. With its rear doors swung wide, it looks like some wild, primeval bird laying an egg—only the egg, in this case, is Larson's stretcher that the paramedics are loading aboard. Two TV choppers are already circling, their cameramen shooting footage from the open bays.

Though Wright's sweaty and aching and exhausted, he's for the most part no longer even aware of any of that. Instead, the full weight of his situation pummels him with the noise and the grit. He smiles: he's quite literally up the creek again. Raisani and Maggie left before the bullet-nosed rescue chopper arrived. By this time, hopefully, they're safely back in Larson's cave. Raisani had real difficulty parting from Larson, but she understood that she and Maggie had to disappear. There was no point in having all of them dragged in for questioning. A male voice had made the distress call, and explaining what a female doctor was doing this far up the canyon with a TV personality who just happened to stumble on a badly wounded but as yet unidentified man would have more than strained credulity.

Not that Wright's account is going to have a goddamned shred of plausibility anyway. After all, there's really nothing he can adequately explain. Why, hobbled as he is, he happened to be hiking in the canyon, how he found Larson in such a remote and inaccessible spot, why he happened to be carrying first aid supplies, why there are so many different shoeprints in the area, how and why Larson was shot, who shot him, why Larson was wearing a bullet-proof vest, and a dozen other equally obvious questions will be asked of him—and, though he knows the answers to all of them, he can't, of course, answer any of them frankly. And he can't, like Raisani and Maggie, simply vanish now that Larson's safely aboard the chopper.

Wright wipes grime from his sweating face, rolls his neck in a vain attempt to get the kinks out, and squints up at the TV choppers. The paramedics were not particularly hopeful, but Larson was still alive when they lowered him from the ledge. And that, at least, is something. Naturally, one of the paramedics, a rock-solid fiftyish guy with a bull neck and the sloping shoulders of an ex-athlete, recognized Wright, even with the hat and battered mug. He knows he's supposed to wait for the team of park rangers and cops hiking up the canyon trail to investigate the shooting—but the paramedics have offered to fly him to the hospital, too. They apparently think, even after providing him with two liters of water, that he still looks bedraggled enough to visit the emergency room as, in their words, *a precautionary measure*. Which is fine by him. He may not be able to disappear entirely, but the fact that he'll be gone when the investigative team arrives is a small blessing—there will be one fewer group to fabricate ludicrous answers for and act monumentally dumb with.

The paramedics pull the rear doors shut after them, and the co-pilot, a sturdy woman with a long brown ponytail, waves Wright over. Holding his hat on, he limps to the side door and, with her help, climbs aboard. The pounding rotors and rushing air make the inside of the chopper deafening. The paramedics have already begun an intravenous blood transfusion and a glucose and saline solution. As Wright straps himself into the padded steel seat behind the pilot, he thinks of the scene from *Catch-22* in which Yossarian tends to a dying comrade, diligently staunching a superficial wound while the guy bleeds to death beneath his flight suit. And, he can't help concluding that they're all treating the minor wound while the fatal wound hemorrhages undetected.

Wright shivers, cold again after being so warm in the sun. His mind, despite the chopper's din and his fatigue, begins to spin like a rotor. From his seat, he can see out the nose between the pilot and co-pilot. The chopper has barely risen before Las Vegas, a gleaming metallic beast, roars toward them across the desert. For a moment, he feels stuck in time between the canyon and the city, held fast between stark natural beauty and glittering human folly. But that's exactly the paradox. Nobody can really survive alone in the desert; anybody, even somebody like Larson, is always sucked back by the human factor into the teeming chaos of society. Raisani's deep love and Grant's cold hate reflect the species equally; each carries the seed of the other. Other people are inevitably, necessarily, our salvation and our doom.

When the chopper circles before landing at the helipad on the UMC Trauma Center roof, Wright glimpses the Stratosphere Tower, the Strip, McCarran International Airport, and the web of highways leading into the city. He'll stop the Virin's use, as Larson so clearly intended to, in some deep way, *needed* to. He doesn't yet know how, but he'll find a way to prevent Wengelt and Smith and Grant from implementing their goddamned plan.

But what the hell is that plan? What are these guys trying to prove with the goddamned Virin anyway? Wengelt, that his conception of spirituality, the divine spark, is the only one that's true? Or worse, that his aberrant take on religion should be imposed on all Americans? And Smith, that his racist bullshit can enable even a fat-assed goddamned pig to foist his personal failures off on everybody who is most unlike him. Or Grant, that his corrupt form of militarism can flout, even annihilate, the American military's most basic function, the protection of the nation's citizens.

As the helicopter lands and its rotors rev down, Wright can't slow his own spinning. Yes, he'll stop the Virin's use, whatever it takes. He'll take up Larson's...What is it—a burden, a cross, a quest? And he'll do so for the simple reason that *he* needs to. It's not exactly a sense of duty to society, or an obligation to other Americans, or even a personal commitment to Maggie or Fereshteh. It's all of those, but something deeper, too—something inside him, something he didn't know was there, something he's not sure he understands.

The pilots and paramedics rush Larson to the hospital's rooftop entrance, but Wright remains strapped in his seat. Looking out over the rooftops at the Stratosphere, he takes the phone from his pocket and taps the number.

61

Joseph Wengelt paces the floor of the Commons. His left hand holds the phone to his ear, and his right hand rakes his hair. Mr. Gary Babington Smith, that contemptible upstart imbecile, is again making demands on him—on this, the Day of the Lord. "No!" he roars into the phone. "Absolutely not. You will not come here today!"

He stops, stares at the grate in the stone fireplace, and presses the fingers of his free hand against his temple. Michael was right, damn it. This philistine deserves to suffer eternal damnation, everlasting hellfire. If only Michael was here, he, the Prophet, would order the vermin's extermination this instant. But Michael isn't here. Michael is absent without leave. He took the Wrangler and left during Matins without consulting with his Prophet. Maybe, just maybe, he timed his departure so he would not have to heed his Prophet's commands. Michael didn't disobey orders. He would never do that. No, he simply left without his Prophet's blessing, without a word of any kind.

He must retain his faith in Michael. Absolutely must. Yet, the Prophet has had, since he received no sign from the Lord earlier this morning, a gnawing in his gut, a sickening feeling that the Lord is displeased with his handling of events the last twenty-four hours. He must commune with the Lord—not listen to this blowhard barbarian. "What?" he shouts into the phone. "You can't be serious! Out of the...I will not..." The bastard—Smith *is* a bastard—is demanding twenty-five thousand dollars and one container of the poison. The moron has no idea in hell what he's asking for, but he's still insisting that if he doesn't get both the cash and the poison he'll tell all to the media. Today. At noon. At the warehouse. "You...!"

The Prophet's ire erupts, a burning in his throat and chest, an internal fire. Gasping for air, he slouches into the armchair and fixes his gaze on Remington's Bronco Buster. Panic mixes with the anger, and he rubs his sweaty hand down the leg of his pressed jeans. He needs Michael. Michael fixes things when they're not right. Smith, that damnable heathen, says he's got evidence of a conspiracy. What in holy hell could he have? His eyes dart around the Commons. Has the scoundrel stolen something of import? Something that could implicate the Divine Eagle Institute? Implicate the Prophet himself?

"Listen to me, you…" he yells into the phone. "How dare…You can't speak to me…You can't do this now, you…bastard!" He wipes his face repeatedly as he shouts. "This is the Day of the Lord's Wrath. The Apocalypse is at hand! The Lord wills that the unwashed masses —all those mudheads you so despise—must perish. And today is the day! Their dead bodies shall lie in the street. All along the Strip! I am the Will of the Lord! You work for me, Mr. Smith." He says the name as though it is unclean. "And I forbid you to speak to the media. They are the tool of the devil, and you damn well know it. How dare you even…"

Out of the corner of his eye, the Prophet sees Christine peaking through the doorway, that pretty, befuddled look on her face. When he was informed that this call was urgent, he came into the Commons to get away from his flock. They are all, even the Elders, twittering this morning, sensing something, but not, of course, understanding anything. They comprehend only what he explains, and he has not mentioned the Day of the Lord, except in grand generalities concerning an impending Sign of the End Times. He has said nothing to indicate that today is the Day and that this Day is his doing.

He waves Christine away, but she steps forward. He can clearly see in the light streaming through the front windows that she wears nothing beneath her white nightgown. She must *never* flit about the Institute like this. "Go to your quarters, young woman," he commands. "You should be ashamed."

She takes a small step back, her eyes filling. "Prophet," she says, "I was in my…but the Elders came…They've sent me…" She clutches her hands at her waist, her arms pressing her ample breasts together against the flimsy white cloth. Tears roll down her cheeks. "The Canyon…On TV…They told me to…"

"Not now, damn it!" the Prophet thunders.

Cringing before his rage, she flees from the Commons.

The Prophet waits until he can no longer hear her feet slapping the tile floor, and then he turns his full wrath upon the philistine. "Damn you to hell!" he shouts. "Never make demands on me, Mr. Smith. I am the Prophet!" A storm brews in his head as he stands and stalks over toward the wall with his wooden snakes. "I answer only to the Lord! To no one else! I am the Lord's Will! I will not meet you at the warehouse at noon, you impertinent bastard. I will never meet you. Not anywhere. Not any time."

The snakes are all lightning bolts, the wall a furious storm sweeping across the desert. "And I will not ever consider your diabolic demands. Not for money. And not for the Virin either." When he squeezes his eyes shut, the storm only intensifies, thunderstrokes flashing in his mind. "You'll rot in hell before I give into your demonic blackmail! Rot in hell, I say! Rot in hell!"

62

Grinning, Gary B. Smith uses the public phone's receiver to scratch his scalp above his ear. Reverend Dickhead's really ranting now. He loves to piss off pompous assholes like the Dickhead. Always has fuckin' loved it, even in grade school. High school, the army, the jobs he used to work—it's always been pure fuckin' fun. He takes a deep drag on the Marlboro, blows the smoke out through his nose, and snorts contemptuously. All the stuck-up dicks like the Rev lose it sooner or later. They all fuckin' crash and burn big time.

Letting the Dickhead shoot his wad, Smith glances at the phone numbers scraped into the dark wood above the phone. He's Downtown at Binion's, where his mother loved to play Keno. This isn't one of those overblown Strip casinos where aliens and fairies go to drop fifty large a night and be seen doing it. It's plenty fancy, though, with more real people and less fuckin' mudheads. In fact, from where he's leaning against the wall near the spiral staircase, he can see through the smoke these two little old ladies playing the penny slots—*Wheel of Fortune* and *Red White & Blue*. Both of them are dressed up like it's a Sunday church meeting. They're both much tinier than his mother, but she used to dress up on Sunday, too, 'specially if she was between boyfriends. One of these two, the more shrunken one with blue hair, has on white gloves and a Mickey Mouse cap, probably for luck. The other one's in one of those electric wheelchairs pulled right up to the bandit. She's got her Virginia Slims and a silver lighter stacked in front of her, and she's arm-wrestling the bandit for all she's fuckin' worth.

When the Dickhead finally shuts his fuckin' yap, Smith takes another deep drag and blows smoke at the mouthpiece. "You heard me right, Rev," he says, his voice almost fuckin' chatty. "And you know what, Rev? You'll do exactly what I'm fuckin' tellin' you."

The Dickhead's starting to bluster, not even forming words, almost fuckin' speechless. Just incoherent slobbering coming through the line. And the madder they get, the happier he gets because he knows he's got 'em by the balls. "We meet at noon at the warehouse. You with the twenty-five grand and the poison, and me with the evidence." His tone becomes downright friendly. "You gotta be completely alone, Rev. No Michael fuckin' Grant or any of those holy fuckin' hulks you got hangin' around." It's so easy sometimes with these pole-up-their-ass idiots. He started by demanding they meet at the Institute, the last fuckin' thing he really wanted. The Rev about shit over that. And though he's still playing hard-ass with all that *I am the Prophet* and *you'll rot in hell* bullshit he's spouting into the phone, the Dickhead's gonna make the meeting. He'll fuckin' be there, all right.

"Otherwise I go to the TV dudes with what I got." Smith lets out a little chuckle, just enough to really piss the Rev off. "I've already got meetin's set for this afternoon. These dudes already know me, and they got hard-ons waitin' to see what I got to show 'em. And you can bet your ass I ain't fuckin' bluffin', Rev." He isn't. Or, at least, not about this part of it. He's contacted FOX, and they're practically cumming at the idea. He purposely left ABC the fuck out of it so that when they get wind of it, they'll send that tight-assed little bitch Maggie Mac running after the story.

Smith reaches around behind him and scratches his back through the black and silver *Las Vegas USA* T-shirt he just bought. As he tries to reach the itchiest spot, he leers over between the rows of bandits at this one way hot dealer with her skimpy black outfit and white bunny ears bent just so. He may be fuckin' busy, but he's still a man. Now, if everything goes right, and he's starting to think it's gonna for fuckin' once, he'll get the cash and the stuff from the Dickhead *and* have Maggie Mac swing that sweet little ass of hers right into his trap. It won't fuckin' make up for his mother's house or all that other shit, but it'll be something. Der Tag's not gonna work out like he hoped neither for him or his PSF boys. But the day ain't over yet, not nearly fuckin' over. The fat lady sure as shit ain't singing yet.

63

ANDREW WRIGHT SITS ON A LOW, LIGHT BLUE COUCH SET BETWEEN MATCH-
ing armchairs in the hospital's waiting room. The goddamned air conditioning's blasting, and he's shivering despite the camouflage jacket.
The furniture, the yellow floral wallpaper, and the sunlight pouring
through the window give the room an unrelentingly cheery atmo-
sphere that belies Wright's mood as he talks with Sergeant Douglas
Carey, a Las Vegas Police Department Violent Crimes investigator.
Nick Larson's condition is critical; he's still in surgery, and no further
information is available. He's also still listed as a John Doe because
Wright's insisting he's never seen the guy before.

Carey, a tall, pale man who looks out of place in his blue cham-
bray shirt and narrow knit tie, has been diligently taking notes, but
Wright's pretty goddamned sure Carey isn't buying a word. Not that
what Wright's told him is *totally* implausible—that he was out in the
canyon because he was looking for the spot where he'd been injured
earlier in the week. That he was there so early because his biological
clock's still on Eastern time. That he approached the canyon from the
seldom-used western route because he didn't want to bother the park
rangers at the main entrance. That he heard something that could've
been a gunshot, but he doesn't remember exactly what time it was.
That he didn't see anybody else, but he did notice a dark green Jeep
Wrangler parked way off the dirt road—and its license plate had three
or four letters, the first of which may have been a D and the last possibly a G. He noted the vehicle because it was so similar to one driven
by the security chief at the Divine Eagle Institute. Wright's crew
had been there just yesterday working on a story. This final detail
about the Wrangler is, of course, a complete fabrication. Having the

cops look for the Wrangler—and he's sure that's the message Larson scratched into the limestone—is the way to go. But is the remaining Virin *in* the Wrangler? Was that Larson's conclusion? Or, was Larson, *finally,* willing to go to the authorities? There's no way to know. And no goddamned time to figure it out. The trick, which he's not pulling off well, is to seem to know nothing but still provide Carey with critical information. To get the cops onto Grant without spilling the whole goddamned can of beans—yet.

Wright wants to tell the whole story, to come clean, or at least to blurt Grant's name—even if it's only a goddamned alias. But he just can't do it. Once he does, he's finished. And the sense that he's *not* finished, at least not yet, has him by the throat. It's irrational, but it's also true on some goddamned level beyond logic. A deep shiver runs through his body, and his breath catches. Even the sunshine is a deluge flooding his thoughts. He has to buy himself time. Just a little goddamned time, that's all.

He could give the cops Larson's photo of Grant, but it's back in the cave. All he really has is the Wrangler's license. Grant's somewhere in Las Vegas, and having the cops pick him up, detain him for questioning in the shooting, might keep him from deploying the Virin —at least for a few hours. Or, if Grant sees the cops coming, which he probably would, it might trigger his use of the Virin. Or Wengelt's. Or Smith's. Or somebody's, goddamn it. There's no way out.

Benjamin Kupferberg sweeps through the door and strides across the waiting room. "Sergeant Carey," he says, shaking the officer's hand. "Everything's all right here, I hope." He's sporting a tan Armani suit, a tasteful gold and blue tie, and a wide smile. He's clean shaven and bright-eyed, with no hint that he's been up all night marshaling casino owners and their private security forces. Already knowing the cop's name is, Wright thinks, a quintessential Kupferberg touch.

When Carey stands, he towers over Kupferberg, but both his handshake and his nod suggest deference as well as recognition. "Mr. Kupferberg," he says, "I…What can I do for you?"

Kupferberg tugs at the monogrammed cuff of his starched white shirt and then waves toward the television suspended from the ceiling in the corner of the room. The TV is on with the sound muted, the image on the screen showing a high angle shot of half a dozen uniformed men and women milling along a narrow creek running steeply between red sandstone boulders. "Tell me," Kupferberg says, "that neither of you noticed Andy on the tube."

As Carey shakes his head, Wright struggles stiffly to his feet. When he was weaving his web of lies for Carey, he did notice on the screen over the officer's shoulder the shot of himself, standing like some hunched waif waiting for his ride in the chopper—but he didn't see the need to point it out. Nor for that matter, did he mention that he made two calls from the helicopter after it landed, the second of which was a plea to Kupferberg to find some way to get him the hell out of the hospital and away from the goddamned cops.

His voice lowering to an almost conspiratorial level, Kupferberg says, "Andy did a very nice piece on The Tahitian yesterday morning, despite the fact that he'd taken a tumble in Red Rock Canyon the day before." He touches Carey's elbow and shrugs. "And he looked on television like he'd been dropped from—not picked up by—that helicopter." Glancing at Wright's disheveled appearance, he smiles again. "With Andy being something of a hero for finding that wounded man, I thought I should check on him." His tone suggests that there's nothing in the world more important he has to do this morning. "See if there's anything I could do for him."

Wright can tell from Carey's bemused expression that the cop isn't buying Kupferberg's spiel any more than he did Wright's, but that he's going to let Kupferberg get away with whatever his wealth and power and charm allow him.

Kupferberg pulls a gold case from his suitcoat's inside breast pocket and slips out an embossed card. "Are you gentlemen about finished here?" he asks.

Carey gazes at the television for a moment, clears his throat, and says, "Yes, Mr. Kupferberg, Mr. Wright and I are pretty much done for the time being." He scratches his eyebrow. "But I'll definitely have more questions when the ETs are finished out in the canyon."

He nods at the television. "And when—and if—the victim regains consciousness."

"Of course," Kupferberg says, jotting a phone number on the back of the business card before handing it to Carey.

Turning to Wright, Carey asks, "You'll be staying on in town, at least for the next day or so?"

Almost smiling, Wright nods. Given the circumstances, the question seems absurd.

"He'll be at The Tahitian," Kupferberg says, "recuperating." He smiles yet again. "And avoiding the media that will, no doubt, attempt to knight him for what he's done." He points at the business card that Carey's turning over in his hand. "I can *always* be reached at that number. Call whenever you need to contact Andy."

64

Just north of the Thomas and Mack Center, Michael Grant brakes slowly. Not wanting to draw attention, he turns into the University of Nevada Las Vegas campus, winds past tennis courts, and pulls into the Lied Gymnasium lot. He takes a spot between a black Blazer and an old purple Tracker, shifts into neutral, yanks the parking brake, and checks the rearview mirror. He can't quite believe what he's hearing on the radio. *Newscaster Andy Wright saves unidentified shooting victim in Red Rock Canyon?* What the fucking fuck? Though he feels no panic, he's genuinely confused. True, he didn't confirm the kill. But that target was hit, bleeding badly, left for dead. Had to have died out there in the canyon. The caveman's alive, though, in surgery in a hospital only a few minutes from here.

Grant removes his reflective wrap-around Raybans, brushes his hand across his face, and switches to the all-news station. He listens patiently for five minutes, gathering all the pertinent intelligence. Andy Wright, that television doofus, has saved the caveman. They're some sort of tag-team conspiracy. He slams the heel of his hand against the steering wheel. Something's sure as hell not right here in Sin City, and these meddling assholes could still jeopardize the mission, which, despite Smith's snafus and the alterations they caused in the plan, has been going well—in fact, much better now that the Prophet has completely subtracted that idiot from the operational equation.

Once he left the canyon, Grant has been between ten and twenty minutes ahead of schedule—until now, anyway. Six of the canisters are already in position, and the seventh is safely cached so that he can deploy it this evening. He'll move efficiently and clandestinely from site to site unleashing the canisters' lethal contents, staying one step ahead of the SHIT all along the way. He thinks of his actions both this morning and this evening as working a trapline—and what's more American than that? Only his traps are modern wonders that'll snare tens of thousands in a snap.

He takes his phone from the dashboard charger. He should check in with the Prophet, but then he'd have to admit he blew the caveman assignment—an assignment he coerced the Prophet into giving him. He'll call his source at the LVPD first, see if there's any information the…But what the hell is this on the radio now? A report that Andy Wright identified a vehicle near the site of the shooting. A Wrangler? The doofus must've been having drug-induced flashbacks. There was no fucking vehicle anywhere near…And then it hits him. That son of a bitch is setting him up! That TV shit can't know about the trapline, of course, but must have obtained some fucking intelligence about *something*. He slams the steering wheel again, hard, with both hands, shattering the phone. Staring at his right hand, he glares at the demolished plastic and the blood oozing from his palm.

He retrieves the medical kit from under the passenger seat. The gash is long but not deep, and it shouldn't impede him at all. When he pours the hydrogen peroxide on the wound, his hand trembles in an involuntary spasm. Using the butterfly strips and gauze, he dresses the wound. As he tapes the hand, he considers his next moves. The Wrangler, obviously a liability now, must be left here among all the SUVs where it won't be noticed. If the SHIT have the license, it won't take long before the Wrangler is traced to the Institute. Though the Wrangler is his personal vehicle, a perk from the Prophet, it has never been registered in his name simply because the Prophet writes it off as a DEI expense, thereby screwing the IRS in one more small way. The question then is, will the Prophet cover for him? The answer should be, *Absolutely, yes.* And even a few days ago that would've been the only conceivable answer. But the Prophet has been going soft as the Day of the Lord approached. The Prophet won't cave immediately—he's too cocksure of his own Truth. But if things get hot, the Prophet might give up even his most trusted cohort, his archangel, to save that candy ass of his.

Grant makes a fist, opens his hand, and makes a fist again, admiring his work. There's almost complete movement and only negligible pain. A good job, but the phone's completely out of commission. That may, though, be a blessing in disguise because, the more he thinks about it, the more he realizes it's necessary to go to deep cover. He'll need another vehicle, and he'll be thrown approximately ninety minutes off schedule, but both of these facts are, like the wound, mere irritations that won't, at the end of the day, negatively impact the plan.

He cleans up the remnants of the phone, closes the medical kit, and stows it again. He puts on his Raybans and steps out of the Wrangler, scattering sparrows that were picking at a bagel on the pavement. A skinny blonde in a black nylon jogging suit is heading into the gymnasium, but the perimeter's otherwise quiet. Sunlight reflects off the vehicles, and heat radiates from the asphalt—but he pays scant attention to the torrid conditions that would wilt a lesser man. Prepared as always, he's got a change of clothes in back. He'll also have to select a weapon from the Wrangler's hidden compartment. The Remington would be of little use in close quarters, and, in any case, it's locked in his gun rack at the Institute. But the Smith and Wesson .357 Combat Magnum will be just the ticket. It'll drop any fucker in his tracks, and only men of his strength and physique can handle it.

Yes, he'll go to deep cover. Michael Grant will disappear, and George Grisham, the wealthy Texas oil and cattle baron, will land at McCarran and rent himself a fully-equipped Suburban, the cowboy Cadillac. And then he'll implement the *final solution*. The eighth canister is, after all, his alone. The final solution is a radical and irrevocable move that will conjure memories of Jonestown and Heaven's Gate, but, given this turn of events, it's necessary. Without it, there can be no real closure to the operation, no absolute assurance that he'll come through the mission unmarked and that the Alien-in-Chief will fall and the Great Republic will rise again.

65

FERESHTEH RAISANI REWINDS THE SURVEILLANCE TAPE SO THAT THEY CAN review it carefully. She has been struggling to stay focused on the task at hand rather than on Nick's surgery. Though she and McNamara retrieved the satchel with the Suzuki's key and found the motorcycle on their way back here, she has thus far successfully stifled the urge to race to the hospital herself. A friend at the hospital, one of the few who has any inkling she has a relationship at all much less with whom, has promised to call the moment Nick is out of surgery. And Andy Wright, who called when the helicopter touched down, will check in again as well. She is, though, still stunned by the depth of her need to be there when Nick regains consciousness. She's acutely aware that she must remain here doing what she's doing—and that this is exactly what Nick would want. But that doesn't alter the feeling in her marrow.

Her hands on the back of Raisani's chair, Maggie McNamara peers over the doctor's shoulder at the video screen. "Reverend Joe," she says, "is becoming unhinged."

"I agree," Raisani answers as she starts the tape again.

They watch and listen as Wengelt slumps into the chair, shouts into the phone, yells at the young woman, and stalks toward the wall with the snakes.

"Is that her?" McNamara asks.

Raisani nods without turning around.

When the phone call with Smith ends, Wengelt remains standing, staring at the wall, seemingly transfixed, as though the snakes are alive and slithering before him. He then hurls the phone against the floor, shattering it and sending shards skittering across the tiles. Finally, his face contorted, he stomps from the room.

Letting go of the chair, McNamara says, "We've got him, Doctor Raisani." She leans against the console and taps the monitor with her forefinger. "In his own words. No vague religious platitudes. Just straightforward homicidal mania."

Raisani pauses the video. "Yes," she says. "In his anger, he finally let the truth escape."

"Burn three copies," McNamara says.

Raisani turns and looks at her—this small woman with all this energy. McNamara's eyes are bright, her posture erect, her hands partially balled, not combative, but definitely assertive. "Why three?" Raisani asks. She's not used to receiving commands, and she needs to understand McNamara's thinking before they do anything.

McNamara holds Raisani's gaze. "One for the police," she says. "You told Andy earlier that you weren't going to the authorities because you lacked hard evidence. Now you've got it."

Shaking her head, Raisani says, "No. We told him we could not go to the authorities until we had accounted for all the canisters. There are still ones we've failed to locate."

"Time's running out."

"The canisters must be loca…"

"Doctor Raisani," McNamara interrupts, "We've got to contact the police."

"Yes," Raisani admits, glancing at the video screen. "You're right." Nick would never involve the police, but this is the first time they've actually caught Wengelt on tape making direct references to poison and to deaths he has ordered. And, as McNamara points out, time is critical at this juncture. Though Nick would remind her that the government's response could be catastrophic in and of itself, he would also note the differences in the situation now. "What about the other two copies?" she asks.

Folding her hands, McNamara says, "As a contingency, I'll get the second copy to my guys at ABC to be aired if they don't hear from us again by…" She gazes at her watch. "…three o'clock our time."

Raisani bites her lower lip. "In time for the national news?"

McNamara nods. "And the local news."

"I cannot do that." Raisani stands up, facing McNamara. "It would cause widespread panic. We don't know how the Virin really works, how it's transmitted, what it…"

"And if we don't warn people," McNamara says, *"before* those lunatics use the Virin, everything'll be much worse." She places her hands on her hips. "The death toll will be far greater."

Raisani stares into McNamara's eyes. She does not like the principle of the greater good—or, in this case, the concept of the lesser of two evils—being used against her.

"And the third copy," McNamara says, "I'll personally deliver to Gary Smith." She's almost smiling. "At the warehouse—before noon."

"What?" Raisani asks, taken aback by the idea.

"He wants evidence to use against Wengelt. The video shows that Wengelt's the ringleader. That he views Smith as an employee…a hired hand working for him."

Raisani sits down in the chair. The idea is intriguing—but flawed. "The man is threatening blackmail."

"He's threatening to go to the authorities with what he knows," McNamara retorts.

"Not the authorities. The media. And he's completely untrustworthy."

McNamara *is* smiling now. "Don't you think I know that?" she says. "Whatever he does with the video, we'll be better off."

"Wengelt will know he's being watched."

"Damn right. It'll scare the crap out of him. Maybe he'll run before he uses the Virin." McNamara waves at the video monitor. "It's not like he's being rational now."

Raisani glances at the screen, weighing the pros and cons of this rash plan. She paused the tape at the point at which the large man lumbered from the room. Gazing at Maya's photograph, she wonders what Nick would do—and then she's pulled again by her emotions into the operating theater, holding her breath, worrying over what is happening to him at this moment.

66

As Andrew Wright and Benjamin Kupferberg pass the angular woman who guards the entrance to The Tahitian's executive offices, she hands Kupferberg a folder and coldly assesses Wright. With his hat rolled in the pocket of his khakis and no other discernible bloodstains, he must look better than he did on his last visit—even if he is wearing a camouflage jacket. But he's still battered, bandaged, and hobbling, which is not, he suspects, the look of most of Kupferberg's guests. Kupferberg talked on his phone in the limousine all the way to The Tahitian, and Wright gleaned from the conversations that though security measures all along the Strip were still being upgraded, no suspicious canisters had been located. And it seemed like the Inner Circle's egos needed some serious stroking.

When they're finally in his office behind closed doors, Kupferberg slides the folder onto his desk, waves Wright to the dark leather armchairs, and asks, "The guy in the hospital, he's your source?"

Nodding, Wright gazes at the Gauguin and then sits in the chair facing away from the painting.

Kupferberg lifts the manila envelope from his desk and holds it gingerly with his thumb and two fingers as he carries it over. "What did you tell Sergeant Carey?" he asks.

"Nothing about the canisters," Wright answers. "Only that the Divine Eagle security chief could've been the shooter."

"Andy," Kupferberg says as he takes the chair across from Wright, "you're probably their next target."

That's already occurred to Wright, but he's hoping both Wengelt and Grant are too preoccupied with the Day of the Lord to bother eliminating him. He realizes, though, that Nick Larson likely had similar thoughts before he was shot. "Yeah," he says. "It's a possibility."

Kupferberg crosses his leg. "I'll assign you a team of bodyguards," he says.

"That's not necessary," Wright answers. He doesn't want someone like Hans following him around. Worse, he suspects that Kupferberg may want to keep an eye on him every bit as much as to protect him. He's sure Kupferberg's not at all inclined to fetch him again at the hospital or anywhere else.

"At least today," Kupferberg says, smiling amiably, "for a few hours."

"It's really not necessary." Wright shifts his weight to relieve the pain in his ribs.

"I insist," Kupferberg says, his smile waning. "After all, you're my guest here."

Wright nods. "Okay," he says finally, but the word *guest* doesn't ring quite right. Pointing to the envelope, he adds, "You can hold on to those for a while. They're safer with you, at least for now."

Kupferberg taps the edge of the envelope against the chair's arm. "All right," he answers. "They sure as hell had the desired effect on the Circle."

"But nobody's found anything?" Wright asks.

"Not yet," Kupferberg says. He stands, goes to the desk, places the envelope next to the folder, and glances at his Rolex. "I've got a video conference in ten minutes to update the Circle." Picking up a slim remote, he shakes his head. "The shooting out in the canyon really set them off. I got a lot of calls asking what the hell you were doing out there." He points the remote at the framed photographs on the wall opposite the rosewood bookcase. As the panels slide open to reveal a sixty-inch flat-screen video monitor, he clicks the remote again. "You've got to lay your cards on the table, Andy, if you want these guys to back you." An image appears, and he scrolls through the channels until he finds a shot of the creek running through the red rocks. "You, not me, have got to tell them what the hell's going on." He raises the sound so that it's clearly audible but not loud. As he pulls a sheaf of papers from the folder, he adds, "I've got to go through this stuff before the conference."

Wright turns to the monitor and watches the shot of officers milling along the creek. By now, he assumes, they've discovered the petroglyph and traced the tracks back to the shooting site. They know others have been there before them. In short, they already know, or will soon figure out, that the story he told Carey is a complete goddamned crock. The video image cuts to a tan, square-faced announcer with a deep voice, who says, "In a major development related to yesterday's WNTS Big Story, police investigators are reporting they've recovered a portion of what may be the gas can used to ignite the Harold Street fire and explosion that killed two LVFD firefighters." The man cocks his head and smiles at the camera. "We'll be back after this brief pause."

Shit, Wright thinks, pushing himself up from the chair. "Where's the john?" he asks. "I need to wash up before I talk to your guys."

Kupferberg looks up from the papers he's shuffling. "Yeah, sure," he says. He points the remote at the wall to the left of the television screen and clicks twice. The panel swings open a couple of inches, and a bright shaft of light cuts across the carpet. When Wright reaches the hidden doorway, Kupferberg adds, "And, ditch that jacket while you're at it, Andy."

The bathroom's all green Italian marble, mirrors, and bright light. Wright's face in the expanse of mirror over the sink looks bad—older, worn, and world-weary. The swelling's even worse, and the look in his eyes is closer to that of a combat veteran than a TV correspondent. As he splashes cold water on his face, trying to rub life back into it and welcoming the rush of pain on his bruised skin, he wonders if there are fingerprints on the chunk of the gas can the police found. He can't yet have the cops link him to Smith's house. Inevitably, that'll happen—but not yet.

He wipes his face with a plush white towel. He hoped there would be another exit from the bathroom, an escape route through a private suite, perhaps, or out into the hall. Talking to the Inner Circle via the video hookup is no big deal, but he doesn't want to answer questions. Refolding the towel, he's aware that he doesn't mind the mini news conference, but he doesn't want to put up with the sort of grilling reporters routinely inflict on the subjects of their stories.

When Wright returns to the office, Kupferberg's on the flip phone asking, "Where?" Nodding, he pauses. "When?" Turning to Wright, he waves him over to the desk. "Hold on a second," he says into the phone. Then, lowering the phone against his hip, he whispers, "They've found a canister at Paris."

Wright's eyes lock on Kupferberg's as he asks, "Where?"

"On the casino roof." Kupferberg shrugs. "Concealed in a trash can near the swimming pool."

Reaching into the pocket of his khakis, Wright asks, "The sprinkler system? Is the pool the source of the water?"

"Yeah." Kupferberg nods. "All the newer hotels, the pools feed the sprinkler systems. If there's a fire…" He seems to realize the implication of his words. "George," he says into the phone, "shut down your…"

"No!" Wright interrupts. "Not yet." When Kupferberg begins to protest, he adds, "Get the serial number." He unfolds the index card that Raisani gave him. "There's a series of yellow letters and numbers on the canister."

"We need the serial number, George," Kupferberg says into the phone.

As the two men wait, Wright says, "Some of the canisters are inert. Lars…my source switched the contents."

Kupferberg drums his fingers on the desk. "Even if it's not inert, we might be better off leaving the canister. Set a trap for the lunatics."

Leaning his unbruised hip against the desk, Wright weighs that idea. Leaving even one canister of Virin in place is hugely risky, but if Grant is flying solo at this point, it might be worth it. Is it possible, he wonders, to safely exchange the contents *and* set the trap? He realizes he needs to talk with Raisani immediately.

Kupferberg takes the gold pen from his pocket. As he jots the number on the folder, he says aloud, "V9189NA003."

Wright checks the list twice, knowing before the second time that the number isn't there, but still hoping he'll somehow find it. "It's real," he says to Kupferberg. "It's the goddamned Virin."

67

JOSEPH WENGELT SLOUCHES IN THE CHAIR IN HIS SANCTUARY. THE LIGHT'S on, and the ventilator's humming. This sanctum sanctorum is the only place left to him, the only untainted spot where he may yet commune with the Lord on this Day. His left hand clutches the golden fist. The fingers of his right hand massage his temple. His head keeps thundering, and his breathing's shallow. While he was still watching that manure on TV about the caveman surviving Michael's vengeance, the cops were already on the phone, two of them at once, interrogating him about Michael's Wrangler. He was alone in his quarters, everyone, acolytes and Elders, too terrified of his rage to approach him. But they know the news report about the shooting in the canyon has something to do with the Divine Eagle Institute. They know Andy Wright was just here, and the most innocent among them, even Christine, have begun to whisper again about Michael's tendencies.

The cops pretended during the call to be respectful, but he could hear the contempt in their voices. Their words dripped with secular disdain for the Prophet. He did not lower himself to their level, did not once lie to them; he admitted that a vehicle like the one they described was registered to his religious foundation. He pointed out, truthfully, that he did not know the current whereabouts of the vehicle, that he had not personally seen the vehicle in days, and that he did not, in fact, know if the vehicle had been legally taken from his Institute. It could well have been stolen, given the conflicting information he has received to this point.

He handled the buffoons masterfully, but the root of the problem persists: Michael has gone AWOL with the Wrangler. Though the guardians twice logged Michael's departures, they, of course, know

nothing of his destinations. Arrogant, beautiful Michael, his archangel, the disciple he most counts on, is unaccounted for. Michael,
who is most obsessed with the Institute's security, has caused this
monumental lapse, this unforgivable breach. On this Day of the Lord,
Michael has blatantly attracted attention—almost as flagrantly as
that bastard, Smith. And then, to fuel the flames of his transgression,
Michael has flown—vanished into the world outside the Divine Eagle
Institute.

The Prophet squeezes the golden fist. He needs Michael *now*. He
needs to know what went wrong in the canyon—*how* the caveman
survived, *what* evidence, other than the vehicle, can conceivably con-
nect DEI to the shooting, *who* else might possibly be a witness, and
why in God's name Andy Wright was out there at dawn. It can't be
coincidence. No, damn it, not at all. There's a connection, a sex tri-
angle probably, that includes that Arab woman doctor. The Prophet
also needs to know what has transpired with the deployment of the
seven canisters—whether each canister is in place and exactly when
each will do the Lord's Will. Michael had a clear timetable, but there's
no way of knowing if he's adhering to it. The Prophet has called
Michael repeatedly on the mobile telephone, a phone the Prophet
purchased and continues to pay for. But the phone is off-line. Michael
has deliberately cut communications.

The Prophet loosens his collar, but it does little to help his breathing. He presses his eyelids in a vain attempt to stop the storms. Finally,
of almost greater import, he needs to know what to do about that
vile philistine, Gary Babington Smith. He cannot let the imbecile
enter the Institute accompanied by those violent, unclean skinhead
dregs of his. True, the Prophet possesses the firepower to repel the
bastard forcibly. In the last year, Michael has procured at great expense a sophisticated arsenal for the Divine Eagle Institute. But, with
the media hordes invading the canyon and without Michael's martial tactics, using the weaponry is questionable. Worse, without
Michael's input, the Prophet's only choice is to meet Smith at the
warehouse. He won't, however, meet the bastard's demands. He has
ten times the twenty-five grand safely set aside in his *private* coffers,

but it'll be a cold day in hell before he gives in to that blackmailing son of a bitch. He'll have to throw some cash Smith's way, but he needs to determine just how little will placate the bastard. And how he will keep Smith from coming back and making even more outrageous demands. Michael's way is the only way, but the Prophet has not as yet sullied his own hands in the name of the Lord—and he refuses to start with Smith.

The Prophet couldn't provide Virin for Smith even if he wanted to. He'll substitute snake venom for the Virin, that's what he'll do. The imbecile won't know the difference. But what he'd really like to do is loose a pair of diamondbacks on the bastard. To do that, though, he'd have to transport the snakes, handle the fanged, diabolic creatures himself. He shudders at the thought. Michael, vain and disdainful Michael, has abandoned his Prophet in the moment of greatest need.

He opens his eyes and stares at the gold *crux commissa*. It levitates there, a symbol—but more than a symbol, a holy presence. He bows his head before the cross, yearning to commune with the Lord. This is the Day of the Lord's Will, and yet the Lord remains inaccessible, totally mute. The storm in his head blows through the Lord's silence, sucking away his breath. His large hands clenched, he gapes at the cross, almost begging for a Sign. He is the Word of the Lord, the Will of the Lord, but he feels absolutely forsaken.

68

A<small>NDREW</small> W<small>RIGHT</small> <small>AND</small> B<small>ENJAMIN</small> K<small>UPFERBERG</small> <small>STAND UNDER THE FAUX</small> tree across from the double arched entrance to the Paris Hotel and Casino's elevators. Hans lurks to the left of the arches under the *Le Boulevard* sign scanning the patrons wending their way in both directions along the ersatz avenue. The video conference was postponed an hour so that they could get here faster, and now they're not doing a goddamned thing. Wright tightens and reties the camouflage jacket he's rolled and knotted around his waist. He's into some zone, well beyond fatigue and physical discomfort, that he's never experienced before. It makes no sense. He knows he's running on empty and that he may crash at any moment, but he's feeling as clear and focused as he has ever felt.

Kupferberg taps his foot on the cobblestones, glances at his Rolex, and says, "Three more minutes, Andy. If she's not here, we go up without her."

Wright nods, but he knows they're not heading to the casino's rooftop pool without Raisani. When he called her from The Tahitian, she was adamant that the pool area be cleared and that no one do anything until she got there with the biohazard suits. Though Kupferberg easily convinced the Paris manager to temporarily shut down and secure the pool, he had trouble persuading him to wait to remove the canister. When Wright and Kupferberg arrived at the hotel, the manager, a pear-shaped man in a gray European-cut suit, took one look at Wright and lisped in an affected French accent, "So, Benjamin, is this the chemical specialist you mentioned?" After Wright informed him that, in fact, he was not but that *she* would be arriving shortly, the manager and his loss prevention chief took the elevator up to the pool without waiting for Raisani. Only Wright's hand on Kupferberg's shoulder prevented him from joining them.

Kupferberg's phone rings just as Wright spots Raisani. Carrying a large dark duffel bag, she pauses under a black wrought-iron street lamp. He can, even at that distance, see the light in her eyes.

"Yes. Who...?" Kupferberg says into the phone. "Sergeant Carey... yes." He looks askance at Wright. "Not at the moment. But I expect him."

As Raisani approaches, Wright asks her, "Any more word on Nick?"

"I'll have him call you," Kupferberg says into the phone. "Within ten minutes...Good."

Raisani shakes her head, the light fading for a moment from her eyes. "He's in post-op. Still critical." She lowers her shoulder and slips the duffel to the floor. Forcing a smile, she adds, "He survived the surgery."

"That's something, Fereshteh," Wright says, touching her shoulder. "He was in such good shape that if he's made it this far..."

She nods and then gazes up at the wisps of painted white clouds on the blue domed ceiling.

"What about Maggie?" Wright asks. "Where is she?"

"We took the bike to my house," she answers, still looking at the ceiling. "I borrowed a friend's pick-up." She focuses again on him. "Maggie went to...do some things."

"Things...?" Wright says. "What things?"

Kupferberg flips his phone shut and extends his hand, saying, "Doctor Raisani."

"Mr. Kupferberg," she says, shaking his hand. "What've we got here?" She grabs the duffel by its strap and hoists it back onto her shoulder.

"Sergeant Carey needs to talk with you," Kupferberg says to Wright. He then glances at Hans, who motions toward the elevators.

I'll bet Carey does, Wright thinks.

"The pool's on the casino roof," Kupferberg says to Raisani. "A couple of guys went up there about..."

244

"What?" Raisani's eyes spark as she glares at Kupferberg. "We agreed that no one…"

"The hotel manager and his…" Kupferberg says as they pass *Le Journal*.

"They have no idea what they're dealing with," she says, striding into the elevator.

Hans keeps pressing the elevator's call button until Wright and Kupferberg enter after her, and then he follows. He stands stiffly to one side, away from the others. The elevator's rise is swift, smooth, and quiet.

Crouching and unzipping the duffel, Raisani repeats, "No idea at all." Her hair, pulled back in a single thick braid, falls across her shoulder.

"Doctor," Kupferberg says, "precautions were…" His phone rings again, and he frowns as he answers it. "Where?" he asks. "Shit. Get the serial number. Yeah, the stenciled numbers. Yes, *immediately!*"

Taking the list from his pocket, Wright looks at Kupferberg.

"Bellagio," Kupferberg says. "Right across the street." He glances down at Raisani, who's pulling surgical gloves from the bag. "In the sub-basement."

"Damn," Wright says. "I was hoping there'd be a pattern. All swimming pools or something."

The elevator opens to a posh, brightly lit foyer with glass doors leading to the pool.

"V9189NA0…" Kupferberg begins as Wright squints at the list.

"Where are they?" Raisani exclaims, rising and staring out into the sunshine. "The two men, where are they?"

Glancing up from the list, Wright follows her gaze into the brightness. A security guard, dressed as a French gendarme in a white cap and powder blue jacket with white epaulets, stands alone by the pool entrance. Beyond him, sunlight gleams on the green steel arches and white tile, reflects from the eight oversized white planters spaced around the pool, and sparks the water's surface—but no one else is visible anywhere in the pool area.

Raisani pushes the glass doors open, and Kupferberg, still holding the phone to his ear, follows her. Heat and light wash over Wright as he steps out the door. Sparrows flutter from sculpted bushes, and a French woman's sultry voice accompanied by a jazz combo diffuses from hidden speakers. Directly across the pool, the Eiffel Tower replica rises fifty stories into the sky. Alternating groups of concrete and canvas cabanas ring the periphery of the pool area. Hans brushes by Wright and reaches behind his back under his navy blue sport coat.

"Where are the men who came up here?" Raisani asks the security guard as she accosts him.

The guard looks at her blankly for a moment and then directs his answer to Kupferberg. "I...In...They went into the cabana," he stammers, pointing to a pair of neoclassical mausoleum-like structures between the base of the Eiffel Tower and the blue and gold Paris balloon.

"How long've they been in there?" Raisani asks.

"I...I'm not..." The security guard looks at Kupferberg. "More than ten...Maybe ten minutes."

Squeezing his fists hard, Wright murmurs, "Jesus shit."

"What the hell...?" Kupferberg says, color draining from his face.

"They're dead," she says. "Your friends are dead." She shakes her head again. "The Virin...I hope, for everyone's sake, they didn't spill it."

"I'll call back in a minute, Carl," Kupferberg says before flipping the phone shut. "I'll...What do we do, Doctor Raisani?"

His hand inside the back of his jacket, Hans gapes wide-eyed at his boss.

"*You,*" she says as she heads by the first row of blue and white striped chaise lounges, "need to keep everyone away from here, Mr. Kupferberg." She glances at Wright. "Andy, come with me. We'll change in the tent to the..."

"Andy's not..." Kupferberg says. "I'll work with you."

Raisani stops and stares at Kupferberg. "Andy will help me," she says. "I know him." Her tone is business-like, but it's clear to Wright, as it must be to Kupferberg, that there's no possibility for negotiation. "Find out about the next canister, Mr. Kupferberg. And keep people away from here."

As Wright hands Kupferberg the index card with the list of the canisters' serial numbers, his heart's pounding—not in fear or excitement, but something deeper, the anticipation of a moment that matters. He's going out to face a horrific killer and, maybe, see the future of the city.

"Figure out who's left in charge here," Raisani says to Kupferberg. "And we're going to need large, leak-proof bags, at least four of them."

Kupferberg nods to her and then waves Hans over. Turning a slow circle, Wright scans the pool area. The hotel forms an arc around one side of the pool, and the Eiffel Tower looks directly down on it. Surveillance of the pool deck could readily be done from any of a thousand vantage points. Wright glances at Kupferberg, but there's nothing to say. Kupferberg claps him once on the back and flips his phone open.

69

Fereshteh Raisani leads Andrew Wright to a tent cabana fifteen yards from the spot at which the security guard last saw the two men. The shaded interior of the cabana has the feel of a patio at night —a striped couch and easy chair with footstool form an L around an oval table. Raisani slips the duffel onto the table's glass top and pulls out surgical scrubs and a blue biohazard bodysuit with a clear faceplate and a dark ventilator. "Andy," she says as she takes off her turtleneck and hangs it over the back of one of the four steel chairs surrounding the table, "this will be…"

"Ugly," he answers. He slips off his loafers. It's already occurred to him that the bodies will be gruesome as well as hazardous.

Nodding, she pries one shoe off with the toe of the other. She then puts on the scrub shirt before untying the drawstring of her black pants.

Wright's sweating hard by the time he's fully into the second biohazard suit, which is a little tight on him. Once Raisani locks down his faceplate, he has to consciously control his breathing. It's difficult to talk through the ventilators so Raisani makes eye contact, nods, and raises the thumb of her double-gloved hand.

The sunlight is dazzling as Wright steps out again onto the rooftop deck, and he's disoriented, feeling almost as though he's scuba diving rather than walking. He stays just behind Raisani's shoulder, following her as she cuts among the lounges. His breathing echoes around him. The sky is an ocean, and he's light-headed, as though a surge of sky might, at any moment, wash him from the roof.

As Raisani pushes open the cabana's white shuttered door, Wright's arrested mid-step. Unable to draw his eyes away, he's just not prepared—couldn't possibly be prepared—for what he sees. The two corpses are far more hideous than any pictures could ever be. The manager lies on his back, his limbs rigid, blood still trickling from his nose and ears. His eyes protrude, and his partially severed tongue sticks out between his clenched teeth. An overturned chair lies next to him as though he tumbled into it or, convulsing, kicked it over. His neck wrenched, the security chief lies on his side in a sticky pool of blood. Black bile smears his white shirt, and shit stains his khakis. Feeling vomit rising, Wright swallows hard, forcing it back down.

Between the two men, the open canister stands on the floor, its outer and inner lids removed. Wider but no taller than a thermos bottle, it looks commonplace with its stenciled yellow letters. Wright's amazed at how his mind works—he's noticing in this grisly moment the cabana's mundane details. The ceiling fan turns slowly. There's a print of Claude Monet's *Hotel des Roches Noires* on the wall. And live plants. In the corner, a tall potted fern with stems like snakes.

Raisani yanks his arm. As he turns toward her, she pulls him back through the entrance. Behind her faceplate, her eyes—those beautiful eyes—are wide with horror. When they're out in the sun-washed sea of the deck, she slams the door. Shaken, much more so even than when they found Larson, she clutches both his arms, tilts her head close to his, and shouts.

He can hear her but can't at first make sense of what she's saying. Her words echo in his head as though his mind is some aquatic canyon.

"…Airborne!…Can't handle this ourselves." Her hands on his sleeves are trembling. "Undiluted, the Virin's airborne! We have to close the lid…and get out of there."

Finally, he nods. The Virin's even more lethal than she thought. They're in over their heads. They have been all along, of course, but now she knows it. They both know it. And yet they have to go back into the cabana to close the canister.

Holding his arm, she pauses before opening the door again. She's steeling herself, composing herself for what they face. He should be, too, but he feels drawn back into the cabana, toward the grotesque

249

corpses. *What did those guys do?* he wonders. They knew about the Virin. Knew what it could do. Kupferberg briefed them. They saw the pictures…Or did they? More probably, their boss was briefed, and they knew only what they were told—which might merely have been that they were dealing with poison, a toxic chemical agent. Still, only an idiot would open a sealed canister containing a toxic chemical. True, it's something he might've done for the camera in a past life—but *they* should've had more sense. Did they actually touch the Virin? Or just sniff the stuff? Or, was merely opening the canister enough to kill them?

Raisani flicks the wall switch to stop the ceiling fan. She and Wright stoop together on each side of the canister. It's too wide to hold with one hand, and she gestures for him to brace it. He focuses on the canister, tunneling his vision so that it's all he can see. Once he gets a good grip, she replaces, turns, and locks the inner lid. He's hunched over, and his elbow's almost touching the blood around the security chief's head. Pain stabs his ribs, but all his energy is in his hands. The roof could collapse, and he'd plummet into the casino still clasping the canister.

She needs to force the outer lid with both hands, and, for a moment, he feels his grip slipping. He transfers his full focus to his fingers, willing his gloved hands to hold firm, watching them as though they're separate from him. When she finally secures the lid, he glances up into her eyes, which tell him to lift the canister. Aware that he has been holding his breath, he exhales slowly, keeping his eyes on her and away from the corpses on either side of him. Cradling the canister, he kneels awkwardly and then wobbles to his feet.

He has no idea what to do next. The exterior of the canister may be contaminated. His gloves may hold minute amounts of Virin. His suit may have touched the blood. Panic steals his breath. The canister has hold of him every bit as much as he has it. Then, he looks over at Raisani, who's rising after him, nodding to him. Stepping away from the corpses, he reaches out and, hands quivering, gives her the canister. She cradles it in her arms as though its some newborn infant, its hour come round at last.

70

GARY B. SMITH DOES A COUPLE OF QUICK DRIVE-BYS IN THE BUICK BEFORE parking by the curb in front of Reverend Dickhead's warehouse. He's come to the meeting forty minutes early to make sure nothing's doing. The place looks like any other warehouse thrown up on the cheap—cinderblock walls painted white and a flat roof that makes it hotter than a witch's tit inside. The Dickhead doesn't really use the warehouse for anything except secret fuckin' meetings with guys like him the Rev doesn't want to be seen with. There's a bunch of books inside, but nothing else, not even a fuckin' john that works.

He turns off *New Country 95.5,* fires up a Marlboro, and watches the place for a couple of minutes. Nothing's happening—no holy hulks setting a trap, no Michael fuckin' Grant getting a hard-on over the possibility of kicking the shit out of him. Nothing. Just fuckin' heat bouncing off of everything—the warehouse walls, the Buick's hood, and 'specially all the aluminum air conditioning ducts and vents piled in the fenced yard across the street. Actually, nothing much is going on anywhere around. A couple of beaners are leaning against a flat-bed truck heaped with more a.c. ducts. They're smoking butts— maybe on a break from loading up the truck. Those lazy asses have been on break their whole fuckin' lives. A jumbo jetliner, probably full of more mudheads and fairies itching to blow their fuckin' wads on the Strip, is circling low for a landing over at McCarran.

Shit, he wishes the Buick's air conditioning still worked. There's no fuckin' breeze, and the smoke's just hangin' in front of him, a cloud in the windshield. He's been sweating all morning, 'specially since he picked up the six of Bud. Bud's the real breakfast of champions, no doubt about it. He's only had two so far—one more before the meeting with Reverend Dickhead won't hurt, but that's all. It's too fuckin' hot out, and he's got to be ready, have his wits about him, for the meeting. He grabs a can from the seat and presses it against his forehead. The can's not cold, but it's not nearly as hot as he feels. It's like he's got a fuckin' fever or something. When he was a kid, his mother used to put a cool washcloth on his forehead whenever he was, like she said, *runnin' a temp.* But now the Bud's as good as he can do, and it's not really fuckin' working.

He pops the Bud's top, sucks the foam, and belches. One good thing about sweating his ass off like this—he hasn't had to piss once. Pissing just reminds him of how much his balls still hurt. He downs half the Bud, belches again, and wipes his mouth with the back of his hand. He can still smell the smoke and sweat and whatever the hell else is oozing out of him. The new *Las Vegas USA* t-shirt didn't do shit to get rid of the stench. It's like it's coming from inside him. But fuck it. He doesn't need to smell like no fuckin' roses for the Rev or anybody else.

He's got to stop thinking about the smell and cover his back, that's what he's got to do. He's got to be ready—scout out the place on foot. He finishes the Bud, belches a third time, crushes the can with one hand, and tosses it out the window. The beaners look over for a second when the can hits the street, but then they go back to chattering about whatever the hell beaners jabber about. He grabs the keys, his smokes, and the Luger, elbows the door open, and steps out. It can't be fuckin' hotter outside than in the car, but it is. He sucks in his stomach and stuffs the Luger in his belt under his shirt. The keys go into the pocket with the wad of cash, and the smokes get rolled into the sleeve of the t-shirt. His knee's stiff as hell, and he still can't remember when he banged the shit out of it. Those pigs must've done it when they arrested him. Yeah, they fuckin' did it to him. He kicks at some cement droppings on the sidewalk and then starts to cross the shitty little parking lot toward the warehouse—just to make sure nobody's there. And walking helps loosen the knee.

He's about half way to the door when Maggie Mac, the pixie bitch herself, comes strutting around the building's corner toward him. He stops dead. It can't be. He must be dreaming. He's so fuckin' blown away by the sight of her that he doesn't even think to pull out the Luger. And, she's walking right at him with a brown binder or folder or something held against her chest like she's some virgin school girl and he's the all-star jock meeting in the hallway. Her hair's bouncing with each step, and she looks even hotter than before, if that's fuckin' possible. She's so out of place and this is so fuckin' unbelievable, that he's frozen—can't move a muscle.

When she's only about twenty feet away, she pulls the Colt automatic, his fuckin' Colt, from behind the folder and points it at his chest. "Don't move, you shithead!" she says in that same voice she used when she kicked him in the balls.

The voice both freezes him worse and unfreezes him. This is no fuckin' dream, and she's pointing his gun at him again, goddamn her sweet fuckin' ass.

"Listen up, Gary," she says.

Her green eyes are gleaming like emeralds or something in the sunshine. And she knows his name. What the fuck gives here? She knows his goddamn name. She's been watching the reports on the fuckin' tube. That must be it.

"I'm making you an offer, Gary," she goes on like they've been doing a deal or something. "You're meeting with Reverend Wengelt. But you don't really have anything on him, do you, Gary?"

Now his mind's totally blown. How in holy fuckin' hell does she know about the meetin'? Nothing about that's been on the tube. He raises his hand to wipe the sweat that's suddenly pouring down his face.

"I said, don't move, Gary!" she hisses at him.

He lowers his arm slowly. He could go for the Luger, but she's pointing the Colt at him like she knows how to use it. Like she fuckin' *wants* to use it.

"Answer my question, Gary," she says. "You don't have a thing on Wengelt, do you?"

"What...?" he stammers. "How do you know...?" He shakes his head.

253

She takes the brown folder-envelope thing she's been pressing against her boobs and holds it out like it's a fuckin' present or something. "Take it with both hands, Gary," she says. "Very slowly. And keep holding it with both hands."

As he steps forward and reaches for the accordion file—that's what you call the fuckin' thing—his hands are shaking. He can't believe it. The pixie bitch is really getting to him again. He's getting fuckin' hard. Clutching the file with both hands, he props it on top of his belly.

"It's a surveillance tape, Gary," she says, "of Reverend Wengelt when you were talking to him on the phone this morning." She's actually smiling at him now. "You know, the call in which you were blackmailing him, and he went off about how he's having all those people killed."

She knows. His head's pounding bad, and his breathing's all fucked up. She has a fuckin' tape of Wengelt at the compound. "What...? How...?" he begins.

"Don't ask questions, Gary," she says, still smiling at him. "The tape's worth a lot more than twenty-five grand. It may even save your sorry ass from death row." Her smile disappears. "Now lie down on the ground, Gary."

"What?" No fuckin' way he's gonna do that. She'll kick him in the balls again.

"On your stomach, Gary! Hands behind your head. Keep holding that file." She's yelling at him like he's a fuckin' kid or something. "Kneel, now!" She reaches under his shirt and yanks the Luger out. Shaking her head, she adds, "Boys and their toys."

He kneels down and, glaring up at her, sees in those beautiful green eyes that she really wants to kill him but she's using him instead for something. But what the fuck for? When he reaches out and puts one hand on the pavement, it's so fuckin' hot he knows he's gonna fry.

She pulls out the Luger's clip and then ejects the cartridge in the chamber. Dropping the gun by a broken concrete wheel guard, she says, "I hope Wengelt doesn't notice it's not loaded, Gary. Now, down!"

Madder than hell, he flops onto his belly and puts the hand with the file behind his head. That way he can just barely keep his face up.

"Both hands!"

His cheek burns against the blacktop, but he does what she says.

"Use your brain for once, Gary," she says.

That's something his mother used to yell at him when he was in trouble, and he wants to choke the living shit out of the pixie bitch for saying it.

"Count to fifty, Gary," she demands. "And don't move that fat ass of yours. Don't even look up. Count!"

"One," he begins. "Two." As he counts, the anger and humiliation boil over. The blacktop's hotter than hell, and dirt and gravel are burning into his face. His new shirt's sopped with sweat, and his neck already hurts from holding the file…What the hell is the tape? How the hell did she get her hands on it? And, what the fuck did she mean by it being worth a lot more than twenty-five grand?

By the time he gets to twenty-two, he can't take it anymore. He moves his arms, raises his head, and pulls himself up on his elbows. She's gone—fuckin' vamoosed. But the two beaners are over there standing by some smashed skids between the truck and the dumpster, staring at him, not laughing at him, but smiling, those wide, white-toothed smiles—this big gringo taken down by some bitch half his size. Must be pretty fuckin' good entertainment. Can't wait to tell all the other fuckin' beaners what they saw!

His elbows are scorching so he hunches up onto his knees. And suddenly the pixie bitch is rocketing around from behind the warehouse on some black motorcycle. She doesn't even look at him as she shoots by. But it's her, all right, her pixie-do slicked back by the wind. It's got to be a fuckin' dream. The bike looks like one of those whiny off-road Jap jobs, but it's not making any noise—and she's gone before he can even turn to see which direction she went.

71

MICHAEL GRANT PASSES THROUGH HIS SECRET ENTRANCE TO THE INSTI-
tute. It's just past noon, cloudless, one-hundred-and-three in the
shade—and even he's sweating hard. Everything's taking too much
time, but if he stays on task, which he will, he'll finish here in plenty
of time to spring his traps on schedule at twenty-one hundred. He
has changed back into his fatigues after posing as George Grisham
to procure the Suburban at the airport. It's a damn fine vehicle, but
it's still no good out here. He had to leave it at a concealed site five
clicks back along the road and hike in by the western route. The pack
he's wearing—which contains only his supplies, the Magnum, a flare
gun, and water—is light, but humping the western rocks in this heat
takes its toll on any man.

He pauses among the pines, takes off his black sweatband, and
brushes away the sweat. After consuming his second liter-bottle of
water, he discards it in the underbrush, puts the sweatband back
on, and begins to work his way through the trees toward the buildings. This is, in some ways, the most difficult mission of the day. The
Prophet has been more than just his employer—almost, during the
planning of the operation, a brother-in-arms. Some of the Elders
have been like uncles, and a few of the acolytes useful. But it's absolutely necessary. He has examined the situation from every conceivable angle, and, particularly after the Wrangler was identified, this
is the most obvious solution, the most logical conclusion, the most
sensible course of action. And, it'll also serve as a test run for the
larger mission on the Strip.

When he reaches the inner perimeter, he crouches behind a scrub
pine in order to control his breathing and allow his senses to sharpen.

Just as he suspected, there's minimal activity outside. The sound of a single hammer pounding down by the garage echoes over the general hum of air conditioning and electronics. The smell of onions rises from the communal kitchen's exhaust fans. He checks his watch, deciding to wait another five minutes before commencing with the operation. Everyone should already have gathered in the refectory for the mid-day prayer and meal. That's something you've got to say for the Divine Eagle Institute—the place runs on schedule. As he counts the seconds, he scans the compound. He has seized the high ground, but he still doesn't have clear sight lines throughout the area—and though he can handle anything, he wants no surprises.

He's about to make his move when the refectory door opens, and Christine waddles out. She hurries toward the Prophet's house, hoofing right along, as if she has a purpose—but he knows she has no thoughts without the Prophet's permission.

When she's again out of sight, he moves to the cistern. Both the base and the bowl are plain steel, but the delivery system is highly sophisticated. Out here, water is *the* commodity. The solar panels produce plenty of electricity—sometimes, in fact, a surplus that the Prophet can sell back to the State. But there's never an abundance of water. Neither rain nor the well alone can produce sufficient water for the Institute's needs, so the low-slung shed near the base of the cistern houses a system that combines the two sources, purifies the water, and delivers it to the buildings. Much of the water is then recycled, repurified, and redistributed. It's an efficient system—and one that's perfect for his purposes.

Ducking by the side of the shed, he flips the door's latch. The shed's interior is close and dark, almost suffocating, but, ignoring the physical discomfort, he steps in, removes his pack, opens it, and lifts out the eighth canister. He concealed this canister from the Prophet because he knew its implementation might become a necessary phase in the operation. He must protect himself from those at the Institute who, already jealous of his status with the Prophet, would lay blame for the Lord's Retribution on him. Collateral damage is unavoidable in any operation. And these people are not truly Patriots. They are devoted only to the Prophet's words, not to the Stars and Stripes.

He places the canister on the concrete slab, puts on the protective face mask and rubber gloves he brought in the pack, and begins his work. It's easy enough to detach the top of the drip system that adds the purifying agents, the fluoride and other chemicals, to the Institute's water. He's done it a dozen times before. But he's still careful. When he opens the canister's outer lid, he feels a quickening of his pulse despite his confidence in himself. The mask and gloves are both topnotch Level Seven issue, but this is still the first time he's uncorked a canister without wearing a biohazard suit. Before opening the inner lid, he takes a deep breath and holds it. He swiftly twists the cap and turns the canister. Deftly, he empties the canister into the drip system's container. It's not all that different from adding motor oil to a vehicle's engine, except that even a minor spill here would prove lethal. He realizes that using the entire canister is overkill—definite overkill—but he doesn't want to carry out a partially filled canister and he's certainly not going to leave it here. Once the canister is empty, he quickly replaces both the inner and outer lids and reattaches the drip system's cap. Only then does he lean back and take a breath.

Waiting for the Virin to work its way through the system would be inefficient, and leaving without checking at least the preliminary results would be unprofessional—so he moves immediately on to the second stage of his mission. Once he's outside the confines of the shed, the temperature feels ten degrees cooler. He removes and bags the mask and gloves, tucks the flare gun into his fatigues, closes his pack, shuts the shed door, and sets the pack against the shed wall. Crouching low, he scurries to the refectory's main entrance and locks the door with his master key. Then, staying below the windows, he rounds the corner of the building and locks the kitchen door. Without pausing, he scales the wall next to the chimney and slips out the small section of siding he cut under the eaves two nights ago.

He inserts the flare gun's muzzle through the hole into the dark space between the refectory's interior ceiling and the roof. He smiles as he fires. With the air conditioning going full blast, no one inside will have heard the shot. The heat building between the ceiling and

258

roof will set off the sprinkler system within ninety seconds. Though half a dozen Elders have keys to the refectory doors, the ensuing panic should prevent their use. Even if someone—the Prophet, maybe—keeps his composure, he should only be able to restore order by about the time that the Virin has worked its way through the sprinkler system. Those inside the refectory will never know the real, insurmountable obstacle they faced.

He scuttles back to the shed and positions himself so he has a clear view of the refectory. He must see the Virin do its work before he retrieves the Remington and his other personal effects. Loose ends remain—the sentries at the main gate, whoever's hammering, Christine, and maybe a couple of others. But, allowing a few of the DEI faithful, who did not actually witness his work, to survive will prove beneficial. They know nothing about who he really is, and Christine, at least, will be too hysterical to call the authorities. In fact, the Prophet has his followers so stirred into a religious frenzy that they'll blame the devil or government agents or both for the annihilation. In any case, they're just guinea pigs that don't have a fucking prayer of comprehending what's really going on. And they won't contact the media either, at least not right away. They won't do anything but cower during the first critical hours. And eventually the survivors will tell a tale of a diabolic disaster, maybe even laying the blame for the upcoming Strip devastation on the devil, too. The casualties will become martyrs, the Divine Eagle Institute another Waco.

72

Joseph Wengelt sits, steaming, in his Cadillac. The Caddy, parked next to his warehouse, is cool enough with the air conditioning blowing on him full blast. But there's a new storm brewing in his head even before the last one's over. He's still suffering occasional flashes, like heat lightning, and thunder still rumbles in the distance. It's that bastard Smith's fault. He's already twenty minutes late. It's just like that philistine to demand a meeting and then not show up on time.

The plain brown envelope with the five grand in it lies on the seat next to him. Fifty crisp one hundred dollar bills with that bulbous head of Benjamin Franklin. There's no Virin with the cash, though, no poison of any kind. Not even snake venom. The imbecile will complain, but he'll be salivating so hard over the cash that he'll take the deal. And it'll keep the son-of-a-bitch at bay at least for a little while. Long enough, anyway, for Michael to find a better solution. Just in case, he has his Colt .45 with the pearl handle under the seat. But he's not really expecting any problems. He's Smith's meal ticket, and the philistine knows it. Not even that son-of-a-bitch is dumb enough to bite the hand that feeds him.

When he hears the screeching of tires, he glances out the window. It's Smith's beater of a Buick, all right, whipping around the corner and slamming to a halt along the curb by the telephone pole. The lardass heaves himself out of the Buick and lumbers over carrying an accordion file. He's got on some grimy black Las Vegas t-shirt, dirty jeans, and those black boots misfits wear. Between his driving and the clothes, the bastard might as well advertise the meeting. The Prophet turns off the Caddy and swings open the door. The warehouse will be hotter than hell, but that porker isn't, under any circumstances, parking his fat grimy ass on the Caddy's clean leather seats.

"Hey, Rev," Smith says, his voice full of mockery. "How the fuck ya doin'?"

The Prophet reaches for the envelope, gets out of the Caddy, shuts the door, and pulls himself up to his full height. "I'm a busy man, Mr. Smith," he says, fixing the philistine with his gaze. "I've already missed the mid-day meal with my flock because of this meeting." He holds up the envelope and then waves it toward the warehouse. "Step inside so that we can complete our business."

"Not so fast, Rev," Smith says. His smile is yellow, like he's brushing his teeth with nicotine. And the man stinks worse than a chicken coop.

The Prophet notices the bulge under Smith's shirt where the material stretches below his gut. The bastard's carrying, and for a second the Prophet thinks about going for the Colt under the seat. But he stops himself. He's in charge here, and the vermin won't try anything. He steps back to get away from the stench. "Tell me what your evidence is, Mr. Smith." The lightning's coming on strong, and he opens his eyes wide to keep from squeezing them shut. He points the envelope at the accordion file.

Smith's smirk is diabolic. "The fuckin' evidence, Rev," he says, stepping forward and holding up the accordion file, "is a surveillance tape of you tellin' me on the phone this morning about Der Tag. You tellin' me I work for you, and how you're havin' all those mudheads and fairies on the Strip snuffed."

It's the Prophet's turn to scoff. He thought it might be something like an indecipherable audiotape of one of their meetings. But this is ludicrous. Surveillance of him *inside* the Divine Eagle Institute? Preposterous. How does this imbecile expect him to believe it?

The son-of-a-bitch is starting to laugh. He's actually laughing at the Prophet. His belly jiggles in that dirty t-shirt like he's some demonic Santa Claus. "Well, Rev," he says, "what were ya thinkin' when you were sittin' in that chair starin' at that fuckin' cowboy statue?"

The Prophet sucks in his breath, but he quickly regains control. The bastard could've guessed that easily enough.

"And what the fuck was happenin'," Smith asks, that damned smirk plastered all over his face now, "when you were starin' at those fuckin' wooden snakes after your little bitch interrupted us?" The fat ass is so infernally gleeful that he's starting to bounce up and down. "You looked like you were gettin' one motherfuckin' headache, Rev. A real Mr.-Gary-Babington-Smith's-got-me-by-the-balls fuckin' corker!"

Thunder booms everywhere as the storm blows the Prophet back against the Caddy's door. His breath tears from his chest. Lightning strikes behind his eyes. One of his flock has betrayed…It can't…The Lord would not…Judas walks the Institute's grounds! The envelope slips from his hand and falls to the pavement.

73

GARY B. SMITH SAVORS IT ALL. REVEREND DICKHEAD IS CRASHING HARD, burning bad. Eyes bugging, the fucker can't hardly stand up. He's clawing at his silver eagle bolo, ripping the top button off his starched white shirt. "Yeah, Rev," he says, "I got it all right here on a DV-fuckin'-D." He pulls the disc from the file, waves it in front of the Dickhead's face, and plops it back in the file. You gotta kick a guy when he's down. That way he don't get up.

"Who?" the Dickhead gasps. "Who…?"

"My source?" Smith says. He's sure as shit not gonna admit it's Maggie Mac, the pixie bitch. And that she's fuckin' humiliated him again. "I'm not, Rev, at liberty to divulge that information." Laughing, he puts on his best news-dude voice. "My source wishes to remain anonymous."

The Rev clutches his bolo and stares hard, but he just can't seem to get any words out.

Smith's knee hurts like hell as he stoops to get the envelope. There's a wad in it, but it's no fuckin' twenty-five large. He balances the envelope in his hand for a minute in front of the Dickhead, and then he rips it open with his teeth. There's five, maybe six grand— a shitload of cash, all clean, crisp C-notes, too. But its nothing close to what he demanded from the Rev. Looking into the Cadillac, he sees there's no fuckin' poison neither.

Maggie Mac said the tape was worth a lot more than twenty-five G's, and she was right about that. When he watched the DVD alone in the back room of the video store, he couldn't believe his eyes. He still can't figure out why Maggie Mac gave it to him—or how the fuck she got it, 'specially so fast. But he's using his head. Had this dude in the video store make two quick copies. He had to lay a couple of Grants on him for five minutes work. Had to watch the dude do it the whole time, too, so he didn't bootleg his own copy. But it was fuckin' worth it. He's got the DVDs hidden under the spare in the Buick's trunk. All that work made him a little late for the meeting, but so fuckin' what. With this tape, he can twist the Dickhead's nuts whenever he wants.

He waves the envelope in front of Reverend Dickhead's nose. "What's this?" he asks. "Six fuckin' grand? And where's the poison? You can do better than this, Joey." He closes in, smiles wide, and watches the Rev turn his head away. "I'll tell you what…" His mouth's just six inches from the Dickhead's cheek, and he's spitting the words. "Take the DVD. Watch it a coupla times. Then tell me what the other copies I got are fuckin' worth."

The Dickhead turns and glares at him. He's sweating bullets, and his face is all red. The hatred's obvious, but there's fear, too. The famous TV preacher is afraid of Mr. Gary Babington Smith. And he still can't get no words out.

"You're gonna do exactly like I tell…" Smith begins.

Suddenly, the Rev lunges forward, grabbing Smith by the neck with both hands. Those big fuckin' hands are choking the living shit out of him. It's like a vice is squeezing his neck. The warehouse, the sky, the world's turning. As everything starts going gray, he tries to knee the fucker in the balls. But his other knee fuckin' gives out, and he topples sideways, hitting the blacktop hard, the Rev still half on top of him. The Rev's just as stunned as he is, and he wiggles out from under the hulk. And then the Dickhead's ripping at his pants. No, he's going for the Luger. And he's got it.

"You…You'll rot in hell!" the Rev screams in his face. "Rot in hell!"

They're both on their knees now, facing each other, the world still half-spinning around them. The Rev's pointing the Luger at him, yanking the trigger again and again. Not getting it that there's no clip. As the Rev climbs to his feet, Smith stands, too, not putting much weight on his gimpy leg. They're still facing each other, and the Rev's still fuckin' pulling the trigger. His face is all screwed up like he's blowing his lid.

The Rev throws the Luger at him, missing his head by an inch. And then the Dickhead's lurching back to the Cadillac. Swinging the door open, fumbling under the seat for something. Another fuckin' gun!

Smith takes off for the Buick, running like fuckin' Chester. As he hears the first shot, he dives behind the Buick, scraping the shit out of his belly. There's three more shots, one of them clanging into the side of the Buick. Staying low, he opens the driver's door and crawls in. Two more shots. The fuckin' window on the other side shatters, spraying glass. He turns the key that's already in the ignition, and, still keeping his head down, rips the shift into drive. Panting hard, he sits up and floors it. The door he left open slams shut against his side. He looks back where the Rev stands by the Cadillac, the gun held at his side and both the accordion file and the envelope lying by his feet.

He turns and looks forward just before the Buick slams into the rear of some parked piece of shit camper-back pick up. Turning the wheel does no fuckin' good. "Shi...!" he screams, but it's drowned by the smashing of steel into steel full throttle. The camper-back slices through the windshield like some fuckin' razor from hell. And a fuckin' wad of white heat smears him.

74

ANDREW WRIGHT SLUMPS ONTO THE COUCH IN THE SHADE OF THE TENT cabana. He's wearing only his boxer briefs, and his bruised skin is damp with sweat. Fereshteh Raisani stands on the other side of the oval table wiping her forehead with the back of her hand. Her surgical scrubs, stained with sweat, cling to her. They sealed the concrete cabana with the canister inside, then disinfected and bagged the gloves and biohazard suits—but they can't do anything else. The bleedout and the corpses are too hot for them to even think about handling.

Outside, the water in the pool gleams, and the rows of chaise longues shine. Over the French torch singer's voice, Wright can hear the thwapping of a TV helicopter circling above the Strip. Some alarm's gone out, some information leaked, but the helicopter cameraman hasn't yet zoomed in on Paris as opposed to the other casino-hotels. Sirens blare, but they're distant, heading somewhere else. It's only a matter of time, though. The complete absence of people on the Paris pool deck should be enough to tip the helicopter crew.

A shadow passes the tent's entrance, and Benjamin Kupferberg steps in carrying two bottles of water. "The deal's done," he says, giving a bottle to each of them. "The LVPD'll be here any minute."

"You absolutely have to get a military decon team," Raisani says. "Immediately." Her eyes are both bright and bleary. "The police aren't equipped to…"

"I know," Kupferberg interrupts. He still looks neat and trim, but the skin around his eyes is becoming puffy. "You're sure the Virin's airborne?"

"No, not completely. But at least to some extent—in its undiluted state." She shakes her head. "Those men didn't touch it. They must have breathed the vapors when they unsealed the canister."

"And when it's diluted?" Kupferberg asks. His voice suggests a note of resignation—perhaps fatigue and fear, too—that surprises Wright. Knowing those two men bled out or, perhaps, the thought that he almost went to the rooftop with them seems to have sobered him, slowed him down a lot. He certainly knows now, just as Wright does, that the goddamned Virin isn't something his security teams can mess with.

"Diluted, it's probably not airborne." She brushes damp strands of hair from her face. "But the point is, we don't know. That's why we need the decon team right away. No one, and I mean *no one* else should go anywhere near that site. The police…"

"The wheels are in motion," Kupferberg says. "The LVPD won't move without the military. In the meantime, they'll keep a lid on news about what's happened." The police chief's a personal friend of his, and they spoke directly about both the LVPD response and military involvement.

"They'll never be able to," Wright says. "Not for long." He twists the cap off the water bottle and drinks deeply. His body's slipping though another trough of pain and weariness, but his mind's still clear. A cold shower or a dive in a pool—some *other* pool—would help. The staff here at Paris knows something has gone radically wrong. The cops' arrival will cause a local media swarm. And once the military intervenes, the network guys'll be goddamned flies on shit.

"We've found another canister," Kupferberg says. "At the Garden Arena. It's on your list."

Raisani sips her water and looks over at the concrete cabana.

"Good," Wright says. But that still leaves—what?—four or five more, at least one of which is horrendously lethal. And even the canisters with water in them might still be dangerous to anybody handling them.

Raisani hands Wright his shirt and pants. It's clearly too late to go ahead with Larson's plan to locate and exchange the rest of the Virin. But they've got to still somehow stop Wengelt. And Wright's flat out of ideas. The helicopter's rotors beat louder as it hovers lower, and he assumes they're finally focusing in on Paris.

"Andy," Kupferberg says, "Sergeant Carey keeps calling. You've got to contact him."

Wright glances at Raisani, who shakes out her dark cotton pants as though this part of the conversation has nothing to do with her.

"Right away," Kupferberg says. "Something about evidence they found in the canyon." He looks at his Rolex and smiles ironically. "Carey's actually threatening to haul me in if you're not at the station before one-thirty."

"You better get moving, then, Andy," Raisani says. Turning, she adds, "Will you excuse me, Mr. Kupferberg, while I change?"

Kupferberg looks at her for a moment, seeming to question whether he can trust her, before saying, "Of course, Dr. Raisani." He checks his watch again. "I've got to meet with Allan Imrem, the owner. I'll have the security people here escort you to the the executive offices when you're dressed."

"And you'll get me to the police station?" Wright asks. He stands to pull on his pants, but he still can't put much weight on his ankle— and he feels like he's doing some goddamned clown act that's bound to end in a pratfall.

"I've got a car and driver waiting," Kupferberg says as he turns toward the cabana's entrance.

When Kupferberg's gone, Raisani says, "Andy, the police will have figured out that you weren't alone in the canyon."

Nodding, he struggles to get his shirt on over his injured shoulder. That's not all the cops will have concluded by now, he suspects.

"They'll probably hold you." She pulls off her scrub shirt and wipes her sweating shoulders with it.

"Yeah." He's already thought of that, too. Without tucking in his shirt, he knots the jacket around his waist and then stoops to get his shoes and hat from beside the couch.

"We…Maggie still needs you to do things," Raisani says. "She's waiting for you at your hotel."

268

He glances up at her holding the damp scrub shirt in front of herself. "What..? What about the other canisters?"

"I'll work with Mr. Kupferberg. You won't do any of us any good in jail."

He stands and looks across the glimmering pool.

She raises her head and swabs her neck and chest. "Maggie and I," she says, "made tapes of Mr. Wengelt yelling at Mr. Smith on the telephone, admitting he ordered mass deaths by poison." She tosses the scrub shirt on the table.

"In so many words?" He tries to wedge his bare swollen foot into the shoe.

"Almost, yes." She unties her pants' drawstring. "For the first time. Finally."

"Maggie's errands?"

"Yes. She'll explain. She should have met up with your TV crew by now. She is going to deliver one of the copies of the tape to the police." The bleariness is gone from her eyes, and the lilt's returning to her voice. "As soon as we leave the elevator, I'll ask whoever's waiting for us to take the duffel. That's your signal to go."

"Fereshteh..." he begins, "I..."

"That's the plan, Andy," she says, her voice firm.

75

When Joseph Wengelt drives up to the front gate of the Divine Eagle Institute, the guardians are not on duty—an egregious breach of security that exacerbates the storm in his head. Though none of the shots struck home, unloading the Colt at that bastard Smith had an oddly calming effect—but the storm has returned. He did not wait to see if Smith survived the crash and fire. It was just like the imbecile to drive headlong into a parked pickup truck. And it was exactly what the barbarian deserved for making those diabolic demands on the Prophet and for treating him with such a total lack of respect. Yes, the bastard received his just desserts. And the Prophet was able to absent himself from the scene before any police vehicles arrived.

Honking the Caddy's horn repeatedly, he stares down at the DVD he removed from the accordion file. The bastard was so impudent about it that there must be something truly damning. More importantly, who was the Judas? Who among his flock betrayed him so infernally? And, how? Why? They are believers, one and all. Every one heeds his word. They all fear the Lord's Will. Only Michael would have both the technological skills and the audacity to install a camera. And Michael would never...But where the hell is Michael? He still hasn't contacted the Prophet, not since he barged into the Prophet's quarters, parading his body before Christine and flaunting his arrogance before the Prophet. Just how much does Michael, in his pride, still fear the Lord?

Leaving the engine and the air-conditioning running, he climbs from the Caddy. The mid-afternoon heat and light blast him so quickly he can't for a moment breathe. The Caddy's exterior is too hot even to touch, so he leaves the door open. The steel gate is also broiling, but he presses against it and strains for the keypad. Even with his long wingspan, it's too far. He and Michael did too good a job of making sure that an intruder, even with the code, could not open the gate. But this lack of guardians is inexcusable, absolutely inexcusable. In fact, this whole situation is intolerable. Someone will pay for this transgression. Someone will pay dearly.

His head thunders louder as he stomps back to the Caddy. Inside, he takes a single deep breath, shifts into reverse, floors it, slams the brakes, flings the gearshift into drive, and floors it again. The gates fly open more easily than he expected, shattering only one head-light and leaving the hood barely scratched. Fury flooding through him, he keeps the pedal hard to the metal all the way up the winding driveway until he's twenty-five yards from his front door, and then he slams the brakes again and spins the steering wheel. The Caddy fishtails against the wide front step, rocks twice, and stalls. Despite the screech of tires and the clang of metal against stone, there's still no sign of anybody. He could set off a bomb, and nobody, it seems, would check what's going on. There will be hell to pay.

He gets out of the Caddy, stalks to the front door, and throws it open. No one is in the Commons, and the rest of the house is eerily quiet. Only a few hours ago he had to retreat to his Sanctuary to find silence, and now it reigns in the house. He still sees no one as he marches to his quarters. He seldom takes medication, doesn't believe in it—one must trust in the Lord in all things! But he needs to do something about the storm, and he remembers that Christine keeps pain relievers in the medicine cabinet in his private bath. He'll get those first and then proceed to the cloister to make some heads roll.

As he passes through his bedroom, which is cool and dark with the blinds pulled, he drops the DVD and envelope on the wild stallion bedspread. He switches on the light, turns on the sink's faucet so that the water will run cool, and opens the mirrored medicine cabinet. As he reaches for the plastic bottle of Anacin, he hears a sniffling coming from the shower stall. Turning, he slides the translucent shower door aside.

Christine sits against the wall in a long plain white frock. She is hugging her knees pulled up against her rounded stomach. Her hair is tangled, and her face is buried in her breasts. Crying softly, she does not look up.

"Christine, my child," he says. "What in the name…?"

She curls herself tighter and shakes her head but still does not look at him.

Stooping, he says more sternly, "Christine, it's me, your Prophet."

"No," she murmurs. "No…no…no."

"Christine!" His voice booms in the confines of the bathroom.

She turns her head toward him but does not stop whimpering. Her eyes are welling, and her cheeks are damp with tears. "Prophet," she mumbles, "the refec…" She breaks into a series of sobs, gasping for air like an infant.

He doesn't really have time for her pathetic crying…over what? Some slight during the mid-day meal? Some unkind reference concerning her special status or her pregnancy? He has more important matters to tend to—finding out why the gate wasn't manned, watching that philistine's disc, locating Michael, checking on the Day of the Lord deployment…"Christine," he says, "You must…" Her breasts are heaving with each choking sob. "Here, I'll get you some water." He dips the plastic cup under the faucet and fills it half way. He's meticulous, and not a single drop spills.

She goes on shaking her head, unable to catch her breath enough even to form a sentence. "The…Prophet, I…" she sputters. "The… refectory…"

"Drink this!" he says.

She wobbles to her feet and reaches a quavering hand for the cup —then recoils.

"Take it," His tone is grave. "Now!"

"No!" she shrieks, her tears streaming.

Focusing on Christine has caused the storm to abate some, but he has no time for this frantic insubordination. He must get on to the other, more important, matters. He puts down the cup, turns off the spigot, and takes the Anacin bottle from the medicine cabinet.

"Don't!" She seizes the cup and hurls it into the shower stall, where it rattles against the tiles and spins toward the drain.

He raises his free hand to strike her, but the look in her eyes stops him.

She stares at him with an intensity he has never before witnessed in her. "The refectory!" she screeches, balling her fists. "They're…" She shudders as though she is possessed.

The storm roars anew. He drops the Anacin bottle, grasps her shoulders, and shakes her hard.

Her eyes roll. "Blood," she moans. "Everywhere."

When he loosens his grip, she hunches forward, opens her hands, and gapes at her palms. Her chest heaves. "Blood…blood…blood…" she mutters. Her head twists as though the devil has her by the throat. "Death," she murmurs. "Hell."

He flings her down, and she crashes hard onto the floor. Clutching her stomach and keening, she gnaws her lower lip and stares up at him. Blood stains her front teeth.

And then the lightning flashes. The storm rages as never before, a single word thundering in his chest. "Virin!" he bellows. "Oh, my Lord!" He throws himself back against a ceramic towel rack, shattering it. "My Lord!" He lifts his arms to heaven. "My Lord! My Lord!"

He lowers his arms, claws at his temples, stares between his hands at her squirming on the floor. The roar rolling from his throat is beyond words, a wailing for the Lord…to the Lord…at the Lord… *against* the Lord. He takes a step toward her, then stumbles backward out of the bathroom.

He careens blindly down the hallway, fumbling with his keys, finally reaching the Sanctuary's doorway. Tumbling inside, he collapses into the chair and covers his face despite the chapel's darkness. The storm spins, a twister now, a tornado. He must think, but he can see only the seven canisters of Virin at the eye of the storm.

He presses his fingertips against his eyelids, wanting to rip out his eyes. Is Michael Judas? Has Michael sacrificed the Divine Eagle Institute's faithful? Beautiful Michael. Damnable Michael! That's what

Christine was trying to tell him. She was spared so she could deliver the message. If she had not been curled there in the shower, the Prophet would have swallowed that water, suffered that unthinkable fate. How can this be the Lord's Will? It cannot be. No, it is Lucifer's work. Michael, the Prophet's archangel, his favorite, has forsaken the Lord to become Lucifer's disciple—a heinous betrayal. Worse, the Prophet blessed Michael's mission. There is no way to stop him now. No way in hell.

He cannot bear even to look up into the darkness. Yet he must go to the refectory, witness whatever atrocity has occurred there. It robbed Christine of speech, but he must confront it. How can the Lord permit this? Why is the Lord so absolutely silent now?

But no voice speaks, no answer comes. There is only the raging storm, darkness lit intermittently by flashes, a gale blowing across desolate territory. He staggers to his feet and swings his arm in the darkness until his wrist catches the golden chain. Grasping it tightly, he yanks with all his might.

76

MAGGIE MCNAMARA NUDGES ANDREW WRIGHT ON THE SHOULDER, waking him from a dream of battlefield carnage. He was huddled in a shallow foxhole, head low, the dark sky lit intermittently by exploding canisters of deadly yellow gas. Star-shells burst occasionally as well, revealing a tortuous maze of trenches and fortifications. Bloated, rotting corpses lay everywhere, and hulking rats infested each trench. He pressed his gas mask hard against his face, but the gas swirled around him, seeping into his pores.

"Right, Boss?" Miguel Ramirez yells from the van's front seat.

Wright starts. He has no idea whether he has been asleep for ten seconds or ten minutes. The desert seems tinged with yellow.

Maggie runs her fingers lightly along Wright's forearm. Just before they crept away from The Tahitian in the van, she'd talked with Fereshteh Raisani. Two more canisters had been located, one at Mirage and one at Caesars Palace. Both were inert. Only one inert canister remains, but one or two lethal ones are still out there somewhere.

Wright is coughing and sweating; his heart's racing. The last thing he remembers is watching three burros rummaging on the open range after Arnuz Jones turned the van onto West Canyon Road. They'd all been riding in strained silence, Arnuz and Miguel sullen, barely holding back their anger. Now the van's passing low scrub pines as it rumbles up hill, and there's some answer Miguel expects.

"God-fuckin'-damnit!" Arnuz shouts over his shoulder. "It's got to be that dude!"

Maggie's eyes are wide as she looks at Wright.

"What?" he asks.

Just as the red and white Divine Eagle Institute's warning sign comes into view, Arnuz slams on the brakes. Miguel straight-arms the dashboard, and Maggie and Wright lunge against their seat belts.

Maggie still somehow holds Wright's gaze. "The story on the radio," she says. "That guy in the car crash, he's been identified as Gary Smith." She adjusts the strap of the large, loosely woven green shoulder bag she has in her lap.

As the dream fades, Wright's mind begins to clear. They're on their way back to Larson's cave to retrieve the BluRay Disc with the video they shot of the DEI compound. They didn't all *have* to come, but Maggie insisted. In less than three hours, she's going to have a piece —nothing like *The Wright Stuff*—on Wengelt and his goddamned homicidal plan ready to air. She wanted the whole crew involved in every step. It's what they do best, and, as she said to Wright at the hotel, it's all they *can* do now. But neither of the guys looks too goddamned happy about it at the moment.

Arnuz glances at Miguel and then stares into the rearview mirror. His eyes are screaming, *Mutiny!* "We ain't movin' one fuckin' foot farther," he says, "until one of ya tells us what the fuck's goin' down here!"

Miguel turns, loops his muscular arm over the the seat, and glares at Wright. "You been dickin' us around for two days, Boss!" he shouts. "You keep disappearing and getting the shit kicked outa you. Then you leave us in the middle of a fuckin' shoot, and we take all kinds of shit from New York! I mean, the full fuckin' brown helmet, Boss!"

"Damn straight," Arnuz yells, cheering the cameraman on.

"And Tank keeps disappearing, too," Miguel shouts. "Leavin' us hangin'. And we had to send in that whole disaster story ourselves. And, naturally, we get more shit from New York. Even though we gave 'em some quality fuckin' footage of that house all blown to hell!"

"Ya got that right!" Arnuz yells.

"Then this morning there's a shootin' out in this canyon. Somebody's trying to off some mystery dude nobody's ever even fuckin' seen before." Miguel's getting so worked up he's beginning to spit the words. "But who finds the dude? Whose fuckin' face gets plastered all over the tube? On fuckin' NBC geezer news, no less! Andy fuckin' Wright Stuff, our boss! Imagine the shit we're in! It's like all those suits are screaming, *Coffee break's over, now kneel in it, suckers!*"

"It's not fuckin' fair," Arnuz says, his voice calmer, but the resentment even deeper.

"Then Tank shows up," Miguel keeps shouting, "with some fuckin' DVD that's more important than our jobs. And just when she's finally gonna show it to us so we at last get a clue about what's happening, you bust in on us like there's a fuckin' posse or something after you." He's slapping the back of the goddamned seat now, really rolling. "And we gotta hustle our asses the hell outa town to get some disc that you dumped in the fuckin' desert in the first place." He wipes his mouth with the back of his hand. "Okay, we're a fuckin' team. Or was! But now this same dirtbag you wigged out over yesterday when his house blew up rams his beater into a parked truck or something, practically killing hisself." He slams the dashboard with his other hand. "And now we're hearing reports of bullet holes in the side of his car! Two fuckin' shootin's in the same morning, and we're the only ones that know what the fuckin' connection is. Our fuckin' boss!"

"What the fuck are ya makin' us accessories to, huh, Andy?" Arnuz asks, his voice cold.

Wright stares out the front window of the van at the warning sign. This is the third day he's seen it, and he's blown right by it every time. Or, maybe, he saw it years ago, has always seen it, every day, this same sign in that same life he's left behind but keeps flashing back to. He takes a deep breath and exhales. Not upset or even disconcerted by the sign or the flashbacks or his friends' anger, he glances at Maggie. He has no idea why Smith crashed or why there were bullet holes in the car, but he suspects she knows. Turning, he looks first at Miguel and then at Arnuz. "Joseph Wengelt," he says, "is attempting to murder tens of thousands of people on the Strip. He's targeting the fight crowd and tourists at the hotels. I fell onto the lunatic's scheme by chance. I've been trying to stop him. Maggie has been, too."

Miguel and Arnuz look at each other for a second.

"*You?*" Arnuz says to Wright. "What the fuck?"

"You're a talkin' head, Boss!" Miguel shouts. "Not some goddamn Rambo fuckin' cowboy!"

Maggie unclips her seatbelt and leans forward. "The DVD I was going to show you," she says to the guys in the front seat, "presents the first hard evidence we've got that Wengelt's planning to poison people."

"The poison," Wright says, "is the most lethal ever made." He's not absolutely certain that's true, but it sure as hell seems like it. The image of the Paris manager wavers before him like some hideous Power Point slide. "Two guys died—horribly—from it on the Strip this morning. I was at the scene." He turns to Maggie. "As far as I could tell, they didn't even touch it. Just sniffed it."

Arnuz looks at Wright in the rearview mirror before turning to Maggie. "You at least got some sense, Tank," he says. "Why didn't ya just go to the cops?"

Maggie stares into Wright's eyes for a moment and then leans again toward Arnuz and Miguel. "A courier's delivering a copy of that DVD to the LVPD as we speak. Then, we're breaking the story. And you know New York's going to want all the footage, all that other Wengelt video ASAP."

"Gary Smith," Wright says, "worked for Wengelt."

"The video," she says, "is of Wengelt talking to Smith on the phone, yelling at him about what they're planning to do, all the people, particularly minorities, they're going to murder."

As she speaks, Wright suddenly understands the pattern. He needs to see that surveillance tape, to hear exactly what Wengelt actually said, but he already gets what was in Wengelt's and Grant's and Smith's minds as they planned the Day of the Lord. They all have different agendas, different shit they think they're going to prove to the world, but racial hatred is the goddamned glue, the common bond. And they'd have had no goddamned problem agreeing to target foreigners and minorities.

His elbow propped on the seat, Miguel nods as though all of Wright's behavior is finally starting to make sense, but Arnuz turns and stares at Wright. "We got to know, Andy," he says. "Did ya do all that shit to that dude?"

Wright meets Arnuz's gaze. "I started the fire yesterday, but I didn't…"

"I gave Smith a copy of the surveillance tape," Maggie interrupts, "before he was to meet with Wengelt this morning. They must've gotten into a fight over it or…"

Arnuz looks at her. "Tank," he begins, "you was…" Then he stops and shakes his head.

No one in the van says anything for a minute. Maggie scratches the polish off her thumbnail. Wright gazes at her, aware that she must have known that Smith and Wengelt would double-cross each other over the tape or that they'd try to take each other out. Miguel nods slowly, and Arnuz looks out the driver's side window at the large rectangular mirror with the circular mirror inside it.

Finally, Miguel says, "Shit, Boss, those firemen…You…There's no fuckin' way out for you."

"Ya in too deep," Arnuz says to the mirror.

"Yeah," Wright answers, "I know that. But you guys aren't. All I need you to do is wait while we get the BluRay. You'll just pick up the disc and go. That's it." And it is, except that he's not entirely clear on what he'll do after that.

77

ANDREW WRIGHT FOLLOWS MAGGIE MCNAMARA THROUGH THE BARRIER of clear plastic strips into Larson's cave. They left Arnuz and Miguel in the van by the fork in the road and hiked through the desert up to the cave. He's not sure he could've found the place on his own, but she scrambled right to it along a rocky route that would be difficult, if not impossible, to trace. He hobbled after her, his body aching, and let her help him over the most treacherous terrain. Sweating after the climb, he's chilled by the cave's coolness.

Maggie goes immediately to the console and begins sorting through the discs stacked on the shelf above the bank of video monitors. Wright takes off his hat, tucks it in his back pocket, and flips through the manila folders until he finds the one with the photograph of Michael Grant. Grant's not his real name, and neither the police nor anybody else knows what the guy looks like. Providing a picture is something he should've done earlier, goddamn it.

As he slides the photo back into the folder, Maggie says, "Uh, oh." She fiddles with one of the monitor's controls. "Shit! What the hell are those guys thinking?"

He rubs his burning eyes, rests his free hand on her shoulder, and looks at the monitor. The white van stands in front of the open gates of the Divine Eagle Institute. "Goddamn it," he mutters. "They... Have you seen them?"

"No. Just the van."

Both Maggie and Wright lean closer to the screen. The van is clearly in view of the DEI security camera, but there's no sign of Arnuz or Miguel or anybody else. The gates are thrown wide open, and the one on the right looks like its bent. Wright lifts his hand from her shoulder, sinks into the armchair, and scans all of the monitors. There's no goddamned movement on any of the screens. None whatsoever. No Arnuz and Miguel. In fact, it seems like nobody's home. It isn't meal-time, but they must all be in the goddamned refectory, which isn't on any of the monitors.

"Do you think Wengelt's got the guys?" she asks.

Drumming his fingers on the console, he squints at the monitor showing the van and the gates, but he can't find any marks on the pavement or in the nearby dirt. No signs of a struggle at all. "I don't know," he answers. "Doesn't look like it."

"Why would Arn…?" She leans across him and taps the monitor of Wengelt's goddamned Grotto. "Andy, look at this!"

He sees the red altar cloth on which the canisters stood but does not, at first, notice what she's pointing to. Then, there it is, the image of a boot just to the left of the altar—a cowboy boot. And it's moving, the toe digging into the dirt.

"What the…?" Maggie says.

He glances at the other screens, but there's no movement anywhere.

"Something's wrong!" she says.

As she stuffs the disc into her shoulder bag, he looks back at the monitor of the cavern.

"Andy!" she exclaims. "Come on!"

He grabs her arm as she turns. She wrenches free and yells, "Andy!"

But he's staring, riveted, at the screen. Dirty and disheveled, Reverend Joseph Wengelt crawls on all fours around the corner of the altar. The ends of Wengelt's bolo hang below his chin as he swings his head at an angle like a horse before a race. His filthy hair is matted, his shirt caked with grime. Something's wrapped around his fist and dragging in the dirt—a length of glinting chain attached to the gold T that hung in his chapel, his sanctum sanctorum. His mouth moves as though he's chanting.

"Sound," she says as she reaches for the monitor's control panel.

Wengelt's not speaking so much as mewing. He casts the cross ahead of him like an anchor, flops onto his stomach, stretches out his arms, digs his toes into the earth, and moans, "Or…Or…Or…Or…"

78

ANDREW WRIGHT IS PANTING BY THE TIME HE REACHES THE ROAD TO THE DEI compound. Stopping to catch his breath, he removes his hat, wipes his face with his forearm, and slips the hat back on. Maggie stuck with him most of the way, but in the last quarter mile she jogged ahead, the .45 pulled from her shoulder bag. He's still not sure she'll use it, but he was reminded again that she seems to know how.

He hobbles up the road toward the van that shimmers in the heat rising in waves from the point at which DEI's blacktop drive-way begins. The image of the dead men in the cabana clashes with that of Reverend Joe thrashing in the dirt. What was the guy saying —*Lord, Lord, Lord,* or what?

As he approaches the back of the van, he can hear something— a murmuring or rustling, he's not sure—but he can't see anyone, not even Maggie. Only when he angles cautiously out to the side does he glimpse Miguel slumped by the open gate on his knees, his head low and a hand clutching one of the gate's wrought iron bars. Wright gasps—Miguel's bleeding out! No, he's puking—the dry heaves, nothing coming up anymore, no blood and no spasms. His Sony lies against the bottom of the gate as though he'd dropped it.

His hands on his knees, Arnuz hunches over on the van's front fender. Maggie has one arm around his shoulder; with her other hand, she strokes his head like a mother comforting a sick child— this petite woman offering solace to this tall man. Her shoulder bag rests at their feet. She turns, her green eyes brimming, glisten-ing in the sunshine—but she doesn't say anything.

Arnuz stands, pulls away from her a little, and says, "They all dead, Andy." His voice is choked. "Their innards exploded."

Wright takes a step back and gazes through the gates, seeing nothing but blank sky and the shining black road winding into the trees. "Who?" he asks.

Maggie sucks in her breath. "All of them, apparently. The whole cult."

Miguel clings to the iron bar, still retching, trying to pull himself up with both hands.

Arnuz stares wide-eyed at Wright. "They locked in the cafeteria, Andy. A couple of them're hangin' out the broken windows. It's like their insides blew up."

Jesus Christ, Wright thinks. Did Wengelt sacrifice his goddamned congregation to his Lord? "The dining hall?" he asks.

Arnuz nods.

Or, Wright wonders, did Wengelt return from his meeting with Smith to discover what Arnuz and Miguel have found? It's more likely Grant did it. Used the eighth canister, the one Wengelt didn't even know about. That would explain Wengelt's hegira to the cave. Wright limps over to Miguel, cups his hand under the cameraman's thick arm, and helps him to his feet.

Miguel's chest heaves. "Don't go in there, Boss," he mumbles. "It's the worst...*infierno.*" He leans over and gags.

Wright picks up the Sony and takes Miguel by the elbow. "We need to get you guys out of here fast," he says as he returns to the others.

Maggie lifts her bag and loops the strap over her shoulder.

"Andy," Arnuz says, "we was goin' to shoot footage of the front gate for ya. Then we saw it open...no guards nowhere. We thought maybe we could sneak in. Get some *Wright Stuff* while we waited for ya." He clears his throat. "I ain't never seen nothin' that bad. Not ever. We didn't shoot nothin'."

"Can you drive?" Wright asks him.

"Yeah," Arnuz answers. "Just give me 'nother minute."

"Miguel?" Wright asks. "You...?"

"I'll be okay," he says, reaching for the camera. "I just...It's like... I don't fuckin' know...Like Heavens Gate, maybe. Except it don't look like these dudes had a clue what was gonna happen."

"What about you, Andy?" Maggie asks.

"You guys get going," he says. "The quicker, the better." He hands her the sweat-stained folder containing Grant's photo.

She takes the folder, nods, and looks into his eyes. "What about you?"

"I'm going to stay out here," he says. "For a while, anyway." By this time, he must officially be a fugitive from justice, and he doesn't want any of them seen with him in Vegas. There's also business here he's going to finish. He's not exactly sure what he'll do, but he's already weighing things that both Larson and Wengelt said to him.

79

After the van has backed up and pulled away, Andrew Wright stands off to the side of the road watching it shrivel in the glimmering heat. When he's sure the van's gone, he turns and walks through the gates into the Divine Eagle Institute. His saliva's gummy, but he knows he won't drink any water here. As he hobbles up the road to the ranch house, he keeps picturing Reverend Joe crawling around that altar at the goddamned Grotto. He's aware that he can't kill the man; premeditated murder's just not in him. But neither can he leave Wengelt to the ponderous American justice system. Copping an insanity plea would be almost too easy for the guy, as would keeping the case bogged down in the system until he died a natural death. Justice for what Wengelt planned, for what still may be carried out in his name, will never be served.

The heat blankets Wright, and the scent of pine lingers in the air. Reverend Joe's Cadillac stands hard against the ranch house's front stoop—more evidence that the preacher had no foreknowledge of his congregation's fate. Skid marks mar the pavement, forming a pair of distorted question marks where the car fishtailed to a stop. The thick oak front door is ajar, but Wright doesn't enter the goddamned house. He's far too wary of the Virin to spend any time in the compound's air-conditioned buildings. As he's already seen, merely breathing the poison's vapors may be enough. He skirts the ranch house and stops by the chapel, squinting up into the vast light. The white T rises like a chalky rune against the sky. Feeling a compelling duty to bear witness, he chooses a path up into the trees so that he can circle the refectory. He needs to be close enough to see clearly but far enough away that he won't be contaminated. There's not even enough breeze to tell which direction is upwind.

The devastation is stunning—far more horrible than what he's already witnessed. But the two corpses in the cabana have prepared him at least a little. He's not at all immune—the flies are already feasting on the gore, and the grotesque bodies and contorted faces of the DEI devotees impaled on the broken windows cause him to fall to one knee and bow his head. Like Maggie, he feels his eyes brimming. Like Miguel, he feels himself needing to heave out the evil. Like Arnuz, he feels himself almost inarticulate in the presence of the horror here. He hasn't prayed much in recent years, but he finds himself murmuring not to Wengelt's righteous and vindictive Lord but to some Being beyond time and place. He begs forgiveness for his species' arrogance and self-destructiveness. What is it in us, he asks, that would cause us to synthesize Virin, to take that innate need we have to create and twist it into something so deadly?

And finally, after a few minutes or an eternity—he has no sense of time—he's thankful, despite the horror he's witnessing, for this his life. Thankful, despite the terror we have so often inflicted on ourselves in so many times and so many places, for this gift of life. Thankful even that he can ask the dreadful questions that plague him now. Thankful, ultimately, even in this moment as he raises his head and gazes at the carnage before him, that life is so infinitely precious.

80

ANDREW WRIGHT CUPS HIS HANDS AROUND HIS EYES SO THAT HE CAN SEE into the window of Reverend Joe's herpetology lab. The snakes are still, but when he hammers on the window frame there's enough movement in the cages to tell him the Virin has not permeated the lab or that the snakes are impervious to it. At first, he thought of taking a couple of the cages, returning to the outcropping with the petroglyph, and loosing the rattlesnakes down that shaft. With their heat receptors, the snakes just might find their way to the only warm-blooded creature in the lighted cavern below.

But that idea is neither practical nor right. He's not going to expend his remaining energy toting snakes into the canyon. And anyway, some of the evidence technicians and other investigators might still be there scouring the area for clues. On another level, he's no avenging angel. Even when he gives himself up later, he will not mention Reverend Joe's hideout. His will be a sin of omission, not commission. He will leave Wengelt to himself in that cavern, let the serpents in the preacher's mind continue to slither over him. He suspects that at this point, given the man's writhing and sniveling, there's no escape for Wengelt unless someone saves him, brings him to justice. And this is something Wright won't do, either.

He does not look again at the refectory as he makes his way back through the trees toward the house. When he passes by the semi-circular stone church, he glances once more at the white *crux commissa* jutting into the sky. He remembers glimpsing the cross when he first saw the compound, but he can't recall what he felt or thought driving the Hummer up that rutted track. As he crosses the patio behind the house, he's arrested by a white heap in the shadow by the sliding glass door. He squints at the form on the flagstones—a woman in a white gown turned away and curled into a fetal ball. When he circles closer, he sees that she's breathing, the gown's white cloth rising and falling in quick strokes. She's young and blonde, and her hair's cut short. She's sobbing fitfully—and she seems to have no awareness whatever that he's approaching her.

He stoops and kneels beside her. She's pregnant, well along, maybe starting her third trimester. She could be the woman he caught sight of before his aborted interview with Reverend Joe, but he's not sure. When he touches her shoulder, she flinches and balls herself tighter.

"It's all right," he says, though he knows it's not. He has no idea what else to say, and so he repeats, "It's all right."

"No," she murmurs. "No…no…no." Her voice is small, more a child's than an adult's.

"I'll get you out of here," he says. He can't leave her, but he doubts he'd be able to carry her. When he tries to pull her up by her shoulders, she yelps and yanks her knees and elbows closer.

"It's hell," she whispers. "Hell."

As he glances over his shoulder at the cross, his breath quickens, almost as though he's trying to keep up with her. "It'll be okay," he says softly, but his words are empty. This time, though, when he slides his hand beneath her shoulder, she stiffens but doesn't recoil. As he turns her toward him, he cringes. Blood stains her gown where she'd tucked it between her legs. She's not bleeding out, but she's definitely bleeding. *Shit,* he thinks, but catches himself, continues to turn her, and says, "We'll find help." He has no phone; he left it on the van's seat when he and Maggie set out for Larson's cave. "We'll get help."

Grit lines her temple where her head lay against the flagstone. She's still rigid, but she allows him to rest her head against his knee. Dried blood cakes her lower lip, and her breath is fetid. "Hell," she repeats. "Hell."

When she opens her eyes, he starts. He's seen those pale gray eyes before. They're dry and swollen from weeping, but their color's unmistakable. "Christine?" he says before he thinks.

She turns her head and looks at him, but she doesn't stop sobbing.

"Christine," he says as he brushes the grit from her forehead.

"Hell," she chokes.

"Christine," he says, "we've got to get you to…We need a doctor." With that last word, he understands what to do, how to make this work. "Christine," he says, holding her chin so that their eyes lock, "your father needs you."

"My…"

"Yes," he says, nodding as though what he's saying would be obvious to anyone, "your father. He's waiting for you. I'll take you to him."

They hobble together toward the garage. He limps, and she drags along, most of her weight against him. Her eyes are half closed, and her breathing's a little deeper, a little more regular. He selects from among the Jeeps parked in the open bays the green Cherokee with tinted windows that Grant used to meet the video crew at the compound's gate. The keys are in the ignition, and the gas tank's full.

Helping her up into the back seat, he says, "Lie down, Christine. Rest. I'll take you to your father."

As he's about to close the door, a massive young man, a goddamned behemoth with broad shoulders and short hair, steps out from around the side of the garage. Raising a crowbar in his grimy hand, the guy lumbers toward the Cherokee.

"Don't!" Wright says. Sweat and grease stain the guy's T-shirt. His arms look like logs. "Don't do it."

The behemoth stops four feet from Wright but doesn't lower the crowbar. His eyes are glazed, and his lips quiver.

His voice soft, Wright says, "She needs help. Immediately. I'm taking her to a doctor."

The behemoth glares at him, the crowbar swaying.

"Grant. Michael Grant did that to your sisters and brothers."

The crowbar rises higher against the sky, but it doesn't come crashing down.

Wright turns, shuts the back door, opens the driver's door, and climbs into the Cherokee. He starts the engine, flips the air conditioner's fan to its highest setting, rolls down the window, and shuts the door. "It wasn't Satan," he says to the dumfounded lout. "It was a man. Grant."

81

Michael Grant checks his watch as he saunters through The Tahitian's lobby. He's back in his George Grisham oil and cattle baron mode, looking good but not conspicuous in his ostrich-skin boots, starched jeans, Western shirt, reflective Raybans, and white Stetson. Though he's confident he won't be recognized, he's still feeling some stress. It isn't the afternoon's operation at the Institute that's bothering him. The results there were predictable. The actual panic, once the subjects started to bleed out, was more frantic than he expected —but the timing from the sprinklers starting to the first casualties was well within anticipated parameters.

No, it's the radio news that's jarring. Most of what he heard while parking the Suburban was good—the shit still haven't found his Wrangler, the pretty boy reporter is now the one wanted for questioning in the canyon shooting, and Gary Smith, who bashed his bullet-riddled beater into some parked car, lies unconscious in the UMC ICU. He doesn't know what that fat-assed fuck-up was doing at the warehouse, but the accident is, conveniently, tying up a loose end for him. All that plus the jacked-up, jerk-off fight crowd along with the usual Sin City stupidity will keep the LVPD's attention from him, all right.

But there was also something on the news about the Paris Hotel's swimming pool being shut down because of a fatal but not yet explained accident. Heavy LVPD presence at the site. He'd cased that pool carefully over the last month, and the cabanas are cleaned each morning before eight AM. Using a chunk of the DEI funds earmarked for the Day of the Lord project, he'd rented a Paris suite, the fucking *Suite LeMans,* and the cabana for three days. All done through a dummy corporation so there'd be no way to trace it to DEI, much less to him. And nobody had any business fucking around in that cabana after 8:15 when he set up the cache. It might be just a coincidence. But he doesn't trust coincidences. If the Paris canister has been discovered, the plan will still work because it's not dependent on any single trap and because the SHIT are always too slow to react and deploy their assets. But it will throw off his schedule for springing his traps all along the line. And it'll likely put some of the other targets on the alert. As a matter of fact, it did seem like security was beefed up at The Tahitian's garage entrance. He marched right by, of course, tipping his Stetson and saying, *Howdie*.

Timing is everything—preparation and timing—and he's got both down. He's eighteen minutes ahead of his revised schedule—time enough to head to George Grisham's *fare* out there on stilts all by itself in that lagoon that's off-limits to everybody but the filthiest rich. He could kick back for a few minutes in privacy and watch the WNTS News on the big screen TV. Or he could use the eighteen minutes to just sit in this lobby, visualize his movements along the trapline, smell the damn flowers blooming all over the place, and listen to the medley—the waterfall splashing, the slots chinging in the casino off to one side, and the constant chattering of all these morons hustling around here like their lives matter. But the news about Paris is problematic, and he needs to do additional reconnaissance.

This lobby looks like a fucking United Nations meeting, a melting pot—which is exactly what it's going to be. Not the lobby, actually. There's too many logistical issues here—all that dead air where the water tumbles six stories, too many exits, and SHIT everywhere. It's crowded all right, but not congested enough. He needs sardines, and the casino provides a much better can. Lower ceilings, few exits, video monitoring which does exactly didley-shit in a crisis, and crammed full of aliens and other losers. And the rubes definitely get disoriented, totally fucked up, once they're in the can with all the light and noise. They're just stew for the pot, that's all.

He didn't much enjoy his work at the Institute this afternoon; it was a necessary job, a preliminary sortie to ensure that the Op's a go.

But watching all these UN dweebs bleed out might be fun. He'll do exactly what the good book instructs—"have power over waters to turn them to blood." No more. And definitely no less.

He won't, he decides, remain here among the rabble. He'll cross over to Paris and see for himself what the situation is. He chose The Tahitian as his base because it's the *center* of the trapline. When he begins his work, he'll change yet again in the Suburban and head out on foot as Gabriel Granowski, tourist from Dubuque. He'll be moving light, circling his line, carrying nothing suspicious, just surgical gloves and a mask, a concealed Magnum, and a commando knife. Just an ordinary guy working the Strip like everybody else.

82

NICK LARSON SURFACES SLOWLY. HE CAN SEE LIGHT ABOVE HIM, BUT THE undertow keeps dragging him down into the darkness. Disaster is all he remembers. He knows he's hurt badly but feels no pain. And he should. Pain would help. He strokes again toward light but is towed into the depths.

Someone's there, urging him on. But who? He can hear her voice, a sweet, lilting voice, but he can't make out the words. The voice spurs him, and he almost reaches the surface. A room—well-lit, clean, safe, somewhere far from the undertow.

She can somehow reach him, touch him, grasp his hand. He can understand some of the words now, clear and then fading, clear again, and fading. A name, a beautiful and meaningful name, *Maya*.

"Please, Nick, for Maya. She needs...I need you."

Maya.

Yes, his daughter. His child. He breaks the surface fleetingly. Lights above him and the sound of machines—technology he helped to create. And then he sinks once more. His first child is still lost. His older daughter. He cannot save her.

His hand is held tight. Clasping, fingers meshed. Pulling him out. Saving him.

"Nick, my love. Maya needs you. I need you, my love."

He recognizes Fereshteh's voice. Energy flows down to him with the words. This time, he'll make it. He will...But there's a bell, a ringing. And her hand slips from his, the energy ebbing.

"Yes. Andy! What? Oh, no! At Reverend Wengelt's Institute? Oh, my God, no!"

No lilt. He's submerged but not plunging deeper. Her hand returns, clenching his, needing his now, too—clinging to him. But he will not drag her into the depths with him. He will rise to her.

"No! The entire cult? No! No one here knows yet. I...I'm with Nick."

He's here, on his back in a room with light and purring machines and Fereshteh.

"Christine? She is...? *With you!*"

Her hand squeezes his harder. He's out, away from the undertow, no longer yanked down.

"Yes...At my clinic? Good. Exactly the right idea...Best place... Bleeding? How much? I'll get an OB out there right away."

He's not yet able to open his eyes, but he's here. Not yet able to squeeze her hand, but directing all his will toward that simple act.

"Yes. In the ICU. Stable, but still critical. Not yet conscious."

He's thirsty, a metallic taste, his throat parched. Like a desert. Yes, like a desert. Images form behind his eyelids. He's been hit... His shoulder's torn...He's moving downstream...Doubling back... Climbing with the last of his strength. Climbing through pain. Yes, pain. Excruciating. His shoulder. He's alive. He's here with Fereshteh.

"Yes. Another one. An inert one at NewYorkNewYork. LVPD is taking over. Emergency military teams are flying in from Nellis. Deploying from Area 51. No. I don't..."

His fingers close around hers.

She gasps. A quick scraping—a chair moving. Her breath on his face. Her lips grazing his. But then she's lifting her head away from him. Speaking again.

"What? Yes, Andy. Kupferberg's still organizing internal searches. A pattern? You've found...Yes. But with the one at Wengelt's compound, we may have them all. True...Yes there could...Yes, Nick believed there were eight. Yes, an eighth...The Tahitian? Why The Tahitian?"

Wengelt...Virin...She's talking with the TV guy, Andrew Wright. Disaster has struck. Or, has it? They've found at least some of the canisters. But have others been used? Has the Virin been loosed upon the city? And what about Christine? Fereshteh mentioned her name. He needs to find out what's happening. Though he can do nothing, he needs at least to know.

"*Yes*, Kupferberg's angry! That police sergeant has been all over him."

His fingers are entwined with hers, as though they are grafted and will grow together.

"Kupferberg said he was going to hunt you down himself—as soon as…"

He wills himself to speak, the word forming deep inside him. "Fereshteh!" he says, more coughing than speaking.

Her lips touch his again. His eyes open to her gazing down at him. Her eyes are wide, tears sparkling, her pupils dark, dilated, the whites holding the world. Holding him. Her smile aglow.

83

STANDING AT THE PAY PHONE IN THE BACK CORNER OF THE RED SAPPHIRE Market and Sheriff's Office, Andrew Wright gazes up the aisle at the obese woman seated at the front counter who's pretending she's not looking at him as she flips through the pages of the *Midnight Sun*. She's wearing a paisley, tent-like sundress that hides far too little, and she's got her head cocked so she sees his every move. The back corner seems like an odd place for a public phone, but it's the farthest spot from the whir and clink of the old nickel slot machines. An elderly man and woman are up there now sitting next to each other, yanking the bandits' arms, and whooping whenever nickels spill out. Wright pulls his hat lower over his eyes, turns his back to the woman at the counter, drops his last three quarters into the slot, and calls Benjamin Kupferberg's personal number. Christine is safe at Raisani's clinic up the road, but this is not a call he could make from there.

When Kupferberg answers, Wright says, "Ben, I know where the canister is."

"Andy? Where the hell are you?" Kupferberg's voice flares.

"It doesn't matter. I know..."

"Fuck *it doesn't matter,* Andy!" The suave negotiator's gone, replaced by a pissed off liquor salesman. "Listen, you son of a bitch, Carey's got a warrant out on you. And if you're not at the station..." There's a brief pause. "...ten fucking minutes ago, he's pulling me in. The Chief says he can't interfere in an ongoing investigation. And, Andy, you cocksucker, I can't find the canisters if I'm spending all my time trying to explain where the fuck you are. Got that, asshole?"

"Red Sapphire," Wright says, glancing over his shoulder at the obese lady who's now staring blatantly in his direction. By now, the police must have reviewed Maggie's tape and made the connections among Reverend Joe's Institute, the shooting in Red Rock Canyon, the deaths at the Paris pool, and Smith's car crash. They should be well on their way to making their gruesome discovery at Wengelt's cafeteria. Still, Carey may not be in the loop yet—and it might not take the heat off even if he were. "I'm at a pay phone in Red Sapphire."

"Red Sapphire?" Kupferberg's voice suggests Bangkok would make more goddamned sense.

"Ben," Wright shouts into the phone, "listen to me." He lowers his voice again. "There's only one left. The eighth canister, the last one. It's at The Tahitian."

"Wh…what?" Kupferberg says.

"One of the canisters was used at Wengelt's compound out on West Canyon Road."

"Shit." Kupferberg sucks in his breath. "The people?"

"Dead. Almost all of them." Wright glances at *lisa licks Dicks* scribbled on the wall above the phone.

"That's…"

"Ben, you're sitting on the last canister. It's at The Tahitian."

"My people have been over this whole place." Anger's returning to Kupferberg's voice. "Twice, God fucking damn it!"

"It's there, Ben. Somewhere." Wright looks over his shoulder again. The obese woman's waddling along the aisle pretending like she's straightening cereal boxes, but she's really angling closer.

"Yeah? You gonna bet the whole fucking ranch on that?"

"Evacuate the hotel, Ben." Wright's calm certainty is scaring him almost as much as it's angering Kupferberg. "Get everybody out."

"I…we can't fucking do that, and you know it." Nothing smooth or glib is left in Kupferberg's voice. "I'd lose…It'd cause the whole fucking Strip to panic."

"It's there, Ben," he says. "At the Tahitian. Get every…"

"What makes you so fucking sure?" Kupferberg explodes. "I can't evacuate the whole fucking hotel on your fucking hunch!"

"Weng…They're targeting foreigners and minorities, Ben." Wright's tone is firm, like Raisani's when she knows she's right. "Tonight's fight. The canister at the arena." The woman's only eight feet away, shifting shampoo bottles. Her cheek is pink with powder, and the flaccid skin under her arm jiggles as she moves. "The other hotels…involved…all have significant…"

"But…"

"Ben, which property on the Strip is most *international*—has the highest percentage of minorities and foreigners?" Wright keeps his voice conversational, as though he's just doing a business deal. "Both as guests and investors?"

The phone is silent.

"Which property, Ben?" Wright asks again.

84

THE SERPENTS SWARM THE FLOOR AND WALLS. THEY SLITHER, SCORES OF them, in every direction. Joseph Wengelt loops the gold-link chain around his right hand. The chain and *crux commissa* will be his mace. He will strike at the serpents, smite them—but there are far too many for him alone. Forsaken here, without his favorite, fallen arch-angel and his vanished, silent Lord, he will fight one last, great battle. Satan's forces are aligned against him, hideous battalions, rank upon rank. He rises to his feet, takes the scarlet cloth from the altar, and wraps it around himself, girding his loins for battle.

The storm, incessant and unrelenting, flashes and roars above him, deafening him but not blinding him to the vast desolation and horror. Black clouds lower upon him, roll over him, driving him to his knees. The dirt all around him seethes with serpents. He swings the cross back and forth, striking them again and again. Those he severs multiply—eyeless beasts with fangs and flicking tongues. Sweat pours like blood from his brow as he thrashes the dreadful demons. His heart pounds with the exertion; his breath comes only in short gasps.

Shrieks pierce the unholy din. When he looks up, the clouds part. The Elders march toward him down a fiery ramp. They are naked, covered with blood, their eyes gory holes and their mouths aflame. They chant, but he cannot hear their words over the thunder and the screeching. As the Elders file past him, their facial features and appendages shrivel and char like burnt bacon.

Behind the Elders, Michael and Christine descend the ramp. His manhood engorged, Michael grips Christine by the arm, leading her though the inferno. Her breasts droop over her distended belly. The clouds close behind them, and the storm rages. Michael smirks, his teeth bared. Crimson tears fall from Christine's eyes. Michael seizes her by the neck with his right hand and cleaves her belly with his left. The world itself rends! Her mouth gapes—a shrill scream coming from some nether region within her. Michael rips out the bloody baby, a dark malformed monstrosity with cloven feet, jagged claws, and barbed fangs. Laughing diabolically, Michael extends his arms and offers this unholy malignancy to his Prophet.

"No!" Wengelt wails, pitching backward. Satan's Spawn, Michael's offspring, glares at him with flaming eyes. "No!" Tearing his way through the mass of serpents, he rolls over and buries his face in the earth by the altar. He inhales the russet, sandy dirt—inhales deeply. Chokes. Coughs. Gasps. Sand sticks to his skin and stings his eyes. The storm rages—thunderbolt upon thunderbolt. And the interminable roaring.

A chasm opens behind Michael and Christine—a fissure spewing fire. Flames roil. Sulfuric fumes rise, choking him worse. His lungs burn. He's trapped here with this fiendish Spawn and these snakes on this smoldering island. And Michael is stepping inexorably toward him bearing his unspeakable gift. The serpents wriggle before the Spawn in some rhythmic, horrific, worshipful rite. Still coughing and gasping, Wengelt cowers under the altar. He tries to swing the *crux commissa,* but the chain's caught in the crimson cloth. Michael stands over him, the Spawn's blood pouring forth, staining him. And then Michael genuflects, forcing his offering upon the Prophet.

He worms away behind the altar, pulls himself up, and, still gagging on the gritty earth, fumbles for the cross. Screaming "No!" a third time, he hurls the cross at Michael's execrable gift. The cross ignites in mid-air, flames furling back along the chain.

"Horror!" he moans again. "Horror...! Horror...!" Unable to breathe, he stumbles around the altar past the hideous child. The serpents sink their fangs into his heels and ankles. As he careens toward the Grotto's mouth, he trips and sprawls across the hellacious chasm. The lightning is infinite, the thunder omnipresent—and the chasm's hellfire sears him.

85

MICHAEL GRANT SLIPS INTO THE SEAT AT THE PARIS SPORTS BOOK. *Le Bar du Sport,* it's called—the pretentious fucking Frogs. He's looking perfectly dorky dressed as Gabe Granowski in his worn white gym shoes, pressed jeans, denim shirt, generic shades, and green John Deere billed cap—just like any dweeb from Dubuque who's wandered in to lose his nest egg laying bets on ball games. The dark wig with the shaggy hair spilling down the nape of his neck completes the illusion. A waitress brushes her silicone boob against his shoulder as she takes his order for a Mich. He leans forward, his elbows on the console, and stares at the wagering keyboard and the personal mini-monitor with some fuckin' snoozer of a baseball game on it. The big screens all around the room are showing everything from harness racing to soccer, sports for kings and wimps, neither of which deserve to live.

He's totally pissed off, burning with anger, ready to explode. The whole fucking trapline's been sprung—all his traps except for the last one. The whole Op's been compromised. There's SHIT everywhere, like fucking dysentery, setting their own traps along his trapline so they can snare him—which they don't have a fucking prayer of doing. He even saw one of his old Area 51 Crisis Response Teams deploying outside the arena. And they're not like the SHIT. The CRT's good—they're trained to kill on sight. There's no way, even if the SHIT haven't discovered the cache at the arena, that he can get anywhere near it. Too bad, too, because the arena was to be the headliner, the media grabber with all those Hollywood hippies, hoods in hoodies, and foreign fags bleeding out for live pay-per-view.

The hotels are almost as bad—rings of surveillance, most of it heavy-handed, around each cache—all overt crap he easily circumvented, but there's still no way in hell he can spring those traps. The Divine Eagle Institute is all over the radio and tv, though the media morons don't yet have a clue about what really happened and haven't yet made any connection to Paris or the rest of the Strip, even if the SHIT have. And the SHIT do somehow know. There's an informant. But how in hell…? Could the Prophet have survived the operation at the Institute?

Now that Grant thinks about it, he doesn't remember seeing the Caddy anywhere at the Institute when he reconnoitered the perimeter. What the hell was the Prophet doing away from there? The SHIT must've gotten to him, and the old man must've spilled his guts—that's the only way they could've found out about the traps here along the Strip so fast. But did they get to the Prophet before or after the DEI operation? Fuck it. It doesn't matter. The Prophet was a good man gone soft at exactly the wrong time. That's what matters, damn it.

The waitress slides a cold bottle of Michelob onto the console and pulsates away. He came in here to the Paris sports book because it's the last place the SHIT will look for anybody. The pool deck's quarantined, and most of the dupes have bolted. But not all of them—the casino's still going pretty strong, and there's more than a dozen dolts glued to the screens here. He's got to think, got to work through the anger. He's sure it's not showing. The waitress didn't notice a fucking thing. But he can feel the tightness in his neck and shoulders. He sips the Mich just for show. He never drinks during an Op, but he's got to look like a dumb-ass from Dubuque blowing his dough. Fuck, he's got to burn some energy bad. Pump iron. Bash somebody's brains.

He pulls off his shades and hunches forward with the Mich like he's studying the mini-monitor. What he's *really* got to do is spring his final trap—save the operation and, thus, the Republic. If he sets off the last trap, he can still start the New American Revolution. The Brotherhood grows mightier day by day. Has since even before the Millennium. A lot of valorous Patriots will follow him. All they have been waiting for is a strong leader, a man of action instead of some talk-show druggie. Even if he has only one shot left, he can still be the New Minuteman. It's simple, really. As always, he just has to suck it up and fucking do it.

He takes a longer pull on the Mich and then wipes his mouth with the back of his bandaged hand. The hand has stiffened, but it's nothing he can't deal with. Springing the trap, though, isn't that fuckin' simple. The sortie at the Institute's gone public, as has the "accident" here at the Paris pool. The SHIT'll be waiting for him everywhere, especially The Tahitian. It's good the Prophet never knew the specific sites for the caches—just the venues, but not the particulars. God is in the details, but the Prophet was much better on ideas than logistics. The old man was too busy communing with the Lord and boffing the acolytes to cross his T's and dot his I's. Always counted on the Elders to run the Institute and on him to upgrade security, enforce the rules, and, most importantly, implement the Day of the Lord—which is still going to succeed, damn it.

He slips the shades back on and glances around, needing to relieve himself before he moves out. The john's over by the exit—*Les Toilettes,* the fucking sign says. He presses the shades to the bridge of his nose, turns the bill of his cap around, and swigs the rest of the Mich. Adrenaline's pumping, flooding his head, pouring through the tightness in his neck and shoulders, and flowing down his spine. It's time to saddle up. Get the hell out of here and over to his base, then set and spring his final trap.

86

GARY B. SMITH DREAMS. HE LIES IN HIS MOTHER'S BED, FEVERISH, THE cool washcloth she's placed on his forehead doing nothing to relieve the burning. His eyes are closed, but he can hear the rattle of the air conditioner and other noises, too, that aren't so familiar. And he hears her voice clearly—that high, nasal voice with a twang that mostly scolds him but sometimes heaps praise and love on him. "Gary Babington Smith," she says, "you've really done it this time, young man. Gotten yourself into a heap of trouble. Wait till your daddy gets home. You'll be sorry!"

But he knows, even in his delirium, that his father's not coming home. Never has. Never will.

He can feel the mattress sag as she sits on the side of the bed and takes away the washcloth. "I just don't know, Gar-*ree*," she sighs. "I don't know what to do with you anymore. Nothin' I do is ever enough." He hates it when she calls him Gar-*ree*, emphasizing the last part. Sometimes in public, in front of other kids even, she'll tweak his ear and call him Gar-*ree*. The guys at school mock him with that fruity name—"Gar-*ree*, Fair-*ree*! Gar-*ree*, Fair-*ree*!" They know it drives him crazy, makes him madder than hell. And no matter how much he chases 'em, he can never catch 'em, guffawing and taunting— "Gar-*ree*, Fair-*ree*!"

"You've just got no respect for your elders," his mother sobs. "You don't even respect yourself, Gar-*ree*." If he's been really bad, she takes him aside, even at the playground or in the back of church or at the bus stop, and pinches the soft skin under his arm above his elbow so hard it turns black and blue. He always tries to fight the tears till he's alone, staring down at the dark marks. "How can you expect others to respect you when you don't respect yourself?" she asks. "You're hopeless, Gar-*ree*. Completely hopeless."

The dream begins to fade, but his eyes remain shut—taped shut, bound up, and it's no fuckin' dream neither. Where is he? It's like he's floating on air, but he can't move his arms or legs. He's tied down, but flyin', too. And the pain, the searing pain, is real bad. But he also can't feel it, like he's somebody else. Or, he just doesn't care. How can he be hurt so bad and not hurt at all? He must be fuckin' dead.

Is he fuckin' burning in hell, like she always warned him? No— hell's got no machines. His mother's gone, the dream's gone, but the noise of the machines is still all around him. Wherever he is, it sure as shit ain't heaven. If he's not dead, where the fuck is he? And, how'd he get here?

Something's coming back. His mother's house is on fire, smoke's everywhere, and he's hauling ass out of there. Maybe his hands got burned. Or his hair got singed. But there's more. After the house blew up, he was locked up in a pig holding cell. So that can't be right neither. Something happened later, but he doesn't know what.

There's voices now along with the machine noises. Ladies, but not his mother. Different sounding. And the words aren't lining up into sentences.

"Third degree...Forty percent."

Forty percent? Is he flunking again?

"Even if he pulls through.... The face...eyes, both totally...No quality of life...None."

Some weird accents. Foreigners? Lady doctors? Nurses? Fuckin' mudhead voices. Yeah, that's it. Whatever happened, it's the mud-heads.

"The face...nothing's left."

Something's happened. Something real bad. And the mudheads did it to him. The mudheads did something to him. It's all their fuckin' fault.

87

ANDREW WRIGHT CAN'T FEEL HIS SHOES TOUCHING THE CEMENT AS HE steps out of the jeep and limps across The Tahitian's garage to the elevator. He's so far beyond fatigue and pain now, so far into the emptiness he has been running on, that he no longer even wonders when he'll finally crash. The Divine Eagle Institute disaster is on every AM and FM station. The police have cordoned off the compound, and military teams have been deployed—but no official statement has been released yet. They're trying to produce a major response without causing so much as a minor goddamned stir—a governmental oxymoron. The media reports are confused, often contradictory. One thing, though, is certain: the story is already feeding on itself. Reporters are getting much of their information from other reporters, and nobody has his facts right. The military presence at the arena is fanning media rumors about the cancellation of the title fight. And the current bullshit rampant on the radio has foreign—Islamic—terrorists sighted at McCarran.

In the elevator, Wright goes over his calls to Kupferberg and Raisani. He's right about the last canister, goddamn it. Despite what Kupferberg says, it's here at The Tahitian somewhere. But Kupferberg is still trying to carry on business as usual, and not a single one of the other casinos, not even Paris, has been evacuated either. It's truly insane, but this is, after all, Las Vegas. Grant's around here somewhere, too, and Wright's going to stop the bastard. Two guards in white uniform are standing at the entranceway acting as though they're just hanging out there on break. They lean against the concrete wall on either side of the doorway, talk, and pretend not to scrutinize everyone entering the hotel. When they see that Wright's not carrying anything, they merely nod to him as he passes.

Before Wright heads to the lobby, where he's supposed to meet Maggie by the waterfall, he stops at the hotel's tobacco shop for a couple of Snickers and a bottle of water. The sales clerk, a red-haired teenager wearing a gardenia behind her ear, stares at his hat rather than at him. She has probably never watched morning news, has no idea who he is—but, given the appalled look on her face, she's certain that nothing bearing The Tahitian logo should ever look as gross as that hat.

Wright gazes for a moment through the locked glass door at the private inner lagoon. It's goddamned idyllic, really—the long board-walk running out toward the black sand beach, the finger piers crossing to the thatched-roof *fares,* and the palm trees absolutely still in the tranquil early evening. The lobby itself, with its cascading waterfall, dark wood, soft music, bamboo furniture, and lush plants, also belies the lethal threat Wright knows is imminent. The people milling in the lobby, the casino, and the walkways to the mall and public lagoon heighten his sense that time's running out. Maggie stands near the front desk, but Kupferberg and one of his goddamned guys are there, too. The guy, who's either the engineer or the security chief Wright met during The Tahitian tour that now seems so long ago, fiddles with his ear-piece and then folds his hands in front of himself like he's a funeral director.

"Andy," Kupferberg says as Wright approaches, "come with me." He doesn't offer to shake hands. "Sergeant Carey is on his way."

"The canister," Wright says, looking at Maggie, his eyes screaming, *Is this some fucking set up?*

"Not here," Kupferberg says. "In my office. Now."

"The goddamned canister, Ben…"

"We've tightened the lid. Nothing's coming in, nothing…"

"It's already here," Wright says.

Kupferberg glances at the guy who takes a step toward Wright. He's half a foot taller than his boss, fair-skinned, close to forty, strongly built, and well-dressed in a gray tailored suit. Foreign. Probably ex-military. German. *Gunter something,* Wright remembers—that's his name. He's Loss Prevention.

"We have inspected every centimeter of public and corporate property," Gunter says. His English, though excellent, is stilted.

"The canister's here, Gunter," Wright says.

"We cannot verify anything you have said," Gunter answers as he puts his hand on Wright's shoulder. "We must question…"

Talk to the manager at Paris, Wright thinks, but he knows ticking this guy off won't help. He needs Kupferberg to do certain things fast. He takes off his hat and looks up ninety feet at the peak of the roof that tapers in tiers of glass and hanging plants back down toward the casino's twelve-foot ceiling. Pain slides across his chest as he shrugs Gunter's hand from his shoulder. "How does your sprinkler system work?" he asks. That's got to be it. The DEI annihilation was set up that way. Paris, too. True, the arena and a couple of the other hotels weren't, but he's still sure.

Gunter glances at Kupferberg, who stares at Wright for a moment before nodding. Maggie's peering at Wright now, too. It's hard to say which of them looks more tired. Kupferberg has shaved again, but his face looks like it's turning to putty. Maggie's eyes are bleary, and the skin under them is dark and puffy. He suspects, though, that he looks a whole lot worse than the two of them combined.

"Fire pumps drive the water from the lagoons," Gunter says. "The system pumps 750 gallons every minute."

Wright glances over at the casino entrance, which looks from this angle like a well-lit tropical cavern. The casino is fairly crowded, the lobby less so. "Shut the system down," he says, turning to Kupferberg.

"We cannot," Gunter says. "It is locked open."

"What about an over-ride?" Maggie asks.

Gunter shakes his head. "No. There is no master switch. It is constructed that way so it *cannot* be sabotaged."

"Shit," Wright begins. "There's got to…"

"Andy," Kupferberg says, "there are manual valves. Three per floor. No short cuts."

Glancing again at the crowd surging into the casino, Wright says, "Shut 'em off." A man with a green baseball cap is following a gaggle of hefty sixty-something women past the first bank of slot machines. "Shut the valves off."

Gunter runs his hand over his close-cropped brown hair. "It will take four to five minutes for *each* valve," he says.

"Start with this floor," Wright says. "The casino *first*." Green baseball cap has a slouching hayseed gait that's exaggerated—not quite natural. "Which lagoon does the system…? Shit! It's him!" Wright starts to hobble through the crowd. "It's Grant, goddamn it!"

"Andy," Kupferberg shouts, "Get the fu…" He stops, apparently aware that it's a bad idea to scream obscenities across the opulent lobby of his own hotel.

Wright pushes past two women, one of whom calls him a son of a bitch in a heavy Russian accent. Maggie reaches into her mesh handbag as she knifes past him. He clips his shin on the corner of an end table, stumbles, and loses sight of the green baseball cap. The going's even slower at the periphery of the casino, and by the time he's in among the slot machines, Maggie has stopped. She's on her toes, holding the handbag across her chest and craning her neck as she surveys the area. He scans the crowd, too, but there's no green baseball cap anywhere.

"He's gone," she says, turning and looking into Wright's eyes. "Are you sure…"

"It was him, goddamn it," Wright says. He tries to remember where the casino's other exits lead.

Kupferberg and Loss Prevention Gunter approach them with Hans, who has materialized from somewhere in the lobby, following behind. Gunter is talking into his lapel radio, and Hans has his hand at his belt inside his sportcoat.

"It's him—Grant," Wright says, even though he's acutely aware that the guy he just followed doesn't much look like the man in the photograph that Maggie has had distributed to the cops and hotel security people. He licks his lips, which taste of metal. "Scruffy hair." He turns to Gunter. "Denim shirt and a green baseball cap."

309

Gunter repeats the description into his radio.

All around them, people have stopped punching the slots' buttons in order to gape at this madman who's muttering "it was him, goddamn it" while holding a filthy hat and two Snickers in one hand and a bottle of water in the other.

"Andy, we're moving somewhere private," Kupferberg says under his breath.

Hans grips Wright's arm.

"It was Grant, goddamn it," Wright says, yanking his arm free. He stares into Kupferberg's skeptical eyes. "It was him." Even he, though, understands there's no way to convince the others unless Gunter's security people grab the guy fast. And there's no sign of him anywhere among the players and the tourists.

88

As Michael Grant takes his beige linen sport coat from the hanger in the oversized wooden wardrobe in his swanky *fare*, he gazes for a moment at the last canister suspended by a cord slung around the hanger. Security has gone on full alert—there was even some bullshit sweep while he was in the casino men's room ditching the Gabe Granowski hat, wig, and shirt before circling around here to George Grisham's *fare*. But security would never find the canister *hanging* in a wardrobe of one of The Tahitian's most expensive rooms. Hell, housekeeping could clean right around it and never notice it. This thatched-roof hut out here on stilts in the lagoon, connected to the hotel only by its long wooden pier, has got everything from a jacuzzi in the john to a satellite link for the internet. It cost the Prophet more than two thousand dollars a night, but, for Grant's purposes, it's the perfect bargain. Location, location, location—and a private deck overhanging the lagoon.

He drops the sportcoat on the king-sized bed with the fancy carved wooden headboard, pulls his suitcase from the wardrobe, and pops the false bottom. He takes out the special shoulder holster he himself designed so that the outlines of both flare guns and the Magnum won't show beneath the sportcoat. After loading the flare guns and checking the Magnum, he pulls the beige cowboy hat from the wardrobe's top shelf, brushes the rim with his fingertips, and puts it on.

He marks the time on his watch. Once he begins, timing is critical —and there's no turning back. This is it. The Prophet may've lost his nerve, and the SHIT may've fucked with his other traps. But he's going to finish this operation. Bugles resound and drums beat in his head.

He's going to lead the Revolution. Turning, he gazes into the mirror above the dresser. A smile crosses his face. He's got his shirt off and his hat on—just the right look for a rich Texan lounging on his private deck right here in paradise. The adrenaline's really pumping now. He's fucking ready to rock and roll.

He unslings the canister, wraps it in a towel, and tosses another towel over his shoulder. Before sliding the glass door open, he rechecks his watch, glances again in the mirror, and nods to himself. It's a go. His boots clap the wooden deck. It's a fine evening, the sky still blue even though the sun's below the hotel's roof. It's warm but not hot with no wind at all—only a touch of coolness from the open door of the air-conditioned *fare*. The water's dead calm, reflective, almost black in this light. A couple of dark women, tits bare and flowers in their hair, are still chatting on the beach fifty yards away, but mostly it's quiet and peaceful around the lagoon.

He sits side-saddle on the chaise lounge he positioned earlier right near the edge of the deck. His back to the beach, he sets the covered canister between his legs. For exactly three minutes, he doesn't make a move. It's just long enough for any wimps who noticed the rich Texan saunter out onto the deck to lose interest. He's got to look totally relaxed but work fucking fast, and he's counting, no doubt correctly, on the fact that any peeping-toms leering out the hotel room windows will be eyeing the boobs on the beach. He's got no gloves or mask this time either because they might draw attention, too—but he'll be so quick and careful that he won't make any contact with the material or its fumes.

Using the towel from his shoulder, he twists off the canister's outer lid and drops it into the lagoon. Then, holding his breath, he turns the inner seal, flips it into the water, and takes the canister in both hands. In one smooth, seamless motion, he leans over the deck's edge and shoves the open canister head down into the water under the decking. Seven, maybe eight seconds tops, it's a done deal. The canister's sinking, the Virin diffusing. Nobody saw a thing, except maybe a Texan holding a towel lean over and glance into the water. He drops the towel on the deck, stands, stretches as though he's got all the time in the world, saunters back inside the *fare*, shuts the door, and only then exhales.

He's dressed and crossing the pier in under three minutes. Another two minutes gets him to the casino entrance where he halts to check security. He has built these stops into the operation so he is never hurried even at top speed. In his hat and tinted shades, he looks nothing like he did before. His posture's more erect, his broad shoulders causing the sportcoat to conceal the weaponry perfectly. Even his walk is different—big-time Texas money, the lucky man born between the Red and Rio Grande.

The casino is packed. Almost wall to wall. Sardines, baby, sardines. They're all hot to hit the jackpot, and nobody's got a fucking clue. These dipshits are going to fucking trample each other in exactly three-point-five minutes. He almost wishes for a moment that the Prophet was here to see this, that the old man hadn't wimped out so bad. Because here it is, The Day of the Lord, the Lord's Retribution. He feels another little pop of adrenaline as he makes his move. Snaking his way easily through the crowd, he heads toward the semi-private high-stakes poker parlor set off with bamboo and lots of plants that form a curtain and wall.

When he reaches the exact spot he'd marked during each of his three dry runs, he turns so his back is to the bamboo. He unbuttons his sportcoat, folds his arms in front of him, and scans the crush of stiffs one last time. Swiftly, with the ease of a practiced stroke, he draws the flare guns and raises his arms, outstretched in opposite directions. His eyes light as he fires the flares into the casino's false ceiling. *The shot heard round the world!*

He's already stashed the flare guns among the ferns and entered the high-stakes poker hut before the report's echo dies. There's stunned quiet in the casino, not silence but a murmur, as he flashes a winning smile at the waitress and strolls among the tables to the private exit. He waves the VIP electronic key card, the *fare's* most important perk, and the private high-roller exit swings open to him. There's noise now from the casino, confusion—the sardines know some weird thundering is starting in the ceiling above them, but there's no panic yet. No reason for it—the flares' fireworks are all out of sight. Heat not smoke sets off the sprinklers, and it'll be another five seconds or so before there's heat enough in the ceiling. They smell the phosphorescence, but the sprinklers'll go on before flames appear. They'll get drenched before they're smoked. Then, as the lagoon water pumps through the system, all hell will break loose. As the Prophet predicted, the four horsemen will ride roughshod through the casino. Death and hell will cast all the idolaters into this lake of fire. And from the ashes, true natural-born Patriots will rise.

89

THE FIRE ALARMS GO OFF AT THE SAME TIME BENJAMIN KUPFERBERG receives the code red call. The whole group—Maggie, Wright, Kupferberg, Hans, and half a dozen other Tahitian staffers—are viewing the security video of a guy in a green hat entering the casino's washroom. Loss Prevention's sweepers have found a John Deere baseball cap, wig, and denim shirt under the black plastic liner in the washroom's trash can. Gunter himself left earlier to supervise the closing of the sprinkler system's valves. And Wright doesn't look quite so much like a goddamned lunatic.

Fereshteh Raisani just called, and she'll be here after she checks on Christine. Now, though, something's going wrong in the casino, and Wright, hobbling after Kupferberg into the lobby, fears the worst. Images of the Paris pool and the DEI cafeteria well in his mind. Smoke swirls up the lobby's sloping ceiling. An acrid odor pervades the area, causing the surge of people flowing away from the casino to cough and cup their noses. But there are no flames, no water from the sprinklers, and no panic. There's smoke but no fire—almost like it's a goddamned fire drill. Kupferberg's people are ushering everybody toward the exits in a disorderly but not chaotic fashion. The crowd is shuffling pretty fast, but nobody's pushing or shoving anybody else.

Sirens echo around the lobby. His phone held to his ear, Kupferberg stops near the waterfall. He's shouting into the phone, but whoever he's talking to probably can't hear a word over the alarms, the sirens, and the clamor of the crowd. Sergeant Carey's head is visible among the firemen trying to make their way through the throng. At least three uniforms are with him.

Maggie wraps both hands around Wright's arm and yells up into his ear, "What the hell's Grant doing, Andy?"

Wright doesn't know. He feels like he's floating above everyone, looking down on the scene. The mass of people seem to be moving as one undulating creature, a Chinese dragon with a tail of orange curling smoke. Time's coming unstuck, too, slowing then lurching and slowing again. Grant somehow set a fire in the casino, but Gunter must've already closed the valve because nobody evacuating through the lobby is wet. And nobody's bleeding out, thank God. *Nobody's bleeding out!* He wants to grab Maggie and shout it—*Nobody's bleeding out!*—but his breath catches. If Grant started this fire, the Virin's already in the system. The Tahitian's water's already contaminated. Horrific stuff could still…He's got to…

"The fire's in the ceiling," Kupferberg shouts to them over his shoulder.

Wright's looking around, not wildly, but with an absolute sense of urgency. Sergeant Carey's forty-five feet away but temporarily blocked by a group of Asian tourists in matching blue tropical shirts. The Chinese dragon is sagging and reeling, bloating in its midriff as though it has swallowed some prey whole.

And there's Grant, goddamn it! Over by the elevators standing under a palm tree. He's got on a beige cowboy hat, sunglasses, a Western shirt, a pale sportcoat, and a silver bolo. His feet set apart and his hands clasped behind his back, he looks like he's viewing a military parade, the goddamned bastard.

90

MICHAEL GRANT'S HEAD POUNDS. HIS TIMING HAS BEEN SPOT ON. HE HAS done his job *perfectly*, but nothing's working. These morons stumbling out of the casino should be drenched, bleeding out through every fucking orifice, piling up like so much shit in the Lord's own outhouse. But they're not even damp. Dry as a fucking bone. The sprinkler system failed. But it's built so it *can't* fail. It's supposed to be dickproof, but somebody still dicked with it somehow. Somebody...it can't be the SHIT. They'd shut down the whole place...barge right in like they were doing over at the arena...evacuate the whole fucking hotel... ransack the place and ask questions later.

He slowly scans the sheep being herded to the exits. Cops are clomping through the herd. The LVFD's dragging hoses from their trucks—their response time almost double the two minutes they brag so much about. The SHIT should all be packing right into the Virin, but they're not. Everything's going down exactly as he planned —except that the fucking sprinklers aren't spewing Virin. Who the hell's respons...?

Some twit over by the front desk is raising his arm like he's some kind of cripple...He's got some stupid hat on, and he's with some small dark-haired...He's pointing this way...It's Andy fucking Pretty Boy Wright and his producer! Could...? Did Wright fuck up the Op...? Is he the one who's...? The hotel owner is there, too, in this knot of people...Wright's practically fucking waving now.

Grant reacts swiftly and decisively, spinning into a crouch and drawing the Magnum. Some suit is stepping in front of the knot, aiming at him with a thirty-eight. But the knot untangles faster than hell when he drops the suit with two shots.

The Magnum's reports echo all over the fucking place, panicking the herd. They screech and stampede around the SHIT, who've got no fucking clue where the shots came from. He'd like to stay and finish off the Pretty Boy and his producer, but if he does he'll draw a fusillade. And there is nothing Patriotic about dying under this palm tree. Nothing at all. It's time for a strategic withdrawal. He ducks low, just in case there's incoming, skitters to the private entrance to the lagoon, and flashes his VIP electronic key card. The glass door swings open, and he's through, moving with all deliberate speed.

91

WRIGHT SCRAMBLES TO HIS FEET. HANS HAS BEEN HIT TWICE, ONCE IN the chest and once in the arm. He's down, but nobody else has been shot. At least, not yet. Smoke is snaking out of the casino, getting denser without the sprinklers to douse the fire. The Chinese dragon is blowing apart, the panic-stricken crowd scattering through the lobby. People are starting to trample each other in their terror. And nobody's going to hear, much less obey, any orders in the melee. The firemen can't make it over to the casino, and Carey and his cops don't have a prayer of getting after Grant.

Kupferberg is kneeling next to Hans, yelling into his phone. Maggie is already running for the exit Grant must've taken. Skirting the distended dragon, Wright limps after her. Nobody else is heading that way because it's *toward* the billowing smoke. When she reaches the door, she shoulders it—but it's on auto-lock and doesn't budge. She pulls Smith's Colt from the bag, drops the bag on the floor, and slams the door's glass with the Colt's barrel. When it fails to break, she takes a half step back, raises the Colt, and fires, shattering the glass. She climbs through the opening like it's some goddamned playground jungle gym.

Wright cuts his left forearm but gets through the door, too. Maggie is raising the Colt, holding it steady with both hands, squaring her shoulders. Grant's thirty yards ahead along the boardwalk that leads to the lagoon's beach. He's not running but walking fast, his gun out of sight. He's not doing anything to draw the attention of the two security guards in white uniforms hurrying toward the lobby.

Grant glances over his shoulder just as Maggie fires. He lurches, his hat and sunglasses fly off into the lagoon, and he topples sideways.

Maggie jogs along the pier, and Wright hobbles after her as fast as he can.

Grant has fallen at the edge of the boardwalk where it forms a T with a finger pier to one of the *fares*. As she approaches, he rises to one knee. A bright red stain spreads along the hip of his jeans, and a darker stain marks his crotch.

"Give it up, asshole!" Maggie shouts.

By the time Wright catches up to her, he's gasping for breath.

As Grant wobbles to his feet, his eyes are gleaming.

"It's over, asshole!" she shouts.

Wright looks around, but there are still no cops. The two security guards are twenty-five yards away, frozen, spectators to whatever's about to happen. Maggie is wide-eyed, unblinking. Separated by less than ten feet, she and Grant measure each other.

Grant takes a step back so he has one foot on the finger pier. He's unsteady, but he's smiling.

Widening her stance, Maggie stares at him.

Grant's smile broadens as reaches with a bandaged hand inside his sportcoat.

Wright's breath catches in his throat again. A deep clarity wells in him: Maggie may be good with guns, but she's no killer.

Time slows. The lagoon glistens darkly.

Grant pulls out a gun.

The sweet, heavy odor of tropical flowers hangs in the air. The alarms and the sirens, the shouting and the screaming blend into one remote chord. The slide that began with the storm in Red Rock Canyon has all been one moment, a singularity. Wright has been waiting for this moment. The moment.

Grant will shoot; Maggie won't.

It takes Grant a second, a crucial second, to switch the gun from his bandaged hand to his left hand.

A solitary star shines in the fading sky. The air is perfectly still.

Wright gathers his remaining energy, focuses all of it, everything.

"Andy!" It's as though Maggie knows.

Time stops in this crystalline second. As Grant raises the gun, Wright pushes off on his good ankle. Dives forward. Slams the crown of his hat into Grant's chest. The gun fires into the sky, its report held fast in the moment. Both men take flight, arc away from the pier, and sail out over the lagoon's dark water, light bursting all about them.

EPILOGUE

As the sun sparks the ridge to the east, Maggie McNamara cradles the plain steel urn to her chest. The wind freshens with the rising sun—a warm, tangy breeze that tickles her skin. The four of them —she, Fereshteh Raisani, Nick Larson, and Ben Kupferberg—stand in a semi-circle around a dark, clear pool formed by the narrow creek running down through the red rock. They are somewhere high along Lost Creek Canyon gathered at the spot Larson chose for this covert ceremony. Birds call, and the water chimes as it cascades into the pool.

Three weeks have passed since Andy head-butted Grant into the lagoon. She has wakened every night to Grant's stunned face disintegrating. Andy, at least, had his face down in the water, that goofy hat of his hiding much of the horror. The media have, predictably, uncovered a lot of facts but not the truth, and she has become their darling, a national hero, the heir to *The Wright Stuff*. According to the story playing out—a potpourri of fragmentary information, clever equivocation, and outright bullshit—she gunned down some fanatic hell-bent on setting off a fire-bomb at The Tahitian. Andrew Wright died bravely, the only real truth in the whole byzantine fabrication, and she saved the hotel and city by stepping forward and plugging the mad-bomber with the Colt. She has had to do daily *Wright Stuff* updates, of course, but she has spent more of her time retelling her story for other sources. And part of the story, at least, is also the truth: her father, a Kankakee cop, trained her in the use of a handgun when she was twelve. Later, before he was willing to let her move to New York to be an ABC TV producer, he made her practice each day for a month. He trained her well—too well, in fact. She has, dozens of times in the last three weeks, castigated herself silently for aiming at Grant's ass to stop his flight rather than simply taking the back of his head off.

Andy's *faux* funeral was held at Saint Patrick's Cathedral. CNN ran fifteen minute updates, and that night ABC aired a ninety-minute prime-time retrospective of *The Wright Stuff*. Andy's cremated ashes, his *real* ashes, which she is pressing harder to herself now, were only given to her three days ago—and would never have been released at all except that she demanded a *real* funeral as part of the deal she cut with the government to keep her mouth shut about what actually happened in the days leading up to *The Tahitian Tragedy*, as her colleagues in the media are calling it. Nobody else, not even Arnuz and Miguel, knows the whole truth.

Raisani has been in touch every day, and she has, McNamara suspects, filled in Larson. Though he is recovering well, he should probably not have hiked up to this spot this morning. A blue sling holds his arm across him while the reconstructed shoulder heals. He kept his balance amazingly well as they clambered up the backside of the canyon, but he sweated hard and had to stop a couple of times to drink from the canteens Raisani carried clipped to the belt of her khakis. Because of Andy's saving Larson in the canyon only hours before he himself died on the Strip, speculation has been rife in the media about Larson's identity and his role—but his name was never released publicly, and he has seemingly disappeared since his furtive departure from the hospital. A few people at UMC recognized him, but his privacy, at least so far, has been protected. In fact, only McNamara knows that he has been convalescing in Red Sapphire with both his daughters. Maya is keeping him focused on the living. Christine, though, harbors appalling demons following her miscarriage and the holocaust she witnessed at the Divine Eagle Institute. She spends most of her time alone, curled into herself, but just yesterday, Raisani reported, Maya got her to play catch with a nerf ball for a couple of minutes. Raisani herself has shunned any attention, and though her name surfaced briefly in the media the day after Andy's death, she has held stoically, even rigidly, to her privacy as well.

"Shall we begin?" Kupferberg says, nodding to Larson.

Kupferberg sweated hard, too, coming up the canyon, but McNamara knows he would not have missed this moment. He knows most of what happened, but not everything. Raisani never informed him, as she did Maggie, that she found Joseph Wengelt's corpse, blown apart by one of Grant's defensive tripwires just inside the Grotto. The Rev, it seems, blundered to his death in his hysteria. Raisani will later today report the location of Wengelt's decaying, vermin-ridden corpse to the Las Vegas police partly because various loonies have already made Wengelt sightings from Arkansas to Montana and partly because the Rev is becoming, in absentia, a cult figure and Waco-esque rallying point. There's no such notoriety for Gary Smith, who remains paralyzed and disfigured in the UMC intensive care burn unit. According to a nurse McNamara contacted, Smith hasn't had a single visitor.

Kupferberg knows most of the rest, though. And the fact that he's here means that he understands that Andy saved him and his hotel. Dozens of people were injured in the crush to flee the gunfire, but no one died. And none of the injuries was caused *directly* by the shut valve. Questions remain not only about why the valve wasn't functioning but also about the sequence of events between the start of the fire in the casino's ceiling and the deaths of the two men at the lagoon. Kupferberg has been spinning the story, doctoring it expertly. Hans, his bodyguard, has survived three surgeries and will eventually recover, but he's not saying word one to the media. And Kupferberg has the cash to keep him and anybody else from going public with any fragments of the story they possess.

The Tahitian is still shut down, but its Grand Reopening is scheduled for the first of October. And given the culture's peculiar logic—notorious *is* famous—advanced bookings, especially for large corporate outings, are strong. The building remains sealed off from the public, and the inner lagoon is enclosed within an opaque plastic canopy, ostensibly to clean it thoroughly after the two gunshot victims—Andy and Grant—tumbled bloodily into the water. The truth is that though the lagoon was drained that first week through a government system into clandestine holding tanks, cleansed with some super-secret government chemicals, and refilled twice, military chemical warfare specialists are still testing the water daily for any residual traces of Virin. Kupferberg has his bevy of *wahines,* now wearing coconut bras, restationed at the large public lagoon in front of The Tahitian, and the outrigger canoe races are running again at regular intervals. Kupferberg himself was deflated those first few days, but the task of revitalizing The Tahitian has gotten him back to his old self—impatient and twitching with energy. Now, as Larson says a short prayer, Kupferberg rocks on the balls of his feet.

"…Is now and ever shall be, eternally," Larson concludes. He raises his head and looks into Maggie's eyes. He holds her there, his eyes the color of the limestone cliffs lit by the morning sun. He is deeply and utterly thankful, she knows, for his life and the life of his daughter.

Raisani begins to pray in Farsi, a lilting, mournful chant that sounds like the creek streaming down into the pool.

Larson's eyes tell McNamara to say something profound, but she doesn't need to. She understands, as Larson does, what probably would've happened and likely still would be happening if Andy hadn't slid down into that cavern, trusted his own idiosyncratic instincts, and followed his own offbeat but necessary path.

When Raisani finishes her prayer, Kupferberg brushes his hand through his hair but, uncharacteristically, says only, "Andy was a good man. When the chips were down, he did the right thing." Or is it out of character? There's no sales pitch to make here, no opportunity for a sound bite, no spin, at least among the four of them, to put on Andy's death. Kupferberg's brevity speaks more strongly.

McNamara steps forward and takes a deep breath. Morning light flows all around her, washing her. The cliffs and escarpment turn gold and russet. The pool glows blue-green, with silver rippling in concentric circles. The bushes shiver with the freshening breeze. Somewhere nearby, a snake rattles its tail. "Andy…" For a moment, she can't find her voice. "Andy Wright," she says finally, "was my friend. I loved him…" Her voice catches again. "I love him still. And I miss him."

Larson ushers them around the pool to a hidden crevice leading deep into the rock. He asked McNamara a couple of days ago if the site should be marked, and now a petroglyph, etched above and to the right of the crevice, depicts a winged creature in full flight. It is, though, neither fierce nor predatory. Its wings are spread, but it has neither sharp beak nor hooked talons. She raises the urn, and the sun gleams from its smooth surface. It's hermetically sealed so they couldn't cast his ashes to the wind even if they wanted to.

She holds the urn to the sun until a glistening molten spot like the after-image of a gliding bird hovers before her eyes. She then lowers the urn and passes it so that first Kupferberg, then Larson, and finally Raisani hold it one last time. As Raisani returns it, her eyes now hold McNamara, who can see in the dark and the light what Andy must've seen—a world both here and now and beyond space and time.

McNamara stoops on one knee and listens to the water and the birds, the rustle and the rattle. She feels the sun hot on her neck and the tickling wind, smells the juniper and the creosote. The bright air all about her claps softly as she opens her hands and lets the urn drop into the crevice. It tumbles, ringing, into darkness.

ACKNOWLEDGEMENTS

This story has had quite a journey into print. I am grateful to everyone who has provided advice and support along the way. I want to especially thank Marcy McGinnis for sharing her expertise and her insights about television news. Thanks also to Tom and Sally Nieman for their help and hospitality in Las Vegas and to Art and Gail Burton for a place in Cape May to finish the story. The hurricane was impressive.

Thanks yet again to John Manos for his thoughtful reading and editorial acumen.

Finally, I'm grateful to Sarah Koz for her superb designs.

The Healer's Daughters
Bone Box
Cycle
America's Fool
Whale Song
52 Poems for Men
AMIKA PRESS

Doubloon
Blackbird Singing
FORGE BOOKS

Deep Gold
WARNER BOOKS

School Smarts
The Study Skills Handbook
The Creative Writing Handbook
GOOD YEAR BOOKS

Verbal Review and Workbook for the SAT
HARCOURT BRACE JOVANOVICH

JAY AMBERG is the author of twelve books. He has taught high school and college students since 1972. Contact him at jayamberg.com.